"I suppose that means you don't want to sign away your rights as a father."

"No." Mason's expression was intense, serious. "In fact, since I last saw you, I consulted an attorney."

Words to put fear into a girl's heart. "I'm their legal guardian. If you try to take them away from me—"

"Whoa." He put his hands up in a "slow down" motion. "It's just that even though I'm their father, I have no rights because my name isn't on the birth certificates. Now, with DNA proof, I will acknowledge paternity and petition the court to legally claim my paternal rights."

"How long will that take?"

"There's a sixty-day waiting period, then however long it takes to get a court date," he said.

"And then you're going to sue for sole custody?"

"Of course not. No one is talking custody fight here. You clearly love them, Annie."

"I do. But how can you know that?" Where men were concerned, suspicion was her default emotion.

"Because you did copious research on a pacifier. And I just get the feeling if I look at either baby funny, you'd cut my heart out with a spoon."

"You're not wrong." But how did he know her so well? They'd barely met.

His Double Baby Bonus

TERESA SOUTHWICK
&
SUE MacKAY

Previously published as *What Makes a Father*
and *The Nurse's Twin Surprise*

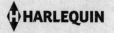

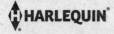

ISBN-13: 978-1-335-61745-3

His Double Baby Bonus

Copyright © 2021 by Harlequin Books S.A.

What Makes a Father
First published in 2019. This edition published in 2021.
Copyright © 2019 by Teresa Southwick

The Nurse's Twin Surprise
First published in 2019. This edition published in 2021.
Copyright © 2019 by Sue MacKay

Recycling programs
for this product may
not exist in your area.

This edition published by arrangement with Harlequin Books S.A.

For questions and comments about the quality of this book, please contact us at CustomerService@Harlequin.com.

Harlequin Enterprises ULC
22 Adelaide St. West, 40th Floor
Toronto, Ontario M5H 4E3, Canada
www.Harlequin.com

Printed in U.S.A.

CONTENTS

Teresa Southwick lives with her husband in Las Vegas, the city that reinvents itself every day. An avid fan of romance novels, she is delighted to be living out her dream of writing for Harlequin.

Books by Teresa Southwick

Harlequin Special Edition

An Unexpected Partnership
What Makes a Father
Daughter on His Doorstep

The Bachelors of Blackwater Lake

A Decent Proposal
The Widow's Bachelor Bargain
How to Land Her Lawman
A Word with the Bachelor
Just a Little Bit Married
The New Guy in Town
His by Christmas
Just What the Cowboy Needed

Montana Mavericks: Six Brides for Six Brothers

Maverick Holiday Magic

Montana Mavericks: The Lonelyhearts Ranch

Unmasking the Maverick

Visit the Author Profile page at Harlequin.com for more titles.

What Makes a Father

TERESA SOUTHWICK

To my parents, Gladys and Frank Boyle.
You made raising six kids look easy.

I love you both and miss you always.

Chapter 1

Annie Campbell didn't know exhaustion of this magnitude was even possible. Since suddenly becoming a mom to newborn twins three months ago, she'd been tired, but in the last week she'd counted sleep in seconds and minutes rather than hours. Either Charlie or Sarah was always awake, hungry, wet, crabby or crying uncontrollably for no apparent reason. Childhood had been challenging for Annie, but raising twins was the hardest thing she'd ever done.

And she wouldn't trade being their mom for anything. With one toothless grin they had her wrapped around their little fingers. Now they had all the symptoms of teething—drooling, gnawing on their fists, crying—and Annie honestly wasn't sure she'd survive it.

Her apartment was small, perfect for a single woman.

Then she brought infants home from the hospital, forced by circumstances to care for two babies at once and too overwhelmed to look for a bigger place. And she was still overwhelmed. On a good day she could sneak in a shower. Today hadn't been a good day but there were hopeful signs.

Sarah was quiet in the crib. Charlie was in her arms but she could feel him relaxing, possibly into sleep. Oh, please God. She would walk until her legs fell off if that's what it took. With luck he'd go quietly in with his sister and Annie could close her eyes. To heck with a shower.

Slowly she did a circuit of the living room, past the bar that separated it from the kitchen, around the oak coffee table, gliding by the window that looked out on the center courtyard of the apartment complex. As the baby grew heavier in her arms, she could almost feel victory in her grasp, the euphoria of having two babies asleep at the same time.

Then some fool rang her doorbell. Charlie jerked awake and started to cry just on general principle. Sarah's wails came from the bedroom.

"Someone is going to pay." Annie cuddled the startled baby closer and kissed his head. "Not you, Charlie bear. You're perfect. But if someone is selling something they'll get more than they bargained for."

She peeked through the front window and saw a man wearing military camouflage. This was probably daddy candidate number three, the last one on her sister's list of men who might be the babies' father. This had to be Mason Blackburne, the army doctor who'd been deployed to Afghanistan. She'd contacted him by email and he'd claimed he'd get back to her right away when he returned to the States. She hadn't expected that he actually would.

In her experience, men were selfish, hurtful and unreliable. His written response was a brush-off any idiot would see. Except maybe not since he was standing outside. Not to be picky, but the least he could have done was call first. Come to think of it, how did he get her address? She'd only given him her phone number in the email. Apparently she was taking too long because he followed up the doorbell ring with an aggressive knock.

The chain locking the door was in place so she opened it just a crack. "Your timing sucks."

"Annie Campbell? I'm Mason Blackburne."

"I gave you my number. You were supposed to call me. How did you get my address?"

"From Jessica."

Pain sliced through Annie when she heard her sister's name. Jess had died shortly after giving birth to the twins. The joy of welcoming her niece and nephew into the world turned to unimaginable grief at losing the person Annie loved most in the world. Her sister had lived with her off and on, couch surfing when she needed somewhere to stay. She didn't trust men in general any more than Annie, so if she'd given the address to this guy, her gut must have said he was okay.

Annie unlocked the door and opened it. For the first time she got a good look at Mason Blackburne. Two things stood out: he was tall, and his eyes were startlingly blue. And he was boyishly handsome. Okay, that was three things, but she was too tired to care. And some part of her worn-out brain was regretting that her hair was in a messy ponytail because she hadn't washed it. Or showered today. Or put on makeup. And she was wearing baggy sweatpants and an oversize T-shirt.

"Come in," she said, stepping back. "I've got a DNA swab right here. Just rub it on the inside of each cheek for thirty seconds and put it back in the tube. I'll send it to the lab with the other one and the results will be back in five business days."

But it wasn't clear whether or not he'd heard her. The guy was staring at Charlie. The baby had stopped crying and was staring suspiciously back at the tall stranger. And he was sucking his thumb. The baby, not the stranger.

She sighed. "Well, baby boy, now all my extensive research into the best pacifier on the planet to prevent thumb-sucking is down the tubes. Somewhere an orthodontist is doing the dance of joy."

Mason had a look of awe on his face. "What's his name?"

"Charlie."

"Did Jessica choose that?"

"No, she didn't get a chance. But she'd narrowed down the choices to Christopher and Charles. Sarah was always the top girls' name."

He looked past her to the hallway where the baby girl was still crying. "Can I see her?"

Annie wanted to say no. She didn't know this guy from a rock, but again, Jess didn't normally share her address with men and she'd given it to him. So maybe it was okay.

After closing the front door, she headed for the hallway with daddy candidate number three following. The master bedroom and bath were on the right, and across from it was her office, now the twins' nursery.

"She's in here. And before you ask, they share the crib. The pediatrician advised not separating them just yet."

"Because they shared quarters for nine months," he said.

"Exactly." They walked into the room where the crib was on the wall opposite her desk. "She probably needs her diaper changed. I'll have to put Charlie down since I haven't yet figured out how to do it one-handed. Fair warning—he's going to cry."

"Could I hold him?"

Annie's gaze snapped to his face. "Why?"

"You need help. And he might be my son." There was an edge to his voice and intensity in his eyes that made her think it really mattered to him.

Annie thought it over. This guy *might* be Charlie's father. Why not push him into the deep end of the pool, let him know what he was getting into. She held Charlie out to him and he took the baby, a little awkwardly.

Annie walked over to the crib and lowered the side rail. She picked up the little girl to comfort her first. "It's okay, Sarah. You're fine. I'm here, sweet girl. I have to put you down again, just for a minute to change that diaper. Trust me on this. You'll feel a lot better."

Three months ago the top of her lateral file cabinet had become the storage area for diaper supplies. She settled the baby back in the crib and quickly swapped the wet diaper for a dry one, then picked her up again for a snuggle.

"What happened to Jessica?" He looked away from the baby and met her gaze.

"I told you in the email. She had a pulmonary embolism, a blood clot in her—"

"Lung. I'm a doctor. I get it. But why didn't she let me know she was pregnant? And that I might be the father of the baby—" He stopped and his gaze settled on Sarah. *"Babies?"*

"I told her more than once that the biological father had a right to know. Even though I suggested she let the guy screw up first, she was convinced that he would desert her anyway. She planned to raise them by herself."

"Why would she think that?" There was a tinge of exasperation and outrage in his tone.

"She had her reasons."

His gaze narrowed and irritation pushed out the baby awe. "So you talked her into it? She didn't intend to share the information."

"Not with you or the other two men she slept with." Annie winced as those words came out of her mouth. That made Jess sound like a slut. Maybe it was a little bit true, but that's not who she was. Her sister liked men and sex. She'd been looking for fun, nothing more. "Men sleep around all the time and no one thinks less of them. But if a woman does it, she's trash. Don't you dare judge her."

"I wasn't judging—"

"Oh, please." When a person was as tired as she was, that person had to dig deep for patience. Hers was dangerously depleted. She looked at him and, judging by the uncertain expression on his face, it was possible that there were flames shooting out of her eyes. "And why is this all on my sister? You were a willing participant. Who didn't wear a condom."

"I just wanted to talk," he protested.

"Right. That's what they all say." Her voice dripped

with sarcasm. "You should know that I'm not normally this abrasive, but I'm tired. And I was much more compassionate the first two times a potential father showed up—"

"What happened with them?"

"First one wasn't a match. Number two finally came by a few days ago. I have his sample for the lab along with a legal document from his attorney relinquishing all rights to the babies in exchange for my signed agreement not to pursue him for child support should he be a match. I was only too happy to do that and send him responsibility-free on his way. Sarah and Charlie deserve to be wanted more than anything. They don't need a person like that in their lives."

"Prince of a guy." Mason was still holding Charlie and lightly rubbed a big hand over the baby's back.

Annie loved her sister but that didn't mean she approved of her choices in men. "A few weeks before she gave birth, Jess had second thoughts and narrowed down potential daddy candidates to three. Before she could contact them, she went into labor and showed symptoms of the embolism. Tests confirmed it and the risks were explained to her. She got scared for the babies if something should happen to her and put in writing that I would be the guardian. It was witnessed by two nurses and is a legally binding agreement. No one really thought she would die, but fate didn't cooperate. Now Charlie and Sarah are my babies and I will do anything and everything to keep them safe."

"I'm a doctor. I took an oath to do no harm."

"There are a lot of ways to damage children besides physically." Annie knew from experience that emotional wounds could be every bit as painful and were the ones you didn't have to hide with makeup or a story about being clumsy. "And I wasn't implying that you would hurt them."

"I would never do that," he said fervently.

For the first time she noticed that he looked every bit as tired as she felt. And he was wearing a military uniform—if camouflage was considered a uniform. What was his deal? "When did you get back from Afghanistan?"

"A couple of hours ago. My family lives in Huntington Hills, but I haven't seen them yet."

"You came here first? From the airport?"

"Yes."

It was hard not to be impressed by that but somehow Annie managed. The adrenaline surge during her outburst had drained her reserves and she wanted to be done with this, and him. "Look, if you'd please just do the DNA swab and leave your contact information for the lab, that would be great. Five business days and we'll know."

"Okay." Gently, he put Charlie down in the crib.

Annie did the same with Sarah and miraculously the two didn't immediately start to cry. "Follow me."

They went to her small kitchen, where the sink was full of baby bottles and dishes waiting to be washed.

"I have the kits here." She grabbed one from the counter and handed it to him. He seemed to know what to do.

Mason took the swab out of the tube and expertly rubbed it on the inside of his cheek for the required amount of time, then packaged it up and filled out the paperwork. "That should do it."

"I'll send it to the lab along with the other one."

"Okay."

"Thank you. Not to be rude, but would you please go?"

He started to say something, then stopped and simply let himself out the front door without a word.

Annie breathed a sigh of relief. The uncertainty would be over in five business days but somehow that didn't ease her mind as much as she'd thought it would. After meeting Mason Blackburne, she wasn't sure whether or not she wanted to share child custody with him. Not because he would be difficult, but because he wouldn't. And that could potentially be worse.

"She researched pacifiers, Mom." Mason stopped pacing the kitchen long enough to look at the woman who'd given birth to him. "I don't know whether or not she's a good mother, but both babies were clean, well-fed and happy. Well, one or the other was crying, but it was normal crying, if you know what I mean."

"I do," Florence Blackburne said wryly. "And it's not like she staged the scene. She had no idea you were going to stop by."

"That's true." He'd arrived home five days ago and told her everything. He'd started his job as an ER doctor and he was house hunting. None of it took his mind off the fact that he might be a father.

"That poor woman. Losing her sister and now raising two infants by herself." His mom was shaking her head and there was sympathy in her eyes. "I don't know what I would have done without your father when you and your siblings were born. And I only had one baby at a time."

"Yeah. She looked really exhausted." Pretty in spite

of that, he thought. He remembered Jessica and Annie looked a lot like her. But their personalities were very different. Jess was a little wild, living on the edge. Annie seemed maternal, nurturing. Protective. Honest. The kind of woman he'd want to raise his children. If they *were* his children.

The lab hadn't notified him yet, but this was business day number five and he kept looking at his phone to make sure he hadn't missed the call.

"Checking your cell isn't going to make the news come any faster. I'm sure the twins are yours." His mother gave him her "mom" look, full of understanding and support.

She loved kids and had four of them, never for a moment letting on that she'd sacrificed anything on their behalf. Mason was wired like her and badly wanted kids of his own. The woman he'd married had shared that dream, and the heartbreak of not being able to realize it had broken them up. The third miscarriage had cost him his child and his wife—he'd lost his whole family. If the experience had taught him anything, it was not to have expectations or get his hopes up.

"If only DNA results happened as fast in real life as they do on TV," he said.

"Did the babies look like you?" Flo asked. "Eye color? Shape of the face? That strong, square jaw," she teased.

"They actually looked a lot like Annie. Their aunt. Hazel eyes. Blond hair. Pretty." Something he didn't share with his mother was that Annie Campbell had a very nice ass. Her baggy sweats had hid that asset, no pun intended, until she'd bent over to pick up a toy on the floor. There was no doubt in his mind that a shower and good night's sleep would transform her into a woman who would turn heads on the street. "DNA is the only way to be sure."

"That's just science. It's no match for maternal instinct. And mine is telling me that those babies are my grandchildren."

"Don't, Mom."

"What?" she asked innocently.

"If you have expectations, you're going to be let down." Mason could give a seminar on strategies to avoid disappointment. The only surefire approach was to turn off emotion. Not until the science said it was okay could you let yourself care.

Flo's face took on a familiar expression, the one that said she knew what he was thinking and wanted to take away his pain. The woman was a force of nature and if she couldn't do something, it couldn't be done. Wisely she stayed silent about his past and the situation that had left him bruised and battered. And bitter.

There was something to be said for Jessica's philosophy of fun without complications. But Annie was right, too. He hadn't used a condom and chose to believe the woman who'd said she had everything taken care of. Now he was on pins and needles waiting for the results of a test that could potentially change his life forever.

It was almost five o'clock and the lab's business hours were nearly over for the day. Maybe Annie hadn't sent the samples as soon as she'd planned to. She did have a lot on her plate with two infants. It was possible—

Mason's phone vibrated, startling him even though he'd been waiting and checking. He stared at the Caller ID for a moment, immobilized.

"For Pete's sake, answer it," his mother urged, nudging him out of his daze.

He did, assured the caller that he was Mason Blackburne, then listened while the information was explained to him. "You're sure?"

They were completely confident in the results. Mason thanked the caller and pressed the off button on his phone.

Flo stared at him anxious and expectant. "Well? Mason, I'm too old for this kind of suspense. Don't make me wait—"

"They're mine," he said simply.

His voice was so calm and controlled when he was anything but. He was a father!

It was a shock to hear the news he'd hoped for but shocks seemed to be just another day in the ER for him these days. Images flashed through his mind of meeting Jessica the day his divorce was final. She'd sat next to him at the bar. He really had only wanted to talk. A distraction from the fact that his carefully constructed life had fallen apart.

For a while talking was all she'd done, telling him about her sister, Annie, living with her between jobs, and that he would like her. Then she'd flirted and charmed her way into his bed. He'd had a rough time of it and she promised sex without complications.

Surprise! Let the complications begin. Oddly enough, complication number one was Annie Campbell.

At least this time Mason called to ask Annie if he could come by. He'd gotten the news from the lab just like she had, so of course she agreed to see him. The problem was now she had to see him.

He was the twins' father, which gave him every right to be a part of their lives. But he made her nervous. Not in a creepy way. More like the cute-guy-at-school-you-had-a-crush-on kind of thing. And she had to figure out how to co-parent with a complete stranger who made her insides quiver like Jell-O.

There was a knock on the door. She noticed he didn't ring the doorbell again, which meant he was capable of learning. And it was a good thing, too, since the babies were asleep at the same time. Although not for long since they needed to eat.

Annie opened the door and Mason stood there, this time in worn jeans and a cotton, button-up shirt with the long sleeves rolled to mid-forearm. The look did nothing to settle her nerves.

"Come in," she said without offering a hello.

But neither did Mason. He walked past her, mumbling something about needing to buy a minivan and save for college.

"I suppose that means you don't want to sign away your rights as a father."

"No." His expression was intense, serious. "In fact, since I last saw you, I consulted an attorney."

Words to put fear into a girl's heart. "I'm their legal guardian. If you try and take them away from me—"

"Whoa." He put his hands up in a slow-down motion. "It's just that even though I'm their father, I have no rights because my name isn't on the birth certificate. Now, with DNA proof, I will acknowledge paternity and petition the court to legally claim my paternal rights."

"How long will that take?"

"There's a sixty-day waiting period, then however long it takes to get a court date," he said.

"And then you're going to sue for sole custody?"

"Of course not. No one is talking custody fight here. You clearly love them."

"I do. But how can you know that?" Where men were concerned, suspicion was her default emotion.

"Because you did copious research on a pacifier. And I just get the feeling that if I look at either baby funny, you'd cut my heart out with a spoon."

"You're not wrong." But how did he know her so well? They'd barely met. "Is that a negative critique on my mothering instincts?"

"Absolutely not. You're protective. And I think that's a plus. I happen to strongly believe in traditional two-parent families. That kind of environment is a positive influence in shaping their lives. It's the way I grew up and I didn't turn out so bad. I'd like my children to have that, too."

"I see." That was good, right? It was something she'd never had and desperately wanted. Especially for the twins she loved so much.

He looked around. "It's awfully quiet. Are the babies here?"

She wanted to say, "Duh." Where else would they be? There was no family to help her out. She'd barely heard from her mother and stepfather after they'd moved to the other side of the country. Jess was all she'd had. But there was no reason to be snarky to Mason.

"They're both asleep at the same time. It's a very

rare occurrence." His grin made her want to fan herself but she managed to hold back.

"Maybe we should have a parade in their honor," he teased.

"Good grief, no. The marching bands would wake them up and I want to enjoy every moment of this quiet for as long as it lasts."

"Good point. A better use of this time would be for you and I to get to know each other."

He probably wouldn't like what she had to say.

Chapter 2

Annie tried to think of a reason getting to know Mason was a bad idea. She wondered how Mr. I Had a Perfect Childhood would feel about co-parenting with someone whose story wasn't so pretty. But he had a right to know.

Common sense dictated that she find out everything possible about her babies' father and she couldn't do that without giving him information about herself. But he made her nervous. To reveal her nerves would require an explanation about why that was and she didn't think she could put it into words. At least not in a rational way. Last time he'd been here, he was less than pleased about not being informed that he might be a father. Annie couldn't really blame him and wondered if he was still resentful.

"Getting to know each other is probably a good

idea," she agreed. "I was going to have a quick bite to eat while Charlie and Sarah are sleeping. It's just leftovers but you're welcome to join me."

"Thanks. What can I do to help?"

"Set the table, I guess." She wasn't used to having help; it was nice. "I'm going to throw together a salad and I have cold fried chicken. I'll nuke some macaroni and cheese." She pointed out the cupboard with the plates and the drawer containing utensils. Napkins were a no-brainer, right in plain sight in a holder on her circular oak table.

"Yes, ma'am."

"One thing about me you should know right now," Annie said as she put prewashed, bagged lettuce into a bowl. "Never call me 'ma'am.' It makes me feel like I need help crossing the street."

"Understood." He set two plates on the table. "So what should I call you? Miss Campbell?"

"Annie works." She put dressing on the greens and handed him the bowl containing long-handled serving spoons. "Toss this, please."

"Yes, ma—" He looked sheepish. "Sorry. I'm a civilian now."

"I guess you can take the man out of the military but you can't take the military out of the man." She felt a little zing in her chest when she looked at him and struggled for something to say. "So, you were in the army."

"Yes. I enlisted."

She put a casserole dish in the microwave and pushed the reheat button. "Why?"

"I wanted to go to medical school and couldn't afford it. My parents wanted to help, but it's a steep price tag and I didn't want them taking out a second mortgage or going into debt. It was the best way to get where I wanted to go without putting a strain on them. When I got my MD, I owed the military four years. The upside is that I was able to serve my country while paying back the government."

Watching him toss the heck out of that lettuce, Annie realized a couple of things. He was way above average-looking and it wasn't as hard to talk to him as she'd thought. Although, he was the one doing the talking. With a little luck he wouldn't notice that she hadn't revealed anything about herself yet.

Keep the conversation on him. She could do this. She was a grown woman now, not the geeky loner she'd once been. "So now you're a doctor."

"That's the rumor. Also known as an emergency medical specialist." He stopped tossing the salad. "I've started my job at Huntington Hills Memorial Hospital. Just so you know I'm not a deadbeat dad."

"I didn't think you were."

"Just wanted to clarify." He shrugged his broad shoulders. "This kind of feels like a job interview. Maybe the most important one I'll ever have."

"I hadn't thought about it that way. And it doesn't matter what I think," she said. "You are their biological father. Time will tell if you can be a dad."

The expression on his face didn't exactly change but his eyes turned a darker navy blue, possibly with disapproval. "Spoken like a true skeptic."

"I am and there are reasons."

"You're not the only one. Your sister wasn't going to tell me I'm a father."

Annie got his meaning. He was wondering if keeping the truth from a man was a shared family trait. Part of her wanted to remind him she was the reason her sister made the daddy candidate list. Part of her respected his skepticism about her. More often than not people let you down and the only way to protect yourself was to expect the worst. So, yay him.

"That was wrong of Jessica. In her defense, I'd like to point out that she was taking steps to do the right thing. It's not her fault that she couldn't see it through."

"Look, Annie, I didn't mean—"

"Sure you did," she interrupted. "And you're not wrong. So this isn't a job interview as much as it's about finding a way to work together for the sake of those babies."

He thought for a moment. "Can't argue with that."

"Okay." The microwave beeped so she pulled out the casserole dish and stirred the macaroni and cheese, then put it back in for another minute. "So you have family here in Huntington Hills?"

"Parents and siblings," he confirmed.

"How many siblings?"

"Two brothers and a sister."

Annie felt the loss of her sister every day and not just because of caring for the twins. No one knew her like Jess had. They'd shared the same crappy childhood and her big sis had run interference at home and at school. She'd always had Annie's back—no matter what.

"You're lucky to have a big family."

"I know you're right, but I'm looking forward to having a place of my own," he said.

"Don't tell me." She grinned. "You're a man in his

thirties living with his mother. You know what they say about that."

"No. And I don't want to know. Besides, it's not as bad as you make it sound." He smiled and the corners of his eyes crinkled in an appealing way.

"There's no way to make it sound good."

"I guess technically I live with my parents here in town. I sold my house before going to Afghanistan. I'm just staying with the folks until I can find a place of my own." His smile disappeared and there was a shadow in his eyes, something he wasn't saying.

And she didn't ask. The microwave beeped again and she retrieved the dish and set it on the table. "Okay, then. That makes it a whole lot less weird."

"Good."

"Dinner is served."

They sat across from each other and filled their plates. Well, he did. A couple pieces of chicken with a healthy portion of macaroni and cheese. He dug in as if he hadn't eaten in a week.

He finished a piece of chicken and set the bone on his plate. "So, what about you?"

"Me?"

"Yeah. I've monopolized the conversation. Now it's your turn."

She really didn't like talking about herself. "What do you want to know?"

"Do you have a job?"

"Other than caring for the twins?" She realized he had no frame of reference yet for how that was a full-time job. "I'm a graphic designer."

"I see." There was a blank look in his eyes.

"You have no idea what I do, right?"

"Not a clue," he admitted. "I was going to wait until you were busy with something else and Google it on my phone."

He was honest, she thought. That was refreshing. "Let me save you the trouble. I create a visual concept, either with computer software or sketches by hand, to communicate an idea."

"So, advertising."

"Yes. But more. Clients are looking for an overall layout and production design for brochures, magazines and corporate reports, too."

"So, you're artistic."

"Beauty is in the eye of the beholder, I guess. But I can honestly say that I've always loved to draw." She didn't have to tell him she was dyslexic and that made anything to do with reading a challenge. Was it genetic? He might need to know at some point but that time wasn't now. "Fortunately, I can do a lot of work from home. Which means I haven't had to leave Charlie and Sarah much. Yet."

"Oh?" He had finished off his second piece of chicken and half a helping of the macaroni. Now he spooned salad onto his plate and started on that.

Annie pushed the food around hers. Talking about herself made her appetite disappear. "We're developing an advertising package and bid for a very large and well-known company. I won't jinx it by telling you who. But if we get it, my workload could increase significantly and that would mean meetings in the office." She speared a piece of lettuce with her fork, a little more forcefully than necessary. "And the twins don't really have much to add to the discussion yet."

"What are you going to do?"

"I'm planning to cross that bridge if and when it needs crossing."

She put a brave and confident note in her voice because she didn't feel especially brave or confident. Leaving her babies with a trusted friend who bailed her out in an emergency was one thing. Turning them over to a stranger, even a seasoned child-care professional who'd passed a thorough background check was something she dreaded.

"It's really something," he said. "Taking in two infants."

"How could I not?" Annie swallowed the lump of emotion in her throat. "Their mother was my sister."

"Still, I know people who wouldn't do it. You and Jessica must have been close."

"We were. She was always there for me. No matter what—" Unexpectedly, tears filled her eyes and Annie didn't want him to see.

She stood, picked up her plate and turned away before walking over to the sink. She felt more than heard Mason come up behind her. Warmth from his body and the subtle scent of his aftershave surrounded her in a really nice way.

"Annie, if I haven't said it already, I'm very sorry for your loss."

"That's exactly what her doctor said to me when he told me she was dead. Is there a class in med school on how to break bad news to loved ones?"

"No. Unfortunately, it's just experience. The kind no doctor wants to get."

It had been three months since Jess died. Annie had thought she was out of tears and didn't want to show weakness in front of this man. Maybe because he was the babies' biological father and had a stronger and more intimate connection to them than she did. The reason didn't matter because she couldn't hold back her shaky breaths any more than she could hide the silent sobs that shook her whole body.

The next thing she knew, his big, strong hands settled gently on her upper arms and he turned her toward him, pulled her against his chest in a comforting embrace. He didn't say anything, just held her. It felt nice. And safe.

That was a feeling Annie had very little experience with in her life. Odd that it came from a relative stranger. Maybe Jess had felt it, too.

Annie got her emotions under control and took a step back. She was embarrassed and couldn't quite meet his gaze. "I'm sorry you had to see that."

"Don't be."

She shrugged. "Can't help it. I don't know why I broke down now. It's not a fresh reality."

"Maybe you haven't had time to grieve. What with suddenly being responsible for two babies."

That actually made a lot of sense to her. "Anyway, thanks."

"You're welcome. I hope it helped." He looked like he sincerely meant that. Apparently the business of helping people was the right one for him.

"Speaking of those babies, I'm going to check on them. It's not their habit to be so quiet and cooperative when I'm having a meal." The first one with their father, she noted.

"You cooked, so I'll do the dishes."

"Cook is a very nebulous term for the way I warmed up leftovers. But I'm taking that deal," she agreed.

The best one she'd had in a long time. She went to the "nursery" and found Charlie and Sarah awake and playing. Standing where they couldn't see her, she watched them exploring fingers and feet and smiling at each other.

Her heart was so full of love for these two tiny humans that it hurt, and was something she experienced daily. But having a man in her kitchen doing dishes didn't happen on a regular basis.

She found herself actually liking Mason Blackburne. So far. But she hadn't known him very long. There was still time for him to screw up and she had every confidence that he would.

Men couldn't seem to help themselves.

Mason was feeding a bottle to Charlie when he heard footsteps coming up the outside stairs followed by the apartment door opening. Annie walked in and looked at him then glanced around.

"Wow, it's quiet in here. And really neat." Was there the tiniest bit of envy in her expression? "I'm feeling a little inadequate because I can't seem to manage two infants and an apartment without leaving a trail of debris and destruction in my wake."

"Oh, well, you know—"

After several weeks of him visiting the babies every chance he could, she'd reluctantly accepted his offer to watch them while she went to her office for a meeting. He wasn't completely sure she hadn't done a background check on him before agreeing. Fortunately he'd already passed the diaper-changing, bottle-feeding and burping tests. Still, Annie had been very obviously conflicted about walking out the door and leaving him in charge. He'd assured her there was nothing to worry about and shooed her off to work.

She'd barely been gone five minutes before all hell had broken loose. Two code browns and a simultaneous red alert on the hunger front. His situational readiness went to DEFCON 1 and he'd done what he'd had to do.

Glancing at the hallway then at her, he said, "I thought you'd be gone longer."

She walked over and kissed Charlie's forehead. The scent of her skin wrapped around Mason as if she'd touched him, too, and he found himself wishing she had. The night she'd cried and he held her in his arms was never far from his mind. She'd felt good there, soft and sweet.

"I stayed for the high points then ducked out of the meeting. I just missed my babies and didn't want to be away from them any longer," she said. "How did it go? Where's Sarah?"

At that moment his mother walked into the room holding the baby in question. Florence Blackburne was inching toward sixty but looked ten years younger. Her brown hair, straight and turned under just shy of her shoulders, was shot with highlights. He'd been about to tell Annie that he'd called her for help, but he was outed now.

"You must be Annie. I'm Florence, Mason's mother."

Annie's hazel eyes opened wide when she looked at him. "I thought you said you could handle everything."

"When I said that, the ratio of adults to babies was one to one. And I did handle it," he said defensively. "I called for reinforcements." He set the bottle on the coffee table and lifted Charlie to his shoulder to coax a burp out of him. It came almost instantly, loud and with spit-up. "That's my boy," he said proudly.

"Seriously?" she said.

"Eventually he'll learn to say excuse me." Mason shrugged then returned to the subject of calling his mom. "I admit that I underestimated my multitasking abilities."

"Oh, please," Flo said. "You just couldn't stand that one of your children was unhappy."

"Yeah, there's that," he acknowledged.

"Even though I told him that crying isn't a bad thing. They'd be fine." Flo was talking to Annie now. "You know this already. You've been doing it by yourself since these little sweethearts were born."

"I have." Annie gave him a look that could mean anything from "You're a child-care jackass" to "Finally someone gets it."

"How nice that you had backup on your first solo mission."

Flo's blue eyes brimmed with sympathy and understanding as only another mother's could. She handed the baby girl to Annie. "You're not alone now, honey. Being a mother is the hardest job you'll ever do times two. And sometimes you need a break. Recharge your batteries. Take a deep breath. Go get your hair trimmed or a pedicure. I just want you to know that I'm here. Don't hesitate to call."

"I would never impose," Annie said.

"These are my grandchildren. It wouldn't be an imposition. I have a part-time job as a receptionist in a dermatology office and my hours are flexible, so we can work around that. Mason will give you my number."

"Thank you." Annie kissed Sarah's cheek. "I appreciate that."

"What are grandmothers for?" She shrugged. "Full disclosure, I might spoil them just a little because I've waited a long time to play the grandmother card. Charlie and Sarah will learn that my house is different, but I will never compromise your rules. I might be prejudiced, but these are the most beautiful babies I've ever seen. Although I don't see much of Mason in them."

"Gee, thanks, Ma," he teased.

"I didn't mean it like that, son." She smiled at him. "It's just that they look a lot like you, Annie."

She pressed her cheek to baby Sarah's. "There was a strong resemblance between my sister and me."

"Then she was very beautiful," his mom said.

"She was," Annie agreed.

The subtext was that Annie was beautiful, too, and Mason couldn't agree more. Today she was professionally dressed in slacks, a silky white blouse and black sweater. Low-heeled pumps completed the outfit, but he missed her bare feet. Her straight, silky blond hair fell past her shoulders and she was wearing makeup for the first time since he'd met her. And he'd been right. She was a knockout.

"Well, you two, now that everything is under control, I'll be going." Florence grabbed her purse, kissed Mason on the cheek and smiled fondly at her grandbabies. "It was wonderful to meet you, Annie. You don't need my approval, but it has to be said that you've done a remarkable job with your children. And I sincerely meant what I said. Call me if you need anything."

"Thank you, Mrs. Blackburne—"

"It's Flo." She patted Annie's shoulder. "'Bye."

And then the two of them were alone, each holding a baby, and Mason wondered what Annie was thinking.

"So that was my mom."

"You have her eyes."

He'd heard that before. "It turns out that when one of my children is crying because he or she has needs that I can't instantly meet, it's not something I manage very well."

"As flaws go, it's not an exceptionally bad one to have," she conceded. "So you called your mom."

"Yeah."

"And if I got home later and your mom was gone, would you have let me believe you sailed through your first time alone with them trouble free?"

He would have wanted to. There was the whole male pride thing, after all. But... "No. I'd have told you she'd been here."

"Why?"

"Because that's the truth and it's the right thing to do." He shrugged and a dozing Charlie squirmed a little against his shoulder.

"I'm not sure I believe you."

He remembered her saying she was a skeptic and had her reasons. Skepticism was rearing its ugly head now. "In time you'll be convinced that I embrace the motto that cheaters never prosper."

"And in time, if I'm convinced, something tells me your mom is responsible for that honest streak."

"Oh?"

"Yeah. She's really something."

"She's just excited and happy to finally have even one grandchild. In her world twins is winning the lottery."

"I didn't mean that as a criticism." There was a baby quilt on the sofa beside him. Annie took it and spread the material on the floor in front of the coffee table. She put Sarah on it then sat next to him. "I meant just the opposite. She's full of energy in the best possible way. The kind of supportive, protective mother I wish my mom had been. The kind I want to be."

That little kernel of information reminded Mason that he didn't know much about her. The night they'd been getting acquainted he'd given her some facts about himself. She'd only offered up what she did for a living and then he'd held her when she'd cried. He hadn't been able to focus on much besides the soft curves of her body and hadn't noticed how little he'd learned. Now he was becoming aware of how guarded she was. And it wasn't just about protecting Charlie and Sarah. She held parts of herself back and he wondered why.

He stood with Charlie in his arms, then moved to the blanket on the floor and gently settled the sleeping baby next to his sister. After stretching his cramped muscles, he met Annie's gaze. "So, what you just said implies that your mother wasn't supportive."

"She had issues."

He waited for more but that was it. "Had? Does that mean she passed away?"

"No. She lives in Florida with her husband." When Sarah let out a whimper, Annie jumped up as if she'd just been waiting for an excuse to end this conversation. "Did she have a bottle?"

"No."

"Okay." Annie scooped up the baby and went into the kitchen to get a bottle from the refrigerator.

Mason didn't claim to be a specialist in the area of feelings but it didn't take a genius to see that Annie wasn't comfortable talking about herself. Either she was hiding something or there was a lot of pain in the memories. So now he knew she was a graphic artist, had adored her sister and missed her terribly. And there was stuff in her past that she didn't want to talk about.

That was okay. She was the mother of his children and he wasn't going anywhere. In his experience as an ER doc, he'd learned that often people held things back but eventually the facts came out. And he wanted all the facts about his children's legal guardian.

Chapter 3

Several weeks after Mason walked into her life Annie got her first really powerful blast of mom guilt. There had been some minor brushes with the feeling, but this one was a doozy.

Because of him, and by extension his mother, Florence, everything had changed. For the better, she admitted. The woman was fantastic with the twins so when she'd offered to watch them while Annie went to a mandatory meeting in the office, she'd gratefully accepted.

It had only been a few hours ago that Annie had walked out of her apartment but it felt like days. She checked her phone to make sure there were no messages. The empty screen mocked her and she felt the tiniest bit disposable, followed by easily replaceable. There was a healthy dose of exhilaration for this unexpected independence mixed with missing her babies terribly. The verdict was in. She was officially conflicted and on the cusp of crazy.

If all that wasn't guilt-inducing enough, she was going to have a grown-up girlfriend lunch. She should call it off and go be with Charlie and Sarah. Even as that thought popped into her head, she saw Carla Kellerman walking toward her with a food bag. Her friend had stopped to pick up something, as promised. So if Annie bugged out now, Carla would be inconvenienced. She would just have to eat fast.

"Hi." Carla came into her cubicle and smiled.

This woman was completely adorable. Perky and shiny. Straight, thick red hair fell past her shoulders and went perfectly with her warm brown eyes. She had the biggest, friendliest smile ever. And a soft, mushy heart. The occasional loss of her temper was almost always on someone else's behalf and made her completely human. As flaws went, it was adorable.

"I forgot how much I love this office," her friend said, looking around. "If I didn't already have a job, I would want to work here."

C&J Graphic Design occupied the top floor of an office building on the corner of C Street and Jones Boulevard in the center of Huntington Hills. The light wood floor stretched from the boss's office at one end of the long, narrow room to the employees' lounge at the other. Overhead track lighting illuminated cubicles separated by glass partitions. The environment had a collaborative vibe and Annie loved seeing her coworkers' creative ideas and them having easy access to hers.

"Hi, yourself." Her stomach growled. Loud.

"Apparently my arrival with provisions isn't a moment too soon." Carla grinned. "I guess I don't have to ask if you're ready to eat."

"Follow me. There are drinks in the break room fridge. Or we could sit outside." It was October but Southern California was still warm. There was a patio with wrought iron tables and chairs shaded by trees and surrounded with grass, shrubs and flowers.

"That. Door number two," her friend said. "I need fresh air."

They grabbed drinks, walked to the elevator and Annie hit the down button.

"Maybe we should go wild today and take the stairs," Carla suggested. "I could use the exercise."

"Since when? Don't get me wrong," Annie added. "I'm a supportive friend who will follow you bravely down eight flights of stairs. But this switch from 'I can't stand sweat' to 'We should take the stairs' is different."

"Not really. I always think about it."

Annie opened the stairway door and they started down. "But I can't read your mind. You never said anything before. What's changed? Got a crush on the boss?"

"Hardly. I work for Lillian Gordon."

"I know. But didn't her nephew come in to help the company over a rough financial patch?"

"Yes. Gabriel Blackburne. But he's kind of a hermit. Keeps to his office, hunched over a computer, presumably strategizing how to turn the company around."

They'd reached the ground floor and both of them were breathing a little harder as they headed for the rear door that led to the patio.

Carla gave her a look. "You have the strangest expression on your face. Why?"

"Because Mason's last name is Blackburne."

"Who's Mason?"

"The babies' father," Annie clarified.

"Small world," her friend said. "We needed this lunch even more than I thought so you can fill me in."

"I wonder if Mason is related to your Gabriel Blackburne. It's not that common a name," Annie said.

"I guess it's possible." Her friend moved decisively to the table with the most shade, put the bag down on it and sat in one of the sturdy metal chairs. "From what Lillian tells me, Gabriel is not a fan of her business plan but he does approve of the branding campaign C&J did for Make Me a Match."

"Well, he sounds a little intimidating, but definitely has good taste in graphic design companies." Annie sat at a right angle to her friend. "You'd expect Mason to be that way, but he's not."

Carla pulled two paper-wrapped sandwiches and napkins from the bag. She handed one over. "I need details. A text saying 'twins' father showed up and DNA confirms' isn't much information."

"I haven't had much time in the last few months."

"Two babies. I get it. And you're a saint, by the way. So tell me everything."

Annie explained about contacting the men Jessica thought could be the father and Mason showing up last. "He's an army doctor just back from Afghanistan. So, military and medical."

Carla took a bite of her turkey sub and chewed thoughtfully before swallowing. "He sounds honorable to me. I haven't known you long but I'm learning that you're good at finding flaws."

Not so far, Annie thought. "You know me pretty well. I'm not holding my breath he'll stay honorable. For now he's good with Charlie and Sarah. Not too proud to ask for help. The first time I left him alone with them, he called his mom for backup." Annie wasn't sure why, but she'd believed him when he'd said he wouldn't have let her think he handled the twins without a problem. "Florence, his mom, is fantastic. Loves kids and thrilled to be a grandmother. She has them now."

"Lillian's sister is Florence. Has to be the same family," her friend concluded. "Like I said, small world."

"No kidding. If Gabriel looks anything like Mason, I can see why you think you could use the exercise."

"He's pretty, but a little too dark and brooding for me. Besides, he keeps reminding everyone that he's only there temporarily." Carla shrugged. "So the twins' father is a hottie? It could be a reality show—*Real Hotties of Huntington Hills.*"

Annie laughed then thoughtfully chewed a bite of her sandwich. "'Hottie' would be an accurate description."

"You like him." Carla's voice had a "gotcha" tone.

"Why in the world would you come to that conclusion from what I just said?"

"Good question," Carla mused. "Maybe the way you were so deliberately aloof."

It was a little scary how well this woman knew her, Annie thought. They'd hit it off when working together on the branding campaign for Make Me a Match. Annie had spent some time in their office to get a feel for the dating service but the nephew had never poked his head out of his inner sanctum. Her friendship with Carla was relatively new but her assessment of Annie's feelings about Mason wasn't too far off the mark. Still, an attraction was no reason to be giddy. Just the opposite, in fact.

"It doesn't matter whether or not I like him. Men are notoriously unreliable."

"You know I agree with you about that." Carla ate the last of her sandwich then wiped her hands on a napkin. "I know we're fairly new friends and this is probably invading your privacy. Feel free to say it's none of my business, but what's your story? Why are you commitment averse?"

"Let's call it daddy issues. And before you ask, it's both biological and step. My mother has terrible taste in men. And you already know about Dwayne." Her ex-boyfriend. The jerk had sworn to always have her back but couldn't get away fast enough when she'd become the twins' legal guardian and brought them home. "I'm not going to be complacent and starry-eyed then get blindsided when Mason decides he can't handle being a father to twins. I can only deal with one day at a time and for now he's doing all the right things."

"Like what?" Carla asked.

"Well…" Annie thought for a moment and fought a smile she knew would look tender and goofy. "Hardly a day has gone by that he hasn't come to see them. He said he's already lost too much time being their father and doesn't want to miss another single moment with his kids that he doesn't absolutely have to."

"How sweet is that? Certainly not the behavior of a man who's going to abandon them," Carla pointed out.

"Maybe." It was hard to argue with that assertion so Annie didn't. "He works in the emergency room at Huntington Hills hospital and he looks so tired sometimes it's a wonder he can stand up, let alone hold one of the babies."

"Wow." Carla stared at her in disbelief. "Do you have recent pictures of the twins?"

"What kind of mom would I be if I didn't?" Annie proudly pulled a cell phone out of her slacks' pocket, found the most recent photos and then handed it over so her friend could scroll through.

"The twins are beautiful. And I say again—wow." Carla's eyebrows went up. "He's such a cutie, and I'm not talking about Charlie. This one of Mason holding both babies is a seriously 'aww moment.'"

Annie glanced at the picture and smiled at the memory of Mason dozing off while they were on his chest. He held them securely in place with a big hand on each of their backs. The moment did have a serious cuteness quotient, which was why she'd taken the photo. "More than once he's fallen asleep on my sofa."

"Oh?"

"Down girl." She hadn't been able to resist snapping the picture, but it didn't mean anything. Certainly not that she was looking at the future. One day at a time worked just fine for her. "Naps on my couch are about a demanding career, work schedule and his children," Annie said. "It has nothing to do with me. Or us."

"Still, he's not a troll and he likes kids. That's a good start."

"There is no start," Annie argued. "How can there be when he doubts my character? He made it clear that he doesn't trust me."

"What does he have against you? The two of you just met."

"He was justifiably curious about why my sister didn't contact him when she found out she was pregnant, about the possibility that he was a father. I got the feeling that, with him, that lie of omission extended to me because I'm Jessica's sister."

"Is it possible that you're inventing reasons to push him away? Like I said, you're good at finding flaws," Carla said. "Does it bother you that Jessica slept with him first?"

"Of course not. And, as you pointed out, I just met him a few weeks ago." Annie analyzed the question a little deeper. "And by *first* you're suggesting that I will sleep with him, too. That's just not going to happen."

Carla shrugged. "If you say so."

"You're seeing a relationship where none exists. Is Lillian working you too hard at Make Me a Match?" Annie teased. "Maybe you can't leave work at the office?"

Her friend laughed ruefully. "We need satisfied customers. And they need to spread the word about the valuable service we provide if the business is going to survive."

"I'll talk it up and, if I can, send clients your way," Annie promised.

But she wouldn't be one of them. She had enough on her hands without falling in love. Lust was a different thing altogether and had a mind of its own. Proof of that was the vision of twisted sheets and strong arms that had been keeping her awake at night. And those arms didn't belong to just anyone. They were definitely Mason's.

* * *

Mason was at the apartment with the twins several days after his mom had watched them. Annie was putting in more hours at her office because the deadline for the high-profile campaign was approaching fast. He'd gotten Sarah to sleep and had spent the last fifteen minutes walking Charlie. Now he carefully lifted the baby from his shoulder and put him on his back in the crib, beside his sister. He held his breath, fingers crossed that the little boy was finally sound enough asleep that the movement wouldn't wake him. No sound, no movement. Mission objective achieved.

He looked down at them—his children—and thought for the billionth time how beautiful and perfect they were. And how lucky he was to have them. Sure, he hadn't known from the beginning about the pregnancy and could whine about that, but it wouldn't have changed anything. A lot of active-duty service members missed out on big family moments because of deployment. The truth was, he couldn't have been there for their birth even if he'd known.

So he hadn't been able to support Annie through the shock and sadness of losing her sister. A little extra help with the babies wouldn't have hurt, either. Somehow she'd had the strength to do it all by herself. On the other hand, he wouldn't be going through the legal maze of securing his paternal rights now if things had been different.

It had been a month since he'd stood at Annie's door for the first time and he could hardly remember a life without his kids—and her—in it. He'd seen the commercials on TV for companies that facilitated meets for people who wanted a relationship. The tagline: Never

More Ready to Fall in Love. Mason was the opposite of that. Never less ready for love.

The collapse of his marriage had been a horrible warning. He found out that even if one made all the right moves and everything was perfect, it was still possible to fail spectacularly. And painfully. Because of things out of his control. He wouldn't make the same mistake.

That didn't mean he couldn't be in awe of Annie Campbell. He thought about her more than he liked, even when he was slammed with patients in the emergency room. She was quite a woman—sexy, beautiful, maternal, funny and smart. Everything a man could want. So why hadn't a guy snatched her up?

The doorbell rang and he swore under his breath, then checked the babies for any sign it woke them. Neither moved so he hurried to the front door, ready to chew out whoever had been stupid enough to ignore the baby sleeping sign.

He opened the door and saw a thirty-something guy standing there. He was well dressed and nice-looking. Mason wanted to strangle him. "Can you read?"

"What?"

"Did you see the sign?" He pointed. "The babies are sleeping."

"Right. Sorry, man. I forgot."

"How to read?" Now he really wanted to strangle this guy.

"No. That the babies are here." He held out his hand. "Dwayne Beller."

Mason hesitated then shook hands. "Mason Blackburne."

"The father?"

"Of the twins? Yeah." Now his curiosity was on high alert. "Who are you?"

"Annie's boyfriend." He shifted uncomfortably. "At least, I was."

"So you're not now?"

"No."

Mason felt an odd sort of relief that she was no longer with this guy. "What happened?"

"Is Annie here?"

"No." He stood feet apart, blocking the doorway.

"Do you mind telling me where she is?"

"Yes." They were sizing each other up. "Mind telling me what happened with you and Annie?"

Dwayne shifted his stance uncomfortably. "Look, man, would you just tell her I stopped by?"

"Why?"

"Because I'd like her to know that I was here."

Mason didn't miss the fact that Dwayne was looking pretty irritated. It didn't bother him at all. "I meant why don't you want to talk about what happened?"

"Because it's none of your business. It's between Annie and me—"

"Dwayne?" Annie was almost at the top of the stairs and her eyes widened at the scene unfolding in front of her door.

She had several bags of groceries in her hands and didn't look happy to see the guy. That didn't bother Mason at all, either.

"Hi, Annie. You look good." The ex-boyfriend had a sheepish expression on his face and glanced at Mason, who was still blocking the door. "Can I come in?"

"Why?" she asked warily.

"To talk," he said. "I really miss talking to you."

There was hurt and disillusionment in her eyes, proof the line wasn't working. "I don't think there's anything left for us to say to each other."

"Please just hear me out."

"These bags are getting heavy." She elbowed past him and Mason stepped aside to let her through. "And you said quite enough the last time I saw you. At Jessica's memorial service. Your timing left a lot to be desired."

Dwayne elbowed his way past Mason and followed her into the apartment, watching her set bags on the table. "Look, Annie, that wasn't my finest hour. I admit it, but—"

"There's no but," she snapped. "At the worst time in my life you walked out on me. That doesn't deserve a but."

"No one feels worse about that than me." The jerk held out his hand, a pleading gesture. "The thought of being a father freaked me out, okay? Two at once is a lot."

"Yeah, tell me about it." Her tone dripped sarcasm.

"You were distracted and I was starting to wonder if you were ever going to be there for me. For us. But I've had time to think. I miss you. I can't forget you."

Mason could understand that. Annie was unforgettable and this idiot had voluntarily walked out on her. The last thing he should get was a do-over.

Fortunately she appeared unmoved by his words. "Honestly, I haven't had time to think about you at all, what with two infants to take care of. The fact is, you never cross my mind. In case that's not clear enough, there is not a snowball's chance in hell I would ever consider taking you back. You abandoned me once. I won't give you a chance to do that to me again."

"I wish you'd reconsider. We were good together. At home and at work."

Dwayne must be desperate, Mason thought. After what she'd just said it was clear she'd made up her mind.

Annie's eyes narrowed. "Oh, now I get it. And the verdict is official. You're a conniving weasel dog and I don't ever want to see you again."

"Annie, please. I really need this—"

"Oh? I needed you," she said. "And you couldn't get out of here fast enough then. I'd like you to do that now. Just go."

"Annie—"

Mason had seen enough. He moved next to her. "The lady asked you to leave."

Dwayne's ingratiating performance disappeared. "What are you going to do? Throw me out?"

"If I have to." Mason stared at him and knew the exact moment the moron realized it was over.

"Your loss, Annie. Remember that."

"In my opinion, I dodged a bullet," she snapped back.

Without another word, the creep left and slammed the door. Hard.

Mason and Annie looked at each other and said at the same time, "The babies."

They hurried down the hall to check on them but Charlie and Sarah were still sleeping soundly. In unison, they heaved a sigh of parental relief then quietly backed out of the room and returned to the kitchen.

She met his gaze. "So, that happened."

"He's determined. I'll give him that."

"Yeah." She closed her eyes for a moment, as if erasing any vision of Dwayne from her mind. After letting out a long breath she said, "I could have called him much worse than a weasel dog."

"Me, too, but that was pretty descriptive."

"It was a compliment compared to what I was thinking. He's lucky I didn't throw something at him."

Mason studied her face and realized he had never seen her furious. The cleansing breath she'd taken hadn't cleansed anything. There was more. "What else did he do? Besides leave you at the worst possible time."

She met his gaze. "The last thing he said before bailing on me was that raising some other guy's brats wasn't what he'd signed up for."

"Son of a bitch—" Mason felt the words like a body blow. He didn't like the guy but Annie had at one time. He couldn't imagine the scope of betrayal she'd experienced. Now he was furious, too. "Good thing you threw him out. I'd have tossed him over the railing."

Surprisingly, she laughed. "That's a very satisfying image."

"What did he mean about working well together?"

"He's a graphic artist, too. It's how we met, collaborating on a job."

So they had something in common, spoke each other's language. "And when he said he needed this? Any idea what that was about?"

"He's employed by a rival firm. My guess is that they're in competition for this big contract I've been working on. If I took him back, he'd have access to my team's creative direction and could take steps to counter in their own presentation."

"So he wanted to steal from you," he said, seething with anger.

"That's my guess."

"Prince of a guy. Just oozing integrity. Damn right you dodged a bullet."

"Wow," she said. "Don't sugarcoat it. Tell me how you really feel."

"I don't mean to hurt your feelings." That was completely sincere. He would never hurt her. Not deliberately. But he couldn't hold this back. "I just have to ask. What the hell did you ever see in that guy?"

Her hazel eyes turned more green than gold. It was a clue that he'd crossed a line. Her next words confirmed that he'd said something wrong.

High color appeared on her cheeks. "It's really easy to be on the outside looking in and draw conclusions. I've known you, what? Fifteen minutes? Yes, we share the babies and you're their father. Calling them brats makes him lower than pond scum. But I get to say that. You don't get a say about my personal life, especially for something that happened before I met you."

"Annie, I—"

She held up a hand. "Now is not a good time to talk. I have another bag of stuff to bring inside. I'll get it," she said when he was about to offer. "I'm embarrassed by what just happened and taking it out on you. I need the exercise to shake off this unreasonable reaction."

Without another word, she walked out the door. Mason let her go even though every instinct was pushing him to go after her. But moments later he heard her cry out just before a scream of pain. He rushed outside and looked down. Annie was in a heap on the cement at the bottom of the stairs.

Chapter 4

One minute Annie was walking down the stairs, the next she was falling and desperately reaching out for something to stop the downward plunge. Something stopped her, all right. It was called cement. A jarring pain shot through her right leg. She cried out just before it took her breath away. Moments later Mason was there.

"Don't move," he ordered.

"Fat chance," she managed to choke out. "Knocked the…wind out…of me."

"Where does it hurt?" He ran his hands over her head and down her body. "Did you hit your head?"

"No. My leg."

After helping her to a sitting position, he gently touched her knee and shin. Searing pain made her cry out. "Ow!"

He slid her sandal off and put two fingers on her ankle, a serious expression on his face. Apparently he noticed her questioning look because he said, "I'm checking the pulse—blood circulation."

"Why?"

"Make sure nothing is restricting it," he said.

She was almost afraid to hear the answer but asked anyway. "What would be doing that?"

"The bone."

Yup, she was right. Didn't want to know that. Then he checked her foot and dragged his thumb lightly across the arch. It tickled and she involuntarily moved, sending a sharp pain up her leg.

"Ow—" She gritted her teeth because she wanted so badly to cry.

"Do you have scissors?"

"Kitchen drawer. What are you—?"

But he was gone and she heard his footsteps racing up the stairs. He was back in less than a minute with her heavy shears in his hand. He positioned them at the hem of her slacks.

"You're going to cut them?"

"Yes. I'm concerned about swelling. They'll do it at the hospital anyway. I think your leg is broken."

"No. I don't have time for that."

He met her gaze, and his was serious and doctorly. "You're going to have to make time. I'm taking you to the hospital."

"Can't you brace it with a couple of tree branches and wrap it in strips from a dirty T-shirt?"

One corner of his mouth curved up. "You've been watching too many action shows on TV."

That was probably true. "You could be wrong.

Maybe it's just a really painful sprain and you're over-reacting."

"I hope I am." His serious tone said he was pretty sure that wasn't the case. "You still need an X-ray to make sure. I'm taking you to my emergency room to get it checked out."

"Oh, bother—" She closed her eyes and tried not to move and make it hurt more. "I've been up and down those stairs more than a hundred times. How did this happen?"

"My guess is you tripped over that box of dispos-able diapers." He pulled his cell phone from his pocket.

"Oh." Vaguely she remembered bringing bags from the car and trying to take as much as possible in one trip. Between her parking spot and the flight of steps, the box started slipping so she'd set it on one of the steps near the bottom, intending to grab it when she got the last bag. What with the Dwayne drama, she'd forgotten all about it. It was a big box because she went through a lot of diapers— "Mason, the babies!"

"It's all right. I'm calling my mom. She'll take care of them."

"But they're my responsibility—"

"And mine," he quietly reminded her. "But every-one needs help sometime, Annie. And you really don't have a choice right now."

She hated that he was right.

While they waited for his mother, he fashioned a splint from a cardboard mailing box and duct tape to immobilize her leg. Then he filled a plastic bag with ice, wrapped it in a towel and put it on the injured limb to reduce swelling. Flo got there in record time and gave Annie a quick hug and reassuring smile before hurrying up the stairs to handle the twins.

"Okay," Mason said, "let's get you to the car." He helped her stand without putting any weight on the injured leg but the movement sent pain grinding through her. There was a grim look on his face when she cried out. "I was afraid of that. Either I carry you or we call paramedics."

"No ambulance."

"That's what I thought. This will be faster and less painful. Brace yourself. Deep breath."

He gently lifted her and she slid her arms around his neck then held on. In spite of the pain, she had that familiar feeling of safety when he held her and closed her eyes while he moved as quickly as he could without jostling her too much. His SUV was at the curb in front of the complex and he got her into the rear, where she propped the bad leg up across the leather seats.

When they arrived at the emergency room entrance, someone in scrubs was waiting at the curb with a wheelchair. Mason quietly but firmly directed that she be taken to Radiology and he would meet them there with paperwork. He was as good as his word and while waiting for the X-ray tech to take her back she filled out medical forms and insurance information.

It turned out that the scrubs guy was an ER nurse who worked closely with Mason—Dr. Blackburne. He told her that Mason was smart, skilled and one of the best diagnosticians he'd ever known. Everyone liked him. And his combat medical experience saved more than one life during a recent MVA trauma—motor vehicle accident involving multiple cars and victims with critical, life-threatening injuries.

"I think this is just a bad leg sprain," Annie told him. "But Mason believes it's broken."

"Hate to say it, but he's probably right."

It turned out that he was.

After the films were taken, Mason got them to the front of the line to be read by the radiologist.

Annie was sitting on a gurney in Emergency with the curtain pulled when he came to give her the results.

"I have good news and bad," he said.

"Don't ask which I want first. Just tell me the worst," she said.

"It's broken." There was sympathy in his eyes, not the satisfaction of being right. "You'll need to be in a cast."

"How long?"

"That's up to the orthopedic doc. In a few minutes he's going to set it—"

"And plaster it?" she asked.

"Probably fiberglass. It's lighter. The goal is to control your pain and swelling, then keep it immobilized while the bone heals."

She folded her arms over her chest and frowned at him. "I see no good news in that scenario."

"It won't require surgery to set the bone."

"Does that mean I can walk on it?" she asked hopefully.

"No. Non-weight-bearing for six to eight weeks depending on how fast you heal and whether or not you follow doctor's orders."

"I'm sorry. Did you say eight weeks?"

"Max. Less if you don't push yourself too soon," he confirmed. "And, in the good news column, a broken bone heals much faster than soft tissue damage, like muscles, tendons, ligaments."

"Oddly enough, that doesn't make me feel a whole lot better. I have two four-month-old infants." This nightmare was expanding exponentially. "How am I going to take care of them? Go to the store? Walk the floor if they're crying?" Then the worst hit her. "I live in a second-floor apartment. I have to go up and down stairs. There's no elevator."

"If you put weight on it before that bone heals, there will be complications," he warned.

"So what am I supposed to do?" She was very close to tears but not from physical discomfort, although her leg was throbbing painfully. Dyslexia had been a challenge in school and the bullying that resulted was emotionally devastating, but she'd learned coping skills. None of that had prepared her to cope with this.

"Move in with me," Mason said.

That sudden declaration kept her from crying. "Just like that? It was the first thing that popped into your head?"

"I've had time to process the situation."

She was still bitter about him being right. "Because you knew all along it was broken."

"Yes. I'm just glad it's not more serious."

"It's more serious to me."

That was self-pity, raw and unattractive. She wasn't proud of it, but couldn't deny the feeling. He probably thought she was being a drama queen, what with seeing patients who had injuries much more serious and life-threatening. But she had her babies to think about. How was she going to take care of them?

Through her shock she was trying to work out the

logistics of what was happening to her. "I can work from home and have groceries delivered. But I can't hold a baby and walk on crutches. I won't be able to pick up Charlie to feed him. Or carry Sarah into the bathroom to bathe her. And it's my right leg. That will make driving difficult, if not impossible." Her heart was breaking. "How will I get them to the pediatrician? Maybe Uber…but the complications—"

"Move in with me," he repeated.

"I don't know you," she blurted.

He sighed. "Look, I know this is upsetting. But it's been a month now. Have I let you down? Have I done anything suspicious or weird?"

"You mean aside from living with your parents?"

"I haven't had a lot of time to go house hunting." He moved closer to the bed and looked down at her. "If it would make you feel better, you could do a background check."

Annie's eyes filled with tears. "I know I'm being silly. You've been terrific and your mom is a goddess. But it's hard for me to deal with the fact that I can't do this on my own."

"My parents have a single-story house and lots of room. Believe me when I say they would love it if you and their grandchildren stayed with them."

"How do you know? Have you talked to them about it?"

"As a matter of fact, I have," he said. "I would tell you if they were hesitant, but they couldn't have been more enthusiastic."

"I don't know—"

"Look, Annie, we can keep this up however long you want, but we'll end up in the same place." He sat on the bed, being careful not to crowd her injured leg, and took her hand in his big warm one. "The thing is, you don't really have a lot of options."

He was right again and she wasn't any happier about it this time. She nodded and one tear trickled down her cheek. "Okay. But only for the babies."

Mason carried the last box from Annie's apartment into her new room. She was sitting in the glider chair with her casted leg elevated on the ottoman. Charlie was sacked out in one of the cribs his parents had bought and Annie was holding a sleeping Sarah in her arms.

He'd spent his day off making trips back and forth for all the baby paraphernalia, her clothes and toiletries. In between carrying the babies to her for feeding and cuddling, he put everything away in the pine armoire and matching dresser. Using the top of it for diaper supplies, the second crib beside it was being turned into the changing table. His parents wanted their grandkids to spend a lot of time there and had insisted on buying a bed for each baby.

That meant Annie would be there, too. He liked the prospect of spending time with her, especially being under the same roof. For the next six weeks at least, he wouldn't fall asleep on that uncomfortable couch of hers.

"Hi," she said.

"Hey."

"What's in the box?"

"Toys." He set the box in a corner, out of the way. With her on crutches, the last thing he wanted was for her to trip and fall.

Two days ago he'd brought her here from the hospital and his mom had helped her care for the twins. This was his brothers' old room. It had bunk beds but was still a little crowded with Annie and the babies. Between working a shift and moving things from the apartment, Mason hadn't had a chance to talk to her. He'd missed it. He didn't want to, but it was pretty hard to ignore how glad he was to see her.

"This is the last of the things on your list. Unless you think of something else."

"You look tired," she said softly.

"Don't feel guilty."

"Who said anything about—?"

"I can hear it in your voice." Funny how he knew her that well in a relatively short period of time. "It's not your fault."

"Yeah, it kind of is," she said. "I left the box of diapers on the stairs."

"That's why it's called an accident. On the plus side, my folks are over the moon about you and the twins being here." And, though he didn't want to be, so was he.

Mason moved closer to the chair and smiled at his beautiful daughter. "How are the kids handling this change of environment?"

"It's different and they know. Not much napping going on today. I could tell they were a little restless and out of sorts." She looked up and there were shadows under her eyes, proving someone besides him was not getting enough sleep. On top of that she was pale and there were traces of pain around her mouth from the recent trauma.

"How are you holding up? Are you staying off the leg per doctor's orders?"

"Have you met your mother? She's the keep-that-leg-elevated police. If I get up for anything other than the bathroom, her feelings are hurt because I didn't ask for help." Her full lips curved upward. "She's completely fantastic, Mason. So is your dad."

"You'll get no argument from me."

"Flo must be exhausted. Basically she's been doing the work of three people, between the babies and me."

"I think she's asleep." The TV in the family room was off and the house quiet when he'd come home with the last box.

"Good." Annie nodded. "She checked in with me when you went for the last load and wanted to put Sarah in the crib for me, but I just want to hold her. Your mom, bless her, completely understood. She was turning in and wanted to make sure I didn't need anything. She said to holler if I did."

"Well, I'm back and just on the other side of the bathroom." There were entrances to it from each bedroom. "If Charlie or Sarah wakes up, I'll hear them."

Annie shifted the baby in her arms. "Can you put her in the crib for me?"

"Sure." Mason leaned down and slid his hands under the little girl and carefully lifted her. After a soft kiss on her forehead, he set her on her back beside her brother. "She's out cold. So is Charlie."

"Excellent."

"Now you can get some rest," he advised.

"Yeah." But she reached for her crutches leaning against the wall beside her. "After I take a shower."

What? He'd started out of the room and froze then turned back. "You can't get the cast wet."

"Not breaking news, Dr. Do Right. The ortho doc was very clear on that."

He could see she was determined to stand and moved the ottoman out of her way. "So it's going to be a hop-in-and-out kind of thing. Quick."

"Believe me, no one gets that better than I do." She pulled herself up awkwardly, winced with discomfort, then arranged the crutches beneath her arms. "But I'm stuck with this obnoxious thing for a while and I have to bathe."

"Of course. But my sister is off tomorrow. She's a nurse and could help you—"

"I can handle this, Mason. Don't try to talk me out of it. Another sponge bath isn't going to cut it. And I'm going to wash my hair or die trying. So get out of my way. I don't want to hurt you."

She looked fierce and beautiful and so cute. Something in his chest squeezed tight for a moment, then he laughed at the idea of a little thing like her hurting him.

She glared at him. "It's not funny. After two days, I can't stand myself."

He could stand her. A lot. What he couldn't stand was her getting hurt. Seeing her at the bottom of the stairs had taken time off his life and he didn't want to speculate on how much. Showering on her own was a disaster in the making. She was still getting used to the crutches and learning to balance on one leg to keep her weight off the other. It wouldn't take much for this to go sideways, literally, real fast.

"Okay. At least let me help you with a strategy. Figure out the steps, pardon the pun, of this operation."

There was a suspicious gleam in her eyes. "Like what?"

"Keeping your cast dry for starters. A few drops on the outside isn't a big deal. But if you get the inside wet it can lead to a skin infection."

"That sounds pretty gross," she agreed. "So what do you have in mind?"

"I'll be back in a minute. Wait here."

"Seriously? You don't want me to hobble along and keep you company?" Letting the crutches take her weight, she stood there with a teasing look in her eyes.

"Right." He grinned then left the room.

The logistics of this maneuver ran through his mind as he hurried to the kitchen and grabbed the things he wanted. That kept him from thinking too much about Annie naked in the shower except for the lime-green cast on her leg.

Actually the vision popped into his mind anyway, along with the steadily increasing urge to kiss her. If he did, that could be a problem. Clearly she didn't trust easily and he wouldn't be another Dwayne in her life who made promises he couldn't keep.

When he came back to the bathroom, it was empty. "Annie?"

"Coming." Her soft voice came from the other side of the door. Then she shuffled back into the light wearing a short, pink terry-cloth robe, under which she probably wore nothing.

Sweat popped out on his forehead and he nearly swallowed his tongue. "I thought you were going to stay put."

"I changed out of my clothes."

"Yeah. Because that's what you do when you take a

shower." He sounded like a moron. *It's what happened when blood flow from your brain rerouted to another part of your anatomy.*

"What's all that stuff for?"

Apparently she was more focused on what he'd brought than what he'd said. Good. "A plastic trash bag, duct tape and a pitcher. Sit down and I'll show you."

She moved over and sat on the closed toilet lid then rested the crutches against the sink. "Now what?"

Now he would do his level best to act professionally and not let on that he was crazy attracted to her. "I'm going to put the bag over your leg. Before I secure it with the tape, I'm going to tuck this hand towel into the top of the cast so that if the bag leaks it will still keep the inside dry."

"Great idea. I love it when a plan comes together."

Not yet, but if his hands didn't shake when he touched her, he'd call it a win.

Mason went down on one knee and put her foot on his thigh. Then he did his thing with the towel. There was no way he could avoid touching her skin and the contact just south of her thigh was sweet torture. He tried not to notice, but the material of her robe separated just a little. Not enough to get a glimpse of anything he shouldn't but enough to torment him with what he couldn't see.

He took a deep breath, as if he was going underwater, then opened the plastic bag and slid it up over her cast. Twisting it closed just below her knee, he wrapped it securely with the tape then ripped it off the roll.

Annie nodded her approval. "That looks watertight."

"You still need to keep it away from the running water. Hang it outside the shower stall."

"What's that for?"

He glanced at the small, plastic sixteen-ounce measuring cup she was pointing to. "I'll help you wash your hair in the sink. The less time you spend in the shower, the better."

Her mouth pulled tight for a moment. "So I need to let go of a long, hot, relaxing wash."

"Like I said, it will be quick. Sorry."

"Not as sorry as I am." She met his gaze. "Let's do this."

"I'll get towels." He went to the linen closet in the hall and brought back two big fluffy ones. "This one is for your hair."

"Okay."

"Ready?"

When she nodded, Mason helped her stand, then put his hand at her waist and tried not to wish she didn't have that robe on. He instructed her to bend over the sink. Her shampoo and conditioner were right where he'd put them after unpacking her toiletries.

He turned on the water and filled the cup to wet all that beautiful blond, silky hair. He was a doctor and had been married, but this was the first time he'd ever washed a woman's hair. There was something incredibly sensual about the soapy strands running through his fingers.

No way could he stop himself from picturing her, him in the shower together with water running over their bodies. Surely he was going to hell for impure thoughts at the expense of an injured woman. He rinsed the soap as thoroughly as possible then used the conditioner and went through the same procedure, wondering if a man could go to hell twice.

"All finished." His voice was a little hoarse and with any luck she was too preoccupied to notice. He helped her straighten then handed her the towel to wrap around her hair while he steadied her. It didn't escape his notice that the pulse at the base of her neck was fluttering a little too fast. If there was any satisfaction from this ordeal at all, it was that she might be as affected by him as he was by her.

"Okay. Now for the hard part. I'll aim the showerhead away from the door so you can stick your leg out."

After he did that, she looked at him pointedly. "You can leave now."

Here was the classic definition of conflict. He wanted to get as far away from her as possible. At the same time, he didn't want to leave her and risk a fall. But the fact was he couldn't stay. He was trying to be a gentleman, not picturing her naked. The last thing he wanted was to be a sleazeball who reinforced all her reasons for being a skeptic. This might just be the hardest thing he'd ever done.

"Okay. But I'll be just on the other side of the door if you need anything."

"Thanks."

He turned his back and walked out, shutting the door behind him. That's as far as he got. He'd never forget her cry of pain when she'd fallen on the cement and hoped to God he didn't hear it now. So he waited right by that door just in case he needed to get to her in seconds.

He waited to hear the shower go on and it was a while because she had to hobble over, take off that sexy little robe, step in and set the crutches aside. The water went off fairly quickly so she'd gotten the message about not standing under it for too long.

And speaking of long, he stood in that same spot by the door for quite a while after he heard her leave the bathroom and go into the other bedroom. What the hell was wrong with him?

Stupid question. If this was a clinical situation, he would be focused on the medicine. Only that wasn't the case.

It was personal. No matter how hard he tried to stop, no matter how hard he tried not to be attracted to Annie, this was getting more personal every day.

Chapter 5

A week after breaking her leg, Annie and the kids were pretty much settled into a routine with Mason's family. He worked twelve-hour shifts for a couple of days, then was off a couple. When he was gone, his mother took over helping with the twins, bringing one or the other to Annie for feeding and cuddles. When Mason's dad, John, got home from work, he pitched in, too. His sister, Kelsey, had nursing shifts at the hospital, but happily lent a hand when she was home. It occurred to Annie to wonder why a grown man living with his parents was weird, but not a grown woman.

Mason swore that as soon as there was time he was going house hunting. And she wondered why he hadn't kept his house before he deployed to Afghanistan instead of selling it. One of these days she planned to ask him.

Right now she was too busy feeling guilty and sorry for herself. She was only good for elevating her bum leg and petting the dog while the rest of the adults took care of her babies. She could hear them in the other room getting baths. There was a lot of laughing and splashing going on and she was missing out on all the fun. Broken legs sucked.

Dogs did not. Lulu was a black shih tzu–poodle mix and completely adorable. Annie rubbed her hand over the animal's soft furry back and smiled when Lulu licked her hand, like kisses to say "Thank you for paying attention to me." When she stopped for a moment, sad brown eyes looked up at her. "Sorry, Lulu. I have to get up off this couch and go see the kids."

Florence Blackburne picked that moment to come in and check on her. "Not so fast, young lady. Your orders are to stay off that leg as much as possible."

"But I'm missing them grow up." Annie knew she was being overly dramatic and…dare she say it? Whining? But she couldn't help it. "You don't understand."

"Maternal guilt? Boredom? Missing your children?"

"Yeah, that." The words backed Annie up a bit.

Flo sat in the club chair at a right angle to her position on the sofa. "When I was pregnant with Kelsey, my youngest, I had a condition known as placenta previa, which could cause complications during labor and delivery. I was put on bed rest until she was developed enough to take her by C-section."

"Oh, my."

"I had three small and very active boys who didn't understand why Mommy couldn't do all the things she did before. I'll never forget Mason's little face when he asked me to throw the ball with him outside and I couldn't. It broke my heart."

"How did you get through it?"

"My in-laws were fantastic. It would have been almost impossible if not for them."

"You were fortunate."

"Don't I know it. The children adored them. We all still miss them." Her voice went soft for a moment. "They died a few years ago, a couple of months apart. She went first and my father-in-law seemed in good health, except for missing her. He didn't know how to go on without her."

"He died of a broken heart," Annie commented.

Flo smiled sadly. "That's what I always thought. My family helped, too. My sister, Lillian, adored the boys and was here as much as possible on top of her full-time job."

"So you had support from both sides of the family."

"I always suspected there was a spreadsheet and schedule," the other woman said teasingly. "Lillian was in charge of that, but business and records weren't her thing. She was always a romantic and said there's nothing sexy about numbers."

Annie grinned. "That depends on who's using the algorithm."

"So I've been told," Flo said. "My son Gabriel is helping her out with her business right now and I'm told he's not hard on the eyes."

"My friend Carla works at Make Me a Match." Annie explained how they'd met. "It's not a rumor that he's a hottie. She has firsthand knowledge."

Flo grinned. "Family can be both difficult and indispensable. So, my advice is, since there's no way your broken leg is going to heal as fast as you want it to, just sit back and enjoy the help. We're happy to be doing it."

"Thank you. It's appreciated more than I can possibly say." Annie smiled when Lulu rested a paw on her left leg and whined just a little to be petted. She happily obliged. "Please don't think I'm not grateful, because I am. And maybe I'm a control freak. But I haven't had very much experience with backup."

"Do you have family?"

"My mother and her husband. Stepfather," she added.

"You don't like him." Flo wasn't asking.

"How did you know? I thought I was hiding my feelings pretty well."

"You didn't call him *your* stepfather." The woman shrugged. "No offense, but you're not a very good actress."

Sometimes Annie wished she was better at it. Like the night Mason had washed her hair and waterproofed her cast. She'd been a bundle of feelings and jumped every time his fingers had grazed her skin. Every touch was like a zing of awareness, but he probably hadn't noticed. He'd never looked at her, just concentrated on positioning duct tape.

The thing was, Annie liked when he touched her. A lot. But since he'd shown up at her apartment, there'd been no signal from him that he had the slightest personal interest, other than being a father to the twins. They had to parent together. That was all. If she let the secret of her attraction show, it would be humiliating, and her life was already filled with enough humiliation.

Annie looked at the other woman. "I don't hide my feelings well. That could be why Jess and I didn't see much of him and my mother after they moved to Florida."

"Did they know she was pregnant?" Flo asked.

Bitterness welled up inside Annie. "They knew. And they know she died after the twins were born. But they haven't seen their grandchildren even once."

Speaking of being an actress, Mason's mother couldn't or wouldn't conceal the shock and disapproval that showed on her face. "Grandchildren are our reward for not strangling our kids as teenagers. But... Never mind."

Flo seemed so open and Annie couldn't figure out why she was reluctant to say more. Just then the dog jumped off the couch and trotted to the kitchen. Moments later the doggie door slapped open and shut.

"What were you going to say?" Annie couldn't stifle her curiosity.

"I shouldn't judge people I don't know."

"But...?" She prodded.

"No. Florida is on the other side of the country. I have zero knowledge about their financial situation."

"I can tell you have an opinion," Annie nudged.

"Of course. I have opinions on everything." Flo shifted in the chair. "How's the leg? Are you comfortable?"

"I'm as comfy as possible." Annie had her leg elevated on the coffee table with the cast resting on a throw pillow. "And you're changing the subject."

"Yes." Flo sighed. "I don't want you to think I'm awful."

"Seriously?" Now it was Annie's turn to be shocked. This woman had been nothing but kind, welcoming and a godsend. "I could never think that. I can't imagine what I'd have done without this whole family and I don't even want to imagine it. I've actually thought this, so I'll just say it straight out. You're a goddess."

"Right back at you. The thing is, maybe I have strong feelings because I've waited for grandkids for quite a long time. I'd hoped Mason would…" Flo checked her words and sadness slipped into her eyes. "That was another life. It's just that I can't picture not knowing my children's children. They're a blessing."

"The babies are for me, too," Annie said.

"Thank you for sharing them with us. I just want to be included. If I overstep, you are to let me know. I mean that, Annie."

"I promise."

"If I do, just know that it comes from a place of love. I don't want to miss out on anything."

"Okay. And you should know that if I don't think to reach out, it's nothing more than me being tired and brain-dead, certainly not deliberate. And you have to tell me."

"Thank you." Flo smiled and reached over to squeeze her hand.

Lulu returned to stand in front of Annie. The little black dog whined softly and Annie had learned this meant she wanted a treat for successfully going potty outside. The jar was beside her and she plucked out a bone-shaped biscuit, holding it just within the animal's reach. Lulu stood on her back legs, opened her mouth and snatched it from Annie's fingers then took it to her favorite spot underneath the dining room table. Annie was happy to be of use, at least to one member of this household.

But back to her folks. Annie thought about them.

"My mom and stepfather have missed everything and don't seem to mind. That's in character. When I was growing up, they seemed happiest when they didn't have to get involved in mine and Jess's life."

"It's hard finding balance between hovering constantly, being a helicopter parent, and backing off to let your child's independence evolve." Flo looked as if she was remembering. "Mason was our oldest and it never seemed fair that we had to practice on him because we had no idea what we were doing. Unfortunately someone has to be first. John and I always joked that he was our prototype."

Annie laughed. "At least Charlie and Sarah have each other and eventually a therapy buddy when they grow up and complain that we did it all wrong. At least me. Mason is so good with them."

It was clearer every day how much he loved his children, as if he'd been waiting a very long time to be a father. Unlike Dwayne, the douche who'd called her precious babies another man's brats. When she'd told Mason that, she'd been afraid he'd chase down the jerk and pop him like the douchebag he was. The thought of that was pretty hot.

"Mason told me about your boyfriend abandoning you," Flo said.

"Ex-boyfriend." Annie was going to add "mind reader" to this woman's list of superpowers. "I couldn't have been more wrong about him. I won't make a mistake like that again."

"Not everyone walks out."

"Couldn't prove that by me." Annie was afraid the other woman could look into her soul and see the feelings she was trying to hide. Then the meaning of her words sank in. "I wasn't talking about you. I must have sounded completely ungrateful. I'm not sure how I would have coped if not for Mason and you guys, his family."

"We're your family, too."

"I appreciate you saying that." But she wouldn't let herself count on it. The *stepfather* had always said she and Jessica wouldn't have been so much trouble if they'd been his blood. The message had been received loud and clear. Mason's family were helping, but only because of the blood connection to the babies. Why else would they bother?

"I mean it, Annie. Of course having trust is hard." Flo hesitated then added, "You don't have any reason to believe someone who just tells you he loves you. Believe someone who shows you he does."

She was right about trust. Annie's biological father physically left. The stepfather emotionally dumped her. Then she made the mistake of letting her guard down with Dwayne. Three strikes and you're out.

Annie didn't believe in love anymore. Disillusionment hurt and the longer she stayed here in this house with Mason, the more she could get sucked into believing. As soon as she could manage on her own, she was going back to her place.

Mason sat in the rocker that was older than he was and held Sarah in his arms. Annie was next to him in the glider chair, her bad leg elevated on the ottoman and Charlie nestled to her chest. It was late and everyone else in the house was asleep. To keep it that way, they were tandem rocking the twins.

He glanced sideways and thought how beautiful she

looked with a baby in her arms. She and the twins had been here for two weeks and it was the best two weeks he'd had in a very long time. Charlie whimpered restlessly and she softly shushed, settling him down.

Annie met his gaze and frowned. "What?" she whispered.

"Nothing." He studied Sarah and knew now that she was sufficiently asleep to handle a quiet conversation.

Annie kept staring. "You have kind of a dweeby look on your face. Why?"

"It's the same look I always have. Guess I'm just a dweeb."

"No." She shook her head.

"So you don't think I'm a dweeb?"

"I didn't say that. Your expression is just dweebier than normal." She rubbed a hand over Charlie's back. "What are you thinking about? It's making you look weird."

He hesitated. "I feel silly telling you."

"Now I have to know." There was a teasing note in her voice.

"You'll mock me."

"Probably. Suck it up, Doc. You're a grown man. A soldier. I can't believe you haven't developed a thicker skin."

Maybe a diversionary tactic would distract her. "Have you?"

"I had to." She laughed but there was no humor in the sound. "For survival. So let me help you exercise those muscles. What were you thinking to put that dopey expression on your face?"

"Well, I should start by saying that I'm sorry you broke your leg." *But not for helping you shower.* It was on his highlight reel of awesome memories, but he didn't think she'd want to know that.

"Not as sorry as I am. But how is that silly?"

"Because I'm not sorry about being under the same roof with you. And my children," he added. "So I can get to know them better. Like now."

"You're rocking Sarah to sleep," she pointed out. "How is that getting to know her?"

"I'm doing it in the rocking chair that my father bought for my mother when she was pregnant with me." It had been out in the garage and brought in because sometimes both babies needed rocking.

"So it's an antique," she teased.

"I'm not going to let you spoil this for me." He smiled at her. "I'm learning about her sleep patterns. And Charlie's. Figuring out what it takes to soothe them when they're upset. Their personalities. I get to just be around. Before it was like visiting hours at the hospital and now— It's not."

"You'd probably rather have them on their own. Without me."

"No," he assured her. "You're their mom. The engine that drives everything. The center of their world."

"And you really don't mind that your world is turned upside down because I broke my leg and the three of us had to move in?"

"Just the opposite. I love what I do for a living. I love being a doctor and helping people, but it doesn't compare to being a father and spending as much time as possible with my children. Like I said, I'm glad you're here. In fact, I'd have to say, for maybe the first time in my life, I'm content."

He wasn't pulling all-nighters for grades to get him

into med school or stressing about the money to go. It wasn't about looking at the calendar to gauge his wife's ovulation date or trying to get pregnant. There was no agenda except to just be. And while he was just being, he could feel Annie's gaze on him.

"What?" he asked.

"You're right. What you were thinking about was dopey. And sweet," she added.

"Haven't you ever experienced contentment?"

"It's hard to feel something you don't believe in. If contentment exists, it's just the bubble of calm between crises."

His mother had mentioned to him that she'd talked with Annie about her absentee parents and Dwayne the Douche. It explained her tendency toward cynicism, but he had the feeling there was more. He saw a lot of people in the emergency room and often they withheld information, reluctant to admit some aspect of their lifestyle might be contributing to whatever condition needed medical intervention. He couldn't help without all the facts and had learned to spot the signs. Annie was holding out, but maybe he could change that.

"Do you want to talk about what happened to you, besides a self-centered boyfriend who left you in the lurch?"

"Life happened," she said. "Dwayne was just the cherry on top of a bad-luck sundae."

"Tell me about it." Sarah was deadweight in his arms, sound asleep. But if he put her in the crib, this moment of quiet reflection would disappear and he didn't want it to.

"My mother got pregnant in her senior year of high school and was pressured to marry the boy she slept with. They were on their own and hardly more than kids themselves. Barely two years later, I was on the way. He couldn't handle the responsibility of two kids and took off."

That explained why Dwayne's desertion had hit a supersensitive nerve. "You mentioned a stepfather."

"Right." Bitterness was thick in her voice. "He's the man my mother married, but calling him a father is really stretching the definition of the word."

"What happened?" It surprised him a little when she answered because she was quiet for so long.

"You should probably know that I have dyslexia. There could be a hereditary component."

"Okay."

"If either of the twins has trouble reading, we need to look into getting them help as soon as possible."

"That's good to know." The tension and snap in her tone told him diagnosis and help had been a problem for her. "What happened to you, Annie?"

She wrapped Charlie a little more securely in her arms and softly kissed his forehead. "In elementary school, they didn't pick it up with me for a couple of years. Most of the kids were reading and comprehending in first and second grade. They were off and running."

"But not you."

"No. They tested us and arranged everyone accordingly, giving each group a color. It was supposed to be discreet, but everyone knew who was high, middle and low. I got help through the school district's resource program but needed more than they could give. My teacher suggested private reading and speech therapy, but my mother's husband said it was a waste of money. That I was just stupid."

"Oh, Annie—" A fierce, protective feeling welled up inside him followed closely by an even fiercer anger. And he didn't know how to vent it. It wasn't like he could fly to Florida and punch the guy's lights out for being an insensitive moron. But he was afraid to say anything, partly because he was so ticked off at the jerk. Partly because he sensed she wasn't finished yet.

"He used to put me down every chance he got. Called me dumb. Idiot. Retarded. Whatever insult popped into his tiny little mind."

"Where was your mom?"

"Right there when he did it. Too timid to say anything that would make him walk out and leave her alone with my sister and me."

"So *you* were all alone." It took a lot of effort to keep his voice neutral, to not let her see how outraged he was on her behalf.

"No. I had Jessica."

"She was just a kid herself," he said.

"Which makes her actions even more special." She looked at him over Charlie's head. "When he'd start in on me for no reason, she would run interference. And sometimes it would distract him and she'd take the brunt of whatever verbal abuse he was handing out."

"Good for her." He remembered a tough self-awareness about the woman he'd spent one night with. And this was where it had come from.

"He liked to ground us for any small thing, but never together because we had fun."

"Piece of work—" Mason said under his breath.

"And at school. There were bullies who used to

make fun of me. But not when my sister was around and she made it a point to be around as much as she could. She was my hero." Annie sighed and it was an achingly sad and profoundly lonely sound. "I miss her so much. She would have been a good mom."

"Her protective instincts were extraordinarily strong even then," he agreed. "Oh, Annie, I wish you hadn't had to go through that. No child should."

"What doesn't kill you makes you stronger, right? And I was convinced reading would kill me. For sure it was a challenge and I hated it. But art—" The dislike in her voice turned to reverence. "There's no right or wrong way to do it. It's about the artist's interpretation. I had fantastic teachers who took me under their wings and gave me the best advice I ever got."

"Which was?"

"Study what you love. I did that and found a career."

"And you're good at it," he said.

"I'm not looking for pity. I just thought you should know because we'll be co-parenting. And—" She caught her bottom lip between her teeth.

"What? You can tell me anything." And he hoped she would.

"You might have noticed that sometimes I have a chip on my shoulder. It's my hard outer shell, my bulletproof vest against humiliation."

"In the army I saw men and women ripped apart even with body armor. It can't protect against everything. Children can be cruel, but most grow out of it to become better human beings. You might want to cut people slack sometimes. No one is perfect."

"Says the guy with the perfect childhood. Raised by

the perfect parents, with a father who bought his wife a rocking chair when she was pregnant."

"It was good," he admitted. "And I wouldn't change a thing. It's the way I want Charlie and Sarah to grow up. But there's no such thing as perfect. You have to learn to roll with the punches."

She lifted Charlie from her shoulder and settled him on his back in her lap. He was getting so big he barely fit. Then she rotated her arm to ease the stiffness. "I'm not looking for perfect. I just learned to take things one mess at a time and always have a plan B."

Mason had studied anatomy, physiology; he knew how to heal bodies. But wounded souls were not his specialty. He wanted to take away her pain, and all the bad stuff in her past, and had no clue how to do that. For a man whose whole life was about fixing people, that was a tough reality.

All he could do was show up so she would know he wasn't going anywhere. They shared the same goal: loving these children. That would never change and it was safe for him.

Romantic love was different—mercurial—even when you thought you had all the bases covered. It was humbling and painful and something he was determined to never do again.

He wanted Annie. No question about that, but that was just anatomy and physiology. He wouldn't let it become more. Because of the children. And speaking of the twins...

"Tomorrow you and I are going to go house hunting," he said.

Chapter 6

The next morning when Annie walked into the kitchen Mason was there, leaning against the counter by the sink with a cup of coffee in his hand. Every time she saw him it was like being starstruck all over again, making her breath catch and her heart pound. Today was no exception. Most women would be excited about the reaction, but Annie wasn't most women.

Last night she hadn't challenged him about the house hunting remark because they were trying to settle the twins. Now she had questions. "About a house…" she said.

"I'm going out with a Realtor today and I'd like you to come along. If you don't have anything pressing at work," he added.

"No, I'm caught up. My boss has all my ideas and sketches related to the account we're going after, but…"

She leaned on her crutches and stared at him. She had another question. "What about the twins?"

"My mom is working half a day and will be home soon to watch them."

Annie's first reaction was no way. She hadn't been alone with him since the drive to the emergency room when she broke her leg. Although, technically, they had been alone that first night in this house when he'd helped her shower. She'd felt the burn ever since and not from hot water. It was all about the hotness of this man. So pretty to look at, which distracted her from the fact that he could not possibly be as good as he seemed. No man was.

"Annie, please say something." He set his mug on the counter.

"You can't want me to go. With these crutches, I'll just slow you down."

"Not that much. You're getting around pretty well now. Are you having any pain?"

"You sound like a doctor."

"Because I am." He smiled. "So, are you? In any pain, I mean."

"No. But my leg is itching like crazy."

"I know it's uncomfortable. Believe it or not, that's a good sign," he said. "On the bright side, getting out and doing something will distract you."

"Why?"

"You'll be focused on something else and not thinking about how much you want to find something that will fit down that cast and scratch the itch."

She couldn't help smiling because he was right about wanting desperately to do just that. But that wasn't what she'd asked. "I meant why do you want me to go along?"

"Since the twins will be with me half the time, I'd really like your input. A mother's perspective on their potential environment. I've been working with a real-estate agent and he's lined up some houses based on the criteria I gave him." Mason folded his arms over his chest. "I could really use another point of view, especially about safety concerns, kid-friendly floor plans. Another pair of eyes to pick up something I might not see or think about."

"You had a house before you deployed. Why did you sell it?" She wouldn't have blurted that out except he'd backed her into a corner. But when the happy look on his face faded to dark and his eyes turned intense, she felt guilty enough to let it go. "If you really want me there, I'll go. But you need to let me know if I'm holding you back. You don't have a lot of time, what with work, and I don't want to slow you down."

"Promise." With his index finger he made an X over his heart. "I'd really like to get this done. Find a place of my own. You know what they say about a guy in his thirties who lives with his mother."

She laughed. "Yeah. People are starting to talk. 'There's something odd about Dr. Blackburne. He still lives at home.'"

"I know, right?" One corner of his mouth curved up and just like that the darkness was gone. "And I think the twins need their own space. Sometimes we just need to let them cry and it's hard to do that here because we don't want them disturbing anyone else."

"Good point. Okay. I need to change." She glanced down at her old sweatpants, legs cut off to accommodate the cast. "If potential neighbors see a bag lady trailing you, no one will sell you an outhouse."

"Yeah." But something shifted in his expression when his gaze skimmed her legs, and humor was replaced by what looked a lot like hunger. He turned away and reached into the sink. "While you do that, I'll wash bottles and get them ready so Mom won't have to deal with it when she comes home."

Annie hobbled out of the room and prayed she wasn't making a big mistake going with him. However, she'd given her word and wouldn't back out. Besides, she had bigger problems. Like what to wear. Fortunately the October weather was still warm, at least during the day. Bermuda shorts would work. She chose white ones and a T-shirt with lime-green horizontal stripes and three-quarter-length sleeves.

Before going in the bathroom, she peeked at the babies in the crib and was glad they were still sleeping soundly. She was getting pretty good at balancing on one leg and braced her midsection against the sink while pulling her hair back into a ponytail. After taking more care with her makeup than normal, she told herself that it had everything to do with making a good impression on a potential neighborhood and nothing to do with impressing Mason. And she almost believed the lie.

Flo came home just as Annie was ready, so it appeared the universe was aligning for her to go with him.

A short time later they'd met the agent, George Watters, and were now pulling up in front of a house. "Note the beautifully maintained landscape," he said. "Brick walkway. Covered front porch. Four bedrooms, two-

and-a-half baths. I'm sorry, Annie, but this is a two-story home."

"That's not a problem," Mason said before she could comment. "We'll check out the first floor and see if it's even necessary to look upstairs."

After everyone exited the SUV and went up the walkway, George extracted a key from the lockbox and let them inside. Using the crutches, Annie swung herself over the threshold and looked around. It was an older home with low ceilings and needed a fresh coat of paint. There was an eat-in kitchen, but not a lot of counter space. Still, the family room was adjacent, so being able to keep an eye on the twins while fixing dinner was a plus.

Annie couldn't tell what Mason thought. She wasn't blown away, but he was the one buying it. "What do you think?"

He was staring out the sliding-glass door into the backyard. Turning, he said, "I was hoping for a little more space for the twins to play."

"No problem," George said. "This is just the first one. I've got more for you and your wife to look at."

"We're not married," Annie said.

"I should know better than to assume." George was silver-haired, in his mid to late fifties, and looked apologetic.

"No problem. It was an honest mistake." Mason didn't elaborate.

That was for the best, Annie thought. The phrase "it's complicated" was tossed around a lot, but with her and Mason and the twins, it really *was* complicated. The situation would be a challenge to clarify in twenty-five words or less.

"So let's go look at option number two," the agent suggested.

They piled back in the SUV and George drove them to another property that wasn't far from the hospital. The front yard was basic but well cared for and there was a front porch. For some reason Annie was drawn to covered front porches, picturing it with a couple of chairs for sitting outside in the evening. Chatting with neighbors. Watching kids play until it was time to go inside to get ready for bed. The vivid fantasy made her wistful.

George unlocked the door and let them in. The walls were painted a neutral shade of beige with contrasting white doors and trim. Mason checked out the rear yard and nodded approvingly. The kitchen had granite countertops, an island and lots of cupboards.

"Thoughts?" Mason said.

"It's nice. Let me take another look." She walked, or rather, hobbled, the complete bottom floor again and stopped by the stairs. "It has possibilities."

"Okay. Let's look upstairs."

"I can't get up there, but you go ahead," she urged Mason. "I'll wait here."

"I want your opinion on the entire house." He instructed her to rest the crutches against the railing, then scooped her up and carried her to the second floor.

Annie protested but slid her arms around his neck. "For a doctor you're not too bright. Your back will not thank you for this."

"I'm showing off." He grinned. "And you don't weigh much."

That made her heart happy and way too soon the top floor was visible. There was an open loft that looked down on the entryway. Mason walked her through three bedrooms and then the master. One very nice feature was a balcony overlooking the backyard, but they both thought the rooms were on the small side. Annie made him look in the closet and she felt it left a lot to be desired.

"But that might not matter to you," she said.

Unless a woman moved in with him. The thought was vaguely unappealing. It shouldn't be, and the fact that it was bothered her more than a little. Then it occurred to her that another woman would be around her children. And she had no right to say anything about who he became involved with. Well, shoot.

"I wouldn't have noticed that," Mason said. "That's why I wanted you to come with me. Still, there are a lot of positive things here. We'll make a list of pros and cons."

"Okay."

Annie found herself wishing the trip back down those stairs wouldn't end too soon. It gave her the opportunity to hold him, to feel her body close to his. She wasn't the one exerting herself but was a little breathless anyway. It didn't mean anything, she told herself. Just that while her leg might be broken, her female parts were working just fine.

At the bottom of the stairs Mason set her down and she missed the warmth of him. He handed her the crutches and looked up to where they'd just been.

"I was just thinking about the twins. When they start crawling. They'll go right for the stairs."

George joined them. "You can get gates for the bottom and the top. Until they're old enough to go up and down by themselves."

"I suppose." But Mason didn't look sure about that.

So they got back in the SUV and went to two more houses. Both were adequate but nothing to get excited about.

"I've got one more," George said. "It just came on the market. And it's one story."

When they stopped at the curb Annie zeroed in on the covered porch. Check, she thought. The yard was landscaped with neatly trimmed bushes and flowers. Inside was a traditional floor plan: living and dining rooms separated by a marble-tiled entryway. There was no furniture and George explained that because of a job transfer, the family had to leave quickly. That meant they'd probably be willing to make a deal and escrow could move fast. But first things first. They needed to look at the whole house.

The kitchen was gorgeous—beautiful granite, white cupboards—and she didn't even care about toddler handprints. There was a copper rack for pots and pans hanging over the island.

The rest of the house had spacious bedrooms and big closets. Mason heartily approved of the backyard and there was a casita. She looked inside and couldn't help thinking what a great home office it could be. But it wouldn't be her home or her office. Or her man. He was the twins' father. That was all.

"What do you think?" Mason asked.

Without hesitation she said, "I love everything about this house."

He smiled at her. "Me, too. I'm going to make an offer."

While he talked details with the Realtor, Annie browsed the rooms again. With every hobbling step she took, the longing for a traditional family grew. What she wouldn't give for the twins to have a father and mother. Correction, they had that. What she yearned for was all of them together in this house, a family unit, a happy home with kids. And marriage. Traditional all the way.

She hated being right about making a mistake coming with Mason to look at houses. Now there was a happy picture in her head, but reality never lived up to the image. If she'd never seen this place, she'd never have known what she was going to miss.

And she was going to miss being a family and living in this house.

Once a month the Blackburne family had dinner together. Attendance was mandatory unless you were bleeding, on fire, working or deployed to a foreign country. This ritual was one of the things Mason had missed most when he was gone. Today the family gathering had grown by two with the twins. Three counting Annie. She was the mother of his children and a part of them now.

Mason put a big blanket on the floor in the family room, set out toys in the center of it, then settled the twins on their backs.

Annie was sitting on the large sofa that separated the kitchen and family rooms. She was sporting a brandnew, hot-pink walking cast since her recent follow-up orthopedic appointment. After a month the bone was healing nicely, but the doc didn't want her to put weight on it for another two weeks. A cautious approach of which Mason highly approved. For any patient, but especially for Annie.

She met his gaze and smiled. "They're not going to stay put on that blanket."

"I know." They'd grown so much in the last two months, rolling all over and getting up on all fours to rock back and forth, the prelude to crawling. That milestone wasn't very far off.

"As you well know, those toys are far less interesting than electrical cords and everything breakable."

"And I couldn't be prouder," he said. "They're curious. Exploring their environment is exactly what they're supposed to do at this age."

His dad took the roast outside to barbecue and his mom walked over to stand behind the couch, wiping her hands on a dish towel. "Gabriel and Dominic aren't used to babies on the floor. Charlie and Sarah aren't like Lulu, who can get out of the way. Will they be okay?"

"My brothers or the twins?"

Flo laughed. "I was talking about the babies. We have to make sure everyone watches their step."

"Don't worry," Annie said. "I'm on it. I may not be able to move very fast, but I can direct traffic and, if all else fails, I've got my crutches. To make a point."

"Funny," Mason said and she smiled. He really liked her smile.

"It's too bad Kelsey had to work." His mom leaned a hip on the back of the sofa. "You're a doctor. You couldn't pull some strings to get her off?"

"Two things, Ma. I haven't been there very long, so zero influence. And I'm not in charge of the nurses' scheduling." He grabbed up Charlie, who'd already rolled off the blanket onto his stomach and had his eye on something across the room. "Hey, bud, where do you think you're going?"

When the doorbell rang, Lulu started barking and rushed to greet whoever was there, waiting patiently for someone taller and with opposable thumbs to open the door.

Mason put a squirming Charlie back on the blanket and looked at Annie. "It's about to get wild. Brace yourself."

"It occurs to me that for the last five months I've lived in a constant state of being braced."

And it looked good on her. Normally her hair was pulled up in a ponytail, out of her way when she was busy with babies. Today it was down and fell past her shoulders, shiny and blond. For some reason the silky strands framing her face made her hazel eyes look more green. Or it might be the pink lip gloss. She was a woman who would turn men's heads and his brothers were both single. The thought had him bracing—for what he wasn't sure.

The two men walked into the room and bro-hugged Mason. They all had blue eyes and brown hair—clones, his mother always said about the family resemblance. Gabe and Dom knew about Annie and the twins but this was the first time they'd met.

Flo smiled at her sons. "I have to finish getting the rest of dinner ready. Mason, you handle introductions."

"Okay." He looked at his brothers. "This is Annie, the twins' mother."

The taller of the two moved closer and shook her hand. "I'm Gabriel. Sorry about your leg. Nice to meet you."

"Same here." She looked ruefully at the cast. "My fault for not watching where I was going."

"I'm Dominic." He was the youngest of the boys and had a thin scar on his chin. The details were never clear but it had something to do with a girl.

"Nice to meet you." She looked past Mason. "And those two little troublemakers are your niece and nephew, color coded. Sarah's in pink and—"

"Charlie's the one in blue who is checking out the movie collection." Mason moved quickly to grab him up before the stack of plastic DVD containers toppled on him. "He's moving faster all the time."

"And Sarah is right behind." Annie indicated the little girl who was scooting in the same direction as her brother. "She's ready to follow into whatever trouble he leads her."

"Cute kids," Dom said. "They look like Annie."

"Subtle, bro." Mason held his son and the curious little boy checked out the neckline of his T-shirt then explored his nose and ear.

"So you're a graphic artist," Gabe said to Annie.

"Yes."

Mason hadn't mentioned anything about her job. "How did you know that?"

"Her firm did a branding campaign for Make Me a Match. It was well-done. Smart. Clever. Visual."

"Thanks." The dog trotted over to Annie and she patted the seat beside her. Lulu didn't have to be asked twice and jumped up for a belly rub. "My friend Carla works for you. We met while I was involved in the project."

"Actually she's my aunt's personal assistant. And I'm only working there temporarily."

"So she said. I understand the business is still not where you'd like, financially speaking," Annie commented.

"True." His mouth pulled tight. "Aunt Lil is more focused on idealistic notions of relationships than numbers."

Their mother walked over to join the conversation and clearly she'd been listening in. "My sister is a romantic and always has been. Did you know she fixed up your father and me?"

The three brothers stared at each other with equally blank expressions. Mason said, "That's news to me."

"Did she charge you for her services?" Gabe asked wryly.

"Of course she didn't."

Lulu barked once and jumped off the couch then trotted over to Sarah, who was reaching for the DVDs her brother had just looked over. Mason put Charlie back on the blanket and picked up his daughter.

"Her romanticism is the problem," Gabe continued. "Aunt Lil is in love with love and wants to give it away for free. It's a business and by definition the purpose of its existence is to provide a service for which customers are prepared to pay. In other words, make money."

Flo looked at Annie. "Lillian is a widow. She and Phil were deeply in love until the day he died. They never had children but she always says they were rich in so many ways because they had each other. She wants everyone to have what she did with her husband."

"They were lucky." Mason wasn't interested in what his aunt was selling. "Not everyone is."

"Is that the voice of experience?" Annie asked.

"Yes. I was married and the magic didn't last."

Annie had asked him why he'd sold his house before he deployed. He could have kept it, shut things down until he returned. But it held nothing but bad memories—loss, pain and a marriage imploding with no way to fix it.

Lulu sat on the baby blanket and Charlie touched her back. The dog was extraordinarily patient with the babies and was loving, even protective. While Mason cuddled Sarah close, he caught Annie considering him, surprise in her eyes.

Then she turned to Gabe. "How do you match people up?"

"Clients fill out a profile, with a picture, then define their likes and dislikes. An algorithm picks up key words to narrow down potentially compatible people. Then we have that group fill out a more detailed questionnaire."

"What kind of questions?" Dom asked. He looked uncharacteristically interested.

Gabe thought for a moment. "Things like 'If you could share dinner with anyone in the world, who would it be?' Or 'If you could be a character in a movie, which one would you choose?' A very revealing one is 'Tattoo—for or against?'"

"Let's try it," his mother suggested. She looked at Annie and Mason. "You take the quiz."

Annie looked a little startled. "I don't know about Mason, but I'm not looking for a match."

"I know. It's just for fun," Flo said. "You're both single. Gabriel, give them a question."

"Okay." He sat on the couch. "How about which character in a movie. You first, Annie."

"Wow. No pressure." She blew out a breath. "Okay. I'd want to be Wonder Woman."

"You're already a superhero," his mom said.

"How sweet. Thanks, Flo."

"I mean it. Twins? That says it all."

"Actually it's not the superpowers I want," Annie clarified. "But that golden lasso would come in pretty handy. A way to know someone is telling the truth."

"Okay. Good answer," Dom said. "Mason, you're probably going to say Superman."

"No." He'd had time to think. "Sherlock Holmes."

"Because the supersleuth is so in touch with his feelings?" Gabe teased.

"No. He notices little things and figures out who's guilty. I can relate to that. I do a lot of mystery-solving in the ER because people don't always give me all the facts. Their symptoms are very general and vague. So I have to read between the lines to help them. It's my job to figure out what's wrong."

"Good answers, both of you," Gabe said. "But I'm not sure they would intersect for a match."

"Okay, next question," his mother said. "I like the tattoo one. How do you feel about them?"

"Not a fan. Don't have one and no plans to get one," Mason answered.

"Okay. The doctor doesn't like needles," Dominic teased.

"But you were in the army," Annie said.

"A tattoo is not a prerequisite for joining," he answered.

"Annie? What about you?" his mother asked.

She squirmed then sighed. "I have one. And I love it."

Mason looked at her, the skin he could see, and couldn't find her ink. His curiosity cranked up by a lot to know what it was and—more important— where. Discovering the location would involve taking clothes off and his body reacted enthusiastically to that thought.

"Strike two." Gabriel shook his head. "Last one. Who would you want to have dinner with?"

"That's easy," Annie said. "Eunice Golden."

"Who?" they all said at the same time.

"I was an art major. She's a painter and a pioneer in her field, focusing on nude male bodies in her earlier work."

Mason noted that the rest of his family looked as clueless and surprised as he felt. And now it was his turn. "I'd like to have dinner with the Surgeon General of the United States Army."

Gabe gave him a pitying look. "Probably no overlap there."

"Even though that person is a woman, appointed for the next couple years?"

"Too subtle." Gabriel shrugged. "If you were clients of Make Me a Match, you would not be paired off."

"Then it's a good thing neither one of us is looking to do that," Annie said.

"Oh, pooh," his mother said. "A few questions on a quiz isn't everything."

Mason had mixed feelings. On the surface they might not look compatible, but he agreed with his mom that a quiz didn't come with a guarantee of success. Everything in his first marriage had looked ideal, but together he and his wife were a disaster. Still, a quiz

was stupid. Right? He agreed with Annie about that.
He wasn't looking for a match any more than she was.
He'd never failed a test in his life. Surely that's what
was bothering him now.

Chapter 7

Her hormones didn't take that matchmaking quiz but you wouldn't know it by the way they were stirred up.

Annie hadn't been able to stop thinking about those questions, through dinner and the rest of the evening. Now it was quiet in the house. Mason's brothers had gone and everyone else was in bed. The two of them were standing side by side, just putting the twins down. She had the crutches under her arms but didn't put much weight on them. Their arms brushed and she felt the contact all the way to her toes.

According to their answers to those questions, they weren't compatible, but her body wasn't paying any attention. Still, she had another question for Mason. She hadn't wanted to interrogate him in front of his family, but no one else was here now.

"Why didn't you tell me you were married?"

He glanced at the babies, who were drowsy but not sound asleep yet, and put a shushing finger to his lips. He angled his head toward the connecting bathroom and indicated she should follow him. Not wanting to disturb the twins, she limped after him. When he flipped the switch on the wall in his room, a nightstand lamp came on. There was a king-size bed with a brass headboard and an oak dresser with matching armoire.

Mason met her gaze. "I wasn't keeping it a secret. If I was still married, I'd have said something. But I'm not. The fact that I was married just never came up and it didn't cross my mind to mention that I'm divorced."

Logically that was true, but somehow it felt very relevant to Annie that she didn't know he'd been legally committed to a woman at one time. He'd taken that step because he'd been in love. It should simply be a fact from his past, just information, but she was having a reaction to this fact and it wasn't positive. She wasn't proud of it, but this feeling had a good many characteristics of jealousy.

And then she really looked into his eyes and saw the sadness. Facts were one thing; emotions were something else.

"Do you want to talk about it?" she asked.

He laughed but there was no humor in the sound. "You know those were the first words your sister said to me."

"Oh?"

He nodded. "My divorce was just final and I went to the bar. She was already there and came over, sat down on the stool next to me."

"She must have thought you looked sad. Like you do now." She moved closer to where he stood at the foot of the bed. Their bodies didn't touch but she could feel the warmth of his. "Did you tell her what was going on?"

"Only that my divorce became final that day but not why it happened in the first place. She heard the *D* word and suggested that there was a rebound activity guaranteed to take my mind off it."

Annie winced. It was hard to hear about her sister's behavior. Jess was always there for her and she'd never forget it. "She wasn't a bad person."

"I know. That night we both needed a way to forget the stuff that was eating away at us."

"What were you trying to block out?" she asked.

"Failure. On so many levels." He sighed. "I fell in love with Christy and that was obviously not a success. I was in town to see my family, on leave from the army, when I met her at Patrick's Place, formerly The Pub. That's where I ran into your sister." He smiled. "She was beautiful and funny."

Annie wanted to hear about the woman he'd loved. "So, on the day your divorce was final you went back to the scene of the crime, so to speak."

"Yeah. I guess closure was on my mind. Coming full circle. A place to reflect on what went wrong." He smiled sadly. "The night Christy and I met, we couldn't stop talking. We were kicked out at closing time and sat on a bench outside for hours. Just talking."

"About what?" Annie asked.

"About what we wanted. Mostly that we both very much wanted to have children." He smiled at her. "I love kids. I'm like my mom that way. In fact, I thought about being a pediatrician for a while."

"Why didn't you?"

"I liked the adrenaline rush of emergency medicine."

"So what happened? With Christy, I mean."

"We had a long-distance relationship, but it worked, and then I proposed. We bought a house here in Huntington Hills. After all, I wouldn't be in the army forever and this town is where we wanted to settle and raise kids. We had a church wedding with both families there. She even got pregnant on our honeymoon. Everything was perfect."

"Magic," she said quietly.

That soul-deep sadness turned his eyes as hard as blue diamonds. "Until it wasn't."

"She lost the baby." Annie was just guessing.

He met her gaze and nodded. "We both took it hard, but she was really sucker punched. After all, she'd had a life inside her. And then it was gone. The doctor said we could try again right away, but I wanted to wait. She insisted we go for it and I gave in to make her happy."

Annie knew what he was going to say and just waited for him to put it into words.

"That time she made it almost through the first trimester before the miscarriage."

"Oh, Mason—" She put a hand over her mouth. "I can't even begin to imagine how hard that was for you both."

"And I don't have the words to explain the devastation we felt. The first time we believed—hoped—it was a fluke. Just one of those things. And the doctor assured us that it happens and no one can explain why. No reason we couldn't have more babies without any problems at all. Other couples did all the time."

"But not you." If this had a happy ending, the two of them wouldn't be standing there right now.

"The second miscarriage meant there was a pattern. Made us doubt we could have what we wanted most. Christy wanted to try again, right away, but this time I held firm on waiting." He dragged his fingers through his hair. "When a body goes through trauma like that, conventional wisdom suggests a sufficient amount of time to rest and rejuvenate." He looked lost in memories that were bad and it seemed as if he was going to stay there, but he finally went on. "She was angry. We both knew there was an overseas deployment in my future and she wanted a baby before that. We were drifting apart emotionally and physically. I suggested date nights, brought her flowers, tried to get back the dream we'd both wanted when we first met."

"And?"

"She was closed off. Until one night she came to me and was so much like the woman she'd been. I thought we were finding our way back. We had sex. She didn't mention that she had stopped birth control."

"She got pregnant?"

"Yes." A muscle in his cheek jerked and his eyes flashed with anger. "And she lost that baby, too."

"I'm so sorry, Mason."

He sighed. "That's when she gave up on us. I wanted to go to counseling, try to make things work. There were other ways to have the family we wanted. Surely we could be like my aunt Lillian and uncle Phil. But I couldn't fix what was wrong all by myself. No matter how much I wanted to."

"That's so sad."

"Yeah, sad. A small word for what I felt. I didn't

just lose my children, I lost my wife. My family. I couldn't save anything. And I hated that house full of sad reminders."

"That's why you sold it before you were deployed," Annie said.

He nodded. "Most guys who shipped out left behind a wife and their kids. They didn't want to go, but sacrificed that time with loved ones in service to their country. But I couldn't wait to get out of here. I was glad to go."

"To leave the bad stuff behind."

"Yes. And to do some good. I couldn't help Christy, but I saved lives. To the best of my ability I stabilized the wounded, made sure soldiers who experienced traumatic injuries didn't lose an arm or leg. They thanked me for healing them, but it was just the opposite. They healed me." He met her gaze. "Then I got your email."

"About the babies possibly being yours."

He nodded. "I didn't know what to feel. So many times before I'd expected and hoped to have children. I didn't want to go all in again and get kicked in the teeth. Or was it just a cruel hoax? A miracle? A scam?"

"You're not the only one who thought that," she said wryly.

"I could have sent you a DNA sample, but I wanted to meet you—" he glanced past her, toward the room where the two babies slept side by side in a crib "—and the twins before doing it. Just being here made me feel more in control." He shrugged and there was a sheepish expression on his face. "Stupid, really. I know better than anyone control is an illusion. Because if it was up to me, those pregnancies would have resulted in healthy babies not miscarriages."

"And you might still be married," she said.

"I'm not so sure about that. I began to wonder if we just needed to believe we were in love because of wanting children so much. Thanks to science there are more options to have a family and I tried to talk to her about that or adoption, but she couldn't stand that everything wasn't normal, neat and tidy. Perfect. If she couldn't have that, she didn't want anything. Including me. By my definition, that isn't love."

It was such a devastating story of life dumping on him and love lost. And Mason looked so incredibly sad at the memories of the children who would never be. Annie couldn't help herself. She had to touch him, offer comfort. She moved one step closer and rested her crutches against the bed then put her arms around him.

"I'm so sorry you went through that, Mason."

He held completely still when her body pressed against his and didn't react for several moments. Annie was afraid that she'd somehow made things worse and started to step away.

"No."

She looked up and saw the conflict in his eyes just before he pulled her against him and lowered his mouth to hers. That achingly sweet touch set off fireworks inside her. It felt as if she'd been waiting for this since the moment she'd opened her door and seen him standing there in military camouflage, looking as exhausted as she'd felt.

Annie pressed her body closer but it wasn't enough as heat poured through her and exploded between them. He settled his hands at her waist then slid them down to her butt and squeezed softly before cupping her breasts in his palms. The kiss turned more intense as he brushed his tongue over her lower lip. She opened to him and let him explore, let the fire burn.

He backed up toward the bed and circled her waist with his arm, half carrying her with him. The only sound in the room was their combined breathing and it was several moments before they both heard a baby's whimper.

"It's Charlie." She pulled away and started to reach for the crutches but he stopped her.

"Should I apologize, Annie?"

That would mean he was sorry, and she didn't want him to be. She just wanted him so much.

"Annie?"

The whimper became more insistent and she put the crutches under her arms before turning away. "He's going to wake Sarah. You need to grab him, Mason."

He nodded and hurried into the other room.

She was sorry but only because of how very much she wanted him. Giving him that information wasn't smart. He didn't believe in love any more than she did. So starting anything wasn't the wisest course of action. It had just happened because they were practically living on top of each other.

She could resist him for just a little bit longer. In a short time the cast would be off and she could go back home. And he would close escrow on the house and move into it. Either way, she wouldn't have to go to bed at night with only a bathroom between them.

Just to prove how spineless she was, Annie wasn't sure whether to be sad or glad about that.

It had been several days since Mason had kissed Annie and his son interrupted them. The kid's timing was bad. And she'd never answered the question about whether or not he should apologize for kissing her, touching her. *Wanting* her.

Now he was in bed, alone and frustrated. It was early and quiet, so the twins were not awake yet. He was, mostly because sleep had been hard to come by ever since that kiss. Might as well get up, he thought. There was a lot of house-buying stuff to do today.

He went in the bathroom and listened for sounds and movement on the other side of the door to the room where Annie slept with the babies. It was still quiet. That was good; she needed her sleep. After a shower and shave, he dressed in jeans and a T-shirt, then went to the kitchen.

His mother was there. More important, she'd made coffee. Moving a little farther into the room, he saw that Annie was there, too, already having a cup.

"Good morning," she said.

His mother was standing by the counter in front of a waffle iron. "Morning, Mason. Did you sleep well?"

"Like a rock," he lied. "Charlie and Sarah were quiet all night. I didn't hear a peep from them."

"I know." Annie sipped her coffee. "If only we could count on that every night."

Flo laughed. "By the time that happens, they'll be teenagers staying out all night."

"It was one time, Mom," he protested. "And I lost the car for a month. Are you ever going to let me forget that?"

"No." She gave him a look before turning back to watch what she was cooking. "And someone got up on the wrong side of the bed this morning. You're crabby."

"For being irritated that you still bring up teenage transgressions?"

"I was joking," she said.

He poured himself a cup of coffee. "Soon I will have my own place and you won't have to put up with me being crabby in the morning."

"Don't remind me."

"It's not like I'm going to the Middle East. The house isn't that far away."

She slid a waffle onto a plate and brought it to the table. "But you'll be gone. Everything's changing around here too fast for my liking."

Annie put butter and syrup on her breakfast and cut off a bite before looking at him. "Your mom and I were just talking about this. My cast is coming off in a couple of days and I'll be going back to my apartment with the babies."

"I'm going to miss all of you terribly," his mother said.

Mason had known this moment would eventually come but hadn't expected the announcement to knock the air out of him. He wasn't ready. "Annie, you need to be careful when the cast comes off and you put weight on the leg. Maybe you should think about staying here a little longer."

"I've already imposed long enough." She looked at his mom, gratitude in her eyes. "As much as I appreciate everything you've done, I don't want to take advantage of your hospitality."

"Please. Use us," Flo pleaded. "Stay as long as you want. We love having you here. It will be too quiet without you. I love those babies so much."

"I know." Annie smiled fondly at the other woman.

"And they love you. I appreciate the offer and everything you've done for us more than I can tell you."

Mason was moving out soon and had deliberately put off thinking about being in the new house alone. After being with her and his kids, that was a lonely prospect. Because she'd helped him pick out the house, he couldn't help picturing Annie there. And the reminder that she wouldn't be didn't improve his mood. For that reason, he kept his mouth shut. No point in opening it and proving what his mother had pointed out. That he was crabby. If he did, there would be questions and he wouldn't want to answer them.

Annie was almost finished with her breakfast and sighed with satisfaction. "That was so good."

"If you stay, I'll make them every morning. I'm not above using food as a bribe," his mother said.

"Tempting." Annie grinned.

"At the risk of being pushy, since the twins are still asleep, it might be a good idea to get a shower in before they wake up," Flo said.

"That's not pushy. I was thinking the same thing." She stood and grabbed the crutches resting nearby. "Thanks for breakfast."

"You're very welcome. I'll listen for the babies and bring their bottles to you when they wake up."

"Thanks." She hobbled out of the room and smiled up at him as she passed.

Mason's heart skipped a beat and he resisted the urge to turn and watch her limp away. He'd gotten used to watching her, seeing a smile light up her face. And when he couldn't see it every day, there would be a significant withdrawal period.

His mother poured more coffee into her mug and blew on the top. "You should marry that girl."

It took a couple of moments for the words to sink in. And he still wasn't sure he'd heard her right. "What?"

"You should marry Annie," she said again, as if there was any doubt who "that girl" was.

"I can't believe you just said that. It's outrageous even for you."

"What does that mean? Even for me."

"I mean you can't just say whatever pops into your mind."

"I don't." She cradled her cup between her hands and leaned back against the counter. "That thought came to me when I saw your face. After Annie said she was moving back to her apartment. I didn't say it then. I waited."

"My face? What about it?"

"You looked as if someone just punched you in the gut," his mother said calmly.

"No, I didn't."

"Mason—" It was the dreaded Mom voice. "I know you. And if I'm being honest—"

"When are you not?" he asked wryly.

"It's a gift." She smiled at him. "I've never seen you happier than now—since Annie moved in here with Charlie and Sarah. It gives me such joy to see you this way."

He wanted to tell her she was wrong but he couldn't. It was true. He'd told Annie as much and risked her calling him silly. But from here to marriage was a big leap. "Mom, seriously—"

"I can see how much you like each other." At his

look of irritation, she sighed. "I'm old, not dead. And I can see when two people have a connection."

"No one said anything about love. I respect and admire her very much but— And, in case you forgot, we were zero for three on Gabriel's questionnaire."

"I'll deny it if you ever tell him I said this, but that quiz is not helpful. I see the way you and Annie look at each other."

"How is that?"

"Like you want to be alone. There were sparks, Mason, and it's more than respect and admiration."

He didn't want to discuss this. It was crazy. Although there was that really hot kiss. "You're imagining things, Mom."

"I have an imagination, I'll admit. But trust me on this, you and Annie have sparks. Successful marriages have started with less. Including me and your dad."

"You weren't in love when you got married?"

"We were young, wildly attracted to each other. And pregnant with you."

"What?" That was a shock. "I never knew that. You had to get married?"

"We didn't have to. Our parents were supportive. But doing the right thing was important to both of us." She shrugged. "The realization of how much we loved each other came after you were born. We were tired and stressed about making ends meet, but our bond and commitment and love grew stronger every day because of how much we both loved you. Your father was the right man for me and my hormones knew it before my heart did."

The union his parents shared was the bar by which Mason judged success. He had no idea their deepest commitment to each other had started with him. "Still, Mom—"

"You and Annie have two children together. You're parents and good ones. In spite of Gabriel's dopey quiz, you're compatible. I can see it the way you work together with the babies. If there were any cracks, the strain of caring for them would break them wide open. If anything, you two have grown stronger from the experience."

That statement had the ring of truth to it. "Maybe, but—"

"Please don't go by those completely irrelevant questions. Fortunately your aunt Lillian relies on her instincts about a man and woman when she's matchmaking. Her success rate is pretty high, too." She smiled. "That intuition for pairing up a man and woman runs in the family."

"Even if you're right about Annie and me—"

"I am." She pointed at him. "And you're going to say, why rush things? And I will say, why wait? You care and so does she. Together you can give Charlie and Sarah a stable home, a loving environment. And all of that under one roof."

"This idea is crazy, Mom."

She tapped her lip. "And your paternity petition is still pending with the court. It couldn't hurt to show that you're making a legal commitment to their mother, as well."

"We don't have to be married for me to present a strong case. I have the DNA proof."

"Of course you do. And that was one of those things that just popped into my mind. But this isn't. If you don't get out of your own way and marry her, someone else just might snatch her up, right out from under your nose. That old boyfriend could still be lurking."

"Not after what he called my children." Mason still wanted to clock him for that.

"Maybe not him, but Annie is pretty, smart and funny. Someone is going to sweep her off her feet. It should be you."

When Mason was in medical school, there hadn't been a class on jealousy, but that didn't mean he couldn't diagnose it now. The knot in his gut, elevated blood pressure and the pounding in his temples. All symptoms that confirmed the thought of Annie with another guy was just wrong.

But that didn't answer the question.

What was he going to do about it?

Chapter 8

Annie sat on the medical exam table at the orthopedic office and watched Dr. Jack Andrews cut through her cast. Mason had driven and was standing by her, but there was something on his mind other than freedom for her leg. She wasn't sure how she knew that but she did.

The doctor shut off the mini-saw and set it aside, then pried apart the cast and cotton-like material beneath that was sticking to her skin. He smiled. "How does the leg feel?"

"Like heaven. But it looks gross. All white and shriveled and different from the other one." She glanced at Mason, not sure she wanted him to see the grossness and not sure why she should care that he did. And it was a waste of energy because he'd already seen.

"Don't worry. That's normal for what you've been

through." Dr. Andrews was a colleague of Mason's, young and good-looking, but his opinion on the attractiveness of her leg didn't matter.

"It doesn't look normal." She glanced at Mason again to see if he was grossed out. He didn't look repulsed. He looked like Mason. Strong, steady and incredibly cute Mason.

"Soak the limb in warm water twice a day for the first few days and wash it with mild soap. Use a soft cloth or even gauze. That will help remove the dead skin."

"Does she need to take it easy, Jack?" Just like Mason to ask that.

"As you know, the muscles are atrophied from lack of use. I'm going to prescribe physical therapy for a few weeks so the experts can work on teaching you exercises to strengthen it. In a very short time you'll build the leg up again." He met her gaze, his own serious. "Your balance might be somewhat compromised after weeks of not walking normally. Go slow. Use the crutches at first to see how you do. But it won't be long before you'll forget this ever happened."

"I doubt that." His smile was nice, she thought, but her insides didn't quiver at all from it. Not like when Mason smiled at her.

And the experience hadn't been all bad. She'd gotten to know his family, how wonderful they were. He'd been pretty wonderful, too. The twins were lucky to have him for a father. Was he really determined to stay a bachelor? He was so loving with the babies, it was hard to believe he wouldn't meet a woman who would convince him to try again.

"You've been a perfect patient, Annie."

"And you've been a perfect doctor, Doctor," she said. "No offense but I hope I never have to see you again."

Mason laughed. "She means professionally."

"I got that," the other man said. "The feeling is mutual."

She shook his hand. "Seriously, thank you so much for everything."

"You're welcome."

When they were alone, Mason handed her the sneaker she hadn't used for six weeks.

"Thanks, Mason."

"For?"

"Do I have to pick one thing?" She thought for a moment. "First of all for reminding me to bring my sock and shoe. I'd have forgotten if not for you. It seems like forever since I needed it and I'd have crutched right out of the house without it."

"Happy to help."

"I also want to thank you for going above and beyond the call of duty these last weeks. And for being a good father to the twins."

"I should be thanking you. For making sure I knew about them."

"It was the right thing to do." Her stomach did the quivery thing when he smiled.

"Are you ready to get out of here?"

"So ready." The crutches were braced against the exam table and she grabbed them. "Following doctor's orders. No point in setting myself back. But now I can pick up my babies, not just wait for someone to hand them to me."

"How do you feel about grabbing some lunch before we go home to the kids?"

"Would it be all right with your mom? Does she have to be somewhere?"

"It was her idea." He opened the exam room door.

"In that case, I'm on board."

They walked down the hallway with medical offices on either side, then into the lobby area, where automatic doors opened to the outside. Annie was using the crutches to take part of her weight but felt pretty good moving on her own two feet. No dizziness or pain, just some minor weakness. She felt free, happy, and was looking forward to lunch with Mason.

It was one of those perfect fall days in Southern California and she was enthusiastically on board when he suggested getting sandwiches to eat in the park. There was one a short distance from his new house where they found a picnic table with a roof overhead not far off the cement walkway.

They were sitting side by side, looking at the white gazebo surrounded by yellow-, coral-and pink-flowered bushes. There were towering trees, shrubs, green grass and just a perfect amount of breeze.

"It's so beautiful here." Annie sighed contentedly then took the paper-wrapped turkey sub sandwich and napkin he handed her and immediately unwrapped it.

"Yeah." He set his own lunch on the table and didn't do anything but stare at it.

"I can't wait until Charlie and Sarah are big enough to run around and play on the kids' equipment." She pointed to a bright yellow, blue and red structure with tubes and stairs surrounded by rubberized material for unexpected landings.

"Uh-huh," he answered absently. Definitely distracted about something.

Annie wanted to know what was up with him. Maybe her comment about him being a good father had somehow freaked him out, put pressure on him. With her luck, the bum leg making her dependent on him had made him change his mind about wanting to take responsibility for the twins. Showed him he wasn't cut out for being a dad and he wanted off the hook. She couldn't stand it anymore and had to know.

She put her sandwich down without taking a bite. "Look, just spit it out. Get it over with."

"Spit what out?"

"Whatever it is you're so jumpy about."

"I'm not jumpy." But he didn't sound too sure of that.

"You've been preoccupied since we left the house. The whole time we've been gone you hardly said two words. Except to the doctor. So, just tell me what's going on. I can handle it. I've been alone before."

"What are you talking about?"

"You're responsible enough to not feel comfortable telling me but decent enough to do it to my face. You don't want to be tied down by the twins." The quivery feeling in her stomach became something else that made her want to cry.

He stared at her for several moments then shook his head. "You couldn't be more wrong."

"So I've made a fool of myself and you don't have anything on your mind?"

"No, you're right about that," he confirmed. "I'm actually surprised you know me well enough to recognize that."

"Of course I do." Although she was a little surprised, too. And also really anxious about what was going on in his head. "So, I say again, just get it over with. Please."

"That's what someone says when they think it's going to be something bad."

Damn aviator sunglasses were sexy as all get-out but she couldn't see his eyes. The window to the soul. A clue to what he was feeling. "Because it is bad, right?"

"I didn't think so, but I guess it could be interpreted that way."

"Darn it, Mason. Will you just tell me what we're talking about here?"

"Okay." He blew out a breath. "I was going to ask you to marry me."

Shut the front door! Annie's jaw dropped and she blinked at him for several moments. Unsure what to say, she finally asked, "Why?"

"That should be a simple enough answer but in our case it's complicated." He angled his body toward her. "I don't know where to start."

"So we're not talking love here." Please don't be talking love, she thought. They both had the scars to prove that was a losing proposition.

"Different *L* word. We *like* each other."

"True." And that was so much safer.

"And respect," he said. "I respect you a lot and I'm pretty sure you feel the same about me."

"Definitely." Even when she thought he was going to leave, she gave him credit for doing it in person. "Okay, but we could just go back to the way things were before I broke my leg. I'll move back to my apartment and you can visit any time you want."

He sighed. "I want more. I'll be moving into the house. It just seems like a natural transition to do that together. If I hadn't spent time with you and the kids in the same house, it would have taken me longer to get to this place, but I would have eventually."

"And that is?"

"I don't want to visit my kids. I want to live with them under the same roof, together with their mother. You've said that the apartment is too small and you were going to look for a bigger place." He shrugged. "I just happen to have one. And since the broken leg and living with my folks, you're half out of there anyway. If we just move your stuff to my place, it would be easier. You love the house."

"I do. And your points are all good ones. But we could just live together," she suggested. "Share expenses. Babysitting. It's a little unconventional, but this situation is the very definition of that. We don't have to get married to be a family."

He took off his glasses and his eyes were bluer and more intense than ever before. "I want a *traditional* family. For me and for them. With you."

Traditional family. The words struck a chord in Annie's soul, a tune she didn't fully realize had been playing her whole life. She'd never experienced what Mason was offering her. But he had and she'd seen it in action. He knew how to do the family thing. It was as natural to him as breathing. If he was going to abandon her and the twins, he'd have done it already. He wouldn't be offering her a legal commitment.

"Annie?"

"I'm thinking." She met his gaze. "Maybe we should try dating or something first?"

"So you don't want a traditional relationship."

"I didn't say that. Actually, I've wanted that my whole life," she admitted.

"Okay. We could date, but we'll wind up right back here. I feel as if we've been more than dating since we met. And it's been pretty terrific. You. The kids. It's what I want."

His marriage broke up because his wife couldn't have children. She and Mason were already parents. Annie did like him. A lot. It wasn't love, but that was so much better. Who needed drama and heartbreak? He was steady. Supportive. Sweet. She was happy around him and enjoyed spending time together. She looked forward to seeing him after work.

And there was that kiss.

"Come on, Annie." He took her hand and brushed his thumb over her left ring finger. "This is the right thing to do."

Her exact words just a little while ago about letting him know he was a father. She waited for some sign, a knot in her stomach, a shred of doubt in her mind, something to make her say no way. But there was nothing. Just a feeling that this could work really well.

"Okay, Mason. I'll marry you."

Escrow on the house had closed less than a week ago so Annie had been busy helping Mason move things in. It had kept her too busy to be nervous about the wedding. But two weeks after his proposal they were going to take vows. Things had come together quickly, partly because it was small, partly because Florence Blackburne was a tireless volunteer on their behalf and wanted this to happen.

On Thursday evening two weeks after becoming

engaged, Annie and Mason stood in front of someone who was licensed by the State of California to
marry them. Flo had found him on the internet. He
was a skinny twentysomething who looked like a college student earning extra money. Carla was her maid
of honor; Mason's dad was the best man. His mom and
sister held the babies, who looked completely adorable.
Charlie had on a little black suit and red bow tie that he
kept pulling off. Sarah was wearing a pink-tulle, cap-
sleeved dress with a darker pink satin ribbon that tied
in a big bow in the back.

If anyone thought Annie's tea-length red dress was
an odd choice, they kept it to themselves. The bodice
was snug-fitting chiffon and the full, flirty, asymmet-
rical mid-calf hem flattered her figure. Muscle was
building up in her leg but she was a little sensitive
about it being thinner than the other one.

Patrick's Place had been closed for this private function. Carla was BFFs with the owner, Tess Morrow
Wallace, and had facilitated the arrangements. Annie
was aware that Mason had met his ex-wife here, but
the interior was new so she chose to be superstitious
about that, in a positive way.

Tables and chairs were arranged to form an aisle
for Annie to walk down. Now the Blackburne family
formed a semicircle around Annie and Mason in the
center of the room. Together they had written their own
vows to each other and she was glad there wouldn't
be any surprises because the unexpected always had
a way of being bad.

Annie cleared her throat to go first. "I, Annie Campbell, take you, Mason Blackburne, to be my husband,
and father to Sarah and Charlie. You're a good, decent

man who takes care of them and me. In front of everyone gathered here, I promise to honor and cherish you and put the family we're making today above all else."

In his black suit, Mason was more handsome than she'd ever seen him. The blue stripes in his silk tie brought out the intense color of his eyes in the best possible way. And his smile… Her heart fluttered and she wasn't sure if nerves had chosen this moment to trip her up or if it was something else a lot more complicated. He didn't touch her with any part of his body, but their gazes met and locked and made her feel as if he was holding her in his arms.

"I, Mason Blackburne, take you, Annie Campbell, for my wife. I solemnly promise to respect, honor and care for you and our children to the very best of my ability. It's good and right, and I look forward to making a family with you and Sarah and Charlie."

She and Mason exchanged plain gold bands, after which the internet guy said, "I now pronounce you husband and wife."

Neither of them moved and Gabriel Blackburne said, "Isn't this the part where you kiss the bride?"

Annie felt a quiver in her stomach and instinctively turned her face up to look at Mason. He smiled then slowly lowered his mouth as her eyes drifted closed. His lips were soft and chaste but that didn't stop memories of their first kiss from popping into her mind. This felt like a down payment on a promise for later. And it didn't last nearly long enough.

Mason pulled back and said, "Hello, Mrs. Blackburne. How do you feel?"

Good question. This was a done deal now. Legal. She'd made decisions in the past and instantly had second thoughts if not outright regrets. What-the-heck-have-I-done moments. But this wasn't one of them. Mason was all the good things a man should be and there was no denying that sparks happened every time he touched her. Most important, the babies would have their father and a normal life.

"I feel great," she said, smiling back at him.

"Me, too."

"Me, three." Carla hugged both of them. "Congratulations. You make a beautiful couple."

"I couldn't agree more." With Sarah in her arms, Florence gave her son a one-armed hug before doing the same to Annie. "Welcome to the family, sweetheart."

"Thank you." Unexpectedly, Annie's eyes filled with emotional tears. Her voice only caught a little when she said, "It's really nice to have a family."

The rest of the Blackburnes lined up to congratulate them. All but Gabriel, she noticed. The bar was open and he'd walked over for a drink. Then she was swept up in the celebration and Charlie was leaning toward her, wanting to be held. Sarah did the same to Mason.

He met her gaze and there was a tender look in his. "We're a family and as soon as the court recognizes me as their father, we'll be official."

"That won't be long," she said. "But I'm officially starving right now."

"Let's go eat. Mom—"

"On it, honey."

Adjacent to the main bar area was a restaurant where tables had been arranged in long rows to accommodate the family. Two high chairs had been set up on the end for the babies. Florence herded everyone to their assigned places, with Annie and Mason surrounded by their maid of honor and best man.

When they were all in place Flo said, "If Annie and Mason have no objection, I'd like to make the first toast."

He looked at her and she nodded. "Take it away, Mom."

"It gives me great pleasure to welcome Annie to our family. My son is a lucky man." She held up a flute of champagne. "Peace and long life."

Her husband frowned a little. "Isn't that from *Star Trek*?"

"Maybe, but it fits." Flo shrugged and nodded at him. "Okay, best man, it's your turn."

John stood and looked around the table. "It's a blessing to be surrounded by my children and grandchildren to celebrate this happy occasion. Mason, you're a lucky man. Annie, I'm very happy to have another daughter. Congratulations."

For the second time she felt emotion in her throat and tears gather in her eyes. She blinked them away and smiled at him. Everyone clinked glasses, and soon after food was served. There were many volunteers to help keep the babies occupied so that they could eat their wedding dinner without interruption. The meal was followed by a beautiful red-velvet cake garnished with roses around the base. Everyone was mingling, chatting and having a good time.

Then Annie and Mason somehow found themselves alone in the crowd. He had a glass of champagne in his hand and said to her, "So, I have a toast."

"Oh?"

"I'm not a man of words, so don't expect profound."

She smiled. "You do okay."

"Right." He held up his glass. "Here's to us."

"To us," she said, touching her glass to his. "It was a nice wedding."

"Agreed. But on the one-to-ten nice scale, that dress is a fifteen." There was more than a little male interest in his eyes. "Why red?"

"Symbolism and maybe a bit of superstition." She sipped her champagne. "Red can be a sign of good luck, joy, prosperity, celebration, happiness and long life."

He nodded and slid one hand into the pocket of his suit pants, striking a very masculine pose. "All good reasons. And not traditional."

She couldn't tell whether or not that bothered him. "I know we took this step to have a traditional family for the twins, but—"

"You think I'm upset that you didn't wear white?"

"Are you?" she asked.

"No. This couldn't be more different from my first wedding and that's a very good thing. Only—" It looked as if something had just occurred to him. "You've never done this before. It's a really bad time to ask. And, for the record, I'm an idiot for not thinking about it until just now. Are you okay with a small wedding?"

"If I wasn't, you'd have heard. In case you haven't noticed, I'm not shy about standing up for myself."

"Yeah, I figured that out the first time we met. And I quote, 'Do the swab and leave your contact information. Now please go.'"

"Yeah." She grinned. "Not my finest hour. In my defense, I was tired and the twins were teething."

"No, I get it. You're independent and it's one of the

things I like about you. I just wanted to make sure you're fine with the size of this wedding because having something bigger would have meant waiting—"

"Speaking of that—" Gabriel Blackburne joined them and had apparently overheard. He had a tumbler in his hand containing ice and some kind of brown liquor. "Why didn't you?"

"Didn't we what?" Mason asked.

"Wait to get married."

Annie guessed Mason hadn't discussed with his brother why they'd decided to take this step. And she couldn't read the other man's expression. It wasn't animosity exactly, more like concern. There was also something dark and maybe a bit bleak, but she sensed that was personal to Gabriel and had nothing to do with her and Mason.

"Don't get me wrong." Gabriel took a sip from his glass. "I wish you both all the best. But why rush things?"

"It's about being a family," Mason explained. "My escrow closed. Annie and the kids were half moved out of her apartment because of the broken leg. It seemed a good time to merge households."

"A merger. My job is turning around failing businesses, but..." His brother's expression was wry. "Be still my heart."

"Annie and I talked this through and we agreed it was the best thing for the children. We want to give them a conventional home. Like you and I had."

"Yes, we did." Gabriel's expression grew just a little darker. "But a successful family starts with a strong core."

"It does," Annie said. "We are in complete agreement about the twins and raising them in a stable and loving environment."

"So you are in love?" Again he glanced at Annie but his gaze settled squarely on his brother. "Because if I'm not mistaken, you were never going there again."

Mason's eyes narrowed but his voice was even and casual when he responded. "Annie is the most courageous and warm woman I've ever met. And it seems to me that if you're this cynical, you aren't the best person to be working in a business that is supposed to help people find their life partner."

"You are so right. That's why my goal is to make that business profitable again as quickly as possible so I can leave." He finished the last of the liquor in his glass. "I'm not telling you anything you don't already know, but this 'merger' will change everything."

"For the better," Mason said.

Annie knew the man meant well but she shivered at the words. Before she could think that through, she recognized Sarah's tired cry and knew Charlie wouldn't be far behind.

"Mason, I think the grace period on the twins' good mood has just expired."

"Yeah."

"I sincerely wish you all the best," Gabriel said again. "You have a beautiful family. I envy you, brother."

Mason smiled and held out his hand. His brother took it then pulled him in for a bro hug. "See you Sunday at Mom's."

They said good-bye and went to retrieve their children from Mason's mother and father. Annie took Sarah and Mason grabbed Charlie, who rubbed his face against his father's shoulder. It was a classic sign of being overtired.

"We need to get these guys home," she said to Florence.

"Why don't you two stay?" his mother said. "I can keep them at my house overnight."

And that was the exact moment it really sank in for Annie that being married *did* change everything. When you married a man, he became your husband and you were his wife. A couple. And couples had sex on their wedding night.

Chapter 9

After his mother offered to keep the kids, Mason could have kissed the woman. A wedding night alone with Annie sounded just about perfect to him. Not that he didn't love his children to the moon and back, but... Taking that sexy red dress off his new bride sent his imagination and other parts of him into overdrive. There hadn't been a specific conversation about sex but after that kiss he figured they were good. If one of the babies hadn't interrupted them, their first time would already have happened.

But it felt right to have waited until after they were married. Right for Annie somehow. That was probably stupid, but that's the way he felt.

"What do you think?" he asked her.

Annie looked a little pale and her smile was forced. "That is so sweet and thoughtful. I can't thank you enough for the offer. But we got married to be a regular family. It doesn't seem right not to have them with us on our first night."

Mason had mixed feelings. He felt like biomedical waste because it crossed his mind that he wanted her all to himself. That made him a selfish jerk for not wanting to share her. The other part of him realized how important it was to get this right.

"We appreciate it, Mom. But I agree with Annie."

This was better, he told himself. No pressure on either of them. The twins came first and that meant bathing, feeding and rocking them to sleep. That might happen by midnight and they would fall into bed exhausted, too tired for… Anything.

Mason tried not to be disappointed and almost succeeded. Almost.

They bundled the kids into jackets because the October evening was chilly. Buckling them into the carriers that fit into the car was more of a challenge. Being overtired and out of sorts, they cried and fought the restraints, but he and Annie out-stubborned them.

She hugged his mom and dad. "Thank you for everything."

"You're so welcome, sweetheart." Flo smiled. "I think you'll make my son a happy man."

Annie glanced at him but her expression was impossible to read. "I'm glad you think so."

Mason looked around the pub's dining area and noticed a busboy busy loading dirty dishes from their dinner into a plastic tote. Still, he had to ask. "You're sure you don't need us for anything here?"

"No. We have it covered. Take your family home."

"I like the sound of that." He looked at Annie and she nodded. "Good night, all. Thanks for coming."

His parents had picked up Annie and the twins, so her car was at the house. They walked outside, each carrying a crying infant. Even after they were secured in the rear seat of his SUV the crying continued. It was impossible to have a conversation over the high-pitched wails. Fortunately it didn't take long to get home.

He pulled into the driveway beside her small, compact car. Annie opened the front passenger door and the overhead light came on.

"I'm glad they didn't fall asleep," she said.

"Why?" Because she didn't want to be alone with him? Was she trying to tell him something?

"Because I'd be tempted to put them to bed without even undressing them. They need baths, jammies and bottles. Never too soon to start a routine."

"Good point."

In the house they set Sarah and Charlie facing each other on the family room rug. The settling-in process was ongoing so boxes were scattered throughout and furniture was still scarce. Shopping for it hadn't been a priority. The babies' nurseries were put together, each with its own crib. But the cartons lined the walls in the rest of the rooms and needed to be unpacked.

Annie looked around ruefully. "Is this all my stuff or yours?"

"Fifty-fifty." He settled his hands on his hips, pushing back his suit coat. "And I have one more load from my storage unit."

She sighed. "It doesn't feel like we'll be settled anytime soon."

Was she trying to get a message across? Or was he

reading too much darkness into that conversation with Gabriel tonight? Until then he'd felt just fine about this whole thing. Now… Time would tell.

The twins had been quiet since coming into the house, both of them looking around with wide eyes. Charlie rubbed his face, a sure sign of an imminent meltdown.

Annie saw it, too. "I'm going to get out of this dress."

It had been a long shot at best, but there went any chance of him sliding the sexy material off her. She was probably going to slip into something more comfortable but it would likely be sweatpants not lingerie. He wasn't proud of these thoughts, but he was a guy.

"Okay. I'll entertain them while you change for operation bath time."

"Roger that." She smiled then hurried out of the room.

Charlie's whimpers turned to full-blown wails, so Mason unbuckled him and lifted the little guy into his arms. That was Sarah's cue to commence with her own high-pitched vocal demonstration of unhappiness. She arched her back against the straps holding her in, but he didn't want to undo them and have her sliding out of the seat.

He put his son on the rug. *Don't judge*, he thought, grateful the germ police weren't around. He was getting a bath soon. Then he freed Sarah and cuddled her close for a moment while her brother took off on another crying jag.

Mason went down on one knee and put a hand on the boy's belly. "I honestly don't know how your mother did it all by herself."

"It wasn't easy." Annie had quietly entered the room and moved closer.

He looked up. "And yet somehow you made it look easy."

"I doubt that. But thanks." She held out her arms for Sarah. "Now, unless you want soap and water all over that nice suit, you should change into a slicker and rubber boots."

"Understood."

Mason put on jeans and a T-shirt, then grabbed his son off the floor and followed Annie into the bathroom that connected the twins' nurseries. Their small tub was already out on the counter by the sink and she filled it with warm water before handing her baby off to him. He had one in each arm and watched her set out two sets of PJs, diapers and two fluffy towels.

She took Sarah and stripped off the dress, tights and diaper before lowering her into the water. Little hands and feet started moving. Crying stopped and splashing started.

"They do love the water, but there's no playing tonight." Annie washed, rinsed and lifted Sarah out before quickly wrapping the towel around her.

Mason had removed Charlie's clothes while his sister was being bathed. They handed off babies and he took Sarah into her room and dressed her in the clothes Annie had put out. By the time he finished, Charlie was in a towel and on the way to his room. He stood in the doorway, holding his sweet-smelling daughter.

"Assembly line works like a charm," he said.

She looked up for a moment and smiled. "An extra pair of hands makes this so much easier."

"We make a good team."

"Yes, we do." She finished putting on Charlie's one-piece blue sleeper. After picking him up, Annie held him close and brushed a hand over his back while he rubbed his eyes again. "You're a tired boy. Let's give them a bottle and put them to bed."

"The same crib? Or their own?"

She met his gaze, thinking that one over. "I don't know. Thoughts, Doctor?"

"Not a pediatrician but… Sooner or later they have to be in their own rooms. This is a new environment anyway, so it might be a good time to try. The worst that could happen is they won't go to sleep and we put them in the same crib again."

Annie nodded. "And if it works, they might sleep through each other's fussiness and we'd only have one awake at a time. That sounds too good to be true. But I vote we give it a try."

"It's unanimous," he said.

After bottles, the twins were asleep. They carefully put them in their respective rooms then met in the hall to wait for the crying to start. Five minutes went by and all was quiet. Annie held up two fingers, indicating they should give it another couple of minutes. They both held their breaths but there wasn't a sound.

She angled her head toward the family room and he followed her there. "I am cautiously optimistic that this just might work."

"A wild prediction."

"You're a pessimist," she scolded. And sure enough, ten minutes passed without a peep. "Cautious optimism rules. It would appear they're in for the night. What are we going to do with ourselves?"

Then her eyes widened and a blush covered her

cheeks. Any other time the kids would have been fussy and out of sorts, but not now. It had been smooth and easy getting the twins to sleep, but Mason sensed a whole pile of awkward in the room. He knew her pretty well now and there was no question that Annie looked tense.

He had wanted her practically from the first moment he'd seen her and now she was his wife. But he'd been getting vibes from her and not the ones he was hoping for.

There were so many ways this could go sideways and he didn't want to do the wrong thing. He didn't want to be another jerk in her life. That was no way to start out. On the other hand, they *were* married. But one of them had to address this situation.

He cleared his throat. "Annie, you're probably really tired and—"

When he stopped and let the meaning of his words sink in, a charged silence joined the awkwardness dividing them like the wall that once separated East and West Berlin. Her eyes changed color, as if a light had gone out. But that was probably his imagination.

Finally she nodded. "It has been a long day—"

"Right. Sure."

She half turned toward the hall. "I think I'll turn in now."

"Okay."

When she was gone, Mason poured himself a Scotch and leaned against the island that overlooked a family room empty of furniture. If one was into symbolism, this would be a doozy. He had thought marrying her would solve problems and fill up his life. He'd had no idea it would be just the beginning of complications.

What was it she'd said? It was never too early to get into a routine. What did this say about the routine they were starting?

Annie barely slept on her wedding night but not for the reason she should have not slept. And a week later nothing had changed. They slept in the same bed but his long shifts at the hospital and caring for the twins became an excuse for him to avoid intimacy. The rejection hurt on many levels, but what stung most was her poor judgment. How wrong she'd been about the sparks between them. Well, half-wrong, anyway. She was the only one who'd felt them.

They had made legal promises to each other, not physical ones, but she'd assumed that would all work out based on one hot kiss. She'd made the first move then but desperately wanted him to make the first move now. Annie had her pride and didn't want him to sleep with her just because they'd said "I do." Or worse, pity.

She threw back the covers and went into the master bedroom's adjoining bath. Lingering humidity and the sexy male scent of cologne told her Mason had recently showered. Apparently she'd slept harder than she'd thought because she hadn't heard him. Obviously he'd taken care to be quiet. That was thoughtful and he got points, but her anger and hurt refused to budge.

After taking care of business, she checked on the twins and smiled tenderly at each of them still sleeping in their very own rooms. Little angels, she thought. They were safe, secure—loved. That's all that mattered, right? Right.

Still, quiet time was rare and she went down the hall toward the kitchen to make coffee and enjoy a peace-

ful moment before all hell broke loose. The hallway
opened to the family room, which was adjacent to the
kitchen. With his back to her, Mason was standing
there in blue scrubs because he was on his way to work.
She so didn't want to face him. Eventually she'd have
to, just not right this minute.

But before she could scurry back to bed and pull the
blanket over her head, he turned and spotted her. She
froze, feeling like a deer caught in headlights.

"I'm sorry if I woke you," he said.

Don't be nice to me, she thought. *Just don't.* If he
was, she would have to let go of her anger and let down
the only shield she had to keep out the hurt scratching
to get in. She also couldn't ignore him, no matter how
ill at ease she felt.

Annie moved closer, trying to act as if all was fine
and normal, but her legs felt stiff and trying to smile
made her face hurt. "You didn't wake me."

"Good." He nodded a little too enthusiastically, sig-
naling that he felt awkward, too.

She was in the kitchen, but kept her distance from
him. "Charlie and Sarah are still asleep."

His gaze didn't quite meet hers. "They must be
growing."

"I guess so."

After a few moments of tense silence he said, "I
made coffee. Would you like a cup?"

"Yes. Thanks." This was so stiff, tense, awkward
and overly polite, it made her want to scream.

He seemed relieved to have something to do and
immediately took a mug from the cupboard above the
coffee maker, then poured steaming hot liquid into it.
Packets of her artificial sweetener were in a bowl on

the counter and he ripped one open before shaking the powder in. Then he grabbed the container of flavored creamer from the refrigerator and poured that in, lightening the dark color to the exact shade she liked. The thoughtfulness was both incredibly sweet and super annoying. He held out the cup.

"Thanks," she said grudgingly. She took a sip and noted that it was perfect. This was probably where she should meet him halfway. "How late are you working tonight?"

"It's twelve hours, so seven to seven. Probably seven thirty-ish."

"Ish?"

"If an emergency comes in around change of shift, I could be delayed getting out. Every day is different. Why?"

"I was wondering about dinner."

"Right." He leaned back against the counter and folded his arms over his chest.

Annie swallowed against a sudden surge of overwhelming attraction for the man she'd married. She'd seen him in scrubs before as he'd often come by the apartment after work to see Charlie and Sarah. When they'd been living with his folks she'd seen him before he'd left for the hospital, too. In her opinion the lightweight top and pants looked comfortable, like pajamas, and weren't the sexiest ensemble in the world.

But the über masculine pose he struck drew her gaze to the contours of his chest and the width of his shoulders. She had the most powerful urge to be in his arms, held tight against his body. Except he'd shut the door on that and every night since then rejection grew wider and more painful.

"If you get hungry, go ahead and eat without me."

"Hmm?" What were they talking about? Her mind had gone completely blank.

"Dinner. Tonight. If I'm not home and you need to eat, don't wait for me."

"Okay. I'll make you a plate."

"Don't go to any trouble," he said. "And I'm sure I'll be home in time to help with baths."

"Right." A devoted dad. He wanted to help with the nighttime ritual. "Unless they're really fussy, I'll hold off until you get here."

"Great." Again with the enthusiastic nodding. He was going to give himself head trauma.

But again the sweet consideration irrationally ticked her off. It was official. She was crazy. "Okay, then."

She sipped her coffee and looked anywhere but at him. "If you have to leave for work, don't let me keep you."

"I have a few minutes."

She waited for him to say more but he didn't. Since you could cut the tension in the room with a scalpel, she would think he'd have jumped on her suggestion and hit the road. But, oddly, he seemed reluctant to leave. Of course, that was about his children, not her.

"Would you like some breakfast before you go?" It seemed wrong somehow not to offer.

"No. Thanks, though. I'll just grab something in the doctor's dining room. At the hospital," he added.

"Right. Because it's logical that the doctor's dining room would be at the hospital." Was she awful for not resisting the urge to tease him?

"This is what you might call a 'duh' moment." The corners of his mouth curved up, cracking the tension a little. For the first time, he met her gaze. "What's on your agenda for today?"

Look at him. Asking his wife what her plans were for the day. Just like any normal couple. If he could pretend, so could she.

"I'm going to the apartment to clean out the last of my things."

"You should let me help with that," he said.

How ironic was this? She was ending her old life at the same time she was dealing with the unforeseen fallout from her new one.

"I gave my notice and have to be out." She wrapped her hands more tightly around the mug.

"But the cast hasn't been off your leg very long. Let me see if I can work something out and help—"

"It's all right." She was touched that his concern seemed genuine. But she was used to doing things alone. That was self-pity talking. She did have backup, just not from Mason. "I can handle it. Your mom is going to watch the twins. And Carla is meeting me there to help. She took a hooky day. Called in sick. Don't tell Gabriel."

"You think I'd rat her out when she's helping you?" It wasn't clear from his expression whether or not he was kidding. "I'm hurt that you think so little of me." He was talking about his male pride but her pain went a lot deeper than that. A place she'd thought was scabbed over and protected. A wound from childhood that she'd actively worked to heal and forget. As much as she wanted to blame him, it wasn't fair. They had moved quickly to marry. Between taking care of the babies and moving, they'd been so busy. Discussing the finer points of this arrangement hadn't been a priority.

"On the contrary, I think you're incredibly honest." She sincerely meant that. "And on the off chance you might run into your brother, it was simply a reminder not to say anything about Carla."

"My lips are sealed."

And so, apparently, was his heart. She needed to do the same. "Good."

He glanced at the digital clock on the microwave. "It's time. I really have to go."

"Have a good day." Wasn't she the world's most supportive wife?

"Hold down the fort while I'm gone." A husband's automatic response.

"Will do," she said.

He straightened away from the counter and hesitated for a moment. Annie had the feeling he was going to kiss her goodbye, a classic husband move, before heading off to work. She held her breath. But hope was a cruel thing because he didn't move close to her after all.

"I'll see you tonight." He turned away and headed for the front door.

Annie heard the soft click of it closing behind him and thought it was the saddest sound ever. On the way to his car in the driveway he would walk across the porch that had caught her heart and reeled in her hopes. It symbolized the dream for a traditional family that she'd had her whole life. But regret flooded her now because she knew all the front porches in the world couldn't fix what was wrong with this picture.

When she'd first met Mason, he hadn't trusted her, what with being the sister of the woman who hadn't told him he might be a father. And Annie hadn't believed he would stick around and take care of his children. They'd been wrong and had become friends, working side by side to care for the twins both of them loved more than anything. Taking the marriage step had seemed perfectly logical but she never dreamed it would create this awful divide between them. They were together legally but had never been further apart.

Chapter 10

Annie climbed the stairs to her soon-to-be vacant apartment and bittersweet memories scrolled through her mind. Jessica announcing that she was pregnant and didn't know who the father was. The nervous and happy excitement when labor had started. The thrill of the twins' birth turning to fear and unimaginable grief because Jess died. Bringing the babies here when they were so tiny and she couldn't carry both of them up the stairs at the same time. The sheer terror of caring for both infants by herself.

Until Mason showed up and stood right here, she thought, looking at the familiar door. The moment she'd seen him, her life had changed in so many ways—some good, some not so much.

She unlocked the door and carried moving boxes and trash bags inside. The place was empty of furniture. Indentations in the carpet were the only clues that her couch and coffee table had once been there. Now they were in storage until decisions were made about what to do with everything. That seemed inconsequential considering everything else that was going on—or not going on.

"Hello."

Annie turned and Carla stood in the doorway with cups of coffee in her hands. "Hey, you. Thanks for coming."

"Doesn't look like you need much help," she said. "Mostly I came because you promised to take me to lunch."

It felt good to laugh and Annie was grateful to her friend for that. And the coffee. She took the to-go cup Carla held out. "The big stuff is gone, obviously. I need another pair of eyes to make sure I don't miss anything."

"I can do that." Carla looked around. "Where do you want to start?"

"The master bedroom." Also known as the room for sleep because in her world no one was being bedded.

Annie led the way and again only the marks on the rug indicated where the bed and nightstands had been. In the bathroom they set their coffee on the countertop between the two sinks. Annie opened the medicine cabinet while her friend got down in front of the cupboard underneath the sink.

"There's a shower cap here," Carla said. "A couple of gigantic hair rollers. A long-handled back scrubber. Nearly empty bottles of shampoo and conditioner."

Annie glanced away from what she was doing.

"That was when I changed brands to get more volume. I kept those for an emergency."

"Do you want me to put these in a box?"

If only hair products would take care of her current crisis. Come to think of it, if she had better hair, maybe Mason would be attracted to her.

"Annie?"

"Hmm?" She pulled her thoughts back to what she was doing.

Carla held up the plastic bottles. "Keep or toss?"

"Throw them out."

"Done." She pulled out a trash bag and dropped the discards into it.

Annie took bottles out of the medicine cabinet and checked each label. There was one that said "Jessica Campbell." Prenatal vitamins. Her sister had wanted the cheapest over-the-counter brand but Annie had insisted she listen to her obstetrician, who'd said the prescription had the right amounts of what she needed for the baby. That was before she'd known there were two. A sob caught in her throat.

She'd been so busy with Charlie and Sarah that she hadn't had time to grieve, and an unexpected pain settled in her chest. It was emptiness and loss and missing the only person she'd ever truly been able to count on to love her.

"Are you okay?" Carla was staring at her.

"Why do you ask?"

"Oh, please. Your face is an open book. Never play poker, by the way. You suck at bluffing."

Annie handed over the bottle. "It just hit me all over again that she's gone and isn't coming back."

"Oh, sweetie—" Carla took it from her and closed

her hand over the name. "I wish there was something I could say to make it better."

"Me, too. And I feel guilty."

"Why? You were there for her when she needed you most. And you took in her children without missing a beat." Carla sat back on her heels. "What could you possibly have to feel guilty about?"

"I love Charlie and Sarah with all my heart. They are the best thing that ever happened to me. But at what price?" Tears filled her eyes.

"Annie—" Carla stood, moved closer and hugged her. "It's not like you made it happen. If you could bring her back, you'd do it in a heartbeat. And Jess wanted you to have the babies. She gave them to you."

"She didn't have a choice. I'm all she had and she's all I had. Our mother and her husband made it clear no help was coming from them. Not that it ever did. In a meaningful way anyhow."

"Their loss."

"And I'm sad that the babies will never know their mom. She was loyal and brave. She stood up for me when no one else would."

"You'll tell them about her," Carla said gently. "And all of her wonderful qualities aren't gone forever. They'll live on in her children."

"You're right." Annie's mouth trembled but she managed to smile. "I need to think about that."

"You haven't had much time or energy to think about anything. You've been treading water and getting by these last few months," her friend pointed out. "And life is give and take, yin and yang."

"I'm not sure where you're going with that."

"Losing your sister was horrible and tragic. But circumstances brought Mason into your life."

Just hearing his name made Annie's chest tighten, but not with sadness. It was way more complicated than that. "Yes. Mason is in my life."

Annie turned back to the medicine cabinet and pulled out a thermometer, antibiotic ointment, peroxide and Band-Aids. First aid supplies would fix a scrape but not what was ailing her.

It was quiet in the room and she'd been too lost in her own thoughts to realize Carla hadn't said anything in response to her Mason comment. In fact she could almost feel her friend's gaze locked on her like a laser beam.

She glanced over her shoulder and knew her inability to bluff was going to bite her in the butt. "What?"

"Something's bothering you. Something besides losing your sister."

Annie didn't want to talk about this but she faced the other woman and prepared to fake it. "No. I'm just tired. It's been hectic. First my leg. Moving in with Flo and John. Settling the kids. Moving again and cleaning out the apartment."

"Getting married." Carla leaned back against the sink. "How's that going, by the way?"

"It's an adjustment."

"Of course. But in a good way." Her eyes narrowed as she looked closer. "Right, Annie?"

"Yes. Of course—"

"Like I said. You suck at bluffing. Something is bothering you and for the life of me I can't figure out what could possibly be wrong. You just married a great guy. He's a hunk and a doctor. Is there any chance that your standards are just a little bit too high?"

Annie crossed her arms at her waist. "I'll admit that on paper my life looks perfect—good job, two beautiful, healthy children and a really hot husband..."

"But...?" her friend prompted.

Annie shrugged. "He doesn't want me."

"He married you."

"For his kids. To be a family. All of us under one roof for their sake."

Carla looked confused. "I really wish it was happy hour and this place had some furniture."

"What does that mean?"

"We could have wine and sit on a comfortable sofa for this chat." She picked up their coffee cups and slowly settled on the side of the tub, patting the space beside her. "This will have to do. Now sit."

Annie sat. "This isn't something girl talk can actually fix."

"Oh, ye of little faith. Besides, you won't know unless you try. I had no words of comfort for you losing your sister, but I've got plenty to say about you and Mason." Her friend was bossy, in a good way. "Now tell me what's going on. The truth. Don't hold back. What makes you think he doesn't want you?"

"He doesn't want to have sex with me."

Carla nearly spit out the sip of coffee she'd just taken. "Tell me I didn't just hear you say that your marriage hasn't been consummated yet."

"Yeah, that's exactly what you heard." Annie told her what happened on their wedding night.

"Okay. But think about this. Everything went down so fast. Maybe he was giving you time. It's possible he really is what he seems—caring and compassionate. That he was simply being a nice guy."

"It's been a week and he hasn't made a move. No guy is that nice." Annie had been miserable when she got here, but not like this. And, so far, talking things over was making her feel worse. "When he proposed, he said we liked each other, which is true. That we were friends, also true. But clearly he didn't mean anything more than that."

"How do you feel? Do you want to have sex?"

Annie thought about kissing him and he sure hadn't pushed her away. "Yes."

"Okay, then. Do something about it," Carla advised.

"Excuse me?"

"Come on to him. It's not the olden days. Things have evolved. Women can make the first move and not be a hussy."

"I can't. I've had enough rejection in my life. Enough humiliation. From Mason it would be—" Annie didn't have the words to describe what a no from him could do to her.

"Wouldn't it be better to know?" Carla asked gently.

Annie was dyslexic and school had been a challenge for her in more ways than one. She'd learned to compensate and be successful. Now her company was one of two finalists for the biggest contract they'd ever had and it was largely due to her vision and artistic execution of the campaign.

Intellectually she knew all of this but her inner child still heard the other kids ridicule her, tell her she was stupid, ugly, an idiot. School had been isolating and lonely, still she'd made it through. But Mason was honest. If she faced him outright and forced him, he would tell her the truth. That they were married friends without benefits. But could she handle hearing it?

"It probably would be better to know," Annie said. "I'll think about it."

Mason had to do something. The situation with Annie was tense and getting worse every day. And it was all his fault. After the problems in his marriage, then the divorce, followed by a year's deployment, he was apparently pretty rusty, socially speaking. He missed the easy conversation with Annie, the teasing and laughter. And the promise of that wedding kiss. But he'd blown it big-time.

So here he was at Make Me a Match. The office was in a building in the Huntington Hills business complex. He parked and exited the SUV, then walked through the double glass doors into the lobby with its elegant marble floor. The elevator opened when he pushed the up button, and he rode it to the top floor, where his aunt Lillian's business was located.

The elevator doors opened into a reception area with comfortable furniture arranged to facilitate conversation. Carla Kellerman sat behind the desk, and he knew she doubled as greeter and his aunt's assistant.

She looked up when he stopped in front of her. "Hey, Mason. How are you?"

"Fine."

"Really? You look terrible."

"Thank you." He felt that way, too, but tried to make a joke.

"Long hours at the hospital? Twins keeping you up at night?" There was an expression on her face: accusation mixed with pity.

"All of the above," he answered.

"How's Annie?"

"Great," he lied. He got the feeling she didn't buy the deception.

"To what do we owe this visit?" She toyed with a pen on her desk. "Since you got married—what was it, ten days ago?—I wouldn't think you'd be in the market to meet someone."

"I'm here to see Aunt Lil."

"I didn't see your name on her schedule. Do you have an appointment?"

"No." He was just desperate. "She was out of town and couldn't make the wedding. I haven't seen her for a while and just dropped by to surprise her. Maybe take her to lunch."

"Too bad. You just missed her," Carla said. "She had a lunch meeting."

Well, shoot, he thought. "My bad. I should have called first."

"Since you're here, do you want to say hello to Gabriel?"

Mason could truthfully say his brother was the last person he wanted to discuss this problem with. "That's okay. Don't bother him."

"Do you want to leave a message for your aunt?"

"Just tell her I was here and I'll talk to her soon." He lifted a hand. "Thanks, Carla. See you."

"Mason, is there anything I can help you with?"

She was Annie's good friend and the second-to-last person he wanted to talk to about this.

"No. It's all good. I'll just be going now—"

"Mason. What are you doing here?" His brother walked into the reception area from a side hall.

"Just stopped by to say hi to Aunt Lil, but she's not here. So I'm going to take off—"

"What's your hurry? Have you had lunch? I was just going to order takeout. Wouldn't mind some company. Come on back to my office."

"Okay." There was no way to make a graceful exit now. "Nice to see you," he said to Carla.

"You, too. Say hi to Annie for me." The woman looked as if she was going to say something more but instead she just smiled.

"Will do."

Mason followed Gabe to an office at the end of the hall. When both of them had walked inside, his brother closed the door.

"What's wrong?" he asked.

"That's direct."

His brother was wearing a T-shirt, jeans and sneakers. Mason had a hunch that, at least for today, his consulting work was strictly behind the scenes and not with clients.

"That's the way I roll. Now answer the question."

He stood in front of the abnormally tidy desk because there were no visitor's chairs in front of it. "Nothing is wrong. Why would you think that?"

Gabe rested a hip on the corner of his desk. "Because you've never dropped in to see Aunt Lil."

"I was deployed. It was a little difficult to commute for a drop-in," Mason said. "And how do you know that? You haven't been here that long."

"I've been here long enough to know that this visit is out of character for you."

"What do you know about character?"

"Okay." His brother looked down for a moment then

gave him a wry look. "You're going to mock me because math and spreadsheets and data are my thing."

"Well, yes, that was my plan," Mason admitted.

"It's true that I'm not involved very much with the other part of this business. But since you've been back from deployment, you never just dropped by to see Aunt Lil at work. That's not criticism, simply a fact. From that data I can extrapolate that you have a problem and think our aunt is qualified to advise you. Since you so recently got married, I deduce your issue is in some way connected to your wife. I'm right, aren't I?"

Mason sighed. "You're not wrong."

"I'm listening," Gabe said.

Mason figured it was a symptom of his acute desperation that he was actually considering telling Gabe what was going on. The brother who'd warned him that he might be moving too fast and marriage would change everything.

"I want your promise that you won't discuss this with anyone else. Especially anyone in the family," he added.

"Are you serious? I can't promise that. I'm not a priest or lawyer ethically bound to keep our conversation in the strictest confidence. No medical privacy issues, either." Gabe's grin was a clear indication of just how much he was enjoying this.

"Then I'm not going to tell you." Mason half turned toward the door.

"Okay. You win. My lips are sealed. But at least can I have an 'I told you so'?"

"I think you just did." Mason hoped he didn't regret this. "Now I want you to swear that you won't reveal to anyone what I'm going to talk about."

"Like swear on a Bible?"

"On the bond of brotherhood," Mason said.

"That's really deep." His brother made a cross over his heart. "You have my solemn promise."

"Okay." Mason blew out a breath. "I messed up with Annie. On our wedding night."

"Dear God, Mason. I'm probably not the best person to help with that. And, for crying out loud, performance in bed is not in Aunt Lil's wheelhouse, either. Maybe you should see a doctor—"

"It's not *that*." Once again Mason was reminded that he was a healer and not so good with words.

"What a relief. So it's not sex—"

"It kind of is."

Gabe shook his head. "Just tell me what happened."

"Everything was fine when we left after the wedding. We got the twins settled pretty fast. They were both sound asleep at the same time, which almost never happens. It was just Annie and me—" When his brother gave him a get-to-the-point scowl, Mason said, "I was trying to be sensitive. All the men she's known are jerks and I didn't want to be another one. I didn't want her to feel pressure to…you know—"

"Sleep with you?"

For now Mason ignored the irony of a doctor being reluctant to use the words. "It was supposed to be an out if she wanted one."

"What did you say?"

"That she was probably tired."

Gabe gave him a pitying look. "I'll admit I'm better with financial facts than women, but even I know not to tell a woman how she feels."

"I found that out." Mason would never forget the

look in her eyes. Emotions had swirled but he'd had no idea what they were. He'd only known that at that moment everything between them changed. In a bad way. "The thing is, it's awkward and tense now. I don't know how to fix it. Doing the wrong thing could be worse than doing nothing at all."

"I had no idea." Gabe shook his head.

"What?"

"That you suck this bad at romance."

"Now you know," Mason snapped.

"I guess I'm not the only Blackburne who focuses on data and logic instead of emotions."

"If this was an emergency room and you were having a heart attack, I'd know exactly what to do. I'm stethoscope and chest tubes, not a matters-of-the-heart guy."

"I get it."

Mason met his gaze. "Since you just admitted you know very little about women, it's quite possible that I just bared my soul and humiliated myself for no reason. You can't help." Mason started pacing. "You're useless."

"I wouldn't go that far. At least, not completely useless." Gabe looked thoughtful. "I try to avoid the interpersonal part of the business but it's impossible to work here and not absorb some things."

"Such as?"

"How to set a romantic scene." His brother shrugged. "We arrange a lot of first dates. I hear things."

"In my case, it seems a lot like shutting the barn door after the horse got loose."

"Ah, yes. You've already met someone and married her." Gabe nodded. "You moved so fast, I have to ask. Have you ever actually taken Annie out? On a date, I mean?"

"It's been hectic," Mason defended. "We have two babies. Then she broke her leg. It's not easy to align everything for alone time."

"Making the most of what you've got is another conversation and not my point anyway. But there are things you can do to maximize the moments you do have."

"Such as?"

"Bring her flowers. Put rose petals on the bed. A bottle of champagne chilling in the bedroom." Gabe threw up his hands. "Google 'romantic gestures.' Because that's all I've got. Or you can ask Mom."

"I'm going to pretend you didn't just say that." Mason barely held back a wince.

"Too far?" Gabe grinned. "But you must see where I'm going with this."

"You're talking about courting her."

"Finally the clouds part and the light shines through." Then his smile faded, replaced by a lost and angry look. "I'm not sure of the rules anymore, but it used to be a kiss good-night on the first date."

"I've already kissed her," Mason said.

"Before the wedding?"

When he nodded, Gabe asked, "And?"

"Hot. Very, very hot."

"Good, you've got some game. On the second date, more kissing and touching. If that works, seal the deal on the third date." Gabe's expression was ironic. "I can't help pointing out that this is something you should have taken care of before the vows."

Mason glared at his brother. "I've lost count. You've said 'I told you so' how many times now?"

"Sorry."

"No, you're not." But Mason laughed.

"No. I'm not." Then Gabe turned serious. "I like Annie a lot. And those kids are terrific."

"You'll get no argument from me."

"I really wish you luck, Mason."

"Thanks." They shook hands and Mason pulled him into a bro hug. "I have to go. Things to do."

And a first date to plan.

Chapter 11

Annie left work later than usual, partly because a deadline was approaching and she'd felt the need to put in more time on her graphics for the new contract presentation. Partly to avoid Mason. He was off today and had taken over childcare while she'd gone to the office. Now she had to go home. It took so much energy to be chipper and "normal" when she felt anything but and she didn't have the sparkle to spare.

In spite of that, her heart always skipped a beat when she saw him. Tired after a long hospital shift. First thing in the morning, all rumpled and scruffy. Playing with the babies. When they worked together taking care of Sarah and Charlie, the tension went away and everything was like it used to be before they were married. But when they were alone…

Was Carla right? Should she come on to him? She was too oomph-depleted to think about it right now.

She guided her car onto the street where she'd lived only a short time and a knot tightened in her stomach. After pulling her compact car into the driveway and parking, she got out then opened the rear passenger door to retrieve her laptop case from the seat.

She walked to the front door and sighed with satisfaction over her porch. She did love it. Bracing herself, she went inside and made her way to the back of the house. It was eerily quiet. No baby coos, chatter or even crying. That was weird.

She moved into the kitchen, where Mason was at the counter, his back to her. It was a broad back, wide shoulders. And if things were different between them, she would march over and let herself feel those muscles for herself.

He turned and smiled. "I thought I heard you come in."

That grin was like a direct hit to her midsection and the shockwaves went through her whole body. "H... Hi."

"You had a long day." He glanced at the case in her hand and moved close. "Let me take that for you."

"What?" His hand closed over hers and held on maybe a little longer than necessary before he took it and her purse. "Oh... I can—"

"I'll just put these over here on the floor in the family room."

The manly scent of his skin had her senses reeling with awareness and she missed it when he moved away. Although distance allowed her brain to start functioning again.

"Where are the twins?"

"Asleep." He walked back into the kitchen and went to the bottle of wine sitting on the granite countertop. It was already open and breathing. He poured some of the deep burgundy liquid into two stemless glasses then handed one to her.

"They're actually asleep?" she asked.

"Yeah. No nap today, which I kind of planned." He moved close and looked down at her. "We did errands. Then I took them for a long stroller ride in the park and they got lots of fresh air. They were tired and fussy for baths, but it worked out."

"You bathed them, too?"

"Yeah. You've been working hard. I knew you'd be tired."

She had been but right now not so much. This new and different Mason had her attention. After a sip of wine she said, "I better get dinner started."

"I already did. It's not fancy," he said. "Salad, twice-baked potatoes and steaks. I'll grill them."

"Wow." This couldn't be real. She must have stumbled into an alternate reality. "That sounds great. I'll set the table."

"Already done."

She glanced over at her small dinette set in the nook. There was a bouquet of flowers in the center and her heart simply melted. She could feel liquid warmth trickling through her as she stared at the white daisies, baby's breath and strategically positioned yellow roses. She walked over and leaned in to smell the sweet, floral fragrance.

"Mason, they're beautiful."

"Did you know that there are meanings attributed to different colored roses?"

"I think I heard that somewhere, but I'm a little surprised that you know."

"I got quite the education at the florist."

Her eyes widened. These weren't just an impulse buy at the grocery store? "You made a special trip?"

"Yeah. The twins won over everyone in the place and I think that got me extra attention."

The babies might have helped a little, but a man as incredibly good-looking as Mason would get attention from women if he was alone. "I'm pretty clear on the significance of red and white roses. But not yellow."

"According to Cathy, of Flowers by Cathy, it means joy, friendship and the promise of a new beginning."

Be still my heart, she thought. Then her practical self shut down any deeper implication. He probably just liked the color.

"They're really beautiful. So cheerful. Thank you."

"You're welcome." He moved to where she stood by the table and held up his wineglass. "What should we drink to?"

The sounds of silence surrounded her and she smiled. "Our healthy babies."

"To Charlie and Sarah." He touched his glass to hers and they sipped. "You must be starved. I'll cook the steaks."

"I'll toss the salad and warm the potatoes."

He shook his head. "You worked today. And this is our first— This is a…" He hesitated then finally said, "This is my chance to pamper you."

"And I appreciate it." More than she could say. "But I think you worked harder today than me. Like a wife."

His eyebrows rose. "That's high praise."

"I mean it." And she was grateful, from the bottom of her heart.

"I'm happy to do it." Intensity glittered in his eyes. Even though no part of their bodies touched, she felt as if he was touching her everywhere.

"And I'm happy to help. But before I do, I'm going to peek in on the twins."

She saw the baby monitor on the counter and they would hear if there was a problem, but she needed to see them. They grounded her and she needed grounding after Mason's sweet thoughtfulness. That made her feel like an ungrateful witch and she didn't mean to be. But she had a hard time trusting the good stuff.

She looked in on Charlie first and smiled at the soundly sleeping boy. He was on his back, arms and legs outstretched as if he appreciated having space all to himself. She couldn't resist brushing a silky blond strand off his forehead and, fortunately, it didn't disturb him.

Then she tiptoed into Sarah's room. The little girl was a tummy sleeper, no matter how they tried to keep her on her back. Annie put a kiss on her finger and touched it gently to the little girl's round cheek. When Sarah moved, Annie froze. After all Mason's efforts, the last thing she wanted was to wake up this baby. She waited a few moments and all was peaceful, so she quietly backed away.

Annie headed to the kitchen, where the French door was ajar. Through the glass she could see Mason watching over the gently smoking grill. The hunter/gatherer, she thought. Today he'd hunted and gathered the heck out of their survival and she didn't know what to make of it.

By the time the steaks were ready she had the salad bowl and potatoes on the table along with the flowers and wine. It suddenly felt very romantic, in spite of the bright, canned light shining down. They sat across from each other and smiled.

"No candles?" she teased.

"Damn, I knew I forgot something." He actually looked upset with himself.

"Oh, my gosh. I was kidding, Mason. This is amazing. I love it."

"Really?"

"Are you serious? I didn't have to cook it. That makes everything fantastic, like going out to dinner."

"Medical school was no culinary institute, so I didn't learn how to serve elegantly. My service in the army neglected that, too."

"Now you're just fishing for compliments," she said.

"Did it show? And I thought I was being subtle." He grinned then said, "Try your steak. I wasn't sure how you like it. I did both medium-rare and figured I can cook yours more if you want."

"No. Medium is good." She made a cut and looked at the warm, pink center. "This is perfect."

The meat practically melted in her mouth, it was so tender. Suddenly she really was starving and practically inhaled the food and the rest of the wine in her glass.

Feeling the need to explain, she said, "I didn't have time for lunch."

"As a doctor I have to tell you that's not good."

"I was on a creative roll. Doing the last tweaks

before we present our concept to the client." She shrugged. "I don't like all my eggs in one basket, which doesn't help."

He refilled her wineglass and she was reaching out when he set it down. Their fingers brushed. The touch was electric and she was sure something sparked in his eyes, too.

He cleared his throat. "What does that mean? All the eggs in one basket?"

"I don't put my creative energy into one concept. It's important to have a choice. So the team brainstorms two or three and we work them up. If we get the contract, the client will choose a direction and we'll put all the detail into that. But there will be enough that they can visualize each one."

"That's two or three times the work for you."

"It's an investment in our reputation. 'The company that works twice as hard for you.'" She rested her arms on the table and smiled.

"Something tells me you're a girl who puts maximum effort into everything, not just the job."

"I always try my best. Even when I was a little girl."

"And your parents didn't see the effort."

"You remembered," she said. A man who listened. It might be his most attractive feature.

"It's their loss. In case I haven't said it before."

She sighed. "Someday maybe I'll believe that. In the meantime, I don't want to lose out on moments with Charlie and Sarah. But I have to find balance. Being able to work remotely helps. And what you did tonight."

"Just pulling my weight," he said modestly.

Of which he had a lot, all muscle and temptingly

male. And this change in him just might be leading somewhere exciting. Was she a fool to hope?

"Speaking of cooperation, I'll do the dishes since you cooked."

"Not in my restaurant," he said.

"At least let me help. It's the least I can do."

He thought that over. "Okay."

Together they cleared the table. Since there were no leftovers, it was only plates, utensils and a salad bowl. They finished wine while working and Annie was super relaxed and hyperaware. When their hands brushed exchanging plates, her breath caught. Their shoulders touched and her heart started to pound. She saw his eyes darken with something sexy and wild and she was almost positive it wasn't just her feeling this.

Should she jump his bones?

Fear froze her. If he didn't want her, she could lose even this, and she couldn't bear that. It was selfish, but also for the babies. Together they could provide a stable environment. More selfish, she didn't know what she would do without him or the family she finally had because of him. No, if a move was going to be made, he was the one who would have to do it.

When they were finished, he looked down at her. "I had a really nice time tonight."

"Me, too."

He looked away for a moment then met her gaze. "Would it be okay if I kissed you good-night?"

That was sweet and gentlemanly, almost as if they'd just met and… Was this a date? She smiled and nodded.

The corners of his mouth curved up as he cupped her face in his big hands then touched his lips to hers.

The contact was soft and sweet and perfect. Tender and gentle, a gesture of promise.

He pulled back and there was a dash of regret in his eyes when he let her go. "I've got paperwork to do, so I'll say good-night. Sleep well, Annie."

All she could do was nod. She was breathless and wanting and more than a little disappointed. But she knew rejection and this wasn't it. Mason was up to something.

After working three days in a row at the hospital, Mason finally had two days off and planned to put Operation Courting Annie into high gear. He had taken the twins to his parents' house and, after carrying them inside, had gone back to the SUV for diaper bags, favorite blankets and stuffed animals they couldn't get along without.

He put the provisions in the room where the cribs were set up, the same one where Annie had slept. The thought of her sent heat rolling through him. Dinner and flowers had gone well and he had every reason to hope that tonight would, too.

Back in the family room, the babies were on a blanket and Lulu sat patiently between them while they awkwardly patted her furry back. His mom and dad sat on the floor with the kids and the dog; it was a modern Norman Rockwell moment.

Flo stood and walked over to stand beside him. "It feels like forever since I've seen these babies."

"You see them almost every day."

"But it's not the same as having them here," she said wistfully.

Mason watched his daughter crawl over to her

grandfather and into his lap. Watching the man who'd raised him cuddle and interact with his own little girl tugged at his heart. He'd been too young to really remember this amazingly gentle and patient side of his dad, so it was cool to see now.

"Mason?"

"What?" He reluctantly looked away and focused on what his mother was saying.

"I said, where is Annie?"

When he'd called to make sure it was okay to bring the kids over, his mom had been on the phone with someone else. She'd confirmed they weren't busy and would love to babysit the twins. Then she'd cut him off. Now she wanted details.

"Annie is at the office, working."

"So why am I watching your children? Not that I mind."

"No, you're just nosy." He appreciated the fact that she didn't interfere but was deeply committed to knowing whatever was shared willingly. "The thing is, I'm going to surprise her at work and take her out to dinner." When you were raised by Florence Blackburne, a guy knew when he messed up and when he did good. This time he'd definitely done good.

"Oh, Mason, that's a wonderful idea. Very sweet and thoughtful of you."

And selfish. But he hoped it would be positive for both him and Annie. He also chose not to share that he'd actually taken his brother's advice and searched the internet for romantic gestures. Since he couldn't sweep her away to Fiji, surprising her at work followed by a dinner out, with candles this time, would have to do.

"I'm glad you approve, Mom." He looked at his father, who had been listening in. "Any objections, Dad?"

"Nope." He let Sarah pull the cell phone from his shirt pocket and grinned at her. "Say hi to Annie for us."

"You know it's Friday. Your father and I aren't working tomorrow. We can keep Charlie and Sarah overnight. If you'd like."

He had been hoping she would offer. Another piece of the plan clicked into place. "I'd appreciate it, Mom. And I know Annie will, too. Thanks."

"Anytime."

Lulu barked once and drew Mason's attention to Charlie pulling himself to a standing position right in front of the DVD stack.

"Red alert," he said.

"We're going to have to move those." His mother hurried over to grab up her grandson. "Come to think of it, babyproofing this house is now a major priority."

He kissed her cheek. "I have to go or my plan to intercept her before she heads home will be a dismal failure."

"Don't you worry. We'll take good care of these little angels." She gave Charlie loud kisses on his neck and he giggled.

"I'm sure the three of you will do fine with them."

"Who's the third?" she asked.

He pointed to the dog. "Lulu. In fact, Annie and I would like to borrow her."

"That dog does love these little ones," his mother agreed. "Now go. We've got this."

"Roger that."

He shook his father's hand and kissed the kids. And,

this was a first, he got them to imitate his farewell wave. One of them said what sounded like "Bye-bye" and he'd swear on a stack of Bibles that it was first words.

Part two of his plan was officially in motion, he thought as he drove to Annie's office. It didn't take long and he parked in the lot that had more cars at this hour on a Friday night than he'd figured. Probably not all of them worked at C&J Graphic Design, but that didn't matter. The very definition of surprise meant you had to be flexible in the execution of the plan.

He walked into the lobby, pushed the up elevator button and the doors instantly opened. After getting inside and selecting the floor where her office was located, the nerves hit. What if she thought this was a stupid idea? What if he embarrassed her? And the worst: What if she had no desire to be anything more than what they already were?

The doors opened and across from him there was nothing but glass, the center etched with the words "C&J Graphic Design." He exited the elevator to get a better look at her office. He could see wood floors and cubicles divided by more glass. A doctor could do delicate surgery in this room what with the excellent track lighting overhead. All the workspaces were empty, except two.

Mason saw Annie standing just outside her cubicle, talking to a man who was outside the one next door. He looked to be in his early thirties, black hair and dark brown eyes that kind of smoldered. Surprise. Mason could have gone forever not knowing she worked with a guy good-looking enough to be on the cover of *GQ* magazine.

"No guts, no glory," he mumbled as he pushed open one of the heavy doors and walked inside, moving toward the twosome.

"Who are you?" Smoldering Eyes asked.

Annie turned and her eyes widened. "Mason!"

"Hi." He lifted a hand in a wave and stopped beside her.

"What are you doing here?"

"I wanted to surprise you and take you out to dinner." He met the other man's dark, curious gaze, then looked back at her. "Surprise."

"Mission accomplished. I'm definitely surprised." There was a pleased expression on her face before it slipped a little. "Where are the kids?"

"At the house. They'll be fine by themselves." He grinned to let her know he was kidding. "I had you for a second."

"No." But she playfully slugged his arm. "Seriously, where are they really?"

"Three guesses."

"Your parents'."

"Right in one," he said.

"So there really is a husband?" *GQ* asked.

"Yes." Annie looked apologetic. "Sorry. I should have introduced you. Mason Blackburne, this is Cruz Wright, one of my coworkers."

Mason shook the other man's hand. "Nice to meet you."

"Likewise. So you're the twins' father, the dad who got Annie to say yes."

Was there a hidden message in those words? Had this guy been planning to move in on her when Dwayne the Douche was out of the picture? Unclear.

"I am that man, yes." Mason moved close enough that his arm brushed Annie's. Meeting her coworker gave him one more reason to be glad that she could do a lot of work remotely.

Just then an attractive young woman joined them and looked him up and down. "So, who's this?"

"Mason Blackburne, my husband." Annie looked up at him. "This is Ella Lancaster, my boss's assistant, and the woman who keeps things running smoothly around here. And she does it with extraordinary grace and good humor."

He shook her hand. "A pleasure, Miss—"

"Ella." She smiled. "Annie's been through a lot in the last year. We were happy for her when she told us she was getting married. It's about time someone lived up to Annie Campbell's rigorous standards."

"She doesn't suffer fools," Cruz explained.

"I suffered Dwayne." Annie glanced up at him and made an "eek" face. "Calling him a fool is an insult to fools."

"Right on." Cruz studied Mason. "Points to you for sticking around."

"He came to surprise me," she explained to Ella.

The other woman sighed and said to him, "Are there any more at home like you?"

"As a matter of fact, there are," Annie said. "He has two brothers. And a sister."

At the end of the row of offices, a door opened and a man emerged. He was in his fifties. Blond hair with gray at the temples, the lean body of a runner. He joined the group.

Before he could say anything Annie said, "Bob, this is my husband. Mason, this is Bob Clemens, our boss."

The man held out his hand. "Glad to meet you, Mason."

"Same here, sir."

"Annie says you were in the army. Deployed overseas recently."

"Yes, sir. I was assigned to a medical unit in Afghanistan."

"Thank you for your service." Bob looked around the group then settled his gaze on Mason. "To what do we owe the pleasure of this visit?"

"I'm here to surprise Annie and take her to dinner."

The man nodded his approval. "She's been working a lot of hours and deserves some quality downtime. The campaign for the client is ready and she needs to relax and have some fun."

"R and R, that's my plan," Mason said.

"Then what are you waiting for?" Bob asked. "Get her the heck out of here."

"Yes, sir." Mason looked down at her and held out his arm. "Let's go."

There was no hesitation or awkwardness when she put her hand in the crook of his elbow. She looked luminous and happy, and that gave him hope that he wasn't messing this up beyond repair.

Now for the next part of his plan.

Chapter 12

Annie was literally quivering with excitement as she walked out of the office on Mason's arm. Whatever was going on with him, she was giving this new attitude two thumbs-up and a double arm pump. Inside, of course. It took a lot of concentration to not giggle like a schoolgirl and walk normally. And he looked so sexy and handsome in his jeans, white dress shirt and sports coat. He was out of her league, but she would deal with that insecurity at another time.

Waiting for the elevator, she could feel her coworkers staring through the glass. Mason hadn't picked her up and carried her out in front of every employee, but it still felt like *An Officer and a Gentleman* moment.

She started to slide her fingers from his arm, but he put his hand over hers to keep it there. She smiled up at him.

"This is a very nice surprise."

"I'm glad."

"To what do I owe—?"

Before she could finish her question, the elevator doors opened and they walked inside. Mason pushed the button for the first floor and the ride down was fast. When they stepped out into the lobby, it was as if happiness made her see everything brighter and more clearly. Nothing was there that hadn't been there this morning, but that was before Mason had made the effort to surprise her at work.

In the corner by the tall glass windows there was a grouping of pumpkins, pots of rust-colored mums and a scarecrow announcing that fall was in full swing.

"This will be the twins' first Halloween," she said. "Should we take them trick-or-treating?"

"Affirmative." He glanced at the decorations and let his gaze wander over the whole lobby. "The little kids in costume are the best."

"I know. And it will be really different for me this year."

"Really?" He gave her a wry look. "You think? With two babies?"

"And a house. There aren't a lot of kids in my apartment building, but now I live in an actual neighborhood." She grinned. "It's going to be fun giving out candy and seeing all the costumes on the little ones."

"Logistics," he said thoughtfully.

"What?"

"Tactical operations center."

"You're going to have to translate that into nonmilitary terms for us civilians."

"One of us will have to stay home—tactical operations center or TOC—and give out that candy, while the other takes the twins around."

"Divide and conquer," she said, nodding.

"Right."

She sighed happily. "From my perspective that is a quality problem to have."

"I completely agree." He looked down at her, more carefree than the solemn, serious guy who'd knocked on her door to take a DNA test. "But the night is young and I'm starving. We can talk about this at dinner."

After walking outside into the cool, crisp evening air, she said, "My car is over there. I'll meet you at the restaurant. Where are we going?"

"Nope. It's top secret. I'll drive. We can get your car later." He pointed. "Mine is right there in the first row."

"Okay." At that moment she was ready, willing and able to go with him wherever he wanted to take her.

They strolled over to his SUV and he opened the door for her, handing her inside. For a split second, their faces were millimeters apart. She could feel his breath on her cheek and thought he was going to kiss her. And she wanted him to so very much. The streetlight illuminated his features and there was a hungry intensity there that had nothing to do with food. So when he didn't touch his mouth to hers, it wasn't a soul-wrenching blow. As he'd said, the night was young and they were going to dinner. As surprises went, this one was moving its way into her top five.

He got into the driver's seat and turned on the SUV, then guided it out of the lot to merge with street traffic. It was a little congested right now as a majority of people left work and headed home. She actually had no idea of their final destination.

"So, where are you taking me?"

"Like I said, it's a surprise."

"I thought you showing up unexpectedly at my place of employment was the surprise."

"Part of it," he confirmed.

"But I can't change your mind about keeping the dinner location a top secret?"

"Nope. Although, you'll figure it out soon enough. Short of blindfolding you, I can't keep it clandestine all the way there."

But how sweet was it that he was doing it at all? Annie pinched herself, just to make sure she wasn't dreaming. The tweak on her wrist told her she wasn't.

As he drove, making left and right turns, the area became more open, less dense with single-family homes and zones where there were businesses and strip mall shopping. Finally, when he turned onto Summit Highway, she knew.

"Le Chêne," she whispered reverently.

"Affirmative."

It was one of Huntington Hills' most highly rated and exclusive restaurants. Upscale, cozy, romantic, historic. She'd only been there once. It was a spontaneous decision Dwayne the Douche had made without a reservation for the busiest place in town. They'd been turned away. So she knew the restaurant was located on a country estate and vineyards. When they slowly drove closer, she recognized the ivy-covered stone exterior that was reminiscent of a French château.

"This place is hard to get into," she said.

"I made a reservation."

Planning ahead, she thought. It was a very sexy quality.

He parked in the lot, then got out and came around to open her door. When she slid to the ground, he put his hand to the small of her back as they walked inside. The interior was dimly lit and had elegant oak wood beams and recessed lighting. The hostess confirmed a reservation for Dr. Mason Blackburne and showed them to a table for two in a secluded corner. There were candles on the table and that made Annie smile.

Tables were covered with pristine white tablecloths and the chairs were oak. It was country elegance with a wall full of wine bottles and lots of wood-framed mirrors.

The server came right over. "My name is Shelly. Can I get you something to drink?"

Mason asked for a wine list and picked out a bottle. Shelly left menus and promised to be back in a few minutes. It didn't take long and she opened the red blend then poured a small amount in a long-stemmed glass for him to approve. He did and she filled both of their glasses before promising to return to take their orders.

"Let's drink to good surprises always," he said.

Annie touched her elegant crystal glass to his and heard a bell-like tinkling sound. "I can get behind that in a big way."

She took a sip of the dark red liquid and savored the perfect blend of flavors. "This is nice. Thank you for all of this, Mason."

"I have to apologize."

"For bringing me here to this beautiful place?"

"No. For not bringing you sooner," he said.

"You have nothing to be sorry for," she insisted.

"I disagree." He met her gaze across the small, intimate table and the flame in his eyes burned as brightly as the candles between them. "Everything was rushed and clumsy. The house. The wedding. Our first night. It was fast—"

"Is this your way of saying you're having second thoughts?" A familiar knot of apprehension tightened in her stomach. "Do you regret everything?"

"No," he said quickly. "Good God, no."

"Then what?"

"I'm trying to make it up to you."

"And I'll try to communicate my feelings," she said. "You can't read my mind."

"No, but I can read your face. There's been tension between us and it's my fault. I hope this is a new beginning."

Their server, Shelly, returned and took their orders. White sea bass for her and red snapper *meunière* for him. "Are you celebrating anything special?"

"No," Annie said.

"Yes," he said at the same time. "We just got married. No time for a honeymoon and we have twins. But this is a special occasion for us."

"Congratulations," Shelly said. "The twins. Boys or girls?"

"One of each," he said proudly. "This dinner is to celebrate the beginning of our life as a family."

"That's so sweet," the server said. "I'm a sucker for romantic gestures."

Me, too, Annie thought.

When they were alone she cleared the emotion from her throat and said, "So, Halloween logistics."

"Right, it occurs to me that my folks could help. Give out candy at the house while we take the twins out. They won't last long anyway, and it's not like they can eat candy."

She nodded. "Just a symbolic gesture, for pictures and the promise of future family traditions."

"I like the sound of that."

They chatted, laughed and teased until the food came. Everything was delicious and she knew that because he shared his with her and she did the same with him. The service was impeccable and Shelly brought them a piece of cheesecake topped with strawberries, on the house, to memorialize this dinner for them. He paid the bill and they walked outside, complaining about how full they were.

At the SUV Annie hesitated before getting in. She looked up at him and had no idea what he saw in her eyes, but on the inside she was brimming with joy. She couldn't ever remember being this happy.

"Thank you, Mason. I had a wonderful time. I feel like Cinderella and my coach will turn into a pumpkin if I don't leave the ball before midnight."

"This night doesn't have to end," he said softly.

"It does. We have to pick up the twins."

"My folks offered to keep them tonight. I made an executive decision and took them up on it."

Annie knew what he was saying and smiled. "For the record, I'm not tired at all."

"Yeah." He looked sheepish and so darn cute. "That was definitely not my smoothest moment."

"Past history." Annie threw herself into his arms and hugged him then turned her face up to his. He kissed her until she was breathless and finally she said, "I like your executive decisions. Now take me home."

* * *

"Can't this thing go any faster?" Annie was in the passenger seat of Mason's SUV. She was only half kidding but the lights from the dashboard illuminated Mason's grin.

"It *can* go faster actually, but I'd be breaking speed-limit laws. I don't know about you, but getting stopped by a cop right now isn't high on my to-do list."

"Mine, either, darn it." She looked at his profile, outlined by passing lights, and admired the straight nose, strong jaw. He was a handsome man, but beauty was only skin-deep. A pretty face didn't reveal character, but what he'd done tonight definitely did. "Mason?"

"Hmm?" He glanced over then returned his attention to the road.

"In case I forget to tell you later, tonight was the nicest surprise I've ever had. No one has ever done something so special for me."

"I'm full of the unexpected," he declared proudly.

Something in his tone caught her attention. It was mischievous, playful. "What?"

"Just stating a fact." Same roguish tone.

"You have something else up your sleeve," she said. "Give it up."

"You are so impatient."

"If I agree, will you tell me?"

"No."

"That's just mean," she said.

He smiled, completely unmoved by her words. "You'll thank me later."

"I guess I'll just have to trust you on that."

"And that's okay," he said softly. "You can."

Trust was the very hardest thing for her to do. Everyone in her world had let her down. Everyone but Jess. Except, in the end, she'd left, too. Not by choice, by fate. Mason was a good man and Annie wanted to have sex with him. She was going to give him her body by choice, but that didn't mean her heart went along. She wouldn't give that up.

"I'm feeling a serious vibe from your side of the car," he said. "You okay?"

"Better than okay." She was in control.

"We're almost home." His voice was edgy and deep with the subtext of what home would be for them tonight.

A wave of anticipation rolled through her and every nerve ending in her body started to throb. She'd been waiting for this possibly since the first time she'd seen him. Maybe not exactly then because she'd been very tired and pretty crabby. But soon after when he'd kept showing up. That was okay. Falling in love was not.

"Here we are." He drove into the driveway. "Home sweet home."

There was a light on in the living room and the babies weren't there. "Do you think maybe we should call your mom and check on Sarah and Charlie?"

"Yeah." He pulled his cell out of his jeans' pocket and looked at the screen. "There's a text from her."

"What is it?"

"She says, 'Babies fine. Don't call me. I'll call you.'"

"Okay, then. Wow." Annie looked at him. "It's a little scary that she can read minds."

"It's a mom thing. She's one, you're one." He shrugged. "Let's go inside."

"Yeah." She opened her door. "I want to see what the surprise is."

Mason got out and came around to her side. He held out his hand and she put hers into his palm, their fingers intertwining as they walked to the front door and unlocked it.

He pushed it wide and said, "Surprise."

Annie's heart melted when she saw pink rose petals on the entryway floor. The trail continued through the family room and down the hall to the master bedroom. On the dresser was an ice bucket with a bottle of champagne and two flutes.

He lifted the bottle and water rolled off. "The ice is almost melted, but it's still cold."

"Oh, Mason—" She moved closer to him and thought surely he could actually hear her heart hammering. "This is incredibly thoughtful. I didn't think you could top picking me up from work and that beautiful dinner, but I was wrong. You were right. I do thank you."

"Yeah?" He was studying her closely and the words seemed to reassure him. "I'm glad. This could so easily have gone seriously sideways."

"It so didn't, believe me." She put her palms on his chest and met his gaze. "I wasn't tired before, but I'm *really* not tired now."

He grinned sheepishly as his hands settled on her waist and pulled her close. "You're not going to forget that, are you?"

"I think the rose petals and champagne bought you a memory lapse."

"In that case…"

Mason lowered his mouth to hers, a soft kiss, but tension had been building all night. And probably even before that. The touch was like accelerant to a glowing spark, igniting it, turning it into a flame that burned out of control. She opened her mouth and his tongue moved inside, caressing everywhere before dueling with hers.

Annie pushed his sports jacket off his shoulders and he dragged it the rest of the way, turning the sleeves inside out in his rush. She started to undo the buttons on his shirt but her fingers were shaking, her hands uncoordinated. He brushed them aside and dragged it over his head.

Light trickled in from the hallway, enough for her to see the impressive width of his chest and the contour of muscle. It was begging to be touched and Annie couldn't resist. The ever-so-male dusting of hair scraped her palms as she moved them over his skin and down his rib cage. She heard him suck in air and flinch as if it tickled—or turned him on.

"You're very forward," he said.

"I've been told I should take the initiative."

"Do I want to know who told you that?" He picked up her hand and softly caressed the palm with his thumb.

"Probably not."

"Even if I wanted to thank them?" he said in a hoarse voice. "And, just so we're clear, I'm definitely not complaining."

He brought her hand to his mouth and sucked on her index finger. Now it was her turn to gasp as the power of that small contact crackled over the nerve endings in every part of her body. She was breathless and feeling like taking more initiative.

"You have too many clothes on," he said.

"What are you going to do about that?" She gave him a sassy look then unbuckled the belt at his waist.

"I'm going to assist you in disrobing." He turned her around so that her back was to him.

She quickly shrugged off her sweater, making it easier for him to keep his promise. He didn't hesitate, instantly lowering the zipper on the black dress. He did it slowly, and only to her waist, then he pushed the material open wider and kissed the exposed skin.

This exquisite torture was making Annie squirm with need in the best possible way. He must have read her body language because with one quick move he had the zipper all the way down. She let the silky black material slide down her body and pool at her feet before stepping out of it.

She faced him in black panties, matching bra and high heels. He wasn't the only one who could read body language. If the intensity in his eyes was anything to go by, he very much liked what he saw.

"You are so beautiful." His voice was hardly more than a strangled whisper.

He put his hands on her waist, grazing his thumbs over the sensitive bare skin before sliding them higher to brush the undersides of her breasts.

The need to feel his hands on her without any material in the way was so strong she couldn't fight it even if she wanted to. She reached behind and unhooked her bra, letting it fall to the floor with the rest of her clothes. Then she took his hands and placed them on her breasts, holding them there. The touch felt so good, her eyes drifted closed, letting her just take in the sensations.

Moments later she felt his mouth on her and the sensations multiplied exponentially. He kissed first one sensitive peak then the other and her legs went so weak she wasn't sure they would hold her up.

"I want you now," she murmured.

"Twist my arm."

He yanked the bedcovers down then removed the rest of his clothes. Annie stepped out of her heels and let him lead her to their bed. She sat then slid over and made room for him. He followed her, gathered her in his arms and slid his hand over her side to the waistband of her panties. He hooked a thumb then dragged them over her thighs and calves, where she kicked them off.

He ran his hand down her hip and over her belly, resting his palm there as he slid one finger inside her. He brushed his thumb over the sensitive feminine bundle of nerves between her thighs and the intense feeling nearly made her jump off the bed.

All the while he was kissing her—eyelids, nose, cheeks, mouth, neck. He kissed the underside of her jaw then blew softly on the moistness, making her shiver before taking her earlobe between his teeth, biting gently, tenderly. The assault on her senses pushed her to the edge.

"I need you. Now—"

Without a word, he nudged her legs apart with his knee and settled himself over her. His chest was going up and down very fast and the sound of their mingled harsh breaths filled the room. Taking his weight on his forearms, he started to push inside her then stopped.

"What?" she asked.

"A condom—"

"Oh, God! I wasn't thinking—"

"I was." He rolled sideways, reached into the nightstand to retrieve one then put it on. Moments later he was back and kissed her softly. "All squared away. Now, where were we? Oh, yes—"

He entered and her body closed around him, welcoming him. She wrapped her legs around his waist, taking him deeper inside, moving her hips. He got the message and slowly stroked in and out, building the tension with each thrust.

Before she was ready, Annie felt herself let go, break apart, setting free waves of pleasure inside her. Aftershocks made her tremble in the most wonderful way and he held her until they stopped.

Then he began to move in and out again. One thrust then two. Moments later he groaned and breathed her name. She kissed his neck and chest and when he buried his face against her hair, she held him until he sighed into her shoulder.

Annie wasn't sure how long they stayed like that and didn't much care. She hadn't felt this good in a very long time, and that kind of scared her. Sex with Mason was different. Oh, the mechanics were the same, but it was unlike anything she'd ever experienced. And there was only one reason for that.

Her feelings were engaged. She wasn't putting any label on them, but something was stirred up inside her. It was ironic that she'd been bothered when he wouldn't sleep with her. And there was that old saying—be careful what you wish for.

Well, she got it. And she wasn't complaining. It was everything she'd hoped for and more. Mason played her body like a violin and her body was happy. But her heart was a different story.

Chapter 13

Annie didn't trust perfect.

She'd grown up in an environment that was the exact opposite of perfect. The absence of crisis was the bar she used to judge the quality of her life. A rainbows-and-unicorns existence made her uneasy but that's how it had been for the last week. Ever since that magical night when Mason had surprised her at work and taken her to dinner, followed by the best sex she'd ever had.

And it wasn't an aberration because it had happened every night after. Even with babies and work, they managed to be together. It was wonderful but Annie was so afraid to go all in and believe this was how things were going to be from now on. She was a little less confident about her control where Mason was concerned.

He would laugh if she confessed her fears, but he

couldn't understand. Except for that one bad marriage blip, his life had been smooth sailing because he'd won the lottery in terms of fabulous families. She couldn't relate to that, so it was understandable that he had no frame of reference for her insecurity, either.

Today her insecurities were on parade inside her. They were meeting his lawyer and the family court judge to finalize his legal petition of paternal rights. He was with Charlie in the family room waiting for her to get Sarah ready.

She smiled at the little girl on the changing table, playing with a small stuffed bear as Annie secured the tabs on her diaper. "Daddy is your daddy, right? So what could go wrong, baby girl?"

Sarah babbled an incoherent response. "I know. I'm being ridiculous. Daddy would say the same thing. It's just that I'm nervous. And you need to look your best. So Mommy has to put your clothes on. No flashing the judge, baby girl."

She slid white tights over Sarah's feet and legs, then covered the diaper. After sitting the infant up, she slipped a dress over her head, a simple floral print with a smocked bodice, and black ballerina flats. Last, she put on a headband with attached bow that highlighted her cornflower blue eyes and blond curls. For once, the little girl didn't pull it off. And again the perception of perfection reared its ugly head.

"I have a bad feeling about this."

She sighed then picked up the baby and walked into the family room. Mason had Charlie in his arms, holding the little boy closer and more tightly than usual. He was wearing navy slacks and a long-sleeved white dress shirt with a red-and-blue-striped silk tie. There was a serious expression on his face and her stomach knots pulled tighter.

"You're worried," Annie said.

"About?"

"Court."

"Nervous," he clarified. "There's a difference. Unless you work there, no one wants to go in front of a judge."

"But your lawyer said it's just a formality. All the paperwork is in order."

"He did," Mason confirmed. "So smile, Annie."

"You first," she challenged.

At that moment Charlie babbled something that sounded like "Da-da" and patted Mason's shoulder with his chubby little hand. And that got a genuine smile from his father.

"See? Charlie isn't worried," Annie said.

"Only about getting his next bottle." Mason tested the weight of the boy resting on his forearm. "Have you noticed how heavy he's getting?"

"I have." She nuzzled her daughter's soft cheek. "This little princess is petite and delicate."

"She looks beautiful. And so do you." For a moment his eyes glittered with something other than anxiety. "Is that a new dress?"

She looked down at the belted black shirtdress with its long sleeves and white detailing. Her coordinating heels were low and sensible. Practical but not flashy. For the moment, anyway, she was living a rainbows-and-unicorns life, so why not dress the part?

"Yes, and new shoes." She caught her bottom lip between her teeth. "Do we look like we're trying too hard?"

"Maybe. But justice is supposed to be blind. I doubt the judge will turn down my petition because of our fashion choices."

"So, you're saying I'm being ridiculous?"

He smiled. "Those words did not come out of my mouth."

"Uh-huh." She looked at Sarah. "See? I told you Daddy would call me silly."

He moved close enough for her to feel the warmth of his body and hers responded to it. Smiling tenderly, he said, "You are the least silly person I know. If anything, I'd like to see you develop a silly streak and work on cultivating a little carefree-ness."

"So now I'm too serious?" she teased.

"You're perfect."

"Not even close." And of all the things he could have said, that was the least likely to anesthetize her nerves. Because she didn't trust perfect.

"That's my prognosis and I'm sticking to it." He shrugged. "But we're procrastinating and need to get going. No one will care how photo ready we are if we miss the hearing."

"Right."

They shifted into high gear, working together like a meticulously choreographed ballet. Each put a baby into a carrier then took it to the car and secured it in the rear passenger seat. Annie had packed the diaper bag with bottles, changes of clothes and supplies for any emergency imaginable and set it on the floor in front of Charlie. Mason lifted the double stroller into the SUV cargo area. He'd put on his matching suit jacket and looked like a successful doctor and devoted dad.

Annie smiled at him. "You look very handsome. And pretty soon this will all be over."

"Piece of cake." He kissed her, a brief brush of his mouth on hers. "We got this."

They drove to the courthouse located in an older section of Huntington Hills. It was a complex of buildings and Mason's lawyer met them in the lobby of the family court. The high ceilings made their footsteps echo on the marble floor and the twins noticed. Both of them found their outdoor voices and used them in different pitches that made Annie and Mason wince.

She had just met the attorney and wanted their babies to make a good impression. Like that really mattered, but… "Sorry about that."

Cole Brinkman didn't seem perturbed by the noise. "This is normal for family court. They're kids and no one expects them not to make a sound."

"So this won't count against us?" Mason asked.

"Of course not," the lawyer said. "Nothing will. Through no fault of yours, you didn't know about them. Now you do and have the science to back up your claim. It's a slam dunk."

"Okay." Mason nodded.

"Just so you're aware, there are other cases in front of this judge, too. There will be other parents."

"And kids?" Annie asked.

"Yeah." Cole grinned. "It's going to be noisy."

"Okay, then."

"We should go in. Judge Downey is hearing the case and his courtroom is at the end of the hall."

They walked in the direction he pointed and stopped at the tall, wooden double doors. Mason pulled one open so Annie could push the twins' stroller through.

Cole wasn't lying. By Annie's count, there were about eight or ten couples already seated with numerous children of varying ages.

Minutes after they settled in the first row, an older man came in from a side door near the high bench. Since he had on a black robe, one assumed he was the judge. A woman in a sheriff's uniform announced Judge Downey, a man with white hair who looked to be somewhere in his sixties.

"Good morning," he said. "I've reviewed the documents for all of you here today and we'll try to move things along quickly. Children have a short attention span and I want them to go be kids. So, first case."

It wasn't them. From what Annie could pick up, the couple were aunt and uncle to a boy whose parents had been arrested during a drug sting and sent to prison for illegal distribution. The child was born while the mom was in jail and family had petitioned for temporary guardianship of the infant. They were the only parents he'd ever known. Now they were seeking legal custody. Their home environment was stable and loving, but the court bent over backward to keep children with their biological parents unless that became impossible. It was complicated.

Thank goodness Mason's case was simple, Annie thought. Several more couples and kids were called up, but Charlie was getting restless in the stroller so she unbuckled him and set him on her lap. Sarah wouldn't stand for being strapped in if her brother got to be free. So Annie handed off the boy to Mason and released the little girl, holding her close for a moment.

As proceedings dragged on she pulled out bottles from the diaper bag, then toys to entertain them. That worked for a while but then they started rubbing their eyes. After that there were tired cries and she wasn't sure if it was permissible to get up and move around with them. Mercifully their case was called and they could at least walk as far as the judge's bench.

He smiled. "You have a beautiful family, Dr. Blackburne."

"Thank you. I think so, too." He patted Charlie's back.

"A lot of scenarios present in my court, most of them heartbreaking. And I have to make decisions that are in the best interest of a child, decisions that will affect people's lives forever. And not always in a good way."

Annie's stomach lurched. Was he trying to prepare them for the worst? Something no one could have predicted?

Judge Downey smiled then. "Fortunately your situation is not one of those and the facts speak for themselves. Black-and-white. The DNA results are proof that you are the biological father of Charles and Sarah Campbell. They are a conclusive determination of your paternal rights, which I'm pleased to legally affirm."

"Thank you, sir," Mason said.

"Your attorney also filed a concurrent petition to change their last names and that is granted, too."

"So, that's it?" For a second Annie wasn't sure she'd said that out loud.

The judge smiled. "That's it. I wish every case was this easy. Congratulations."

"Thank you, Your Honor." Mason grinned at her, obviously relieved.

They left the courtroom and shook hands with their attorney. Cole took cell phone pictures of them, their first as a legal family.

They left the building and found the SUV. Mason grinned. "We're all Blackburnes now."

"I know." She had been ridiculous to worry.

This was surreal and so wonderful that there were no words to express her feelings. The last piece had fallen into place and she could hardly take it in. She finally had everything she'd ever dreamed of. A traditional family. She had never really believed that happiness like this could happen to someone who'd come from where she had. But she'd beaten the odds.

On paper and in reality her life really was perfect.

Mason drove his family home from the Huntington Hills' government center but he couldn't be sure he wasn't flying. Since getting the DNA results, he'd been there for the babies. He'd fed them, changed diapers, walked the floor at night with either—or both—when necessary. He'd been doing all the right things because he loved them. But there was something profoundly powerful in knowing the t's were crossed and the i's dotted. His status was legal. His name was on their birth certificate. No one could take them away from him.

"I'm pretty happy right now," he said.

"Really?" Annie was in the front passenger seat beside him. "I'd never have guessed. What with you frowning since we left the courtroom."

"I haven't stopped smiling." He was stating the obvious, which she already knew. "It's the weirdest thing. The proof was in the DNA test but I feel as if a weight has been lifted."

"That's good, because you're stuck with me and the twins now, Dr. Blackburne."

"And I can't think of anyone I'd rather share this with."

There was a smile in her voice when she said, "What a sweet thing to say. I feel the same way."

He glanced over and thought again what a pretty picture she made in her new dress. He also thought how very much he was looking forward to getting her out of it. But that was for later. Right now they had to get the kids home for naps. How ordinary that sounded and how wonderful. He vowed never to take it for granted. This was something he'd wanted for a very long time.

Annie seemed happy, too. They'd worked out the sex misunderstanding and were as compatible in bed as they were out of it. She wasn't demanding declarations of love or a definition of his feelings, and he was grateful for that. He cared about her more than he wanted to put into words. A couple of times leaving the house or on the phone when he'd said goodbye and nearly added "I love you," it startled him. But he caught himself. What they had was pretty damn good.

He wasn't going to rock the boat with a four-letter word. He'd said it all the time to his ex, even at the end when he wasn't feeling it anymore. He didn't want anything to mess up what he had with Annie and the kids, especially that one little word.

"We're almost home," he said. Another four-letter word that felt different from when he'd left this morning. Now it was his turn to be silly and Annie would probably make fun of him, but right now he didn't care. "The meaning of home feels more profound to me."

"Like you got a blessing from the angels?"

"At the risk of you laughing at me," he said, "yes."

"I understand." And she wasn't laughing.

He pulled the SUV into the driveway and turned off the engine. "Would it be too corny to say this is the first day of the rest of our lives?"

"Probably. But I get where you're coming from and share the sentiment. Who'd have guessed the big, bad, army doctor, emergency specialist was such a super softy?"

"That's our secret," he said teasingly. "I have a ba-dass reputation to maintain." Belying his words, he took her hand, bringing it to his lips to kiss the back of it. "Let's go be a family."

She glanced into the back seat and smiled tenderly at the sleeping babies. "Car ride works every time."

"Any chance of getting them in their cribs without waking them up?"

"There's always a chance." But the skeptical note in her voice put the brakes on hope. "The odds aren't good."

"That's what I figured. I'll take Sarah and the dia-per bag. You get Charlie." He felt as if he was the com-mander of a military operation, and life with twins was like that sometimes. Double the work. But he wouldn't change it for anything.

"Sounds like a plan."

Coordinating their efforts, they swiftly and effi-ciently and—dare he say it?—expertly got their chil-dren inside and changed out of their perfect family court clothes. One-piece terry-cloth sleepers were just what the doctor ordered. Each of the babies got a bottle and went down for a nap with a minimum of protest. The magic was still holding.

He and Annie tiptoed from the nurseries into the family room and he smiled at her. "That was too easy.

Do you think it's because I'm now legally their father as well as biologically?"

"They're just tired out from a big day," she said. "Or maybe we've banked some good karma."

"Since all is quiet on the home front, would you mind if I went out to do an errand?"

"What do you need to do?"

He grinned. "It's a surprise."

"Oh?" Female appreciation turned her eyes a darker shade of hazel, highlighting the gold flecks. "Maybe champagne and rose petals?"

"You're half-right. We need a really good bottle of champagne to celebrate a really good day."

"But no flowers?" She didn't look the least bit disappointed. "It was a sweet and beautiful gesture that I'll never forget. But those petals were really messy. Until they dried, it was kind of hard to vacuum them up. I watched you struggle with that."

"So the whole thing was wasted on you." He knew better than that.

"Absolutely not." She met his gaze and there was a wicked gleam in hers. "But it's not necessary today."

"Good. Because that's not my plan. I wanted to stop by my mom's and share our good news."

"You definitely should. Flo needs to know," she said emphatically. "I have a little work to do anyway. While the kids are sleeping."

"Okay, then. I shouldn't be too long."

"Take your time."

He nodded and started to turn away, then impulse took over. Moving close, he curved his fingers around her upper arms and pulled her to him, then lowered his mouth to hers. Her body went soft and yielding, and her small sigh of satisfaction made him hot all over. He ran his fingers through her silky blond hair then cupped her cheek in his palm. Her breath caught and she slid her arms around his neck. When he reluctantly lifted his mouth from hers, both of them were breathing hard.

"Are you sure you need to work?" His voice was hoarse.

"Yes. Sorry." And she did look let down. "Bob is doing the presentation to the client tomorrow and I need to go over the sketches and theme one more time, just to make sure it's as perfect as possible."

"Okay. And I really should share our good news."

"Yes."

"'Bye, Annie. I—" He'd almost said it again but stopped just in time. And he wasn't sure how he felt about that.

"What?"

"I'll be back soon. But if you need anything, call the cell."

Mason hurried off and drove to his folks' house not far away. His dad wouldn't be home from work yet but his mom's job was part-time and her car was in the driveway when he got there. He exited the SUV then walked up to the front door and knocked.

Flo answered and smiled instantly when she recognized him. "Mason! This is an unexpected surprise."

"Good or bad?"

She playfully swatted his arm. "Always good to see you. And you know that. Come in."

"Thanks."

"Can I get you something? Iced tea? Coffee? Food?"

"Come to think of it, I'm starving. Didn't have lunch today."

"I'll make you something."

In the kitchen she got out what she needed for a sandwich, even putting on one of the dill pickle slices that he liked. He sat in one of the bar chairs at the island and grabbed the plate she slid over to him.

"Thanks, Mom."

"You're welcome." She walked around the counter and sat in the chair beside his, watching wide-eyed as he wolfed down the food. "Why no lunch? Were you at the hospital? I didn't think you were working today."

"I'm not. But it was a big day. Annie and I went to court with the twins."

"That was today?" Her mouth dropped open and then she gave him the "mom" look. "Why didn't you tell me? I'd have been there."

"That's why we didn't tell you. If something had gone wrong—"

"But your lawyer said there were no problems."

"I just didn't want to take a chance." Now he felt like a little boy caught in a lie. "I know how hard you can take things."

"I admit that, but I'm still pretty good with moral support," she defended. "And you might have needed it. You take things hard, too. Sorry. You got that from me."

"Do you want to keep busting my chops for protecting you? Or do you want to know what happened?"

"Tell me," she said.

He grinned. "It's official. The twins are Charlie and Sarah Blackburne now."

"Oh, Mason." She hugged him. "Congratulations. That's wonderful news."

"It is pretty great."

"And I could have been there to hear it if you'd given me the chance."

"Mom, let it go. I was trying to protect you."

"I'll get over it." She grinned. "I can't wait to tell your dad. Or do you want to talk to him? Since you were obviously trying to protect him, too."

He sighed. "You can tell him. Maybe that will get me off the hook."

"It's a start," she teased.

"Good." He slid off the chair and took his paper plate to the trash. "I have to get back to Annie and the kids. I just wanted to come by and let you know. My next stop before home is for a bottle of champagne."

"You have a lot to celebrate." She hugged him again. "I'm so happy for you, Mason. After all you went through, finally things are going your way."

"Thanks, Mom."

She walked him to the door. "Give my best to Annie and kiss my grandbabies for me. Tell them Grandma will see them soon."

"Will do."

He jogged down the walkway to the SUV parked at the curb and got inside. The next stop was the liquor store and a really expensive bottle of bubbly. He had big plans for it later.

After paying, he got back in the SUV, more than ready to be home with his family.

His cell phone rang and he answered right away, certain it was Annie wanting him to pick up diapers or formula or something. But it wasn't.

"Dr. Blackburne?"

"Yes. Who's this?"

"I'm calling from the lab about the DNA sample you recently had tested."

This was weird. "What about it?"

There was a brief silence before the woman said, "I'm sorry to inform you that the results were incorrect. Recent court action on your motion to claim your parental rights triggered a quality control test here at our company. It turned out there was a mix-up with your sample and the one we received at the same time."

Mason listened to everything the woman said and asked a few questions. He was assured that the tests had been checked and rechecked and the new results were correct. After clicking off the phone, he had no idea how long he sat there. And just like that his world blew up.

"I'm not a father."

Chapter 14

Annie looked at the cell phone in her hand as if it was an alien being. The message from the lab came completely out of the blue and the worst part was that Mason had received the same one. The lab had mixed up the two samples she'd sent. The man who'd signed away his rights to the twins was a DNA match to them. Not Mason.

She couldn't imagine what he was thinking right now. Being a father was so important to him. In fact his first marriage had imploded because his wife had given up on them. Annie didn't quit. She wasn't like that. He would be home soon and they'd talk this through. She would assure him that everything was fine.

But time passed and he didn't come home. She called and he didn't pick up. She left voice messages and he didn't answer. He'd gone radio silent. Once she'd come very close to contacting his parents but decided against it. They would have to know soon, but he should be the one to break that news.

The twins woke up hungry so she fed them then did baths and playtime before getting them down for the night without much fuss. They were obviously still tired from their court outing. It had been several hours and still no Mason.

Another sixty minutes went by. She knew because she counted every one of them. If she didn't hear from him soon, she would find out if his parents had. Worry wasn't something she handled especially stoically.

She was pacing and just about to call Flo when the front door opened. Relief washed over her when he came into the kitchen.

"Mason—"

She moved toward him then saw despair on his face and stopped. He was still wearing his suit but the slacks and jacket were wrinkled, the tie loosened. The crisply pressed-and-perfect exterior was gone and seemed to reflect his inner turmoil.

"Where have you been?" she asked.

"Driving."

"You heard from the lab." She wasn't asking a question.

"I did." He set a bottle of champagne on the granite countertop beside him. A bottle that would probably never be opened. "Turns out we didn't have to get married after all."

The words were like an arrow to her heart and she nearly gasped. She didn't know what she'd expected, but that wasn't it.

"The reasons we got married are still the same."

"What were they again?" His voice was flat, emotionless and just this side of bitter.

"You wanted a family and so did I. Now we have one," she said.

"You do." He dragged his fingers through his hair. "You're their aunt. A blood relative, at least. I, on the other hand, am nothing to them."

"That's not true, Mason. You are Sarah and Charlie's dad. A test done in a lab doesn't change that."

"You're wrong. It changes everything."

"All it means is you probably can't donate bone marrow or a kidney. In every other way you are what you've always been. The man who holds them when they cry. Feeds them when they're hungry. Makes sure their diapers are changed. You keep them safe. Everything a father is supposed to do."

"Annie, it's not that simple."

"It's exactly that simple. You feel the same way about them that you did this morning when you were nervous about what was going to happen in court."

"Yeah." He laughed but the sound was cynical, resentful, frustrated. "The timing of this news is inconvenient. Makes you wonder if fate is having a laugh at our expense."

"What does that mean?"

"I have to notify my attorney about this. It's not as straightforward as it was this morning. The judge should have this information."

"Probably. But I don't think it alters anything. The biological father already signed away his rights. He doesn't want them."

"He did that before test results were in. Knowing

for sure gives you a different perspective. Trust me on that."

Annie looked into his eyes, dark with anger and pain. She prayed for the right words to get through to him. "Tell me you don't love them. In spite of this glitch. I want to hear you say that you don't want to be their father."

"I—" He looked down and shook his head. "That's not the issue."

"Are you serious? It's exactly the issue, the only thing that matters."

"I'm nothing to them." He slashed his hand through the air as if severing ties. "I was something for a while. For a few months I had a son and a daughter. For a few weeks I had it all. Test results matter or we wouldn't do them."

"In a medical situation they do, obviously. But it isn't relative to the heart and soul."

"Relative?" His smile was sarcastic. "Are you making a pun?"

"Stop feeling sorry for yourself, Mason." She took a step closer and realized how badly she wanted him to hold her and to hold him back. "They are your children in every way that counts. And they need you."

"I've lost my children. Again." Rage and hurt blazed in his eyes before they went dark. "And there's nothing I can do about it."

"Let's take a time-out." Annie met his gaze. "This has been a shock for both of us. We need to let the dust settle and let it wear off. Deep breath. Decisions should wait until we've processed this completely."

"It's not complicated, Annie. Time and cooler heads won't change the fact that the twins are not mine."

It wasn't the words so much as the look in his eyes that convinced Annie his mind was made up. Nothing she could say would sway him. "Wow, you're not the man I thought."

"What does that mean?"

"I believed you were someone who didn't put restrictions on love. It never occurred to me that you are a man who can't care about a child unless that child has his genetic material."

"That's not fair," he said.

"I think it is," she snapped. "And what about you and me? What happened to sharing this adventure together? You said that to me just today, but I'm getting a totally different vibe now. The fact is that we're married and we have two children."

"You do," he corrected.

"Back to that." She blew out a breath. He was hurt and betrayed and too big for her to shake some sense into him. "So where does that leave us?"

He opened his mouth then closed it again. But emotions were swirling in his eyes: pain, bitterness, betrayal because of a stupid mistake, regret. And that was the one tearing her apart. He was sorry he married her.

Annie hated being right. Mason Blackburne was one more man abandoning her. She should have been prepared for the fact that sooner or later he would back away. Unfortunately she wasn't. She had let down her guard and got a right hook square in the heart.

"Message received," she said. "This is your house. I'll move out, but I'd appreciate a little time to find something for the babies and me."

"Annie, we—"

She put up a hand to stop him. "You made it clear

there is no we, so it's a little late to play that card. Until I can move out, I'm taking the master bedroom. I'd appreciate it if you'd sleep in the guest room."

"If that's what you want."

No, it's not what she wanted, but it was the only choice he was giving her. This wasn't a misunderstanding about whether or not they would assume traditional husband and wife roles and have sex. He'd all but told her that since his DNA didn't match the twins', he didn't want her.

"Good night, Mason."

Without a backward look, Annie walked away and down the hall. She went into the room she'd so happily shared with Mason and closed the door to shut him out.

She'd been clueless and overconfident believing she was in control of her feelings. Now she knew that what she felt for Mason was too big to contain. She was head over heels in love with him and knew it for a fact. Because letting him go was so much harder than any rejection she'd ever experienced in her life.

He'd only married her to do the right thing for the children he'd believed were his. It was clear to her now that she would never have married him if she hadn't been in love with him. The worst part was she couldn't even blame him. She'd agreed to everything he'd proposed.

She tried to hold back the sobs, but one escaped before she put her hands over her mouth. Mason had broken her heart but she would never let him know how much he'd hurt her.

Mason was a mess.

That was his diagnosis and there wasn't any medication or therapy that would make him better. It had been a few days since finding out he wasn't a father and he still felt as if someone had cut out his heart and left a gaping hole where it used to be. He and Annie had been unfailingly polite when forced to interact, but every night he heard her crying and it ripped him apart. So he'd decided to do something proactive.

He'd gotten in touch with the twins' biological father. Annie had his contact information in a file, along with paperwork relinquishing all rights to them. Mason wasn't their blood relative but Tyler Sherman was. And kids needed a dad. The guy reluctantly agreed to meet him during his lunch break and suggested neutral territory. Patrick's Place.

Mason had pushed back on the location because it had memories, but the man insisted. It wasn't far from his current landscape job. Apparently he wasn't inclined to go out of his way for his children.

So Mason was waiting in a booth. He glanced around the place where he and Annie had taken vows not so long ago. The bar with brass foot rail dominated the room and there were personal family photos of the owners on the wall behind it. A room adjacent to this one had pool tables, flat-screen TVs mounted on the wall and comfortable seating to watch televised sporting events. Next to that was the restaurant where they'd had dinner with his family after the wedding. The tables were nearly full during the lunch hour. Coming here was a really bad idea.

So he turned away and focused on the front door, where he could see everyone who came in. There were couples, groups of women and men, even lone individuals who'd stopped by for something to eat. But no one who seemed to be looking for someone. The meet time came and went and he was beginning to think he'd been stood up until he saw a guy enter by himself then hesitate and look around.

"Tyler?" Mason said quietly.

"Yeah." He was tall, blond and really young. Dressed in jeans and a navy T-shirt with Sherman Landscape silk-screened on the front.

"Mason Blackburne." He stood and held out his hand.

The other man shook it then sat across from him. He looked acutely uncomfortable. "What's this about? You insisted it was important. You said it was about the DNA test."

"Yeah, you are the twins' father." Mason was surprised those words didn't stick in his throat. A lab test didn't change his love for those babies and that meant he wanted them to have everything they deserved.

"Is this some kind of scam? Annie said the DNA would be done in five business days. That was months ago. Why are you telling me this now?"

Mason swallowed hard. "The lab made a mistake and we just found out about it. They mixed up the samples—yours and mine."

Tyler looked down at his hands for a moment then blew out a long breath. "I signed a legal document giving Annie sole custody."

"That was before you knew for sure that you're their father. You might change your mind." Mason pulled out his cell phone and found the pictures he'd taken right after court, the day he'd claimed parental rights he wasn't entitled to. "Here they are."

Tyler scrolled through the series of photographs but

his expression didn't change. "They look healthy. Cute kids. Look like Annie."

"Yeah."

He handed back the phone. "But why would you think I'd change my mind?"

"I just found out that the babies I thought were mine are actually not. I won't lie. This information hit me pretty hard because I've wanted to be a dad very badly and for a long time. It seemed to me that the man who is their biological father would jump at the chance to claim Charlie and Sarah."

"Does Annie know you contacted me?"

"I didn't want to say anything until after I talked to you. But these kids deserve to know their real father." Since he felt like their real father, it tore him up to even say that.

"Look, I'm not father material and maybe I never will be. My childhood was crap and my old man was a son of a bitch, probably still is. I wouldn't know because I refuse to see him. The fact is I doubt I'd be a very good father because my role model sucked."

Mason had always taken his close family life for granted, until he'd met Annie. She'd told him more than once how lucky he was to have his parents and siblings, and this guy was confirming that.

Mason met the other man's gaze. "So you're sure about this? The decision is right for you?"

"Some choices are hard, but this isn't one of them. Especially because they have Annie and you." He shoved his fingers through his blond hair. "Look, I'm not a complete bastard. If there's a health issue, or someday they're curious about me, I'll do what's right.

But as far as raising them? Those kids are better off without me."

"Okay."

Tyler looked at his linked fingers for a moment then back up. "I know what you're thinking."

"I doubt that." Mason almost laughed. There's no way he could possibly know.

"It's nothing I haven't thought about. I should have been more responsible about birth control if I feel so strongly about not having kids."

"Now that you mention it..."

"Believe it or not, I'm very conscientious about that. I wore a condom. It broke, but I didn't think too much about it because Jessica told me she was on the Pill. Those twins were meant to be, I guess."

"Apparently."

"Look, Dr. Blackburne, I made the right call—for me and for them. You obviously care and they're lucky to have you. If it matters, you have my blessing."

Oddly enough, it did matter. "Thanks for not blowing off this meeting, Tyler."

"You're welcome." He slid out of the booth and held out his hand. "Nice to meet you."

"Same here." Mason stood and shook his hand then watched the man exit the way he'd come.

"You look like someone who needs a drink." The voice came from behind him, but it was familiar.

Mason had been so lost in his own thoughts, he hadn't heard anyone approach. He turned and saw Leo "The Wall" Wallace, a former NHL star who co-owned this place with his wife.

"Hi, Leo."

"How are Annie and the kids?"

"Healthy." Physically, anyway. She would barely look at him and cried every night, so there was that.

The big man was studying him intently. "Well, my friend, you look like hell."

"Since when did insulting a customer become a good marketing strategy?" No matter how true it might be.

"It's just an observation and I wasn't kidding about that drink. Have a seat. I'll be right back."

"It's too early," Mason protested.

"You're the doctor but you don't always know what's best."

Mason did as instructed and watched the other man walk over to the bar and say something to the bartender. Instantly the woman got two glasses then took a bottle of some kind of brown liquor from the display behind the bar. She poured, then slid the tumblers across the bar to her boss. Leo carried them to the table, setting one in front of Mason.

"Drink up, Doc. It's medicinal."

Mason looked at it for a moment then, figuring he couldn't feel any worse, he tossed back the contents of his glass. It was smooth going down then burned in his chest and all the way to his gut. At least for a few moments the searing sensation took his mind off the pain eating up his insides.

Leo toyed with his glass. "So, who was that guy you were talking to? The conversation looked pretty intense."

Mason saw no reason not to tell him. His family knew and had tried to help. But what could they say?

Words didn't change the results of the test. Talking this through might help. Although he wasn't sure how. It wouldn't change the fact that the rug had been ripped out from under him and the truth he thought he knew was a lie.

"That guy I talked to is the twins' biological father." He explained about the lab error.

"I'm speechless." Leo looked like he'd just been smacked with a hockey stick. Finally he said, "How is Annie taking this?"

"Better than me. She says it doesn't make any difference. Love is all that matters."

The other man's expression turned dark and serious. "She's right."

"Wait a minute. You're a guy. I thought you'd understand."

"You mean take your side. And I do understand. More than you think." Leo tossed back the liquor in front of him then toyed with the glass. "I was married once before. We had a baby boy and I love him more than I can say."

"Okay. Didn't know that, but I'm not sure what this has to do with my situation."

"He's not mine biologically. She lied to me, said she was pregnant with my child, and I married her. After a couple of years when she was having an affair with the guy, she said her son should be raised by his *real* father."

Pain darkened the man's eyes and he sucked in a breath. "The thing is, I felt like his real father. I changed diapers, fed him, played with him, got up at night when he cried. Loved him more than anything. It doesn't get more real than that, but suddenly I had no say in any decisions concerning my son, simply because he didn't have my DNA." Leo met his gaze. "Everything changed except the way I felt about him."

"Oh, man—" Mason shook his head. "Now I don't know what to say."

"Tess and I got off to a rocky start emotionally, but there was this irresistible physical attraction from the moment we met. One night we gave in to it and she got pregnant. She swore the baby was mine, but I'd been burned once and didn't want to be made a fool of again. It nearly ruined the best thing that ever happened to me."

"That's rough."

"Yeah. But now the most wonderful woman in the world is mine and we have a beautiful little girl." His expression brightened. "My point in telling you this is that I have a pretty good idea what you're going through. And I have to say that meeting with the twins' biological father seems straight up to me."

"I appreciate that." Mason remembered his conversation with Annie the night he'd found out about the error. It was bitter and full of self-pity. "But Annie... I said some things."

"People say stupid stuff when they're dealing with really emotional situations. It's understandable."

"Not this."

Leo frowned. "What did you say to her?"

"That we didn't need to get married."

"I'm sorry... What?"

Mason sighed. "I told her—"

"I heard what you said." His friend stared at him as if he had two heads. "You implied that you only married her because you believed you were the twins' father?"

Mason winced. "When you say it like that—"

"I'm guessing that she wasn't happy."

"She's moving out with the kids as soon as she can find a place to live," he confirmed.

"You are an outstanding doctor, but communication is not really your thing." Leo gave him a pitying look. "So, genius, why *did* you marry Annie?"

Mason was running on pure adrenaline now and just snapped out the answer without overthinking it. "I'm in love with her and the babies. I love her so much that I'll let her go if that's what's best for them. Even if it kills me."

And just saying those words, he died a little more. But he meant it.

"You're a damn fool, Mason."

"What?"

"This isn't some romantic tragedy. This is real life. You have a beautiful woman who loves you." Leo pointed a finger at him. "Don't give me that look. I know what I'm talking about. You may not believe this, but I'm a lot more than just an ex-jock businessman. I saw the way she was looking at you the night you got married. Right here at Patrick's Place. Trust me. Those were not the looks of a woman getting married just for the sake of the kids."

They had deliberately avoided defining anything besides friendship and respect—even in their wedding vows. And what Mason felt was so much more than that or he never would have proposed in the first place.

"Oh, man... I really blew it," Mason said.

"You think?" Leo pointed at him again. "You gotta fix this, pal. And trust me. It won't be easy."

He was right, Mason thought. He had to fix things with Annie. But how?

Chapter 15

"Bob wants to see you in his office."

Annie was working in her cubicle and looked over her shoulder at Ella, who was standing right outside. "What does he want?"

"Don't know. He just told me to tell you. Consider yourself told."

"Did he look happy? Sad? Mad?"

Ella thought about the question. "Not sure. If people's faces were emojis, I could tell you."

"Point taken. And it has to be said, no one can tell what Bob is feeling. He's remarkably even-tempered."

"He is." Ella studied her. "You, on the other hand, wear your heart on your sleeve."

Annie really hoped that wasn't true. Because then everyone would know how crushed she was about why Mason married her. "Really?"

"Are you kidding? Everyone in the office has been wondering what's been bugging you for the last couple of days."

"No way," Annie said. "I'm the same as always."

"That's not what Cruz says, and he's right next door to you."

"What is he saying?"

"That since the night Mason picked you up here and took you to dinner you've been so bright and shiny it makes his head hurt. But the last few days, you look like someone popped your wedded-bliss balloon."

Hmm, she hadn't realized her cubicle buddy was so observant. Or that she was so transparent. Or that she could miss Mason's touch so much it was impossible to hide her feelings about him. Being humiliated in school because of her learning disability had been the training ground for her poker face. Only Jessica had been able to tell when she was concealing her pain and anguish. But apparently now her coworkers could, too.

"I'm fine. Just tired. With two babies in the house, who can sleep?" Duck, cover and conceal.

Old habits died hard and she didn't want to talk about this. The babies had been sleeping better than those first few months after she'd brought them home from the hospital. It was Mason keeping her up. All the what-ifs and if-onlys haunted her. How could she have been stupid enough to fall for him? That was actually the easiest question to answer.

Chemistry. She'd felt it from the beginning and it wasn't something easily ignored. Plus he was so darn nice, a truly good man. Practically perfect, which was ironic because she didn't trust perfect. Yet she'd started to trust him and her heart hadn't stood a chance.

"I'm fine, Ella."

"Okay." The woman's tone said she wasn't buying that. "But if you need someone to talk to, I'm here."

"Thanks." She pushed the chair away from her desk and stood. "I'll go see what Bob wants."

"Right."

Annie could tell by her coworker's expression that she was hurt and just wanted to help. It was much appreciated, but she was on the emotional edge and desperately clinging to her professionalism at work. And just before a meeting with her boss was not a good time to air out her personal problems.

She walked to his office. The door was open and he was at his desk. "You wanted to see me?"

"Annie. Yes." He took off his glasses and tossed them on the desk. "Come in. Would you close the door, please?"

She did as requested then sat in the chair on the other side of his desk. "Are you firing me? Should I be worried?"

"No." He smiled. "Just the opposite."

"The opposite would be not firing me."

"I'm making the announcement in the morning to the staff, but I wanted to tell you first."

"About?"

"I'm putting you in charge of the campaign for our newest client." Bob's face grew rounder when he smiled broadly.

"We got the account."

"Yes. In no small part because of your talent and hard work."

"It was a team effort," she said.

"A team that you organized and led." He nodded at her. "Congratulations."

"Thank you."

This was a real "how do you like me now" moment to everyone who ever bullied, teased and belittled her. To anyone who'd called her stupid. This was what she'd worked her butt off for. Against the odds and while raising two infants, she'd managed to come up with creative concepts and execute them, enough to impress a major company and get them to trust C&J Graphic Design with their business.

Now she would be in charge of that account. How she wished Jessica could see her now. She should be doing the dance of joy, except none of it meant anything to her because she'd lost Mason and the family they had made together.

To her horror and humiliation, Annie burst into tears. She buried her face in her hands for several moments then pulled herself together with an effort to look at her boss. "Sorry. That wasn't weird at all."

"Not quite the reaction I expected," he admitted.

"Tears of joy. Honestly." She tried to smile but knew it was wobbly at best.

"You should be proud, Annie. It was a lot of pressure and you've handled it with grace, intelligence and enthusiasm."

"Thank you." She brushed away tears that just kept leaking out of her eyes for no reason.

"I think you should take the rest of the day off. You deserve it. Go home. Let off some steam. Be with your beautiful family."

That nearly sent her into another meltdown because that family was gone. But she managed to maintain her composure long enough to thank him again and walk out of his office.

Family. The idea of it got to her every time. It was the opposite of her superpower. It was her vulnerability. For a pathetically short period of time she'd had everything. The babies, a husband and father, in-laws she loved. It was idyllic. Then a lab error had torn her perfect world apart.

She grabbed her purse from her cubicle and managed to sneak out without seeing anyone. She found her car in the parking lot and put the key in the ignition. But where was she going? Mason wasn't working today and had the twins. He'd insisted, but that was probably all about guilt.

He was clear on the fact that he had a legal responsibility to the babies but insisted he wasn't allowed to have an emotional one. With her promotion, she would probably have to spend more time in the office and that meant hiring someone to watch her children. She couldn't count on him. Not anymore.

As badly as she wanted to see Sarah and Charlie, to hold them, she couldn't face Mason in this raw state. So she backed the car out of the space and drove out of the lot. Instead of taking the turn to go to his house, she went in the opposite direction.

For a long time she just kept driving as thoughts tumbled through her mind. She was operating on autopilot, but her subconscious took over. That was the only explanation for how she eventually ended up at Florence Blackburne's house and saw the woman's car parked in the driveway.

Annie made a spontaneous decision to stop. She parked in front, walked up to the door then rang the bell. Flo answered almost right away. She was holding Sarah. In the background Charlie was crying.

"Boy am I glad to see you." The other woman acted as if nothing had changed. "These two are both hungry. I know they can hold their own bottles now, but I prefer to hold them."

"Me, too. But sometimes you can't."

"The downside of being a twin is having to share because there aren't enough adults around to help."

"This isn't one of those times. I'll go get him," Annie said.

Working together, they warmed bottles and settled on the sofa in the family room. Each of them had a baby to feed.

Annie couldn't get the bottle into Charlie's mouth fast enough. But when she did, there was silence as he sucked the formula down. "Where did Mason go? Did the hospital call him in?"

"No. He said he had to see someone and was going to Patrick's Place."

Annie felt a knot in her stomach. "Another woman?"

"If so, I don't think he'd have mentioned that to me," Flo said. Then her expression changed from teasing to concern. "What's going on with you two? He told us about the lab error, Annie. But I'm not sure why your first thought would be about him meeting another woman."

Annie sighed. Her subconscious had brought her there for a reason. Talking to Mason's mother certainly couldn't make things worse than they already were. "He all but told me he only married me because he thought he was the babies' father."

The other woman took the bottle away from Sarah

then lifted her up for a burp, and she produced a very unladylike one. Flo rubbed her back and met Annie's gaze. "The truth of finding out he's not their father threw him. Mason is solid and steady, unflappable. But he was rocked by this. And he's a doctor. He relies on lab tests being correct so that he can treat his patients accordingly."

"I get that. He wasn't the only one shocked by it."

"I know, honey. Although it may sound like it, I'm not taking sides. The thing is, when he was married before, having a family was his focus. So many times he got his hopes up, only to be devastated by losing a child. And it was even harder for Christy, his ex." Flo shook her head. "But with Sarah and Charlie, they were here and they were his. And that was a dream come true for him. I don't know what he said to you, but I doubt he was thinking clearly when he said it."

"He said there was no reason to be married."

"Unless you're in love."

When the baby stopped sucking on the bottle, Annie took it away to burp him. "It was a mistake. Gabriel was right. We moved too fast."

"Gabe's experience doesn't make him the best person to be giving out advice. I wouldn't take his words to heart." She smiled at the baby dozing contentedly on her shoulder. "I'm the one who told Mason not to let you get away and implied that your old boyfriend was hovering."

"Why would you do that?"

"Because you're perfect together."

"I don't believe in perfect," Annie said. "And when he proposed, we agreed that love had nothing to do with it."

Flo smiled. "But neither one of you stuck to that, did you?"

"It doesn't matter. I'm moving out of the house with the babies as soon as I can find a place to go."

Mason's mother shook her head. "I can't believe you're really going to split up. Annie, you're part of the family. So are the twins."

"They're not. Now we know you're not related to them by blood. They're not your grandchildren."

"You're wrong about that." Flo's voice was kind and gentle when she said the words. It was also firm. "Sarah and Charlie are my grandchildren and I love them with every fiber of my being. DNA is only science. It cannot tell us who we're supposed to love. That's the heart's job."

"Flo, I can't believe—"

"Believe it," she said. "And I believe with all my heart that Mason loves you with all of his. Don't throw that away because he said something in haste after getting the biggest shock of his life. Fight for your family."

The woman's words were the verbal equivalent of a snap-out-of-it slap. It worked. Annie got the message. Perfect didn't just happen. You had to fight for it.

Mason left Patrick's Place feeling both empowered and idiotic. The things he'd said to Annie... He needed to see her as soon as possible and headed to his mother's house to pick up Sarah and Charlie. After parking at the curb, he jogged to the front door and knocked softly. Because of Annie, he was aware that when there were babies in the house, ringing the bell put a guy at the top of the most endangered species list.

The door opened and his mom put a finger to her

lips and then indicated he should follow her into the family room. "They're asleep."

"I figured. The thing is, I have to get home and—"

"Cool your jets."

"Mom, you don't understand—"

"Baloney. I understand plenty." She gave him a look. "What in the world is wrong with you?"

"That's a broad question. You might want to narrow the scope a bit because there's a lot wrong with me."

"You're so smart in so many ways that it shocks me how you can be so dense about certain things."

"What are you talking about?" he asked.

"I talked to Annie. How could you tell her you didn't have to be married after all?" His mom pointed a warning finger at him. "And don't even accuse her of talking behind your back."

"I wasn't going to—"

"Because I pried the information out of her. She's an amazing young woman and you have handled everything so clumsily."

"Tell me something I don't know."

"This is not a news flash. You really screwed up. I explained how emotionally drained you were after the divorce, but you need to talk to her and work this out."

"I get it—"

"Because Charlie and Sarah *are* my grandbabies and I love them. Annie, too. She's become like a daughter to your father and me—"

When her mouth quivered and tears filled her eyes, Mason felt like toxic waste. What kind of a son was he, making his mother cry? "It's okay—"

"No, it's not. But you're going to sort everything out." She blinked away the tears. "Because ultimately your welfare is on the line. Only you know what's in your heart, but I can say in all honesty that I've never seen you as happy as you've been with Annie and your family."

"I know and—"

"So you have to convince her not to move out. At least encourage her to give it some time, let emotions settle down before making a decision you'll both regret."

"That's my plan. I will—"

"I mean it, Mason. You've always been an over-achiever, so if there's ever been a time to go with your strength, this is it—"

"Mom, stop talking. I just came to get the kids. I'm going to talk to Annie when she gets home from work."

"She got off work early and stopped by to talk to me."

"She didn't take the kids home?"

"I suggested she leave them with me so you two can talk quietly and without interruption. And I'm suggesting the same thing to you. Besides, they're sleeping. Everyone knows you never wake a sleeping baby."

"Okay, thanks."

She smiled. "And, Mason?"

"Yeah?"

"You better explain to Annie who your meeting was with at Patrick's Place."

"How does she know about that?"

His mother shrugged. "She asked where you were so I repeated what you told me, which was next to nothing. She went straight to wondering if it was a woman."

"Great. Like I needed another challenge. And no. I didn't see a woman."

"Make sure she knows that."

He planned to. And it was going to be an uphill battle. She'd told Dwayne the Douche that he'd abandoned her once and she wouldn't give him a chance to do it again. For the first time in his life, Mason wished he was a lawyer instead of a doctor. He needed the right words to heal the harm he'd done to her heart.

The drive from his parents' house wasn't long but it felt like forever. People facing death often said their life flashed before their eyes. Mason had the reverse sensation—life without Annie stretched in front of him. The images were sad and grim, without brilliance or color.

He pulled into the driveway beside her compact car and got out. After gathering his thoughts, he exited the SUV and walked to the front door. He opened it and walked inside. It was unnaturally quiet; a preview of his future if he'd irreparably damaged their relationship.

He couldn't stand the silence and called out, "Annie?"

"In the kitchen."

There was too much square footage between them to accurately diagnose her tone. So he took a deep breath and put one foot in front of the other until he was beside the granite-topped island, face-to-face with her.

"Hi."

"Hi." Her expression was neutral and he didn't know how to take that. If things were normal between them, he would ask about her day. But everything was wrong and what he said to her now would determine whether or not he could make them right again.

He jumped straight into the deep end of the pool.

"I didn't meet a woman at Patrick's Place."

"I believe you. But whatever it was must be pretty important if you had to leave the kids with your mom."

"It had everything to do with their future. And ours," he said. "I talked to Tyler Sherman."

"Their biological father." Her eyes went wide with shock. "Why? He made it clear that he didn't want anything to do with them."

"That was before he knew the test results. I thought he had a right to know."

She mulled that over before asking, "And?"

"The new information didn't change his mind." Mason told her everything the guy had said. "If needed, he'll step up, but feels that day to day the kids are better off without him."

Her expression wasn't neutral now. It was full of doubt. "Were you hoping he did want them now, because you're not their biological father?"

"No. God, no, Annie." He was blowing this. Damn it. "I was trying to do what's right. I would die for Charlie and Sarah. I am and will always be their father. I love them more than I can even put into words. And if he sincerely wanted to be a positive part of their lives, it's my responsibility to look at the big picture and do my damnedest to figure out what's best for them."

"So he doesn't want a role in their lives?"

Mason shook his head. "Not now. But he's not hiding, either. If they have questions eventually, he'll be around to answer them."

"Okay. He sounds like a good guy."

"He seems to be. Self-aware and practical. He cares about the twins, enough to put their welfare first. I respect that."

She took one step back. "Okay, if that's all—"

"That's not even close to all." He wanted so much to have her in his arms, but he was afraid to touch her yet. Afraid she would shrug off his touch and not really *hear* him. "I didn't mean what I said, Annie. About being married. It was a knee-jerk reaction to that call from the lab. Nothing changed for me."

"Oh?" Her eyebrow lifted. "So we're still friends who only like and respect each other?"

"No."

"So we don't like each other?"

"That's not what I meant." This was not going at all the way he'd hoped. "More than anything I want to be married to you. I want a family with you, to raise Charlie and Sarah together with you. They're my kids and it's not in the DNA, it's in the heart. I want to be the best husband and father I can possibly be. Because I love you, Annie."

"Really?"

"With everything I've got. If you give me another chance, I'll prove to you that I will never let you down again."

"Right." She turned away then and walked down the hall toward the master bedroom.

Mason stood there for several moments before reaction kicked in. It was not going to end like this. He wasn't going to let it end at all. Whatever he had to do, however long it took, he was going to prove to her that he loved her and wasn't going away. His military training kicked in and surrender wasn't an option. Army strong.

He marched after her into the room they'd shared awkwardly at first and then with all the passion and intimacy of a married couple. He was so focused on what to say that might persuade her to take a risk on him that it was several moments before he really saw the room.

Rose petals had been tossed on the carpet and the bed. A bottle of champagne was icing in a bucket and two flutes were beside it on the dresser. Best of all— Annie was there smiling at him. She'd set a scene, just like he had, to work out the bumps in their marriage.

"What's this?" he asked.

"My way of fighting for our family."

"It's a good way." He moved close and put his arms around her waist, nestling her against his body. "So, this—the flowers and champagne—is going to be our thing?"

"Could be," she said. "What do you think?"

"Maybe we should invest in a rosebush." He met her gaze and with all the intensity of the feelings inside him said, "I'm in love with you, Annie. More than I can tell you."

"I know." She settled her hands on his chest. "Deep down I knew that when you proposed or I would never have said yes, no matter how much we pushed the friendship angle."

"How could you know when I didn't?"

"It was there in everything you did. Going to work. Feedings in the middle of the night. Walking the floor with a fussy baby." She glanced at the petal-strewn bed. "Making the effort to show me how you felt even when you wouldn't say the words. At night, reaching for me even in your sleep."

"I knew it, too." He pulled her close and whispered against her hair. "Love is also being afraid I'd lost you when you fell down the stairs and broke your leg. I finally know what it means to be in love."

"I love you more." She glanced at the bed again then up at him.

"In case you were wondering," he said, "I'm not the least bit tired."

She grinned. "Me, either."

Epilogue

Christmas Day

Mason parked the SUV in front of his parents' house and smiled at Annie in the passenger seat. The outside looked like a Christmas store had thrown up on it. "So it's the twins' first Christmas."

Annie was staring at the house. Flo had invited the whole family to help decorate, but the scope of it all still amazed her. "Something tells me this has nothing to do with our children."

"You would be right about that. My mom goes all out for Christmas. She's missed having little ones to fuss over and has probably set retail records this year."

A feeling of melancholy slipped into her heart. "Jess would have loved this."

Mason reached over and took her hand, wrapping it protectively in his. "And you still miss her."

"I always will." She had Mason now and the twins. They were happy, healthy and beautiful. Marriage to him was the best thing that had ever happened to her. "I wish she was here."

"She is," he said gently. "She will always be here because a part of her lives on in the twins. And she loved them more than anything."

"How do you know?"

"Because she gave them to you. She trusted you with what she cared about most. And you are honoring her memory by raising them to be the best they can be."

She loved the love shining in his eyes for her. "*We* are loving and caring for them."

"And each other."

"Ma—" That earsplitting screech came from the back seat.

Annie winced. "The pitch of our son's voice could shatter glass."

"Doesn't that make you proud?" he asked. "He's not a year old yet and is pulling himself up to a standing position. Before you know it, he'll be walking. Have you seen how fast he can crawl?"

"Seen it?" she scoffed. "I've had to chase him down. And Sarah is no slouch, either. This 'getting around' thing adds a whole new dimension to parenting."

"I know. Are you as tired as I am?"

"You don't look nearly as tired as I feel. How do men do that?" She studied him. "You complain about being old and tired but you, sir, are better-looking and hotter than ever."

There was a wicked gleam in his eyes. "So, I have a plan. My whole family is here for Christmas. We let them chase after Charlie and Sarah and save our energy. When we get home, I'll have my way with you."

She grinned. "Not if I have my way with you first."

When there was a double outcry of frustration at being immobilized in the back seat, Annie sighed. "I suppose there's no putting it off any longer. We have to set them free."

"Yeah. Here we go."

They exited the SUV and each opened a rear door. While Mason liberated their daughter, Annie released the restraints, lifted Charlie from the car seat and kissed his cheek. "Is that better, Charlie bear?"

The little boy immediately wriggled and squirmed to be let down but she held on. His grandparents had seen him last night in his white shirt, red-and-green-plaid bow tie and little jeans. Sarah had been wearing her red-velvet dress, white tights and black Mary Janes. Pictures had been taken for posterity. Today for the Christmas gathering they were wearing comfortable T-shirts underneath their sweaters.

Annie looked up at Mason and grinned, preparing to hit him with her most recent Daddy observation. "Our daughter has you wrapped around her little finger."

"Does not," he said.

"Does, too."

They grinned at this now familiar debate then walked up to the front door. Of course Charlie wanted to ring the doorbell because one time he'd been allowed to and had never forgotten.

Flo opened the door and instantly smiled at each baby. "Merry Christmas, my little sweethearts!"

Her husband joined her and beamed at his grandchildren. "Who's having their first Christmas at Grandma and Grandpa's house?"

The twins held out their arms to the older couple and, of course, they were swept into loving hugs and kisses. After the affectionate greeting, they all went into the family room, where everyone was gathered.

The *family* room. A place where relatives were together. To celebrate peace on earth and goodwill toward men. Or just to hang out on a Sunday. Most people took it for granted, but not Annie. She would never get tired of this.

"Did you see that?" Mason asked her.

"What?"

"They didn't say a word to us. Just commandeered our children without acknowledging our presence." He sighed. "It's official."

"What's that?"

"We're chopped liver."

Annie laughed then slid her hand into his as they mingled with his brothers, sister and parents. There was a gorgeous tree in the corner and wrapped presents were piled underneath it. Lighted garland draped the fireplace mantel, where stockings for every family member were filled to overflowing. It was perfect.

The twins were in the center of the family room, where their grandparents were removing their sweaters. This was it. Annie looked at Mason and grinned. Everyone was watching as if the process were fascinating. When the outerwear was off, the room got so quiet you could hear a pin drop. The message on the front of their little T-shirts sank in.

"'I'm the big brother. I'm the big sister.'" His mother's expression was priceless as she looked at Mason then Annie. "Another baby?"

"Surprise!" they said together.

The tiny guests of honor were momentarily forgotten as congratulations and hugs were offered all around. It didn't last long because Charlie fast-crawled over to the tree and started investigating the wrapped boxes and gift bags. His sister willingly joined in and they had Uncle Gabe's present nearly opened before intervention arrived.

Annie and Mason watched the happy chaos, their arms around each other's waists.

"Are you happy about the baby?" she asked. "It wasn't planned."

"I'm ecstatic. Thrilled. Proud. So lucky. It's the best gift I could have received." He kissed the top of her head.

"Me, too. I feel so blessed. A traditional family is everything I've ever wanted. And you made it possible. I love you so much."

"I love you more," he said. "It occurs to me that we were meant to find each other. In a perfect world we would have met, dated, fallen in love, had an engagement, married and then had children."

"Our story isn't that," she agreed. "But it's perfect for us."

* * * * *

Sue MacKay lives with her husband in New Zealand's beautiful Marlborough Sounds, with the water on her doorstep and the birds and the trees at her back door. It is the perfect setting to indulge her passions of entertaining friends by cooking them sumptuous meals, drinking fabulous wine, going for hill walks or kayaking around the bay—and, of course, writing stories.

Books by Sue MacKay

Harlequin Medical Romance

London Hospital Midwives

A Fling to Steal Her Heart

SOS Docs

Redeeming Her Brooding Surgeon

Baby Miracle in the ER
Surprise Twins for the Surgeon
ER Doc's Forever Gift
The Italian Surgeon's Secret Baby
Take a Chance on the Single Dad
The Nurse's Twin Surprise
Reclaiming Her Army Doc Husband
The Nurse's Secret

Visit the Author Profile page at Harlequin.com for more titles.

The Nurse's Twin Surprise

SUE MacKAY

Chapter 1

*F*ake *it till you make it.*

Yes, sure. So easy. She did it all the time.

Try harder. Remember yesterday's courier delivery.

The final lock had been undone. She was free. Single again. Two years of waiting for the legal process to finally be over. Today was the first day of the rest of her life, and it was going to be a doozy.

That was once she worked out how to proceed with a newer, wiser, not so damned cautious version of herself that yesterday's delivery must shut the door on. Those baby steps she'd been making were fine, but the time had come to stride out, head high, wearing a 'don't mess with me' attitude. Starting now.

Molly O'Keefe pasted on a facsimile of a smile and turned to glare into Mr Nathan Lupton's eyes. And gasped. Those burnt-coffee eyes were spitting tacks. At her?

'What's wrong?'

That's your idea of don't mess with me? Try again.

'That phone call. Something I need to know?'

'I've just spent valuable time ringing round to put specialists on alert at five-thirty in the morning for a patient who's now been taken to another ED.' His hands gripped his hips.

'The man found lying by the train tracks?' Surely not even he was blaming *her*? They weren't friends, but this was ridiculous. The thumping starting up in her chest was deafening. No, he wouldn't be, but he was angry.

Not at me. I can handle this.

Really?

Absolutely. *Fake it till—*

Yeah, yeah, she knew that line back to front. Still needed some practice, that was all. Beginning right now.

'I wonder why the ambulance was redirected to another hospital when we're closest.'

Nathan was staring at her, though she wasn't certain he was actually seeing her. 'That's something I intend finding out. It's not happening again.' He was still angry. Who could blame him when they'd been flat out busy when the initial call had come through? So much for the patients tapering off in the early hours. 'Shouldn't you be keeping an eye on Archie Banks?' he barked.

Odd how on her first day in Sydney General's emergency department when he'd growled at her to get the defib, which she'd already been in the process of wheeling towards the Resus unit, she hadn't been afraid of him. Mightn't like him much, though to be fair she didn't know him except as a doctor, but she was never on guard around him or ever felt threatened by his grumpiness. Which said a lot. She'd think about that later. Right now an answer was required to placate him, because placating kept everyone happy—except maybe her—but it was an old habit she'd still not managed to dump. *Game face, girl.* Duh. Two seconds and her promise to herself had flown the coop.

'I was coming to see if you'd take another look at him. His pain level is increasing, not decreasing.' Nathan had administered a strong dose of painkiller forty minutes ago.

The anger softened. Of course it did. From what she'd seen around here Nathan adored children. 'Anything from the lab yet?'

'No, and I've only just checked,' she added hastily, raising one of her grandmother's glares in case he found fault with her. Another sign she might be getting her act together.

Dark eyebrows rose in that annoying manner of his that inexplicably riled her beyond reason. Then he swallowed and pulled up a smile. 'Sorry. It wasn't your fault the man was taken elsewhere after I've been chasing my tail preparing for his arrival.'

It wasn't the greatest of apologies, but he had tried, and that was unexpected. 'No problem.' None he need know about. She had a list of them, but nothing to do with work. This was her safe place. 'Archie?'

'On my way.' He strode off, his back ramrod straight, his jaw jutting out, yet she'd swear some of his tension had eased.

'Good girl, not letting him rile you.' Vicki nudged her, and brought her back to focusing on anything other than *Mr* Lupton.

'You think?' she asked around a tight laugh, her eyes still taking in the sight of Nathan despite trying to concentrate on what Vicki had to say.

'I do.' Her fellow nurse was also watching Nathan, now heading into a cubicle, and there was a thoughtful tone to her next question that unsettled Molly. 'Still coming to breakfast?'

'Wouldn't miss it for anything.' She meant every word, even after struggling with a strong reluctance to socialise and get too comfortable when she half expected to be nudged out of the way by people who wanted more from her than she was prepared to share. She had initially hesitated about accepting the invitation, then decided to give it a go. After all, Vicki had been friendly and helpful since she'd begun working in here two months ago.

A flicker of excitement warmed her. Look where *faking it* got her. Right into the middle of her colleagues, whose good intentions had brought her close to tears on occasion, even when she didn't trust them enough to give back anything of herself. Getting out and about with this crowd might go some way to fixing the loneliness that filled her days and nights. Not being a team player had come at a price, one that needed to be dealt with if she was to be happy again.

'Molly? Can you come here, please?' Nathan had reappeared in the cubicle doorway, back to being calm and efficient.

Molly looked at the man and, hiding the uncertainty he created in her belly, nodded. 'Need the phlebotomy kit?' Her voice had returned to non-confrontational, Gran's glare long gone. Situation normal. Previous normal. Lifting her shoulders, she reached for the bag of needles and tubes.

Nathan's smile might be reluctant, but it actually seemed genuine. Meaning it was further unsettling. 'Yes. I want liver functions done while we wait for the orderly to collect him.'

The boy, recovering from an appendicectomy last week, was back with pains in his gut and chest. Nathan suspected septicaemia and had started him on an array of intravenous antibiotics. They were now waiting for the children's ward to collect him.

In the cubicle, she said, 'Hey, Archie, I'm going to find you some dry pyjamas after I've cleaned you up.' With the fever drenching him continually, the boy needed regular wiping down.

Archie was eyeing the kit with trepidation. No hiding what was coming from this kid. 'I don't want another needle.'

'It's annoying, isn't it?' Nathan said as he slid the tourniquet up the boy's thin arm. 'You'll be able to tell all your friends how brave you are.'

Molly sponged Archie's legs, in an attempt to distract him. 'I hope you're not ticklish.' Not that she intended tickling him when Nathan was about to slide a needle into a vein. That would be taking distraction to the next level.

'Mum tickles me.' Archie's eyes were on Nathan, apprehension blinking out of his big eyes.

'There, all done.' Moments later Nathan handed her the tube of blood to name and date. 'Mark it urgent.'

'Right.' She headed for the hub to call for an orderly to take the blood sample to the lab.

Nathan had followed her. 'How're you settling in with us?'

'Fine.' I hope. 'I really like the job, and the people I work with.' Had she done something wrong he was about to mention? Wasn't she good enough at her work? The usual worry over making herself stand out began chugging through her mind.

'Good. We don't like swapping staff too often.' Then, 'So what do you do when you're not here?' Nathan was being friendly? Abnormally friendly, since he wasn't known for idle chitchat.

How to answer without giving herself away? 'There's always heaps of things needing attention where I live and people to check up on and shopping at the mall.' Drivel spilled over her lips. 'And I like going for walks.' Definitely faking it. She rarely left the apartment other than to come to work.

He was regarding her like he was sorry he'd asked. Good, then he wouldn't find any more questions for her. *Wrong.* 'Sounds like your evenings are free so you'll have time to come to our midwinter Christmas barbecue.' Nathan was talking about the out of season party some Aussies celebrated that had come about because of English people living in Australia who missed a cold Christmas. He tapped a sheet of paper lying on the desk. 'I don't see your name here.'

That was because she had no intention of going. She wasn't ready for that level of integration. An hour over breakfast was one thing, a full-on party quite another. *Thought I was starting over, now that I'm free.* 'I haven't thought about it.' What excuse could she come up with? She tried to read the shift roster behind Nathan, but he was blocking her line of vision.

'It's a fortnight away but I like to know who's coming well in advance. Bring a plate and your own alcohol. Meat provided.' He was pointing a pen over his shoulder. 'You're not working that night.'

There went that excuse for not going. Little did he know about how hard it was for her to go anywhere that was attended by lots of people.

He hadn't finished. 'I encourage all the staff to join in. It's good for morale, amongst other things.'

New beginnings, remember? Deep breath. Go for it. Taking the pen from his fingers, mindful of not touching him, Molly scrawled her name beneath Vicki's and added *Dessert* next to it. 'There. Done.' And she hadn't stopped too long to think about it. *Definitely* a first.

'Good.' His tone didn't back his reply. Those toast-coloured eyes were focused on her as though she was a mystery he was trying to unravel. She'd probably surprised him by giving in so quickly when it was well known she didn't go out with any of the staff to movies or breakfasts.

Amazed at how easily she'd signed up, she stood absorbing the slow wave of excitement rolling through her. She could do this. She really, really could. 'Where's the barbecue being held?'

'At my place out in Coogee.' He picked up a patient file and began reading the notes. Dark blond hair fell over his brow, making her itch to push it back in place.

'Oh.' The heavy pounding in her chest had returned, and her mouth began drying up like an overbaked sponge. Why hadn't she noticed before that Nathan was disgustingly good looking? Probably her mas-

sive hang-up about getting close to men had kept the
blinkers on until today, when she'd made the promise to move on, get a life. Did that mean finding love?
Thump, thump, thump. It couldn't. That'd be going too
far, too soon. Molly had learned Paul's lessons well.
An absolute charmer, he'd sworn his undying love for
her and wooed her completely. One year into their marriage the real Paul had come to light when he'd started
hitting her whenever she'd disagreed with him, which
was a sure-fire way of making her keep her mouth
shut. Suddenly noticing Nathan as more than a doctor
was scary. Wasn't it?

'Problem with that?' Nathan asked without looking up.

'Hell, yes.' She wasn't ready. It was too soon—
wasn't part of the plan to move on.

Puzzlement blinked out at her. 'Why? It's usual to
go to someone's house for a party.'

Embarrassment rose. She'd answered her question
to herself out loud. This man was rattling her, which
made no sense when, because of his self-assurance,
she'd pretty much ignored him in the two months she'd
worked here, unless it was to discuss a patient or argue
over small things, like where the order for more sy-
ringes had got to. It'd been years since desire had lit
her up, but if this tightness in her stomach and heat in
her veins were any indication, she might be making up
for lost time right now, in the middle of the ED. 'Um,
of course. I didn't mean that. It's fine. I'll be there.'

The alarm sounded. Code one. Relief had her racing to Resus and the man sprawled on the floor, unconscious.

'Cardiac arrest,' Vicki said, her clasped hands pushing down regularly on the exposed chest.

Molly grabbed the electro pads, handed them to Nathan, who was right behind her. Next she snatched up the ventilator in preparation of a good outcome before kneeling down next to him.

'Fill us in on the details,' Nathan said as he prepared to administer a shock.

'Geoff Baxter, forty-eight, chest pains, readings show a minor cardiac arrest an hour ago,' Vicki intoned. 'He was getting stroppy and didn't want to stay on the bed. Started getting up and collapsed on the floor.'

'Clear.'

On Nathan's command everyone moved away from the patient. The lifeless body jerked. The line on the monitor remained flat. Vicki started back on the compressions and Molly squeezed the oxygen bottle when she reached thirty.

'Clear.' Nathan gave a second shock.

The line blipped, rose, then fell into an erratic pattern.

'That's better,' Molly nodded. 'Not perfect, but we're getting there.' She put the ventilator aside and got up to get the scoop stretcher so they could lift the man off the floor and back onto the bed.

Another nurse, Hank, attached an oxygen mask, then began wiping a bleeding abrasion on Geoff's forehead. 'He hit the floor hard.'

Nathan leaned close to the man. 'Geoff, can you hear me?'

Geoff opened his eyes briefly.

'You've had a cardiac arrest. We're going to keep

you in here for a while, then you'll be admitted to the intensive care unit.'

Geoff shook his head once. 'No.'

'That'll be a yes, then.' Nathan gave one of his megawatt smiles.

Molly's stomach stirred, and he hadn't even been looking in her direction. He'd often smiled at her, particularly whenever he'd wanted something unpleasant dealt with, but not in that full-on, cramp-her-stomach way he saved for others. Not that she'd given him reason to. Unless working hard and caring deeply about their patients counted, and apparently it didn't. That was expected of her, no reward given—or required.

Would a man ever again look at her and think, *She's lovely*? One without hard fists? Did she want a man to notice her, get to know her? This new idea had to be part of moving forward, didn't it? It was funny how in a previous, happy-go-lucky life she'd had her pick of gorgeous men, never had a problem finding a date for the glamorous occasions that came with being her entrepreneurial mother's daughter. Not funny, really. Glancing over her shoulder, she saw no one to frighten her. Not that she expected to, but there were still times she just had to check, even though Paul would be in jail for many years to come. She'd lost a lot, but she was free.

Hold on to that. And, yes, think about maybe one day falling love.

Vicki nudged her. 'Time to knock off, day shift's here.'

Another night done and survived without too much drama amongst the patients. She could relax, except her muscles weren't playing the game. The old tension tightened her stomach and neck, while her shoulder blades tried to meet in the middle of her back. Because of the past? Or did she put this down to the rare heat in her veins, stirred up by Nathan Lupton? Yeah, like that'd be a blast. *It might be.* As if. He'd have to get a lot friendlier first, though he had made an effort earlier. Were things looking up all round? Smiling at Vicki, she asked, 'Which shoes are you wearing this morning?'

'Those orange, thin-strapped ones you were green about last week.' Vicki was a shoeaholic, with an incredible collection that made Molly envious—and that was only over the shoes she'd seen at work.

Molly laughed. Twice in one morning? *Go for it.* 'Clothes are my go to when the urge to have some R and R in the malls beckons. Shoes always come second. Maybe I should try the shoe shops first next time because those ones are amazing. When you're sick of them you know which locker's mine,' she said. 'Let's go change.' As well as her trousers and blouse, she needed to put her game face on.

Nathan turned from the specialist taking over Geoff's case. 'You all right?'

'Why wouldn't I be?' There were a million reasons, but he knew none of them, and never would.

'Because you look ready to bolt.'

Make that one million minus one reasons. Except this morning that had been the last thing on her mind. Disconcerting. She'd been laughing and he'd thought that? She hated that nearly as much as she'd hate him to see the truth. 'Actually, I'm working on how to nab Vicki's shoes without her noticing.'

His expression softened. 'Good luck with that.'

'I reckon.' Unbelievable. They were having a normal conversation for once.

'By the way, you were good with Geoff.'

Surprise stole the retort off her tongue. She hadn't done anything out of the ordinary, and yet he was saying that in front of the other nurses? She looked around at Vicki, then Hank, before locking eyes back on Nathan.

He got the message fast. 'So were you two.' He nodded. 'Right, get out of here while you can.' This time he was talking directly to Vicki.

Molly knew she could relax now that Nathan was no longer focused on her, but it wasn't happening. Instead her body was winding up tighter than a ball of twine, and just as rough. Why did this man in particular make her feel a little lighter in the chest, as though hope was knocking? Hope for love one day? Sadly, never for family. That dream had been smothered as a wet sack would a flame by a fist in her belly that had stolen her baby and quite likely any chance of another.

She looked at Nathan as he laughed with Vicki over something, and her heart dropped. If only she had the courage to let a strong, confident man close enough to trust. Until now it never occurred to her to want the things Paul had stolen. But it couldn't be this man waking her up. They were mostly civil with each other, but it took more than civility for a relationship to succeed. Or maybe it didn't. There hadn't been any of that going on in her now defunct marriage.

Flip-flop went her heart. Her stomach softened as the tension started backing off. As though her body was telling her it was ready to have fun. Had certain parts of her anatomy forgotten the pain of the past?

It wasn't wise. Or safe. But very tempting. And eye-opening. One thing this newer version of herself had in common with the last one was that it needed a man who had his own world sussed and wasn't afraid to stand up and be counted. As long as he didn't hurt her.

Nathan knew he'd overreacted to Molly O'Keefe's false smile about the barbecue, but he'd had enough of those. Two months and not once had she joined the staff for a meal, let alone anything else, despite everyone trying to persuade her. Whether she thought she was too good for them, or she believed she wasn't good enough, the jury was still out.

Yet she'd been quick to sign up for the barbecue. Part of him questioned whether she'd actually show up; another suggested maybe Molly didn't back down once she'd taken a stance. Despite working alongside her, often in trying circumstances, he didn't know her at all, which was unusual given the work they did. She didn't fall over backwards to get on with him. That might make him egotistical, but nothing added up. He got on well with most folk, and socialised enough not to return to being the hermit he'd become after Rosie's death.

Molly's a challenge.

He stumbled, righted himself, his eyes seeking out the woman doing this to him. Did he want her to like him? Now, *that* sounded needy. Hardly true when he had his pick of friends, even women. His gaze cruised across the department to the locker-room door from where a burst of laughter came. Vicki was doing her best to be happy on her thirtieth birthday, but her heart was sad because Cole was supposedly deployed off-shore with the army.

He couldn't wait to see her face when he dropped his best friend off at their apartment this afternoon. It would be a big surprise, one he couldn't justify when he saw the sadness lurking in the back of Vicki's eyes. He'd prefer to tell her the truth, and have her meet Cole, but he'd given his friend his word, and promises were not to be broken.

Molly appeared in the doorway, a rare genuine smile lighting up her face and causing those emerald eyes to sparkle, though she'd glared at him earlier. He shouldn't have pushed her buttons but, hell, it'd been impossible not to when he was exhausted after eight hours dealing with what felt like half of Sydney coming through the ED's doors.

Molly rattled him in ways he couldn't believe. He was not used to having his libido captivated by a woman who wasn't interested in him. What libido? Since Rosie's death there'd been little going on in that department, and when there was it was for relief, not involvement. He couldn't imagine being lucky enough to find love for a second time, hadn't been ready to consider it because who got that lucky? Yet today Molly had him questioning that.

Nathan shrugged. So there might be more nous behind Nurse O'Keefe's non-confrontational looks and that beautiful, heart-stopping face than he thought. He should've wound her up weeks ago if the flaring temper in her expression was the result. Far more interesting than quiet and mousy, as he'd believed. A shiver ripped down his spine, but not because her haughty glare daunted him. Not a bit. Instead it gave him a sharp awareness of the woman behind the glare.

Molly was waking up his body, which he preferred to leave in sleep mode until *he* decided otherwise. The sense of being slightly off balance had come out of left field the day she'd started in the department, and now he'd had enough of feeling out of whack. This morning it'd been time to push her boundaries over not joining in staff events so he could get relief from these frustrating sensations. This reaction confused him, and made him feel more than annoyed. Yeah, frustrated. But as in sexually or more? He didn't have a clue.

'You all going to spend the day in there?' he called out. No way did he intend heading to the café without making sure Molly didn't do a runner, because, say what she liked, she had looked edgy for a moment. Vicki liked her a lot, so Molly doing an about-face wasn't happening.

'Pretty much. How come you waited?' Molly's enticing shoulders had returned to their normal, slightly sloped position and her chin had softened back to quiet and mousy.

Except he no longer trusted his interpretation of that look. There was more to Nurse O'Keefe than met the eye. Deep down, had he always suspected so? And reacted accordingly by keeping his barriers in place to protect himself? For better or worse, there was a need ticking inside him making it impossible to look away, or deny how she intrigued him, or pretend he did not want her in his bed, underneath him. Or on top if she preferred. Jeez. He scrubbed his hands down his face. What was wrong with him?

'You run out of words?'

Something like that. 'I'm making sure no one gets lost.'

Her smile didn't slip a notch. 'I told Vicki I'd be there, and I never go back on my word.' Then doubt — or was it guilt?—slid through her sharp gaze and she looked away.

'Glad to hear it.' What was that about? Had she let someone down? In a big way that had come back to haunt her? Behind his ribs a sense of confusion lurched and an unreal feeling of protectiveness crept over him. For Molly? Hardly. There was definitely far more to this woman than he'd realised, but why spend time wondering what made her tick when it was obvious she wouldn't have a bar of him? She was a challenge. And causing a pool of desire to settle in his gut.

Could be hunger for food doing a number on him. Not Molly. He'd missed snack breaks throughout the night—always a bad thing. But nothing was dispelling that softening sensation in his belly as he watched her. Without even trying, she was doing a number on him. Bet he was the last person she wanted to spend time with, even if only over coffee. Was it time for a change? On both their parts? Could be it was time for him to step outside his secure bubble and poke at life, see where it took him.

As long as it wasn't more than he was prepared to give. More than he was *able* to give. He'd given his heart to Rosie, and she'd taken it to the grave with her. Or so he'd believed, until—until now and the thin ray of hope beginning to pierce his long-held belief that he couldn't be that lucky.

He and Rosie had been childhood sweethearts and so in love it had been unreal at times. Except reality had got in the way of their plans for a house and babies in the form of leukaemia. From the first day Rosie had complained of lethargy and swollen, sore glands they had been on a one-way road to hell. It had been a short trip, lasting little more than three months. He'd been glad for her sake it was over quickly, but for himself he'd only wanted her never to leave him, taking his dreams away for ever.

The disease that had taken Rosie's life had a lot to answer for. He used to picture them together, raising their kids, having a great life. The past four years had been long, and lonely in a way he wouldn't have believed before she'd died.

'Nathan?'

He pulled out of his reverie to find Vicki watching him with amusement forming crinkles at the corners of her eyes. 'Yes?'

'Lead on. We're all good to go.' Her wink was slow, and downright mischievous, reminding him how she and Cole thought it was time he came out of his cave. Grabbing his elbow, Vicki strode ahead of the group, tugging him along with her.

'I'm hangry,' he warned around a smile. His friends cared about him so he let them off their interfering ways.

Vicki only laughed. 'I heard you giving Molly a bit of a roasting this morning about the winter party. One she didn't deserve, by the way.'

'Someone had to tell her to get over staying on the fringe around us.'

Vicki jabbed him with an elbow. 'Others have told you they'll be there and not signed the list. Who needs a list anyway?'

'I do.' He huffed a breath. 'Why did she do that pen-snatching thing and scrawl her name across the page large enough to suggest I might be blind?'

'To rile you? It worked, by the way.'

I know that. Damn her. 'Right.' A spurt of resentment soured his mouth. He swallowed it away, and managed to laugh at himself. So Miss Mousy had got one over him. Game on, Molly O'Keefe.

Vicki hadn't finished. 'I'm glad you nudged her about joining in. It's good for her.' Another jab from that blasted elbow. 'She needs to get out more.'

Nathan stared at his friend. 'Since when has she talked about anything that's not to do with patients?' He'd never heard Molly say something as simple as she'd been to the hair salon. And, yes, he knew when she went because those short, red curls would be quiet, in place, for a few days before returning to their riot of crazy colour. He preferred the wild to the tamed.

A tingling itch sometimes crept over his palms as he wondered about pushing his fingers through her hair. Then he'd remember he didn't have a heart any more and would go and see a patient. See? Early on she *had* disturbed him in ways only Rosie had ever done, yet they were opposites. Rosie had mostly been calm, with little that would upset her. On the other hand, Miss Quiet and Mousy, red head contrasting with her temperament and all, managed to upset his orderly existence without even trying, especially when he was overtired or pressured by a particularly ill child. As of now he was going to delete mousy from the nickname.

Vicki tapped him none too gently on the shoulder to bring his attention back to her. 'Molly lives in an apartment on the third floor of a block in Bondi Junction, takes the train to work, has a regular car that doesn't stand out at the lights, and likes to watch comedy shows on TV. Oh, and she has lots of amazing clothes that suggest a previous life that wasn't so lean.'

'You two are close.'

'Sarcasm is the lowest form of wit.' Vicki grinned. 'But you're forgiven since you're in need of food.'

Nathan shook his head. He'd learned more in two minutes than he had in the past weeks. More than Molly being a superb nurse with a special way with the younger patients that came their way so they all fell in love with her, even when she was cleaning a wound that stung or sliding a needle into their arm. He could also admit to seeing her wearing stunning—and expensive—figure-enhancing outfits when she strode onto the ward heading for the staff changing room at the beginning of her shifts. Not that her figure needed enhancing; it did a damned good job of filling out her uniform and her day clothes all by itself.

Bondi Junction, eh? And here he'd been thinking she probably lived in one of the upmarket suburbs near or on Sydney Harbour's waterfront.

Expensive clothes, average address. Once had money, now getting by? Throw in not mixing with people, the loneliness that sometimes blitzed her eyes, and he had to wonder if she'd been let down big-time. That protective instinct raised its head again. Guess he'd never know what was behind Molly's attitude since she wasn't likely to spill her guts over breakfast. Especially not to him. 'Let's hope she enjoys herself.'

'We'll do our best to make sure she does.' Another wink came his way.

'Stop that. Whatever that wicked mind of yours is

coming up with, it's not happening. You have a birthday to focus on, not someone else's problems.' Suddenly Nathan was more than pleased Molly was here. He understood loneliness, knew how it could drag a person down deep. After Rosie had died he'd holed up in their home, only coming out to attend lectures or work a shift at the hospital, doing what was required to qualify—no more, no less. None of his friends or family had been able to prise him out into the real world to become involved with people and life other than what was required for patients and qualifying as an emergency specialist.

To get past the pain of losing Rosie he'd focused entirely on those things and it had worked for the first couple of years. Then he'd begun to understand he wasn't any use to the people who needed his medical skills if he didn't get out and about, and that he owed the people he loved for sticking around.

'We're having champagne this morning.' Vicki laughed.

'Already sorted,' he agreed, his mood lightening further in anticipation of spending time with this group of chatterboxes.

And Molly. No, forget that. She wouldn't start yabbering on to him. Maybe by the end of breakfast they'd be a little further ahead in knowing each other, but that was all. Bet she'd still have his hands tingling and his gut tightening, though. 'Shows we're in need of a life when this is as exciting as it gets.'

Nathan hated admitting it, but he'd been looking forward to breakfast. His heart felt lighter, and the blood seemed to move faster in his veins. Molly had nothing to do with the happy sensations in his chest, or the sudden urge to be on his best, most charming behaviour. *That* needed a bit of practice anyway, and she'd see straight through him and ignore his attempts.

Chapter 2

As the group approached the café entrance, Molly smoothed down her trousers and jacket, hauled her shoulders back so that she looked and felt confident, before following everyone inside to the reserved table where Nathan was pulling out a chair on the far side.

Why did she seek him out? Because his mood had improved? Out of doctor mode and into something friendlier, less gruff than usual. Still handsome and mouth-watering. He didn't often come across as too confident and charming, even though he could enchant a screaming patient into quietly accepting an injection and his medical knowledge was second to none. Experience had taught her to look behind a man's character traits to find out what really made him tick.

'Vicki?' Nathan indicated the chair he'd pulled out.

'The birthday girl gets to sit at the top of the table.' Hank pulled out another chair.

'You're right.' Vicki grinned and sat down on Hank's chair. 'Molly, why don't you take that chair Nathan's holding?'

Because Nathan had already slung his jacket over the one next to it. Looking around the table, Molly saw seats were filling rapidly, leaving her little choice. *Fake it...* Forcing a smile on her mouth and lifting her chin like nothing was wrong in her world—because it wasn't any more—she strolled around to plonk down on the chair Nathan was holding out. 'Thanks.'

'You want a coffee?' he asked, surprise and something else she couldn't interpret flitting across his face.

Thoughtlessly putting a hand on his arm, she said, 'I'll get it.' She jerked away. She never touched a man. Showed how safe she felt around Nathan, despite his attitude.

He said in his I'm-here-to-help-you voice usually reserved for patients, 'I'm going to check the champagne I've ordered to toast Vicki's birthday is coming out soon. I'll put our coffee orders in at the same time.' His gaze was intent, his eyes searching for something in her expression.

Okay, lighten up. 'That'd be great. A flat white, thanks.' Her tongue felt far too big for her mouth. Just another way he tipped her world off its new axis. 'Are we all putting in for the champagne?' But he was gone, slipping through the crowd building around other tables, aiming for the counter, head and shoulders above everyone he passed.

Since she'd run away from Paul she hadn't gone out with a man, never let one in her home or talked about her past to anyone. At first she'd struggled facing the world as most people she knew had blamed her for Paul's arrest. He was so charismatic they'd believed him until the truth had come out in court and those same people had begun fawning over her, wanting to get back onside. She'd struggled not to turn bitter. At the time, dating men had been an impossibility.

Until now. Looking at Nathan, she thought he'd be protective of those he loved. He always stood up for a patient whenever a family member tried to force proceedings in the department that were wrong. No doubt he'd protect anybody who got into danger if he was close by.

Downright crazy to believe that without proof. Look what happened the last time I trusted a man.

Paul hadn't been kind and gentle with those less fortunate than himself, instead he'd enjoyed showing how much better than others he was. Something she hadn't seen until it had been too late. Hadn't known to look. Paul had been the catch every woman wanted, and with her mother actively encouraging her, she'd gone for him and won. Then lost. The first year of her marriage had been bliss, then the cracks had started appearing. She was a lousy hostess, a simpleton, useless at any damned thing. Then she'd fallen pregnant and it was all over.

Molly shook her head. *Stop right now.* She was out with a bunch of great people. She needed to forget the self-pity and enjoy herself, not turn in on herself and repeat the mistake she'd made with the Roos, the basketball team she'd been a member of. The regret she felt every weekend when she looked up the team's results from the Saturday game made her ache, made her wish she'd stopped worrying about letting anyone close for fear of being hurt and got on with enjoying being a part of a great bunch of women. If only she hadn't given in and quit, she might've moved on with getting a life sooner.

So, get cracking and enjoy this morning.

Straightening her spine and breathing deeply, she then fell into another old habit, checking out the latest suits to walk into the café, swinging briefcases and checking their phones. But today she wasn't looking for trouble, instead comparing the men with Nathan. He came out top every time. Something to think about once she was back in her apartment.

'Here you go. Coffee's on the way.' A glass of water appeared before her. 'As is the champagne,' Nathan told Vicki.

'Great.' Molly sat up straighter. Today she might even celebrate her divorce. One sip of champagne for that, and no one at the table would be any the wiser.

Her gaze returned to Nathan, and instantly her heart forgot that memo about not thumping too hard. Crazy. He was just another male she worked with— one who happened to be bone-meltingly good looking, and currently making her aware of him in ways she'd hadn't known around men for a long time. Yet there was something about him that had her wondering what it would be like to curl up against his chest, be held in those strong arms and just relax, be happy. No, it wasn't happening. She wasn't ready. Could she give it a go? Probably not.

Nathan handed her a menu. 'Here, take a look. Most of us know this off by heart. There are some great choices.'

'Suddenly I'm starving.' Molly began scanning the page.

Nathan grunted. 'I'm past hungry. Could eat a whole sirloin.'

She laughed. 'How about tofu and grains?'

His eyes widened. He hadn't thought she'd tease him? Last week she wouldn't have. 'You can't pull that one. Like I said, I've been here before.'

'Okay, so one whole sirloin, and what?' The whole steak wasn't on offer, but he could order two helpings. 'Chips or hash browns, as well as eggs and bacon?'

'Stop right there.' He was smiling directly at her, and it was making her stomach feel like hot chocolate dropped into cream, swirling, warming, tempting. 'Don't mention food like that when I'm this hungry.'

'But you're smiling.' When she was starving she couldn't smile.

'Don't trust it.'

Sorry, Nathan, but I do believe you. Gazing at him, and especially at his smile, Molly felt no qualms. No fear of him erupting into a rage because he needed to eat now, not in ten minutes. Again, she felt that rare sense of safety around him. Needing to put mental space between them, she'd join in the conversations going on around her and enjoy the birthday celebration. After she told the hovering waitress she'd like the eggs Benedict, that was.

The room was crowded, with a queue waiting at the counter for take-out coffees and pastries. In their corner her group was out of the way and could talk without yelling. The champagne arrived and glasses were filled.

Nathan stood up. 'Happy birthday, Vicki. May all your wishes come true.'

Vicki blinked. 'Thanks. I only have one, and it's not happening.' Another blink, and she raised her glass. 'Cheers, everyone, and thank you for joining me today.'

Molly wanted to hug Vicki and wipe away that sadness. Spontaneous hugs not being her thing any more, the best she could manage was to have fun, and not bring her past into the room. Suddenly she was very glad she'd come. Today she'd started to live, not just exist. It was a tiny step in the right direction, but it was a bigger step than usual. There'd be plenty more. Yes, there would.

Nathan sat down and picked up his glass of water. 'Anyone want to start singing "Happy Birthday"? Not me, I'd empty the place.'

'That'd make it a memorable day for Vicki,' someone joked.

Without a thought, Molly began singing 'Happy Birthday'. Instead of everyone joining in, they stared at her. She faltered to a stop. 'What's wrong?'

'Nothing,' everyone cried. 'Carry on.'

Embarrassed, she shook her head and sipped her water. 'Someone else can have a turn.'

'Not after that, they can't,' Nathan muttered. 'You sing like an angel.'

For a moment she forgot everything except the memories of singing, especially with Gran, and how happy it had made her. 'I inherited my grandmother's singing gene.' Gran had paid for her lessons until she'd decided she didn't want music as a career but rather a happy go-to place. 'She sang for the national opera company.' She'd also been the only one to question her love for Paul before the wedding.

Not now, Moll. Having fun, okay?

She turned to Nathan. 'That's some car you've got. I saw you arrive at work last Wednesday when I drove in for a change.'

Again he was watching her intently, but at least there was no tension lurking behind his gaze this time. *And* he went with her change of subject. 'Not bad, eh? I only bought it a month ago and haven't had time to take it for a spin out on the highway. But it has to happen soon, or else I might as well sell it.'

'That'd be a waste.' She couldn't think of anything more exciting than speeding along the road in that amazing car, forgetting everything and enjoying the moment.

Wrong, Moll. Being with Nathan would be more exciting.

Molly spluttered into her coffee.

Nathan held out a serviette. 'Here, wipe your face.'

Trying to snatch the paper serviette from his fingers only caused her to touch him, and she pulled back. Heat that had nothing to do with stopping the spluttering and everything to do with longing began unfurling deep inside her. It came with a growing awareness of herself as a woman, and of the man beside her. 'You a dad, by any chance? You have a thing about goo on faces?'

The serviette was scrunched into a ball and dropped back on the table. 'No kids,' he muttered and looked away.

Back to upsetting him. She didn't know what to say for fear of further annoying him. Time to talk to someone else. Leaning forward, she eyeballed Emma across the table. 'When do you head over to Queenstown?' The intern was going to New Zealand's winter festival.

'Thursday. I can't wait. Have you been?'

'Years ago. It's an amazing event in an extraordinary location.'

Nathan wasn't going to be ignored. 'Did you go on the jet boat?'

'Of course.'

'You're obviously into speed.' When he smiled his whole face lit up in a way she rarely saw.

'I guess I am. Not that I've done anything extreme. Nor will I be. Safe and sensible is me.'

'Nothing wrong with that.' Nathan was watching her in a way that suggested he wanted to know more about what made her tick outside work. But he waited, didn't push.

Which had her opening up a little. 'I liked my sports, sailing on large yachts, going to rock concerts, things like that.'

'Liked?' he asked quietly. 'Not any more?'

Thump. Reality check. Hurrying to deflect him, she spluttered, 'Still like, but I don't seem to find the time any more. Neither do I know anyone in Sydney with a yacht the size I'm used to.' Actually, she did, but that family was part of the past, so she wasn't paying them a visit any time soon. In fact, never.

'I don't suppose a three-metre Paper Tiger would suffice?' Nathan wasn't laughing at her, just keeping the conversation going on a comfortable level, like he was trying to stop her tripping into the black hole that was her past. He couldn't be. He knew nothing about it. 'My brother-in-law's got one.'

A laugh huffed across her lips, surprising her. 'Me?

Actually sail a small yacht? I don't think so. I'd probably fall off or drop the sail at the wrong moment.'

'All part of learning to sail.' He grinned, then told her about his misadventures on his surfboard.

Nearly an hour later people had finished eating, and were beginning to gather their gear together.

'Guess it's time to head away,' Molly said reluctantly. It had been fun talking and laughing with everyone, but especially with Nathan. He was different away from work, more at ease with her somehow, talking about Queenstown, his car, and other things. He even laughed and smiled often. He was a man she liked and wanted to spend more time learning more about.

Nathan leaned closer, said quietly, 'Feel like a ride in my car?' There was a cheeky smile on that divine mouth, and something in his eyes that asked if she was up to it. 'I can drop you home.'

Molly's mouth dropped open. She snapped it closed. Then spluttered, 'That's not necessary. I'm fine with the train.'

Across the table Vicki rolled her hand from side to side. 'Train or top-of-the-range sports car. I know which I'd prefer.'

So did she. Except the car meant being squashed into a confined space with a man. Not just any man. Nathan. Standing up, she said, oh, so casually, 'It's a long way to Bondi Junction.'

'It's on my way. I live in Coogee.' When she raised her eyebrows, he continued in a voice that suggested he was determined she'd go with him, 'I didn't even finish one glass of champagne so you don't have to worry about my driving.'

'I wasn't.'

Nathan shrugged. 'Let's fix our bills and get the car.'

'Nathan, you don't have to do this.' At least he hadn't offered to pay for her meal. Thank goodness for something, because she'd have argued hotly. Paying her own way meant never owing anyone anything. Her stomach was doing a squeeze and release thing, while her head spun with the thought she'd be crammed into a car with a male she didn't know very well. With Nathan Lupton, sex on legs, kindness in his heart and, don't forget, someone who was quick to get grumpy with her, but who she trusted not to hurt her.

'You said you like fast cars.'

True. She couldn't contain the smile splitting her face. Her first car had been a racy little number bought by her mother for her eighteenth birthday. She'd loved it. 'But you can't get up any speed between here and my apartment.'

'Now, there's a challenge.' He smiled back and flipped a coin in the air, caught it and laughed.

Nathan watched the conflicting emotions zipping across Molly's face and damned if they didn't make him want to spend more time with her, not to prove he could win her over but because he just might like her. The challenge was heating up. Though not in the way he'd intended. The offer of a ride home was because on and off throughout breakfast he'd warmed to her more and more, therefore he didn't want the morning to end.

Today Molly intrigued him. He was not walking away. Nope. The genuine happiness lightening her gaze throughout breakfast had stirred him in places usually unaffected by other people, and had him wishing for more, had him remembering he'd once had a heart and thinking he just might like to get it back—if he could find the courage. She'd be a keeper, if he wanted to get involved, and that was the problem. He didn't. Here was the rub. He might be ready to start dating on a regular basis but the thought of anything permanent still freaked him out. To fall in love and have his heart torn out of his chest a second time was unimaginable.

'Ready when you are.' The smile lifting the enticing corners of Molly's soft mouth was real, and not that strained, 'smile if I absolutely have to' version she was so good at. Seemed she'd quite quickly got over trying to talk him out of giving her a lift.

Because he wanted to believe Molly's smile had been for him, he'd risk being hit over the head by teasing her. 'You could seem more excited.'

'Sure.' She leaned in to give Vicki a hug. 'Happy birthday. If you need some company later, give me a call.'

Vicki's eyes lit up. 'I might just do that. Shoe shopping comes to mind.'

Molly was looking surprised about something. It wouldn't be shoes. Everyone knew of Vicki's fetish for footwear. Something else had put the stunned look on her face.

'You could do worse than hanging out with Vicki.'

She glanced down at her high-heeled, black-with-a-bow shoes. 'I reckon.' Then she looked back at him and shrugged, said with caution in her voice, 'No time like now to get back into it.'

Get back into friendships? Again that protective need nudged, stronger this time. He felt certain something had gone amiss with Molly, something that kept her on edge and wary around her colleagues. 'Vicki, you right for getting home?'

That cheeky grin flicked from him to Molly, then disappeared, unhappiness replacing it. 'I'm fine.'

Only because his car was a two-seater, he nodded. 'See you around three.'

'You don't have to coddle me because it's my birthday. Anyway, I'm going shopping with Molly.'

'Yes, I do.' Or Cole would have his guts for guitar strings. 'Shop as much as you like but be home when I get there.'

Molly eyed first him then Vicki, who gave her a big smile before heading out the door. 'You two are close.' Something strangely like envy darkened her voice.

'Her husband's been my best mate from years back when we were into surfing. We continued our friendship into med school, and never stopped since.' Cole had been there for him in the darkest days. Taking Molly's elbow, he kept his touch light when he longed to pull her closer and breathe in that rich fragrance that was her. Funny but he hadn't realised how often he'd smelled it until now. She really was doing a number on him, and didn't have a clue. Which was something to be grateful for. That, and not how he was spending time with her, breaking down the barrier she kept between them.

'You don't surf now?' When she tilted her head back to stare up at him it was almost impossible not to reach across to tuck some wayward curls behind her ear.

Resisting required effort, so it took time to answer. 'Occasionally I chase a wave out where I live but not as often as I used to. Cole joined the army and I broke an ankle. That didn't prevent me getting back on the board once the bones mended, but around that time specialised study began taking up all my spare hours.'

What was left had been for Rosie. Rosie. His heart wavered. The love of his life. Nothing like Molly. Would he have taken a second look if she had been? It would be too strange.

Hang on. S*econd* look? There'd been a third, fourth and more. He shivered, suddenly afraid of where this might lead. All the moisture in Nathan's mouth dried up. He might be getting closer to stepping off the edge in the hope of finding that deep, loving happiness he'd once known, but what if it all went sour? Turned to dislike instead? Or worse, what if he fell in love with a woman he couldn't make happy because of his past?

They reached his car. 'What's your address in Bondi Junction?'

'I'll put it in the GPS.' Molly settled into the seat and buckled in. 'I know the way, but let's play it safe.' Seemed she wanted to get there as soon as possible.

They didn't talk on the way, but when he pulled up outside the apartment block Molly indicated, he said, 'I'll walk you to the entrance.' The sooner the better. He needed to breathe air not laden with Molly's scent, and to put space between them. Then drive away, windows lowered and music on loud. He needed to stop, think about what he was doing getting to know Molly, before it got out of hand.

'That's not necessary.' She grabbed her bag from the floor and elbowed the door open, snatching up the hairbrush that had fallen out of her bag.

The door shut with a soft click, but Nathan was already moving around to join her on the pavement. 'When I see someone home I go all the way.'

Her emerald eyes widened as something akin to laughter sparkled out at him. 'We don't know each other well enough for that.'

'You know what I meant.'

That was not disappointment blinking out at him. It couldn't be. Then Molly proved it wasn't. 'That's a relief. I wasn't a hundred percent sure what you were saying.' Her eyes cleared, but there was a little twitching going on at the corners of her mouth.

Hell, he'd love to kiss that mouth. He needed to know if those lips were as soft and inviting as they looked. His upper body leaned forward without any input from his brain, but as he began to lift his arms, common sense stepped in. Molly would kick him where no man wanted a shoe if he followed through.

Stepping back, he looked around the area. The entrance was accessed immediately off the footpath where a bus stop was outlined. Nothing wrong in that, but it was so ordinary and Molly was anything but. He sighed, long and slow. It had nothing to do with him where she chose to live. This was getting out of hand. He was making up stuff without Molly saying a word. But he had to ask, 'How long have you lived here?'

She was focused on a pebble, rolling it round on the pavement with the toe of one classy shoe, then, raising her head, she eyeballed him. 'Since I moved to Sydney a year ago. I worked in a medical centre down the road while looking for a job in an emergency department anywhere in the city.'

'I'd have thought there'd be plenty of opportunities in that time. You picky, or something?' He added a smile to take the heat out of his question.

'I got a job within weeks of starting at the medical centre, but a nurse I worked with came down with leptospirosis and when the manager asked me to stay on until she was back up to speed I didn't feel I could let them down. They'd been nothing but good to me from day one.'

How many questions could he get away with? Pushing her wasn't being fair, but he needed to learn more. Maybe the answers would dampen the ardour taking hold of him. 'I'd have thought you'd move closer to the city, where the shops and nightclubs are.'

'I like it out here.' For the first time he heard doubt in her voice. 'Neither do I mind the train trip. It doesn't take long. Judging by the traffic the few times I've driven in, I think the train probably gets me there in less time than it takes you in that fancy car.'

True. 'Where did you move from?' So much for shutting up.

'Adelaide. Before that, Perth.' The pebble flicked across the path as she turned away. 'I'm heading inside for some sleep. Thanks for bringing me home.'

His heart skittered. What was wrong with his last question? 'Wait.' What the hell for? Despite the tightening in his belly and groin brought on by those curves outlining her jacket and trousers, he had to let her go. He wasn't ready for this. He'd bet Molly wasn't either.

She paused to look over her shoulder. 'Go home, Nathan. Get some sleep too. Being Friday, tonight's bound to be hectic.'

Ignoring that, he said, 'You want to come with me sometime when I take this…' he waved at his car '… for a blast along the highway?' What happened to not ready, and thinking things through? Damned if he knew, other than he wasn't giving up that easily now that he'd started.

She stared at him as if he'd just asked her to fly to the moon in a toy box.

He waited, breath stalled between his lungs and his nostrils, hands tightening and loosening. What was the problem? He'd asked Molly to go for a spin, which meant sharing the small space and breathing her scent some more. No big deal. Yet it felt huge. It was a date. So what? *About damned time.* There'd been the occasional romp in the sack with women who understood that was all he was offering.

He knew instinctively that Molly would not want that with him. Then again, maybe she would, and he could have fun and walk away afterwards. Shock hit him in the gut. He didn't want that with this woman. All or nothing. No half-measures. *All* had to be out of the question. She wasn't his type. So it had to be nothing. About to withdraw his offer of a ride, he got a second shock.

Molly was grinning at him, and it was the most amazing sight. Beautiful became stunning, quiet became gorgeous and cheeky. 'Only if I get a turn at the wheel.'

His heart must've stopped. Nothing was going on behind his ribs. His lungs had seized. It didn't surprise him when his knees suddenly turned rubbery. How could he refuse her? Leaning back against the car to prevent landing in a heap on the damp asphalt, he asked, 'You like driving fast?' Fast and dangerous? He hadn't thought dangerous would come into anything Molly did. She appeared too cautious. Appeared, right? Not necessarily correct.

'Strictly safe and sensible, that's me.' The grin dipped.

Phew. He could get back on track, be the colleague who'd brought her home—and ignore the challenge he'd set himself. If only Molly's mouth hadn't flattened, because that got him wanting to make her smile again. 'I promise I'll be so safe you'll want to poke me with needles.' He straightened, took a tentative step and, when he didn't fall over, began walking up to the main door, making sure Molly was with him.

He got no further than the entrance.

'Thanks, again.' Molly punched a set of numbers into the keypad.

'I'll see you to your apartment.'

'I'm on the third floor. Think I can manage,' she muttered. 'See you tonight.' The lock clicked and she nudged the wide door open. 'I'm glad I went to breakfast. It was fun.'

Warmth stole across his skin and he had to refrain from reaching out to touch her. 'Glad you came. Now, I'd better get going. I've got things to do before I pick Cole up from the airport.'

A frown appeared between those fall-into-them eyes. 'I thought he wasn't going to be around for her birthday.'

'It's a surprise. He managed to wangle a weekend's leave. The rest of his contingent is on the way home via Darwin, while he's coming direct from KL.'

'There goes the shopping.' Molly smiled. 'She can't work tonight.'

'I organised that without letting slip what's going on. I'll tell her when I drop Cole off.'

'Good on you. It'd be awful if she had to waste this opportunity of having time out with her man.' Though filled with longing—for what, he had no idea—at least Molly's sigh was better than her quiet, mousy look.

Not mousy. Not any more. Sauntering towards his car, he called over his shoulder, 'See you tonight.' Time to put distance between them before he did something silly, like ask why it had taken weeks for her to front up and socialise with the people she worked with. That would put a stop to getting closer.

Nathan remained beside his car until Molly went inside and the door had closed behind her. Then he got in and drove on to Coogee and his small piece of paradise, his mind busy with all things Molly. She'd tipped him sideways by wanting little to do with him.

Except go for a spin in this beast.

No matter what else came up, he'd find time to follow through on that. Hopefully this weekend, so he could get to spend time unravelling the façade Molly showed the world.

Don't think that's going to happen in a hurry.

Better remember to get her number tonight.

Pulling up at traffic lights, Nathan tapped the steering wheel in time to the rock number playing on the radio. A strident ringing from the passenger side of the car intruded. Leaning over, he fossicked around until his fingers closed over a phone. Had to be Molly's. His finger hovered over the green circle, but of course he couldn't answer it. If for no other reason than she'd kill him.

A smile slowly spread across his face. Now he had a reason to return to her apartment and speak to her, and get her phone number at the same time.

Chapter 3

'Hot damn.'

Molly leaned back against her apartment door as it clicked shut and tried not to think about Nathan. Like that was going to happen.

A grin spread across her face. What a morning. They'd gone from grumping to talking to smiling and then he'd driven her home and insisted on walking to the entrance with her. He'd have come up here if she'd let him.

She looked around the tiny space, smaller than Gran's chicken coop, and sighed, glad he wasn't seeing this. The shoddy apartment block would've already given him reason to wonder why a nurse on a reasonable wage would choose to live here. But it was ordinary, wouldn't attract attention.

She kept the apartment simply furnished with the

bare basics in an attempt to make the rooms feel larger. The polished wood furniture came from her grandmother's cottage after Gran died. The furniture had lain in storage until Molly had moved to Adelaide and set up house on her own. The only good thing about Gran's passing was that she didn't get to hear she had been right about Paul. She would've gone after him with her sewing scissors.

No one came to the apartment. Lizzie, her best friend back in Perth, kept saying she'd visit but never managed to make it happen with her job taking her offshore for weeks at a time. Molly missed her more than anyone from her previous life. They'd done so much together, shared a lot of laughs and tears, always been there for one another. But, more important, Lizzie had believed her right from the beginning when she'd said Paul hit her, and she hated him almost as much as Molly did.

Paul Bollard. Nathan Lupton. They were nothing alike. One evil. The other caring. Both could be charming, strong, over-confident. That spooked her. Paul had wooed her as though she had been a princess, at first making her feel like one. Nathan confused her, sometimes making her cross and occasionally, especially this morning, all soft on the inside.

She huffed the air out of her lungs. Nathan wasn't wooing her and, by the expressions that crossed his face at times, had no intention of doing so. Fine. With a hideous marriage behind her, the wedding ring long gone in the bin, as of this week she was single and wanting to trust and love again, but she was very, very cautious.

Going out to breakfast had been the best thing to

happen to her in a long while. She worked with a great bunch, and from now on she'd attend every get-together anyone proposed. She'd also get involved with more than the charity shop. Fake it till she made it. This latest and final version of herself would not be the socialite of the past, or the cowering abused woman. Married two years, separated for two, now alone. If nothing else, she'd become more caring and understanding of other people. Mrs Molly Bollard was gone for ever.

In the kitchenette she filled the kettle for a cup of tea. Sleep would be elusive while her mind was going over the morning. Pride lifted her chest. She'd managed to fit in with her workmates to the point she'd relaxed enough to forget everything that had brought her to that point. So much so, she'd even managed to sing 'Happy Birthday'. Now, there was a step in the right direction, and she mustn't stop at that. There was a city out there to get to know, and if she was careful not to keep her distrust to the fore, she didn't have to carry on being alone, could make friends in all facets of her life.

Did Nathan go to the meals every time the staff got together? She chuckled. He wouldn't do the shopping expeditions. She mightn't be fully ready for a partner or even a lover, but spending time over a meal with a man who laughed, grumped, looked out for others, could not be time wasted.

The doorbell chimed. Molly spun around. No one visited her. Bang went her heart. Crunch went her stomach.

Knock, knock. 'Molly, it's Nathan. I've got your phone.'

Relief prodded her towards the door. How had he managed to get inside and up to her floor without knowing the apartment number? Peering through the peephole, she got a grainy view of the man who'd driven her home.

'Molly?' That familiar irritation was back.

She opened the door. 'Sorry to be a pain. It must've fallen out of my bag with my hairbrush.'

Nathan was watching her with that intensity that was more familiar than his smiles. 'You had a call. That's how I found it.'

'A call?' she asked. 'Who from?'

He shrugged. 'I didn't look. Figured you'd be cross if I did.'

'You bet,' Molly admitted sheepishly as she checked out the caller ID. An unknown number. Her smile snapped off.

'Problem?'

'What?' She shook her head and glanced up at Nathan to soak up the warmth in his gaze. 'No. Wrong number probably.' As far as she knew, Paul only had access to the prison phone and that number was definitely in her contacts file so she could ignore it if he tried to get in touch. Anyway, he'd stopped calling her after his guilty verdict. Though who knew what receiving the divorce notice might've done to his narcissistic brain. He hated losing control over her more than anything.

The kettle whistled. Molly glanced toward the kitchenette. 'Thanks for this.'

Nathan stepped through the door. 'You into minimalist?'

Closing her eyes, she counted to four. Nathan should have left, not come inside. Yet it didn't feel wrong. More like it was okay for this man to be inside her home; as if she wanted him here. Which was so far out of left field she had to stop and look at him again. All she saw was the good-looking man who'd brought her home gazing around her apartment as if it was a normal thing to do. It probably was, for most people. That had to be in his favour. She was not thinking about the pool of heat in her stomach. Not, not, not. 'I'm making tea. Do you want one?' Ah, okay, maybe that heat was getting the upper hand.

He hesitated, his gaze still cruising her living room.

He was going to say no. She got in first. 'It's okay. You've got things to do before picking up Cole.' She wanted to feel relieved, but it was disappointment settling over her.

'Thought you'd never ask.' His gaze had landed back on her. His hands were in his pockets, his stance relaxed, yet there was something uncertain about him, like he didn't know if he was welcome. Nothing to make her afraid, more the opposite. If such a strong, confident man could feel unsure then he was more real, human—flawed in a good way. 'White with one.'

Her disappointment was gone in a flash. Replaced by a sudden longing for another chance at love. Truly? Yes, truly. Still had to go slowly, though. Turning her back on him before she fell completely under his spell and screwed up big-time, she said, 'Would you mind shutting the door? I don't like leaving it open. Never know who might wander in.'

'No problem.' A moment later, 'In case you're wondering, it was the old lady three doors down who told me which door to knock on after I described you.'

'I guess that goes with the territory.' She'd have to talk to Mrs Porter about telling strangers which apartment was hers. Except Nathan stood in the middle of her tiny one-bed home, waiting for a mug of tea. Not a stranger. 'Take a pew.' She nodded at the pair of wooden chairs at her tiny, gleaming wooden dining table. Her mouth dried as he sat and stretched those endless legs half across the kitchenette.

'Not a lot of space for a party, is there?' He smiled.

She could get to like those smiles far too much. They warmed her in places that had been cold for a long time, places she'd held in lockdown for fear of making another hideous mistake. Reaching for the two mugs on the tiny shelf above the bench, she answered, 'As partying wasn't on my agenda when I needed a roof over my head, I'm not complaining. This suits me fine in that respect.'

He looked around again. 'You're not happy with your neighbour telling people where you live.'

'I'm a bit circumspect about giving out personal info to any old body.' Shut up. Too much information. She was not telling Nathan why she felt that way. Anyway, she needed to move on from all that. Paul was locked up. No one else wanted to hurt her.

Nathan was watching her, apparently casually, yet she'd swear he wasn't missing a thing going on in her head. 'I suppose you wouldn't want just anyone turning up unannounced.'

She needed to be on guard around him. Always. 'Exactly.' Glancing around the room that had gone from tiny to minuscule the moment he'd entered, a flicker of yearning rose. Everything about her lifestyle since moving to Sydney had been average. Average suburb, average apartment, average car. Her job was a lot better than that, but the one at the medical centre had been on a par with the other things in her life. Nobody noticed average, which had been the intention. Except now she was restless.

'I like it here, but it might be time to move somewhere more spacious, a place I can feel more connected. I come and go every day, along with everyone else in the apartment block, and all we ever do is nod and smile at each other.' Once, that had been perfect. Now it seemed to roll out in front of her like an endless dark mat leading to a door going nowhere.

'Where would you like to live?'

The phone rang, saving her from having to find an answer. The idea was new, and using Nathan as a sounding board would be stretching their new relationship a bit far. But then, this morning she'd have laughed if anyone had told her he'd be sitting in her apartment drinking tea right now.

There was no caller ID on her phone, only the same unknown number as previously. It wouldn't be anything untoward, would it? 'Hello?' Molly said, hearing the caution in her voice and forcing a smile on her face. 'Molly O'Keefe speaking.' Easier to be brave when Nathan was sitting opposite her.

'Hi, Molly. It's Jean from the charity shop. The shop phone's playing up so I'm using my personal one.'

Relief threaded through the tension that had begun tightening her body. 'What can I do for you?'

'You said to call if we got stuck for staff. One of the ladies who works Mondays has been called away to look after her sick mother. Is it possible you could help out?'

'I'd love to. I have to be at the ED by three. Does that work for you?'

'Perfect. Thank you so much. See you then.' A dial tone replaced Jean's voice. Just like that?

She dropped the phone on the table. 'That takes care of Monday morning.'

Nathan was looking at her as though expecting more from her.

'I put in a few hours at a charity shop that supports the women's refuge. Fill shelves, run up sales. That sort of thing.' The shop raised quite a lot of money for abused women and their kids, and it gave Molly a sense of satisfaction to contribute to people she understood all too well without having to explain herself. Though sometimes she suspected Jean had figured out why she turned up.

'Go, you,' Nathan said. Then a frown appeared. 'You must get to hear some horror stories. I don't think I could cope with those.'

She hesitated, torn between dodging the bullet and being honest. 'Most of the people I meet come in to spend money and support the charity. Rarely are they the women who've survived abuse. Those who have don't usually talk about it.' *Stop.* This man wasn't stupid. He'd see behind her words if she wasn't careful.

'You're probably right. The rare exceptions being those brave women who go public about their ordeals in order to raise awareness.' Awe shaded his voice, his face and that steady gaze. 'I don't know how they do it.'

'Neither do I,' she muttered truthfully.

Draining his mug, Nathan stood up. 'I'd better get cracking, get things done before heading to the airport. Sleep being one of them. You look like you're in need of some too.'

She might look tired and messy, but for once she felt

more alive and awake than a toddler after a nap. Ready for fun, not sleep. Was Nathan responsible for that? Away from work she didn't get so wound up around him, took his comments on the chin. 'I might go for a run first. That always helps clear my mind.' *Anything to shake you out of my head.*

'Running doesn't wake you up?'

'Not often. I'm usually exhausted and a hot shower finishes me off.'

His eyes widened briefly. 'Right,' was all he said, but he managed one of those devastating smiles.

When she could breathe properly, she growled, 'I thought you were leaving?'

'Can't a guy change his mind?'

The smile was still going on and now her legs were starting to protest about keeping her upright. Legs that were supposed to take her for a run. The couch was looking mighty good right about now. With or without Nathan? She wanted *Nathan*? Hell, when she finally woke up she didn't do it in half-measures. There hadn't been any sex in her life for a long time and now every last cell in her body was sitting up, fighting to be noticed.

'No,' she muttered around the need clogging her throat. Not sure if the 'no' had been directed at Nathan or herself. This was not going anywhere. They worked together. He was confident, she wasn't. That was a work in progress. He'd have a woman in his life. What gorgeous-looking man didn't? She'd get over this lust as soon as he left. Or in the next hour while she was out jogging. Or while she was in bed sleeping. Or on the train going into work tonight. She would. It was only an aberration in her carefully controlled world. A damned distracting aberration, but it would pass. No choice.

'Can I have your phone number?' Nathan pulled his phone from his pocket.

So much for passing. He'd raised the ante. 'Why?'

His dark eyebrows rose. 'So I can call when I'm going to take the car for that spin. Is that all right?'

If she was supposed to be getting over her reaction to him, then why was the thought of going for a ride with Nathan winding her belly tighter than ever? Rattling off the number, she hoped she'd got it right. She could've given him the number for the zoo for all she knew. 'I'll look forward to it.' She headed for the door and hauled it open, needing to get him out of her small space where he took up all the air and made her feel tiny and fragile, and so, so alive.

Guess this was what getting a life meant. She had to pause, evaluate what was happening, figure out why she felt like this with Nathan when no one else brought on these feelings. No, no more pausing, hanging around waiting to see what the universe threw at her next. Try taking control instead. Slowly.

Nathan stepped past her, leaving a faint trail of outdoorsy aftershave scent behind him.

She gulped. Were need, desire, hope rising because she truly was attracted to him? Or was this all about getting a new life and he was merely a stepping stone? It was something else to figure out.

'See you tonight.' Quickly closing the door, she leaned against it and tipped her head back to stare at the ceiling as though the answers to her questions were written there. The excitement tripping through her veins, warming her long-frozen heart, was real.

There'd been nothing slow about this debilitating sensation rocking her. Oh, no. Wham, bam, Nathan Lupton had stormed in and turned up the thermostat, taking her by surprise, and she didn't want to back off. Even if she should.

'Hell and damnation.' Nathan shook his head as he pulled into the drive and parked at the back of his large, sprawling house. Towards the end of last night's shift, quiet Molly had shown another side to herself, had become interesting. Except, having spent time with her dressed in a figure defining, classy blouse and trousers, sexy kept coming to mind, raising more questions than answers about what made her tick than anything had during the previous two months they'd worked together. From now on her stereotype uniform was not going to negate those images.

And the short time he'd spent in her apartment had him wanting to know more about where she came from, the life she'd led before moving to Sydney.

Hah. Know more? Or feel more? Touch more? Enjoy more? Learning all about her had become important. He had no idea why, except his hormones got wound up whenever she was near. Hot, alluring, *tempting* came to mind.

Temptation? The groan that spilled out of his mouth tasted of shock and disbelief. Sure, Molly was beautiful, had his hormones in a dither, but tempting? Yes, damn it all to hell and back. Because this was starting to feel like he was seriously back in the real world, where dating might happen. He'd thought for a while he might be ready, but reality was scary.

Slamming the car door harder than necessary, he

strode around the house and out to the fence lining the front lawn to stare across the public green space on the other side of a wide walking path to the Tasman Sea beyond. The light breeze meant no windsurfers doing their number on the waves. Which was a shame because right now he couldn't think of anything he'd rather do than get up on a board—and no doubt fall off just as quickly, since it had been a while since he'd last surfed. At least that would occupy his mind and put these damned fool ideas to bed.

Bed? Nathan groaned. He was exhausted, and needed sleep more than anything before signing on again that night. More than thinking about Molly.

But the idea of sprawling over his couch in front of the television and trying to doze off turned his blood to thick soup. There'd be no sleep while she rampaged through his mind. The hell of it was he didn't know why she was doing this to him when up until today he'd been more likely to get annoyed with her and wish she'd pester someone else. Sure, he was annoyed with her right now, but for all the wrong reasons. So much for getting her to put that cold shoulder to rest. Instead she'd been winding him up tighter than ever. At least she didn't have a clue how badly she was rattling his cage.

You sure about that?

Good question. He'd been determined not to let her see his reactions to her, to the scent of limes from her fruit basket, to relaxing and laughing in her company.

Yeah, and what was that doubt in her face when she'd picked up her phone and seen no ID displayed? Because something *had* darkened her eyes and tightened her face. Certainly more reaction than called for

by someone wanting to ask why she hadn't paid the
power bill or had she forgotten she was meant to be
at the dentist. One thing he knew for certain—she'd
never tell him.

The apartment had been a shock. 'Poky' had the
place sounding larger than it was. It was tastefully
decorated, though. Was that Molly's taste? Or had she
rented the place fully furnished? The late morning sun
had shone through the large, sparkling windows to
brighten the atmosphere. The place was spotless, her
few possessions gleamed. The two mugs on the shelf,
the two glasses and dinner plates, said lonely.

Turning back towards his house, Nathan hesitated.
Molly had mentioned maybe looking for somewhere
else to live with more space, a place that was connected to the outside world. There was a twist to her
story. Maybe she came from a tight community and
was missing that easy friendship with all the neighbours, except she didn't like the way the old woman
had told him which apartment was hers. He looked left,
right and back to his house. He knew his neighbours.
While they didn't live in each other's pockets, they
were there for each other if the need arose.

Don't even think it.

This place was further from work than her apartment, which meant a bus or car to the train station.

He strode towards the back, stopped and studied
his house. Slowly that familiar sense of belonging, of
having found his new place in the world right here,
rose, pushing other annoying emotions aside. With
each front room opening out onto the veranda that ran
the full width of the house with an overhanging roof,
it was a haven in summer and winter.

He'd said, 'I'm buying it,' the moment the real estate salesman had pulled up outside. An impulsive purchase, made two years after Rosie's death, yet nothing had caused him to regret his decision. At the time he'd been stuck in the past, so he'd gone looking for a new home that didn't echo with Rosie's laughter.

Coogee might be a little way out of the city for travelling to work, but the vista at the end of his lawn cancelled out any annoyance about that. He'd weathered storms that had wrecked the cliffs, baked in unrelenting sun, and surfed the waves, and had finally known a quiet within himself that had been missing for far too long. The large house and sprawling, uncontained grounds were his sanctuary.

It couldn't be more different from the small, cosy, modern home he and Rosie had shared. That one had been like her; everything had had its place and the colour schemes had been perfect, the neat gardens with their carefully spaced plants drawing passers-by to lean over the fence in admiration. While this place—it was more like him. Out of sync.

No. Molly doesn't need something like this.

He didn't need Molly in his space. It wouldn't remain a tranquil place to go when the world got on top of him if temptation came to live in the attached flat.

Occasionally he had tenants for short periods, usually medical personnel moving to Sydney General from out of town who needed temporary accommodation while they got somewhere more permanent sorted. He liked it when people moved in, and he was equally happy when they left again. Easy come, easy go. It was a waste having the flat going empty, and occasionally he'd thought of asking around work to see if anyone wanted to rent it permanently, but then he'd got cold feet. What if they didn't get on? Or if the noise level increased? Or if he plain wanted his whole house to himself?

The flat's more spacious than Molly's apartment.

Molly wouldn't be noisy or intrusive. They did argue quite often. But today he'd learned they could get along just fine.

But he'd find it very difficult to ask her to leave if the day came where he wanted to be alone.

Far safer for him to leave things as they stood.

Chapter 4

'You all right?' Nathan asked from the other side of the counter in the department's central hub where Molly was *supposed* to be writing up patient notes. Her head was so messed up with this new awareness of Nathan and wondering what he was doing that she hadn't seen him approaching.

'Couldn't be better,' she lied. 'I managed some sleep after my run.' It was true, though her kip had been filled with dreams of being held in Nathan's arms while she drove his car. Why were dreams so ridiculous? On all counts? 'What about you?'

He grimaced. 'I managed an hour before going to the airport, and then a couple more after an early dinner.'

That explained the shadows beneath his eyes. 'It goes with the territory.' Night shifts played havoc with sleep patterns.

'At least next week I'm on three to eleven. Back to...' he flicked his fingers in the air '...normal.'

'Me, too.' She glanced at the clipboard in his hand. 'You seeing Colin Montgomery next?'

His thick, brown-blond hair tumbled over his forehead as he nodded. 'I see he's got history of arrhythmia and is presenting with palpitations and chest pain.'

Molly followed him to their seventy-one-year-old patient and immediately noted down Colin's pulse and other obs. 'Did anyone come with you to the hospital?'

Colin shook his head. 'I've lived alone since my wife died two years ago.'

'I'm sorry to hear that. What about other family?' There was nothing in the notes about relatives to contact.

He blinked, and his mouth drooped. 'My son and I haven't spoken in years. Last I heard he lives somewhere in Brisbane.'

'How long have you had arrhythmia?' Nathan read the heart-monitor printout and asked pertinent questions.

'Twelve months, give or take.'

'When did the pain start?'

'Around eleven. When it didn't ease off I phoned for an ambulance. I hope I'm not wasting everyone's time. It's very busy in here.'

'A typical Friday night,' Molly assured him.

'Never think you're wasting our time. With your known condition, it's always best we check you out.' Nathan listened to his chest through a stethoscope. 'You're on warfarin. How steady are your test results?'

'Usually my bleeding times stay within the allowable range. Prothrombin, isn't it?' He didn't wait for an answer. 'But last week the test ran really high and I had to have the test every day until the results returned to normal.'

'Although that's not normal for people not on the drug, it is within the required range for someone taking the anticoagulant drug,' Nathan explained.

Colin looked worried. 'Isn't that dangerous?'

'It's what's preventing you having a stroke. That must've been explained when you first started taking it.'

Colin looked sheepish. 'It probably was, but at the time I was too worried about everything, and not being medically minded just accepted that I needed to take the warfarin to stay alive. I could've gone on the internet to find out more but I'd have confused myself further.'

'Relax. You're not the first to react that way, and you won't be the last.' Nathan locked a steady gaze on his patient. 'I'm referring you to Cardiology so they can run more tests to find out what's going on with this pain and that spike in your prothrombin results.'

'Better safe than sorry?' Colin enquired, his worry-filled eyes glued on his doctor.

Nathan calmed him with his straightforward manner. 'I don't believe there's a major problem but I'd prefer you spent at least the rest of tonight in the hospital, where you can be monitored and not at home alone, worrying about what might or might not be going on inside your chest.' He was good. 'That'd only raise your blood pressure, which we don't want happening.'

Colin relaxed more with every sentence.

While Nathan called Cardiology, Molly went to check on eight-year-old Ollie Brown, who'd fallen out of his bunk and broken an arm. 'Hey, young man, how's that head?' There was concern he'd got a concussion as well and a scan had been ordered.

'Hurts like stink.' Ollie grinned.

The grin vanished as his grandfather snapped, 'You're not on the farm now, lad.'

Molly chuckled. 'So you're a country guy? What are you doing in the middle of Sydney, then?' She wanted to observe Ollie for signs of confusion or amnesia.

'It's the school holidays,' Ollie said, as though she was the dumbest woman out. 'Granddad always lets us come to stay so we can do townie things, like go on the ferries and eat take-out food and stuff.' There was nothing wrong with his coherence.

'You forgot to mention that fighting with your brother was why you fell out of the blasted bunk in the first place.' The granddad scowled, but there was a load of love in his rheumy eyes.

'Connor started it.'

'You know better than to let him rile you, lad.'

Molly clapped her hands. 'Okay, guys, the orderly is on his way down to take you for the scan, Ollie. Mr Brown, you can go with him, if you'd like.'

Mr Brown nodded. 'Someone's got to keep an eye on the young pup.'

Before Ollie could say anything, Molly cut in, 'I'll be here when you get back. Then the doctor will decide if you can leave.'

Suddenly the bright, brave eight-year-old slumped and looked at his grandfather. 'I don't want to stay here. I want to go home.'

'Aw, shucks, lad. You'll have a grand time. The nurses will spoil you rotten.'

Leaving them to it, Molly headed for Kath Burgess's cubicle, only to have Hazel, the only female doctor on duty, call from the hub, 'Molly, I want you with me when I examine Kath. She's spent time with you already, and I think it's important not to bring in too many new faces since you managed to calm her down.'

'I agree.' The woman had been distraught when she'd arrived, clutching her stomach like it was going to split open, howling that she might be losing her baby. It had taken ages to quieten her enough to get some obs done.

'We all heard the commotion and our first instinct was to crowd in to see what we could do, until it quickly became obvious that the screeching was lowering to sobs and you had the situation under control. Nathan and I decided not to interfere unless you called for help. We didn't want to fire her up again.' Hazel was reading the triage notes.

'Thank goodness you did. She refuses to be seen by a male doctor.' That'd immediately put Molly on notice, wondering if Kath had been abused by a man, but when she'd tried to find out she had been told she'd fallen down the stairs at the back of her house. Molly had gone straight to Hazel to explain her concerns, but as Hazel had been about to suture a deep wound in a young male's thigh, she'd flagged Kath's notes instead and kept an eye out for whoever might be going into the cubicle.

'That doesn't sound good,' Hazel commented as she led the way into the small space where Kath lay curled up on the bed, a bunch of tissues clasped in her hand.

Closing the curtains, Molly watched Kath closely

as Hazel asked questions about what had brought her to hospital.

'I fell down the steps.'

'You're complaining of abdominal pain. How did that happen?'

'There was a toolbox there, all right?' Kath's voice was rising. 'I must've landed on that.'

'You don't know for sure?'

'I did.' Tears streamed down the woman's face.

Molly's heart went out to her. If only she could hug her and say, 'Tell us everything, and we'll get you help'—but she knew where that'd lead. The police would have to be informed, and social services would send someone to help. Kath had to be ready for what that involved. It wasn't as easy as someone who hadn't been abused would believe. Of course, Molly could be wrong, but she doubted it. It was like looking into her own eyes from the past.

When Molly had removed the sheet covering Kath and lowered her jeans and panties, she stepped aside for Hazel's examination, talking softly to Kath about anything that didn't broach the subject of her husband.

Finally Hazel straightened and pulled up Kath's clothes. 'You're not miscarrying. But I want you to remain in bed for the next few days, at least until the pain subsides. There's still a risk of miscarriage.'

'He won't be happy,' their patient said in a dead voice.

'About you staying in bed, or about not losing the baby?' Molly asked softly.

'What do you think?'

Both, if she was on the right page. But she kept quiet. Kath was getting wound up again. Better to keep her calm and only mention help was available if she was receptive.

Molly opened the curtains so they could keep an eye on her from the hub.

'Hey, you can't come in here without permission,' Hank said loudly from the other end of the department.

'Try and stop me,' came the angry voice of an unknown male.

'Come here,' Hank demanded.

'Where is she?'

Kath gasped, 'No,' and curled in on herself.

Molly asked, 'Someone you know?'

'My man. He's been drinking since early afternoon.'

Great. Just what they needed. The sound of curtains being jerked open and sliding doors rammed back made her skin crawl. He was getting closer, and it wouldn't be long before he found who he was looking for.

'Stop right there,' Hank ordered.

'This is going to be fun,' Hazel muttered.

'Stop. You are disturbing our patients.' Nathan stood at the central counter, hands tense at his sides, his feet planted slightly apart. 'Tell me who you've come to see and I'll check if you can visit.'

'You've got my wife hiding in here. I'm going to find her. Now,' the man shouted.

Kath buried her head under the pillow.

Then her husband stormed into the cubicle, the rage in his face terrifying. 'Get out of my way,' he yelled at Hazel, raising a fist.

It was instinctive. Molly saw movement out of the corner of her eye. One step closed the gap. Her arm came up, locked with the assailant's. Using his forward motion she hauled him toward her, dropped her weight forward and swung her upper body around, taking him with her, dropping him to the floor before landing on top of him, her knees pressing into his shoulders, her hand still tight around his lower arm.

Silence fell over the department.

Then the man began swearing. He struggled beneath her, trying to push her off, getting madder by the second.

She was about to be tossed aside by a raging man who had no brakes on his temper. Then Nathan planted a foot firmly in the small of the man's back. 'Stay still.' Under his breath he added, 'Or, hell, you're going to regret it.'

She was probably the only person to hear that. Certainly the man underneath her either hadn't or didn't believe Nathan because he was still trying to get up.

Then Hank grabbed the man's flailing arms and slammed them down on the floor. 'Shut up, buster.'

Nathan tapped her lightly. 'You can get off now. We've got him.'

She did, fast, not taking her eyes off her opponent until she'd stepped away. 'Has someone called Security?' Where had they been when this guy had got into the department? Taking a break? At least one security guard had to remain at the main entrance at all times.

'Right here.' Two uniformed men raced towards them and took over.

'You okay?' Nathan asked, his hand on her elbow.

'Sure.' She nodded.

'Molly, he was going to hit me.' Hazel nudged Nathan aside to throw her arms around her and hold tight. 'I froze when I saw his arm come up.'

Molly squeezed back, a trembling starting up in her belly and spreading throughout her body. 'Glad *I* didn't.'

Hazel stepped back and wiped her eyes. 'Seriously, you saved me. He was aiming for my face.'

'You reacted so fast, it had to be instinctive. I'm impressed.' There was something akin to awe in Nathan's voice as his hand moved from her elbow to her shoulder. 'Come and sit down. You look like you've been hit by a bus.'

Now that the adrenaline was ebbing, that was exactly how she felt. Flattened. Shocked. 'I can't believe I did that.'

'How'd you know what to do?' Nathan asked after he had her seated and parked his butt on the counter. 'One second that man was attacking Hazel and the next you threw him on the floor and sat on him.'

'Not quite. I had my knees on his shoulders.' She gulped. That had been so close. Not once had she thought about what she was doing. When she'd caught sight of that swinging arm out of the corner of her eye the rest had followed naturally. As she'd been taught to do in her judo classes. If only she'd done martial arts when she'd been with Paul, she might have stopped him in his tracks permanently. 'I saw a movement and instantly went into defence mode. I've got an orange belt in judo,' she added when she saw the confusion enter Nathan's eyes.

'That explains it.' Maybe, but that confusion remained.

Molly hastened to divert him. 'I've always wondered how I'd react if I needed to. Now I know.'

'Why did you learn judo?' Straight to the point.

'Nathan, not now. I need to get back to Kath. The attack proved what I suspected—she's being abused. She'll need reassuring her husband's not going to get near her while she's in here. We'll also have to convince her to stay in hospital for the rest of the night.'

You're talking too much. He's going to see right through you.

Molly clamped her mouth shut and tried to stand up to pull away from those warm fingers still on her shoulder, but Nathan only tightened his hold.

'Sit down. You're as pale as the walls, and shaking like a leaf in a breeze. I'm getting you a strong coffee.'

Actually, she was damned pleased with herself. Who'd have believed she could take a man down? She opened her mouth to argue, but nothing came out when she locked her eyes with Nathan's and found compassion there, and something else. Something hinting at him beginning to understand what made her tick. Her bout of verbal diarrhoea might bring unwelcome questions.

Then a shudder ripped through her. Sinking deeper onto the chair, she looked away, fidgeting with the hem of her top as nausea crept up her throat. That had been too close. What if he'd hit Hazel? Or her? The guy had been off the scale with rage. Not cold and calculating but hot and loose. Was that how he treated Kath all the time?

Molly's heart pounded. She was safe, but Kath wasn't. Seeing that man come charging through the department as though he had the right to do as he pleased with his wife had turned her blood to ice. And brought back memories of a fist hitting her stomach, slamming against her ribs, under her chin.

Nathan was crouched in front of her, his hands now covering hers. 'Your reaction's normal.'

She nodded, afraid that if she opened her mouth she'd never shut up.

'There's more to this, isn't there?'

Another nod, sharp and uncontrollable.

'Hank,' Nathan called over his shoulder. 'Molly and Hazel could do with coffee, please. Make them sweet.'

'Onto it.'

Molly glanced around, away from those all-seeing eyes in front of her. 'Hazel?'

'I'm right here, and, like you, I've got the shakes. I'm also angry and would love a chance to tell that creep what I think of him, coming in here and trying to hurt people who want to help his wife.' Hazel pulled a chair near to Molly's. 'How're you doing?'

'I'm good.' She wanted to laugh and rejoice in being strong. She wanted to cry and hide, and go home. She wanted to bury her head against Nathan's broad shoulder, breathe him in, and feel those warm muscles under his top against her face. She wanted to be comforted by this man she knew without a doubt would never hurt her. But it wasn't happening.

One, they were in the hub of the ED, surrounded by staff and patients, and there was work to do. Two, what she wanted and what she'd get might be two different things, and right now she couldn't handle the disappointment if she'd misinterpreted that look in Nathan's eyes and he put her aside. So she'd toughen up, drink her coffee and get back to work. It was the only way to go. Once the shaking stopped, and some sense of equilibrium returned to her brain. 'I'll be right in a minute.'

Nathan said, 'Don't rush. We've got you both covered until you're ready. Even if it takes the rest of the shift.' He might be talking to them both but it was her hands he was gently squeezing.

Her bottom lip trembled. 'Thanks.'

'Take pride in what you did.' His return smile slowed her stewing stomach. 'I'd rather have you on my side than against me.'

'Then you're glad we're getting on?' No trembling in her smile now. Pride was appearing. She'd been strong, had helped Hazel. Did this mean that no man would ever again hit her? Not without a fight, anyway. Her chin lifted, and she eyeballed Nathan. 'Seems things are looking up for me.' Her new life was well and truly under way.

'Here, coffee for two.' Hank placed two mugs on the counter. 'I pinched some chocolate biscuits out of the fridge as well. Thought they might be better than sugar in your drinks.'

Nathan stood up. 'I'd better see to some patients. Don't rush, either of you.'

Molly reached for her mug, paused. 'Can I suggest only female staff work with Kath? She was leery of Hazel examining her. She's not going to like any male staff approaching her.'

Nathan nodded. 'I'll ask Myra to take over.' Myra had taken Vicki's place for the night and was a midwife and nurse who did extra shifts in ED for the money.

As Nathan passed Molly to pick up a file, his hand brushed her upper arm, and when she looked at him he gave her another soft, heart-melting smile, but sorrow darkened his eyes.

Damn it, he knew. Without being told, he'd put the pieces together and come up with the correct picture.

He would want to know more. Would demand to be told everything. No, he wouldn't. They worked together, they weren't best buddies or in a relationship. He might like to know but he wasn't going to ask her for details. He was a gentleman. Wasn't he? Guess she'd find out soon enough.

For the remainder of the shift Nathan had trouble remaining calm whenever he glanced around to check on Molly. Anger at an unknown man boiled up. Given half the chance he'd like to tear out of the department to go and find him, beat him to a pulp. Not that he'd ever hit anyone before, but sweet, gorgeous Molly did so not deserve to be beaten. Not that she'd said anything to suggest it'd happened, but he knew. The sudden grief that had filled her eyes as the shock of what she'd done to Kath's husband had worn off told him there was a story behind her usually withdrawn manner.

'Glad that's over.' The woman in his head handed a file to one of the incoming shift nurses. 'I'm ready for my bed.'

Not so fast. 'I'll give you a lift home.' Nathan put on his no-nonsense voice in the hope she'd agree without an argument.

'The train will be quicker.'

He should have known it wouldn't work. 'Throw in breakfast and you'll be able to justify going the slow way.' He'd just asked her out? It might only be breakfast, but in a roundabout way it was a date. He hadn't thought before putting his mouth into gear.

So you want to withdraw the invitation?

Nathan's chest rose. No, he damned well didn't. This wasn't only about what'd happened earlier and the revelations that had come with it. He couldn't deny the need to get to know Molly better, to learn exactly who was behind that façade she presented to the world most of the time. He sucked a breath. Which only showed how deep the mire he was floundering in had become. It had happened so fast he couldn't keep up.

Molly was blinking at him like a possum caught in headlights. 'Do you mean that?'

'About breakfast? Yes. Why wouldn't I?'

'Because you're kind and probably want to be a caring boss, making sure I'm all right. If that's the case then believe me when I say I'm fine, and there's food in my fridge that'll suffice for breakfast.'

That scratched at his calm. He was not playing the boss here. He'd stepped beyond that comfortable zone—into what, he wasn't quite sure, but knew he needed to find out. 'Bet you haven't got eggs and hollandaise sauce.'

'Low blow.' There was a wariness creeping into her eyes. She was worried what he'd ask about the martial arts.

He couldn't deny he was ready to explode over what he perceived had happened in her past, but if she didn't want to talk about it, that was her prerogative and he'd accept that. 'That's me. When I want something I'll try everything in my power to get it.' *Except use my fists.*

Molly obviously had no worries on that score because she gave him an exhausted smile. 'I'd love a ride, and breakfast.'

'Why didn't you just say so?' He grinned and took her elbow, wishing he could put an arm around her shoulders and tuck her in close. But they were still in the department and already there were a couple of raised eyebrows and knowing smiles going on. Neither were they *that* close.

'Don't like to be too obvious,' Molly retorted. Then yawned. 'Thank goodness for weekends. I'm over this week.'

'Evening shift next week, here we come.' After two days off, and hopefully a ride in his car. The Blue Mountains were looking good, and the weather was forecast to be fine and crisp. 'You been to the Blue Mountains?'

'That's a long way to go for breakfast.' Her tempting mouth gave him another smile that struck under his ribs and made his heart lift its pace.

The mountains wouldn't be too far for the morning meal if they went there the day before and stayed over in a hillside lodge, enjoying the views and a superb meal, making the most of a large, soft bed throughout the night. But that wasn't happening. *Not yet.* Nathan tripped over his own flat feet. Where the hell had that come from?

You were going to get her onside, not so close you'd get to know her so well.

He hadn't forgotten, but the rules had changed the moment she'd taken Burgess down. He had yet to figure out where he went with this now. Molly was an enigma that he was getting more than interested in. First he had to find out if he was right about her past or way off the mark. It certainly explained her edginess over mixing socially with people. Until yesterday, when she'd participated in Vicki's celebration, when she'd come out of her shell in a hurry, even singing 'Happy Birthday' in front of everyone. Not that Molly had realised what she was doing at first.

Nathan followed her to the lift, and when the door closed, he tapped the button for the basement and the car park. 'You know people will talk about what happened?'

'Fingers crossed, come Monday something else will have happened that'll take everyone's attention.' She leaned against the wall, looking so tired he wanted to wrap her up and take her home for a few uninterrupted hours' sleep. Followed by…

'How about we go to Coogee for that breakfast?'

Her eyes widened. 'That's a fair way past my apartment.'

'So it is.' What would Rosie have thought of Molly? Would she have liked her? Yes, he thought, she would. Rosie had insisted he had to move on when she'd gone, wasn't to sit around feeling sorry for himself. She'd gone as far as saying bluntly, 'Find another woman to love, have that family you've always wanted. Don't live in regret for what we've lost. That would make our time together worthless.'

But should he really take Molly to his home, show her the vacant flat? Should he start thinking ahead, instead of always looking over his shoulder at the past?

Chapter 5

Why go to Coogee when there were plenty of cafés near the hospital? Or in Bondi Junction. Molly watched Nathan's firm hands with their easy movements as he drove through the morning rush hour traffic. Hands that she now knew could be gentle. Shuffling further down into the luxurious leather seat, she stifled a yawn. Which was rude when Nathan was taking her out, but the night had caught up with her.

'Have you always lived in Coogee?' she asked, in need of a distraction to stay awake. Not that Nathan wasn't one, but he might leave her on the side of the road if she stared at him all the way to the well-known beach.

'Only since I bought the house. I like being near the sea, and Coogee appealed. Before that I lived on the north shore.' His voice hitched on that last sentence.

'The surfing?' He'd told her he used to surf.

'It wasn't a priority, as I rarely rode the board at the time. Though that's turned out to be a bonus, like a lot of things about the property. I do hit the waves these days. Besides, the house ticked a lot of boxes and had that wow factor, so I bought it.'

She'd like to see the place sometime. It would tell her a lot about Nathan. Her head nodded forward, and her eyelids drooped shut. Sitting up straighter, she forced her eyelids up and stared out at the road ahead. She'd buy her own home sometime. A small, warm house that would wrap around her; not a sterile mansion that showed off to her friends how wealthy she was. That particular house hadn't been her choice. It'd had Paul written all over the grand frontage, the sweeping staircase, the expansive rooms. The place had felt more like a mausoleum than a home, and as though she as much as the house was on display to all and sundry.

'Not your first property?'

'No. The one I owned first was cosier and more family orientated.' He paused.

Molly waited, hoping she stayed awake long enough to hear what else he had to say.

'I was married. We were hoping to raise our children there. But four years ago it went horribly wrong.'

Wide awake now, she touched Nathan's arm. 'I'm sorry. Life can play nasty when it chooses.'

'You're not wrong there.' Nathan flicked the indicator and pulled into the outside lane, keeping a safe distance from the truck in front, his fingers tapping impatiently on the steering wheel.

She knew the grief of losing the chance of having a family. It undermined everything she wanted for her future. Unlike her, Nathan could have children if he chose to. Molly returned to watching those fingers as they played a silent, sharp rhythm on the wheel.

'Rosie got ALL.'

Acute lymphatic leukaemia. Molly's heart dropped for Nathan, and his wife. What could she say? No words could help. But a hug might—except hugging Nathan while he was driving along the city highway wasn't conducive to safety. Like her dream? She squeezed his arm softly, and remained quiet for the rest of the ride out to the beach.

Had Nathan told her about his wife in a bid to soften the blow when he asked her about her past? Or were they getting a little closer and he wanted to put it out there straight-up? Yesterday's argument and breakfast seemed a lifetime ago. They'd been scratchy with each other, then friendly to the point he'd had a cup of tea in her apartment. At the time it had seemed a vast improvement in their relationship, and since then she'd exposed the results of her darker side, and he was still happy to spend time alone with her.

Having spent the past two years running solo, to have now shared time talking with a man was hard to take in. It excited her about the future. Seemed she was still capable of mixing and mingling, of having a laugh, of doing things outside her four walls.

'Wakey-wakey.'

A gentle shaking of her arm had Molly sitting up and staring around. 'Sorry.' She never went to sleep in the company of anyone, let alone a man. Another point in Nathan's favour. 'This is Coogee?' The sweeping beach with its golden sand sang to her, reminding her of beach holidays with Gran. Lowering the window, she listened to the waves smacking down on the beach beyond the steps leading down from the street.

'Yes, it sure is.' He glanced along the street, then back at her. 'And, Molly?'

Uh-oh. What had she done? She'd been asleep, couldn't be too serious. 'Yes?'

'Stop saying sorry all the time. Falling asleep isn't a crime. It'd been coming ever since you dropped Burgess in ED. Shock or an adrenaline high does that.'

'I won't get into trouble for throwing him on the floor, will I?' It had only just occurred to her it might be seen as a bad move, she could have endangered others. Not that there'd been any chance of stopping her reaction.

'I'd like to see anyone try to make you out to be the villain. If you hadn't stopped him, Hazel would now have a badly beaten face, at the very least. Believe me, everyone's on your side. The word was going round the hospital within minutes that you stepped up and the question's being asked—where was Security at the time he walked through the doors into the department?'

'He could've gained access by asking to see his wife. He didn't need to get all uptight and angry.' That still would have upset Kath, though.

'Unfortunately you're right. Kath hadn't said she wouldn't see him, and I doubt she would've if asked.' He pushed open his door and unwound his long body to stand upright.

Before Molly had gathered her bag, or her wits, Nathan was opening her door. 'Come on. Let's go and eat.'

She grinned. 'Now you mention it, I'm starving.'

'There's a surprise.' Nathan laughed, and held out a

hand to take hers, which he didn't drop as they began walking along the footpath.

For once she didn't try and pull away, or start filling in the sudden shyness swamping her by talking a load of drivel. Instead she looked around at the massive hotel built against the hill, and the row of small shops lining the street heading up the valley. She enjoyed the sense of freedom at being able to hold a man's hand without being frightened, or wary. A warm, strong hand belonging to a caring, exciting guy who was starting to get under her skin in ways she'd long believed wouldn't happen in this lifetime.

Then she let out a sigh. There was no getting away from telling him the bare facts about her past. Nathan had guessed the basics so to go all quiet on him when he was being so darned kind and friendly wasn't right, even when she hadn't told anyone the sordid details since she'd left Perth two years ago. She'd give him an abridged version. Bare facts, and move on.

After they'd eaten.

'Hello, Nathan.' The waitress placed menus before them. 'How's your week been?'

'Hectic, as per usual. Eva, let me introduce Molly O'Keefe. She's a nurse in the department.'

'Hey, Molly, nice to meet you. Are you living around here?'

The girl looked vaguely familiar, which didn't make sense. Unless she lived in the same apartment block as Molly did, but what were the odds? 'Over in Bondi Junction, unfortunately.' She'd love to have an apartment with those views to wake up to every day. It wasn't happening any time soon. Her bank balance couldn't cope. The money from her half of the marital property was locked in an investment, where it was staying until she decided what to do with it. The money was tainted, as far as she was concerned. Though there was her inheritance from Gran. Hmm. Possibilities started popping up. Her mother would be quick to offer assistance to make up for letting her down in the past, but she'd never ask.

'I know what you mean. It's beautiful around here.' Eva looked at Nathan. 'The usual?'

'You've got steak on the menu?' Molly laughed.

Eva gaped at her. 'Steak? No. The full Aussie breakfast.'

Molly's laugh got louder. 'Do you ever cook your own breakfast?'

'Cook it? Hell, no. Do I tip something out of a cardboard box into a bowl and add milk? Yes, more often than you seem to think.' He grinned before nodding to the waitress. 'Definitely, the works. Molly might take time deciding so can we have a flat white and a long black in the meantime?'

'Coming up.'

As Eva headed across to the barista coffee machine, Molly began scanning the menu. 'I feel I know Eva from somewhere.'

'ED. She came in with burns to her legs after a cook knocked boiling water off the stovetop and onto her.'

'She was in agony. The head chef came with her, and was so upset you had to calm him down as well.' It had happened during her first week in the department, and she'd been impressed with Nathan's handling of the chef's stress when it was Eva who had needed his attention. 'You helped them both.'

'Later, when the chef had gone, Eva told me the restaurant had a bad safety record and she wasn't going back. I put her in touch with Henri, who owns this place.'

'You did me a huge favour.' Eva placed two coffees before them. 'Molly?'

'Mushrooms on toast, and lots of crispy bacon.'

'Good choice.'

It was. The creamy sauce the mushrooms came in was divine, and the bacon done to perfection. 'I might have to reserve my own table after this.' Molly grinned as she pushed her plate aside and dabbed her lips with a paper napkin. Coogee wasn't so far from Bondi Junction that she couldn't make the trip occasionally to eat scrumptious food, check out those shops and dabble her toes in the sea.

'Help yourself to mine.' Nathan smiled, those questions back in his eyes now that breakfast was over.

Even knowing how unlikely it was, she'd been hoping he'd let it go. Yet she also thought that by telling him about Paul she'd be testing the water to see how he reacted. It'd be a barometer for the future and how she went about revealing her past to any man she might get serious about. Draining her water, she set the glass down. 'Feel like walking along the beach?' She could not sit here revealing everything, not with him directly opposite and she firmly in his line of vision.

'You read my mind.'

'Oh, no, I didn't.' She could no more read what he was thinking than ride a wave like two surfers were doing out there.

Only three other individuals were on the beach, two in a hurry to get their walk done, probably to head back indoors where it was warmer. Molly zipped her jacket up to her chin.

Beside her, Nathan slipped his hands into his pockets and matched her pace. They were halfway along the beach before she said, 'My divorce came through last Monday. I got the paperwork on Thursday.'

'Was that why you had a toast to yourself at Vicki's breakfast?'

'You noticed?' Was there anything she could keep from this man? Was that good? Or bad? She'd go for good, with a wary eye.

'I've started observing lots of things about you.' Then Nathan stopped. 'If that sounds creepy, I apologise. It's not meant to. It's only that my opinion of you has changed since yesterday morning.'

She glanced across, and couldn't resist smiling. 'We didn't exactly get off to a great start, did we?' Could be that deep down she'd sensed how he could affect her if she let him near, and so subconsciously she'd been protecting herself by pushing him away. 'Of course we might go back to being grumpy with each other next time we're at work.' Fingers crossed that didn't happen. She liked the man, more than liked, but that emotion was for another day further down the track—if they spent more time together outside the hospital. Nathan had mentioned a car trip. Should she go? It meant making herself vulnerable, if only because he was so considerate towards her, something that still had her defence mechanisms coming to the fore.

'How long were you married?' Nathan brought her back to reality with a bump.

'Two years.' Her voice had taken on an emotionless tone, designed not to give anything away she didn't choose to. 'At first it was wonderful.' Deep breath, stare at the sand ahead. 'And then it wasn't.'

'I'm sorry to hear that.'

She was sorry she had reason to say it. 'He hit me. Often, towards the end. There was no pleasing him when he was in a mood.'

'I figured that out when you talked about Kath's problem. You understand what she's dealing with.' Nathan came closer, his arm touching hers, his hand now between them—relaxed and there for her. Or so she hoped.

'Every last emotion,' she admitted.

'I hoped I was wrong.' Then he asked, 'Can I hold you?'

She didn't know whether to laugh or cry. Nathan was asking if it was all right to hold her. Pausing in her mad dash along the beach, she faced him square on. 'Yes, please.'

As his arms wrapped around her she became aware of the tension gripping his torso. It didn't frighten her. Again unusual. It only went to show how much she instinctively trusted this man. 'Nathan?'

His forehead rested against hers. 'I am spitting mad. No man has the right to hurt a woman physically. It's appalling.'

'And degrading, and terrifying, and soul destroying,' she whispered.

'Yet you were brave and left him.'

That sounded so simple. Pack a bag and walk out the front door, never to return. Don't look over her shoulder—except she'd been doing that ever since, though not any more. Other than on bad days when she was feeling down.

Nathan continued. 'You're still looking out in case

he turns up. At one stage I saw you checking every male that came into the café yesterday.'

She pulled back in his arms to watch the expressions crossing his face. He was angry. For her. The tension eased. No one had done that for her since this appalling situation had begun. Not even the people who should've been there for her. 'He can't. He's locked up for years to come.'

'At least that's good.'

She could get to like this man a lot. Like? Or love? Why not? She was allowed to love again, she just had to get it right next time. 'He escaped once and came after me in Adelaide where I'd moved to get away from the people who thought I'd made it all up. They changed their attitude after the trial, but for me it was too late.' Except for her mum, and that was still a work in progress. 'I tried staying on in Adelaide but there were too many shadows at the corners so I moved here.'

'I'm surprised you can get through a day without checking behind every door in the department and studying each male patient who comes in.' So far Nathan had accepted everything she'd told him without criticism. He'd never understand just how much that meant.

'I used to when I began working at the medical centre in Bondi Junction, but it's exhausting so one day I made up my mind to stop. Not that it happened instantly, but I'm heaps better than I used to be.'

'That says you're comfortable here. Am I right?'

'I'm getting there, and, yes, I want to make a life for myself in Sydney. I will never return to Perth.' Her mother had finally accepted that, right about when she'd acknowledged she'd let her daughter down by not believing her about Paul in the beginning.

Nathan leaned in and his lips touched her forehead, brushed over her skin, before he straightened. 'Good answer. You're one tough lady, Molly O'Keefe.'

The wind gusted sharply, flicking sand at them, and Molly shuddered. From the cold or the memories she wasn't sure. Both, most likely. 'I'm starting to believe that.'

'So you should. I'll say this once, and then I'll keep quiet unless you ever want to talk about it again.' Nathan's hand entwined with hers, and she had no compulsion to pull away. 'You are so brave.' Then he kissed both her cheeks and straightened. 'Let's go find somewhere warmer.'

Molly hadn't told him everything. Nothing about the real possibility she'd never get pregnant again. That was just too close, too painful, to reveal. A huge negative when she was trying to be positive. When they reached his car, she asked, 'Where shall we go now?' She wasn't ready for this to end. She hadn't felt so at ease in years, and it was addictive. She wanted more time with Nathan. Plain and simple. Complicated and interesting.

Nathan looked at her over the roof of his car, a look of disbelief darkening his features as he said, 'I want to show you something.'

Was he sure about that? From the way he was looking at her she thought he was more inclined to take her to the bus station and buy her a ticket out of town. 'What?'

'Wait and see.'
Quick, think of somewhere to take her to. Avoid

going home. Because once you show her the self-contained flat you're sunk. There'll be no backing out.

Nathan sucked in chilly air and drove through town, berating himself silently for giving in to the horror with which Molly's story had filled him. Rosie would understand how he had to make sure she was always safe, to protect her from those shadows that haunted her and probably would for a long time to come despite her courageous words. Only then would that beautiful, heart-wrenching smile return more and more readily. A smile that rocked him off his steady stride and woke up parts of him that had been asleep for way too long. Not only his libido, but emotions of longing, caring and wanting to nurture.

Because of that smile he felt as though he'd stepped off the edge of a cliff and had no idea how far below he'd land, or in what condition. Neither did he care.

'No one's said that to me since Gran died. Wait and see,' Molly mimicked in a funny voice. 'Don't be impatient, girl.'

Despite the mire in his head, he laughed. Because Molly made him forget what he'd survived and had him wanting to do whatever it took to get her life back. And his. 'You were close to your grandmother?'

'She was my rock, especially as a child. Believed in me, and taught me a lot about being strong, and not taking for granted everything my mother provided.' Molly hiccupped and turned to stare out the window at the passing scenery. 'If only I'd listened harder before I got married.'

Anger rose in Nathan. Give him ten minutes with the man who'd done this to her. But it wasn't happening, which was probably just as well. He had to accept she was recovering—without any input from him. He swallowed, flicked the music on, and pointed out some landmarks as he drove.

Molly stared out the window. 'It's a beautiful spot.' A gasp erupted from that soft mouth as he turned onto his street. 'You're taking me to your house.'

No fooling her. 'Yes. If I'm keeping you from getting some sleep then I'm sorry. We don't have to stay long and then I'll run you home.'

If I haven't found another reason for bringing you here apart from the real one.

'I stopped wanting to go to sleep before the mushrooms arrived at the table.'

'Good to know I haven't been boring you the whole morning.' He laughed. Again. See? Molly did that to him. It was scary. Yes, and a little bit fun—exciting, even. Could Rosie have been right when she'd said he would love again? Pulling into his drive, he slowed, braked, and breathed deeply. Who'd have known lungs could ache so sharply when deprived of oxygen? 'This is the back. Come around the front.'

She was quiet as they walked along the pebbled pathway to the fenced edge of his property and looked over the public walkway to the grass area and the ocean beyond. Her silence continued for a good five minutes, making Nathan nervous, though he had no idea why. About to ask her what she was thinking, he hesitated, and was rewarded with a big smile. One of those ones that warmed him from his heart to the tips of his toes, and all places in between.

'It's stunning,' she said with a spark in her eyes he hadn't seen before. 'Truly fabulous.'

Then she might be open to his suggestion. If it was

the right thing to offer. Hell, he was nervous. Strange. It wasn't as if he was putting his heart on the line— he was merely helping Molly out. No, he'd been lucky in love once. No one got a second crack at that. Spinning around, he began striding back towards the house. There was no denying, though, that to have Molly in his space meant never getting her out of his head. Did he want to? So much for a challenge. Now he had another one. To love or to walk away while he still could. He stumbled. Damn, but he needed to get a new pair of shoes. These ones were tripping him left and right.

'Nathan? Are you all right?' Molly called from a little way behind him.

'I'm fine,' he replied tersely. 'Come inside.' His alter ego wasn't letting him away with not saying why he'd brought her home. Pressing the numbers to the security system a little too hard, he ground his teeth in frustration. He didn't know if he was coming or going, but helping Molly out was suddenly top of his list. Spontaneity was not one of his strong characteristics, and yet...

At the entrance Molly hesitated, making him feel uncomfortable. His fault. He should have told her straight away why he'd brought her here. 'You mentioned looking for somewhere bigger than your apartment. I have a self-contained flat you might be interested in renting.' There. He couldn't retract it. Heading down the hall, he held his breath. Would she follow? Or would she run out of the house screaming he'd gone too far? No, she wasn't running. Neither was she saying anything. Walking into the flat's living area, he turned to face her. Stunned was the only way to describe her expression. 'Molly?'

'Why would you offer me somewhere to live?'

I have no idea. Except for this strange sensation poking me in the belly—and the chest.

'If you want somewhere temporary, that's fine. Your call.'

Stunned turned to irritated. 'Thanks.' Sarcasm dripped between them. She wasn't looking around, that fierce look he'd only got to know yesterday was back. Worse, her hands were on her hips, fingers tight.

Obviously he wasn't going to be let off the question swinging between them. 'This is going to waste, and if you can use it, why not?' Totally true, just not all the truth.

Her hands dropped away, the fierceness softened.

A return to her good books? He hoped so. He believed more than he could have imagined that he needed her to accept he had her back.

'Thank you,' Molly said. He'd have missed the lifting of her lips if he hadn't been so focused on her. 'I'm a bit surprised. Actually, forget a bit. I'm shocked. I mean, we haven't exactly been the best of friends— until now—yet you're saying I should move into your house?'

'Take a look around, Molly. That's all I'm suggesting.'

And don't ask me anything I'm not prepared to answer—because I don't actually have the answers.

Relief spiralled through him as she wandered away to peek into the double bedroom and then the bathroom, and back to the living room with the kitchen in the corner. At least she was looking. That had to be a good sign. She wasn't about to chop his head off with one of those fast judo moves. He opened the glass doors leading onto the small deck overlooking the sweeping front lawn, which gave the flat a sense of more space than was real. He knew the instant she came to stand beside him, his whole body being on Molly alert.

'It's lovely. And private.'

That had to be a plus, surely? Or maybe not, given her need for security. 'Like I said, I fell in love with this place the moment I set eyes on it and have no regrets.' Nathan looked around and felt happiness swelling in his chest. He'd got it right, and could picture his children running around the lawn one day in the future, when his heart got back to being more than a pump. Something else Rosie had been right about.

'I can see why.' Molly was stalling.

His gut tightened. He *wanted* her to move in. Why? As she'd pointed out, they'd hardly got on until yesterday, their norm not having been overly friendly. Yet in little more than twenty-four hours they had done a complete flip. He'd held her in his arms, caressed her with his lips, held her hand as they'd walked to the café, breathed her scent. And found none of that was nearly enough.

'Come on. You need to see the water up close.' Once again her hand was in his as he strode out, heading back towards the grass strip and sea beyond. Now who was stalling? He did not want to hear her say, no, thanks, and that she'd find somewhere else more suitable to live in her own time.

Damn. He should be grateful if she came out with that. What was wrong with him? A few hours in Molly's company and he acted crazy, inviting her to live in his house and holding her hand like they had something going on. His fingers relaxed their grip on hers and he put a bit of space between them. Tried for sane and sensible. Boring.

'Nathan, do you honestly think it would work with me living here when we're usually on the same shifts in the ED? We'll never get away from each other.'

Go for ordinary, light and friendly. 'You don't think two breakfasts makes us best friends now?'

She stared up at him, those hands back on her hips, this time a hold that didn't indicate her life depended on it, fingers still pink. 'I'm not sure that's what I want.'

'You prefer us being aloof with each other?'

The riotous curls flicked all over her scalp as she shook her head. 'I know you better than that now.' Her mouth lifted, those lips curving seductively. The green in her eyes gleamed like sun on an emerald.

His heart skittered. What the hell? Reaching for her, he brought his mouth to rest on hers, waited in case she didn't want this. When she didn't move away, the need clawing throughout his body won out, and he pressed his lips against hers, and proceeded to kiss her as he'd been thinking of doing since yesterday. Apparently since the day she'd arrived in the ED, if his sense of finally getting somewhere, of the future opening up, was to be believed.

Molly O'Keefe had done a number on him, good and proper. Funny thing was, he didn't give a damn.

Chapter 6

Molly fell against Nathan, her breasts pressing into him, her hands wound around his back to feel those muscles tighten under her palms as the kiss deepened. This was Nathan Lupton, and they were kissing. Not any old kiss either, but something that turned her on and made her knees weak and her heart rate go off the scale. She should stop, pull away.

She didn't want to. Couldn't. It was as though they'd been building towards this moment once they'd found themselves sitting together at breakfast yesterday. It was like being stuck in the path of a tornado with nowhere to hide. Not that she wanted to. So much for not trusting people. Except, not once had Nathan made her think he'd ever hurt her. Instead he'd indicated he'd go after anyone who tried to get to her.

This was starting over, getting on with a new life,

and if it involved getting closer to a man then she had to take the chance. She was done with stagnating. Why wouldn't she want an exciting man in her life? It wasn't as though she'd been neutered. Everything might have been on hold, yet now the barriers were falling fast, not one at a time, as she'd expected, but crashing at her feet in a pile. Leaning closer, she increased the pressure of her mouth on his and went with the wonderful moment, let the exquisite sensations his kiss created have their way and tease her with yearnings long forgotten.

Now? With Nathan? But was she truly ready for this? She jerked, tugged her mouth free. And didn't know what to say. Words, cohesive thoughts, were as hard to catch as a handful of air.

Nathan's eyes flew open, intense with desire. For her.

Forget trying to think what she might say. Instead, she shivered; a delicious shiver that warmed her skin as it raised soft goose bumps on it. Her arms tightened around him. Why had she stopped kissing him?

'Molly?'

Don't say sorry. 'It's good. I didn't want to stop.' She'd had to, though, or lose control.

'Which, I suspect, is why you did.' His mouth twitched.

'It's too soon.' Regret had her tongue lapping at her lips, and his eyes followed, causing a knot to form in her stomach.

His nod was slow. 'You're right. It's the same for me.'

'I'd better get going.'

Nathan shook his head. 'Come inside.'

Not to continue kissing. No, he'd agreed they'd moved too quickly, wouldn't expect a rerun of that kiss. She was coming down to earth now. It was unlikely to be comfortable when the kissing was done and they were back to being professional with each other in the department. Though he was fast becoming a friend, if not something more.

You don't kiss friends like that.

Being in Nathan's arms felt safe. Exciting. Nothing like friendship. Also—and this was big—how certain was she that she wanted this after so long denying her needs?

She tramped along beside Nathan, trying to straighten her thinking, getting nowhere except inside his house, where he led her to a sitting room overlooking the lawn and beyond. A large-screen TV dominated one wall, an enormous couch placed strategically in front.

'Take a seat,' he instructed in a voice that said he was about to get serious. Over what? Their kiss?

Please don't. She'd hate that. It would spoil the moment and hurt, when she'd enjoyed it so much. She didn't need to hear it hadn't been wonderful for Nathan. He could keep that to himself. Talk about out of practice. Gone was the confident girl prior to Paul who used to kiss and leave, or occasionally kiss and stay for the night and then leave. Look at her. She was a blithering wreck because of a kiss. She so wanted to follow up with another, and wasn't going to. She needed to be circumspect. Parking her backside on the edge of the couch, she crossed her legs, folded her arms and waited.

'Whoa, relax, Molly. I'm not about to bite your head off.' He took the opposite end of the couch, and stretched his legs out for ever. Turning in her direction, he eyeballed her. 'Neither am I going to say I regret kissing you.'

Her arms loosened and her hands splayed over her thighs. 'Go on.'

He laughed. 'What more can I say? Other than I'd like to do it again.'

So would she. But—

'But I'm not sure where we're going with this,' Nathan continued. 'I don't know what you expect from men after what's happened to you in the past.'

That makes two of us.

Or did it? Her lungs expanded as she drew a long breath. 'If I hadn't felt comfortable with you it wouldn't have happened.' She'd have backed away, run more like, not leaned in and made the most of Nathan's mouth on hers. 'What happened in the past has to stay there, not taint anyone I get close to in the future. That might sound naïve, but I firmly believe it's the only way to get back a normal, happy life, hopefully with some loving in it eventually.'

'Gutsy comes to mind. How do you do it?'

Fake it till you make it.

'Dig deep for smiles, start trusting those around me, and have fun.'

'Honest too. Though I'm sure there's a lot you haven't told me.' Nathan held his hand up, palm out. 'It's all right. I don't expect you to. All I ask is that you take me seriously, and don't treat me as an experiment to see how you're managing.'

Nathan had been hurt in the past too and wouldn't be rushing to fall in love again. Her eyes widened. 'Now who's being honest?'

'Would you want it any other way?'

This in-depth conversation with a man was foreign—and interesting. 'No. I've never tried to hurt
anyone or, to my knowledge, been so thoughtless as to
do so. You've got things that upset you too, and I don't
want to be the one who reminds you of what you've
lost.' A tremor shook Molly. So much for relaxed.

'We've learned a lot about each other in a short
time.' Nathan was studying her, and she felt completely
comfortable.

'Which is one reason why I can't move into your
flat.' She'd like to get to know Nathan a whole lot better, bit by bit, and that would be best if they weren't
living in each other's breathing space. If they were to
have a relationship she needed a place to be alone at
times while she got used to someone else in her life.
Knowing he was on the other side of the wall could
encroach on her solitude.

She'd become fiercely independent over the time
she'd been alone, and it would take a lot to give up even
a little of that. Not even sensational kisses suggesting
sensational lovemaking would do the trick. Not yet.
Nathan was kind and sincere, or so she believed. While
Paul had fooled her with his charm, she doubted Nathan would ever be anything but up-front and caring.
But she'd got it wrong once, and that niggled a little.

'Any other reasons for not moving into my flat?'

'We work together.'

'People share living arrangements with work colleagues all the time.' His smile nearly undid her re-
solve not to give in.

It would take a nanosecond to lean forward and
wrap her hand around his arm and bring them closer.
Nathan was that damned gorgeous. The air stuck in her

throat. The knot tightened in her belly. She could do this—far too easily. But she hadn't thought it through. She needed to do that first. She was considering it? After the arguments she'd put up moments ago? 'I'm not ready.'

'I'd have your back.'

'I know.' Molly sighed her gratitude. It was true. 'And no one's out there trying to track me down any more. I don't need to check every person who comes within spitting distance.' She believed it, which had to be an improvement on her previous attitude to getting out and about.

Nathan nodded. 'Fair enough. I'm not pushing you to do something you don't want to.'

Settling back into the comfortable, soft, cosy couch, she looked around. A computer sat on a desk in the corner, an up-to-date stereo system in another. 'You've made yourself quite the den, haven't you?' There was a maleness to the sharp white décor with dashes of black in the curtains and the furniture. There was also a loneliness she recognised from her own apartment. The room here was on a far grander scale, but the emptiness felt the same.

'I spend most of my down time in here.' He picked up a remote and pressed some buttons, then music filled the air, a low female voice that lifted the hairs on the back of her neck.

Molly swallowed the urge to sing along. 'Not often, then.' She'd keep digging for info while he was so relaxed with her.

'More than you'd credit me with. I put in a fair amount of time studying and keeping up-to-date with medical programmes and the latest drugs and procedures, even though emergency medicine doesn't change a lot.'

'Why that particular field, instead of, say, surgery or paediatrics?'

'It's when people are most vulnerable. I rise to that. It brings out the best in me.'

'You'd be the same in any area of medicine.'

'True.' He shrugged those eloquent shoulders that she'd held while being kissed. 'There's also a lot of variety in an ED. A bit like a GP practice, I imagine, only lots more cases where there's an urgency about the situation. Sometimes I regret not having the follow-up and knowing how a patient fared long term. At the same time, I don't get to see it all go bad and watch someone I've got to know a little go downhill and have to face the families trying to cope.'

That wouldn't be his thing. Not that it was any-body's. 'You've suffered loss. You'd feel for those pa-tients and their families.' To think this was the man she'd thought irritating and infuriating. He still could be, but now she'd seen behind that mask she'd never accept it at face value again. She might get cross with him but from now on it would take longer to really wind her up. She didn't need to be on guard with Na-than or protective of herself over every word he spoke.

'Yes,' he muttered. 'But then I'm not alone in that.' He stood up, walked to the glass sliding doors lead-ing outside and stared out, his hands on his hips, legs slightly splayed.

She'd gone too far, shouldn't have mentioned his loss. But there was no taking it back. She went to join him, shoulder to shoulder, gazing outward. 'I'm sorry.'

'Do you realise how often you apologise for something?'

'One habit yet to be annihilated.' Sorry hadn't stopped the fists, but she'd always tried.

Pushing a hand through his thick hair, Nathan shook his head. 'Don't be apologetic for what you said. I prefer people don't dodge the issue. I did enough of that all by myself for the first couple of years. Rosie was my life. I cannot deny that, or how what happened has altered the way I go about things now. But I think I'm leading a balanced life again.'

He was ahead of her there, but she was working on catching up fast. 'Receiving my divorce papers knocked down the final block preventing me from getting back on track. I'd been taking baby steps, now I'm ready to take some leaps.'

'Finding somewhere new to live might be one.' He remained staring outside as he continued. 'The offer to move into my flat stands. Despite your arguments, I believe we could make it work just fine. We can talk terms and conditions any time you like.' He was serious, in control of things, but she could do control too.

'The next place I live in will be where I'd like to spend the next few years at least. Permanent, rather than a stopgap.'

'Buy or rent?'

'I haven't given it much thought. I could afford to buy a small house or a bigger apartment in a similar area to where I am now.' That'd mean using the money she'd sworn not to touch, but maybe it was time to let go of that gremlin too. 'I'm not sure where I want to live. There's no hurry.'

'Feel free to run any ideas past me. I've spent all my life in and around Sydney and know where not to buy.'

'Thanks.' Glad he'd dropped the subject of renting his flat for now, Molly headed back to the couch and sank down onto it, smothering a surprised yawn on the way. That was the answer to all this nonsense going on in her head. She was tired from working all night and tossing a man on the floor. She grinned.

I did it. Cool.

Tipping her head back, she stared up at the ceiling and thought, *I really must get going.* She couldn't hang around with Nathan all day. He'd want to catch up on sleep, and probably had plans for the afternoon when he woke up. But it was so comfortable here. She'd take another minute before calling a taxi to take her home.

Nathan woke and raised his hands behind his head on the pillow, stretched his feet towards the bottom of the bed. He'd slept like a baby. His watch showed he'd had nearly four hours. More than enough if he was to get back into his regular pattern tonight.

Was Molly still asleep? She hadn't budged when he'd tucked the blanket around her. It had taken all his self-control not to swing her up into his arms and carry her down to his bedroom so he could lie spooned behind her while they slept. Except there probably wouldn't have been much sleep going on—for him anyway. She flicked every switch he had, and then some.

Who'd have thought it after the way they'd started out? But there was no denying he wanted Molly. She was sexy, sweet, strong, and still recovering from an appalling past. He wouldn't have kissed her for so long but she hadn't stopped, and how was a man supposed to ignore that when the woman fitted perfectly in his arms? Pressed those soft breasts against his chest?

He sat up, swinging his legs over the edge of the bed and leaning his elbows on his knees, then dropped his head into his hands. It had to be a case of wanting what he couldn't have. There hadn't been a woman who'd rattled him like Molly was doing. Not since Rosie. Strange how different they were. Rosie tall, tough, focused; Molly small, soft, trying to be focused on the future and not the past.

A fact that should have him running for the waves. Hadn't seen that coming. All he'd intended was to make her like him. Like? Or desire him? He did want to love again. 'I what?' The question roared across his tongue. 'Yes, I want to love another woman.' Molly?

Leaping to his feet, he crossed to the mirror in the en suite bathroom and stared at the face glaring back at him. Nothing looked any different from what he'd seen last night while shaving before work. He'd been tracking along nicely, and now look at him. Toast. Over a woman he hadn't even liked let alone wanted to kiss at the beginning of the week. Or had he? Had he been in denial all along? Afraid he might actually want to start looking for a future that involved more than himself? Was love possible a second time?

Spinning away from the mirror, he reached into the shower and turned the knob to hot. Cold would be better for what ailed him, but he was a wuss when it came to freezing temperatures; he far preferred the warmth. Even the extreme heat of the outback made him happier than in winter, and Sydney wasn't exactly freezing.

Standing under the water, he knuckled his head. Molly was in there, teasing, taunting with that sassy

way she'd used before she'd realised what she was
doing. As for her kisses—man, could the woman kiss.
His groin tightened just thinking about Molly's mouth
on his.

Molly had mentioned baby steps. That's how he
needed to approach this. For both their sakes. She
might say she was on the road to recovery, but now
he knew what to look for he'd seen the sadness, anger
and pain in her face and darkening those beautiful eyes
at moments when she thought no one was watching.
That might go on for a long time even after she found
someone to trust and love again.

Like the nights when he still woke to a sodden pillow. Those were rare occurrences now, but they did
happen. Rosie would never leave him completely. Likewise, that monster would always be a part of Molly, of
who she'd become and where she went from here. But
it seemed she was ready to reach out with *him*. He'd
better not let her down.

Once dressed in jeans and a navy shirt, he went to
see if Molly had woken up.

She was standing in the middle of the kitchen, looking lost. 'So much for calling a taxi. I fell asleep.'

'You needed it.'

'Blame the couch. It's so comfortable.'

When he'd taken the blanket in, Molly had been on
her side, her knees drawn up and her hands crossed
over her breasts, accentuating their curves and making him wish they knew each better so he could've
wrapped her in his arms instead of the blanket. Her
face had been relaxed, without the caution that was her
everyday approach to people. 'Now you know why I

often spend my sleep time there and not in my bed-room.'

'You got any tea?' she asked, then blushed. 'Sorry. I'll get out of here.'

Bet asking that was one of those steps she'd mentioned. 'Tea, coffee, hot chocolate. I've got the works.' He stepped round her and reached inside the pantry.

'Tea, thanks.' Her soft laugh hit him in the gut. 'Cake?'

He winced. 'There's some in here.' He handed her the box of tea bags and reached for a plastic container. 'This has been in here for a while.' Left by his sister when she'd visited last weekend, the banana cake might be a little the worse for not being eaten.

'You have cake lying around?' She shook her head at him.

'I haven't got a sweet tooth.' Which Allie knew, but still insisted on making him cakes every time she visited, a habit started in the bleak days of Rosie's illness as a way to cheer everyone up. Not that it had worked.

'What a waste.' Molly had the container in her hand. 'The icing's got a distinct blue tinge.'

The disappointment on her face made him chuckle as he slid out the bin so she could dump the cake. 'I've got frozen sausage rolls that won't take too long to heat, if you're starving.' Breakfast had been a long time ago. His stomach was growling quietly, and it wouldn't be long before it got really noisy. He flicked the oven on and opened the freezer.

Again her laughter got to him, tightening one tell-tale part of his body while softening others. 'How do you keep in such good shape if you're eating things like that?'

'Obviously I don't eat them or that lemon icing would never have had time to change colour.' Molly thought he was in good shape? 'I go for a run most days.' Which paid off in dividends, but he was lucky to have a metabolism that let him get away with quite a variety of delicious foods. Then he looked at her and saw the deep pink shade of her cheeks.

'Yes, right. You know I run too.' She busied herself with tea bags and mugs and getting the milk out of the fridge.

'As well as being into those martial arts.' A picture of Molly dropping that irate man flashed across his mind, tightened his jaw. So much for Security. She should never have been put in that position. She could've been hurt. So could Hazel. 'Your moves looked so easy, as though the man was lighter than a bag of spuds.' His heart had been trying to beat a way out of his chest. Not even seeing Molly had been unharmed had slowed the rate. That'd taken minutes of deep breathing, and pretending all was right in the department once Security finally turned up and removed the guy.

She grinned. 'It was pretty cool, wasn't it? I've worked hard at being able to protect myself, but never has that instinctive reaction taken over to make me do what was necessary. Until now I've only ever thrown a judo partner on the mat, where I get to think about the best throw to make and how to execute it properly.' Her grin slipped. 'It makes me wonder what I'd do if someone on the train or in the street raised an arm to reach for something and I reacted without thinking.'

'I bet it was the atmosphere as much as the man's actions that made you react. We were all tense, him in particular.' Nathan hoped he was right, or Molly would get a complex about something she'd learned for her own protection. Placing the pastries on a tray, he slid them into the oven and slammed the door. 'Ten minutes and we'll be into those.'

'Afterwards, I'll get out of your hair and go home.'

It wasn't his hair she was messing with; it was his mind. 'I'll drop you off. I've got to go to the supermarket anyway.'

Handing him a mug of tea in a steady hand, she nodded. 'Thanks.'

No argument? There was a first. He found the tomato sauce and placed it on the bench alongside some plates. 'Need anything else with your sausage rolls?'

'No.' She sipped her tea while moving to the counter and sitting on a stool, plonking her elbows on the bench with her mug gripped in both hands. Looking around the kitchen made for a large family with its counters and eight-seater table, intrigue filled her gaze. 'Did you furnish the house?'

Darn. One of them was behaving sensibly, and it wasn't him. Guess she wasn't feeling the vibes hitting him. He got serious, put aside the hot sensations ramping up his temperature. 'The people I bought it off were moving into an apartment in Rose Bay and wanted to start over with decorating and furnishings so I bought some pieces from them, mainly for the bedrooms and in here. While the table's massive, it gets put to good use when my sister and her lot come to stay.'

'Big family?'

'Allie's got four kids, and a very patient partner. She's like an Energizer battery, no stopping her. She wears everyone out.'

Molly was smiling. 'She sounds like fun.'

'I think you'd like her. And the other two and their broods.' He was getting ahead of himself. Molly did not need to meet any of his family. Not yet, anyway.

'You've got three sisters?'

'Yep.' He jerked the oven door open. 'Let's eat.'

Then he'd take her home before going for a run to work out the kinks in his body put there by being too close to Molly. Nathan muttered an oath under his breath. He had this bad. 'You got plans for the afternoon?'

'Not a lot. Groceries, washing, a run, do the crossword, wash my hair.' She grinned.

'Sounds action packed.' He grinned back. 'Phone me if you're stuck for a word.'

Then her eyes lit up. 'Actually, I think I'll go watch a game of basketball.'

Chapter 7

After a quick shower Molly dressed in fitted black jeans and a pink jersey that deliberately did not match the red curls she attacked with a hairbrush, then followed up with styling gel that did nothing to tame the wildest of them. With a shrug she selected a black leather jacket from the array in her wardrobe. It had been years since she'd worn anything bright pink, and she felt great. Never again would anyone tell her to get changed into something that toned down her complexion. No one.

Halfway out the door she turned back and snatched up the sports bag at the back of her wardrobe. Chances were it would languish in her car, but she was feeling lucky so she might as well go prepared. Humming was another first as she made her way down and outside to where her car sat in a massive puddle by the kerb. Thank goodness for her red, thick-heeled, soft-as-down leather ankle boots. Not only did they look gorgeous but they could keep water at bay without tarnishing the leather.

Grr, grr. The engine gave a metallic groan. Molly turned the ignition off, counted to four, tried again. Bingo. The motor coughed but kept going. She had power. Perfect. She really needed to start it at least every second day if she was going to leave the car out in the weather. Where else could she park it? The apartment didn't come with an internal garage. Or any designated place for vehicles.

Wind rocked the car as she drove away. Hunching her shoulders so her chin was snug against her turtleneck jersey, her humming turned to singing a cheerful song she'd sung often back in the days she'd been truly happy, getting louder with every corner she turned. By the time she reached the indoor sports arena her jaws were aching and a smile was reaching from ear to ear. Hot damn. That was the first time she'd sung her favourite song in years.

Going to watch the Roos team she'd been a part of until two months ago had been a brainwave. They were playing against one of the strongest teams in the local competition, the odds slightly in their favour. She began to hurry. The game had started ten minutes ago and she hated to miss any more. The idea to come here had arrived out of the blue, but with every passing moment it seemed better and better. Catching up with the women she'd played with, and hopefully making up for being so remote whenever they'd tried to get her to join in the after-match sessions in a nearby bar, had become imperative if she was to keep getting up to speed with her new life.

Inside the stadium she searched out the coach and reserves sitting on the benches, watching the game. 'Hello, Coach. Mind if I sit with you to watch the game?'

Georgia flipped her intent gaze from the team to her, and tapped the chair beside her with her notebook. 'Get your butt down here, girl. Where've you been?'

'Hey, Molly, how are you?'

'Molly, I tried to get hold of you to come to a party last month.'

'Hi, how's that new job going?'

'I'm great. I'll give you my number. The job's wonderful.' Wow. No knots of anxiety needed loosening. Everyone was friendlier than she deserved. Sinking onto the seat, she looked around. 'I see you trashed the Blue Heelers last week.' It was the one team everyone had believed might knock them off the top of the leader board.

'Annihilated them.' Coach laughed. 'Glad you're keeping up with us.'

'First thing I look for in the local news on Monday mornings. I miss you guys.' More than she'd realised. When she'd played for the team she'd focused on not letting anyone close, afraid they'd let her down if she needed them in any way, as her friends back in Perth had when it had come out about what had been happening. In the end, staying with the team, not going out for drinks after a game or attending the barbecues that they had once a month, not getting involved as everyone else did, had got hard to face, which in turn had exhausted her, so she'd left.

'You chose to leave.' Coach never minced her words.

'I did.' Molly turned to watch the game on the court. 'How's Sarah doing?' The girl who'd replaced her had spent four weeks on the bench after breaking a wrist in a particularly tough match but had resumed playing a fortnight ago.

'Back to her usual Rottweiler attitude and earning us points to boot. I think the wrist still gives her grief, but I'm the last person she'll admit that to.'

'No one likes telling you anything that might give cause to be sat on the bench for a game.'

'That why you left?' Georgia was watching the game, writing shorthand notes in the notebook, but she wouldn't miss a breath, word or a movement Molly made.

'I felt crowded.'

'Being part of a good, functioning team means being in each other's pockets at times.'

'I wasn't ready for that.'

'You kept to yourself a lot.'

Modus operandi. It had worked. It had kept her safe and—lonely. 'Can't deny that.' Her eyes were on the ball as Emma threw it to Sarah, who lobbed it into the net. 'Go, Roos. Good one, Sarah.' Molly leapt to her feet, stabbing the air with her fists, left, right, left, right. 'You beauty.'

Georgia was calmly making notes. 'Never seen you fly out of your skin before.'

Molly sat back down, a grin on her face. How had she not got all excited over being a part of this team? When she'd played for the under eighteens in Perth she'd been the loudest, most enthusiastic member of the team. Today it seemed she really might be getting her life back. Her grin widened as relief soared.

'Guess you didn't know me very well.' Hell, she hadn't realised how far down the ladder she'd dropped. Yet all of a sudden she was here, getting out and *looking* for fun, not just hoping it might come her way if someone had time to spare for her. When she'd determined to get out and start living she hadn't expected it to happen so fast. It was Nathan. By believing in her, he'd pushed her boundaries and helped her open up some more. 'I'm adept at keeping hidden in plain sight.'

Past tense, Mol. You're over that now.

Georgia's gaze was on every move happening on the court. 'I figured.'

Coach was the second person she'd opened up to, though only briefly. There'd been no in-depth talk about Paul and the abuse, but just admitting she had problems had been huge and had felt good in a way she'd never have believed.

It was good the barriers were dropping here too, but there were some she wouldn't let go. The likelihood of infertility for one. Today Nathan had learned more than she was prepared to share with just anyone. She'd spent so long trying to make people believe she was being abused it was hard to let go of the reticence to talk about it now. What if she woke up tomorrow to find it was all a load of bulldust and she wasn't any further on? That people thought what happened was her own fault?

Then you'll try again, and again, until you get it right. Until people accept you for who you are.

Nathan hadn't laughed or told her she was attention-seeking. No, he'd believed her from the get-go. Her grin had slipped, so she dug deep for another and found it wasn't as hard to do as it used to be.

Molly focused on the game.

The score was twenty-seven all.

The opposing team called for a substitute.

Coach stood up. 'Eloise on. Carmen off.'

At half-time the team swilled water from bottles, wiped faces with towels, crowded around Coach for instructions, and said hi to Molly as though she'd never been away.

The third quarter got under way, and the score continued to climb, each team matching the other, the Roos getting ahead only to have the Snakes catch up and pass them, before they took back the lead.

Sarah snatched the ball, blocked an opposition player and swung around to throw for a goal, and tripped over the other player's foot. Down she went, hard, her elbow cracking on the floor, reaching out with her other hand to prevent hitting the deck with her head. Pain contorted her face as she cried out, pulling her wrist against her midriff.

The coach's expletives were the more damning for being spoken quietly. 'That's the last thing Sarah needs. To do her wrist in again.'

Molly rushed on court with Georgia and knelt down beside Sarah. 'Tell me where the pain is.'

'Same place as last time.'

'Where you fractured it?'

Sarah nodded abruptly, her lips white. 'Yeah.'

'Can I take a look?'

Another nod, and Sarah pushed her arm towards her. 'It feels just the same as before. It's broken again.'

Molly carefully touched the rapidly swelling wrist,

then felt up Sarah's arm and over the hand. 'Okay, I agree with you. We need to get you to the emergency department.'

A first-aider sank down on his knees beside them. 'Let me look at that.'

Georgia glared at the young man. 'Molly here's an emergency nurse, and she thinks Sarah has broken her wrist. I'll take her word on it.'

'All right, then. We need to get her to hospital.'

Molly stood up. 'I'll take her.'

Sarah glared at them. 'I'm not going anywhere until the game's finished. I want to watch the last quarter.'

'That's not a great idea. You're in pain,' Molly said.

'You're telling me?' The woman's eyes widened. 'I know what the damage is, know how the pain works, and I can deal with it for a little while longer. Now, help me off the court so the game can resume.'

Molly smiled at her courage as she took an elbow and Georgia put an arm around her waist. 'You're one tough cookie.'

'Better believe it,' Sarah said, then gasped with pain. Locking eyes on Molly, she growled, 'Don't say a word.'

'Okay.' But she wanted to bundle her up and rush her to an ED to get painkillers on board.

Once they had Sarah settled on the bench, and the game was under way again, Georgia leaned close to Molly. 'I don't suppose you've got some sports shoes with you?'

Her heart thumped once, loud and hard. 'Yes. But I'm out of practice.'

'You still run every day?'

'Yes. What about the other players?' The ones who turned up every week all season.

Standing up, Georgia growled, 'Don't you want us to win this game?'

That was one mighty compliment. 'Back in a minute.'

Shorts and a shirt in the bright yellow team colour were shoved into her hands. 'Put these on while you're at it.'

'Bottoms up.' Eloise raised her glass and tipped the contents down her throat, and most of the other team members followed suit.

Molly sipped her sparkling water. It tasted like the best champagne out there. They'd won. She'd scored eight points. Unreal.

'Glad you dropped by,' Georgia muttered beside her. 'But don't think you're getting out of Wednesday night practice from now on.'

So she was back on the team, whether she liked it or not. Thing was, she *loved* it. *And* this getting together with everyone. Once, she'd gone out of her way to avoid it; now she felt like she belonged with these women. 'One problem. I'm on shift this Wednesday night from three to eleven.'

'Some of the girls are working out here tomorrow at nine. Don't be late.'

'Yes, boss.'

'Better believe it.' Georgia winked. Then pulled her phone from her pocket. 'Sarah's texted. She's having surgery tomorrow. That'll put an end to her playing for the rest of the season.'

'Unfortunately you're probably right.' A second

fracture on top of the previous one was not good. Molly felt her phone vibrate in her pocket. 'Nathan' showed up on the screen. Her heart went flip-flop. He was the last person she'd expected to hear from, despite their harmonious morning. 'Hi. How's things?'

'I saw your car parked downtown and thought I'd see what you were up to, if you'd like some company. But…' and he chuckled '…it sounds as though you're in the middle of a party.'

'I'm at the Lane Bar with the Roos basketball team. I used to play for them.'

Played for them today and made some points. Yeeha.

'Feel free to join me. Us.' He wouldn't come. She'd been rash suggesting it. 'Some of the others' partners are here.'

'Two minutes.' Gone.

She stared at the phone. Had that really just happened? Nathan was coming to have a drink with her? Her heart raced.

You did kiss him this morning. Maybe he wants another.

He could get as many kisses as he wanted from most single females he crossed paths with. He was drop-dead gorgeous and damned nice with it. Nice? Okay, kind, considerate, opinionated and bumptious. But if he made to kiss her again then she wasn't saying no. Yeah, well. She sighed. The kiss had been pretty darned awesome. Her knees still knocked thinking about it.

That might be exhaustion from charging around the court, not desire, Mol.

Sipping her drink, she stifled a yawn. It had been a long, emotional roller-coaster of a day and suddenly she felt shattered. Just when Nathan was about to join her.

* * *

One good thing about Molly's red hair was she was easy to find in a crowd. Another—maybe not so good?—she drove him wild with need, but that was on hold as he tried to slow down his pursuit of her. Yeah, right. If that was so, why was he here? The challenge had got out of hand fast, to the point he didn't know who was challenging who. Hopefully Molly was unaware she rocked him off his usually steady feet.

He stood watching her for a moment as she chatted with the women surrounding the table they stood at, her finger running down her cheek as she laughed over something someone said. This was a whole new Molly from the one he thought he knew in the ED. Yet the vulnerability was still there in the guarded way she stood, one shoulder slightly turned, ready to spin around if she sensed trouble approaching.

'Hey, Molly,' he called, a little louder than necessary, not wanting to disturb her comfort zone.

The curls flicked left then right as her head shot up and around. The smile spreading across her mouth hit him hard in the belly. 'Hey, you, too.' She shuffled sideways to make room for him.

Nathan stepped up beside her, happy when she leaned his way so that their arms touched. 'Looks like you're all celebrating.' He nodded at the array of glasses on the table.

Her smile extended into a grin. 'We won. Against the hardest team we have to play all season.'

'We? You played?' Hadn't she said she was going to *watch* a game?

'Since Coach knew me she asked if I'd fill in for the

last ten minutes after one of the girls broke her wrist. Re-broke it.'

'Why did you leave in the first place?'

Molly's look told him to shut up, so he did, for now.

'What Molly's not telling you is that she scored eight points,' one of the women said in a very loud voice.

Molly shook her head. 'It was a team effort. Nathan, let me introduce everyone.' She went around the table, stumbling when it came to naming the men and laughing when they teased her about her memory. 'This is Nathan Lupton, a—a friend of mine.' Colour filled her cheeks. 'We work together.'

She didn't have a definite slot to fit him into. Friend, colleague. What else? He had no answer either. 'Can I get you a drink?' He needed a beer, fast, before he came up with some whack-a-doo ideas and put them out there.

Molly shook her head. 'No, thanks. I'm good.'

'Be right back.' *Don't go anywhere.* Luck was on his side. The bar was momentarily quiet, no doubt a hiatus in a busy night. 'Thanks, mate.' He took his beer and handed over some cash before returning to his reason for being there.

She was toying with her glass. 'I was struggling with fitting into the group. On court, fine. Off court, not so good.'

Nathan nodded. 'Same as you've been with your workmates. I'm picking same reasons too.'

'Yes. At least I'm doing something about it now.' Her eyes met his. 'Were you headed somewhere in particular when you saw my car? How did you recognise it, by the way? It's so ordinary even I have trouble finding it in a parking garage.'

'I wasn't a hundred percent certain. That's why I gave you a buzz instead of checking out the bars first. How long have you been here?' Molly looked tired, and her eyes were a little glassy. Too many of those bubbly wines that she seemed to be enjoying? That on top of last night's shift, and only a few hours' sleep today, would knock anyone off their perch.

She glanced at her watch, and gasped. 'It's after ten? I think we got here around five thirty. No wonder I'm zonked.' Then she glanced at him, and guilt filled those eyes. 'Sorry. That's rude when you've just arrived. We had a celebratory drink, then a meal and some more drinks. Everyone's stoked to have won. I'm going to the training session tomorrow morning since I can't make Wednesday night practice. I'll probably ache in places I don't know I've got afterwards.' She drained her glass and dropped it back on the table with a thud. 'Damn, I'm talking too much.'

'Yes, but it beats the cold shoulder routine.' He smiled to show he wasn't looking for trouble. 'I like the Molly I'm getting to know.'

She stared at him.

'What? Have I grown a wart on my nose?'

'Not quite.' Finally she dropped her eyes to focus on her hands clasped together in front of her.

'Molly?'

She blinked, sighed, looked at him again, this time with remorse clouding her expression. 'Thank you for not running a mile when I told you everything this morning.'

Oh, Mol. 'As if I'd do that.' Nathan lifted one of her hands and wrapped his fingers around it.

'I knew you wouldn't before I told you or I wouldn't

have said a word. It was blatantly clear you'd have my back right from the moment I tossed that creep onto the floor. Actually, I think I'd already reached that conclusion before then.'

'So what's the problem?'

'I probably haven't got one that a good night's sleep won't fix.'

'Then let's go.'

Her curls flicked. 'You just got here.'

'I can leave just as quickly. Come on.'

A tight smile flitted across her mouth. 'Okay. Sorry, everyone, but I'm heading home. I'm knackered.'

'Yeah, yeah.' Someone laughed. 'Your man turns up and suddenly you're tired. We get it.'

Heat spilled into Molly's cheeks, but she didn't give one of her sharp retorts. Instead she managed a quiet, 'Whatever,' and slung her bag over her shoulder to walk out of the bar, her hand still firmly in Nathan's.

On the footpath Molly turned right.

Nathan tugged her gently to the left. 'My car's this way.'

Pulling her hand free, she nodded. 'Mine's the opposite way, as you must know if you saw it parked.'

'I'll give you a lift.'

Those curls moved sharply. 'I'm fine. I need my car in the morning.'

Okay, now he had to be brutal. 'Molly, you've been drinking. You cannot drive.'

Her mouth fell open. Her eyes widened. Then she found her voice. 'You think I'm drunk?' she screeched.

'Yes, I do. You said you've been in the bar for hours. Drinking was mentioned.' No way was she getting behind the wheel of her car. 'Your eyes are glassy and you were talking the hind leg off a rabbit in there.' He jerked a thumb over his shoulder in the direction of the bar. 'Which is unlike you.' Unless she was nervous, but he didn't believe her nerves had anything to do with this.

'You're wrong.' She spun away to storm down the road.

'Molly.' He caught up with her. 'Please be sensible and let me take you home. It would be safer for everyone.'

She stopped so abruptly he had to duck sideways to avoid knocking into her. 'I had one alcoholic drink when we first arrived. Since then I have been downing sparkling water by the litre. I am not a danger to anyone.'

'Right.' Even to him his sarcasm was a bit heavy as he stepped in front of her.

Stabbing his chest with her forefinger, she glared at him, the anger ramping up fast in those wide eyes. 'I am tired. Not drunk. Please get out of my way. Now.'

'Even exhaustion is a good reason not to drive.' Lame, but true. And desperate. He didn't want her driving. Giving her a lift would make him happy. Apparently not her. He should let this go, but deep inside was a clawing itch that made him try harder to win her over. Reaching for her hand, he tried to pull her in the opposite direction.

She jerked free, stretched up on her toes and said in the coldest voice he'd ever heard, 'Out of my way, Lupton. Damn, but you're so cocky and infuriating.'

When he didn't move she stomped around him and continued down to her car, head high, boots pounding the tarmac. 'I'll follow you,' he called, and headed for his vehicle so as not to lose her. He was going to make sure she got home safely, one way or another.

Cocky and infuriating. What the hell was that about? Putting him in his place? He'd laugh if it didn't sting. Here he'd been thinking they were getting somewhere. Into a deep, murky hole at the moment.

Slamming the stick into drive, he pulled out and caught up to her at the lights. So he'd infuriated her. No surprises there.

He'd insisted she get into his car.

He hadn't listened to her when she'd said she hadn't been drinking.

He had tried to force his opinion on her.

Starting to sound like her ex.

One very big difference. He would never, ever, use his fists. Molly knew that, or she wouldn't have gone to his house with him that morning. Wouldn't have fallen asleep on his couch, leaving herself vulnerable.

She might not have kissed him either. Keeping a respectable distance, he followed Molly's car to her apartment.

He owed her an apology for being such a prat.

Even if he still thought she should've come with him, he had to say sorry. This argument was bigger than what he'd wanted her to do. It was about not believing her, not letting her make her own decisions—in other words, control. He didn't do control, unless it was about himself. People were allowed to make their own mistakes, unless they endangered someone else in the process. Unfortunately he didn't want Molly making a hideous mistake and so he'd overreacted. She'd had her share of bad deals. She didn't need any more.

Now he had to find a way back into her favour.

* * *

Molly closed her door with a firm click, leaned back against it and stared up at the ceiling. 'Damn you, Nathan. Your bossy manner had me reacting faster than a bullet train.'

Her bag slid off her shoulder and hit the tiles with a bang, making her jump. She was wired. And cold. Driving home with her window down to blast the tiredness and keep her alert had chilled her while her temper had combated some of the cold. Now both were backing off. She'd let Nathan get to her—again. Back to how it'd always been between them before birthday breakfasts and judo throws and spilling the beans about her past. It might be for the best. If she hadn't kissed him and been kissed back. Because now she wanted more. Lots more. If she could forgive him for believing she was drunk—*and* telling her what to do.

Picking up her bag, she headed to the kitchen and the kettle. A cup of tea was supposed to remedy lots of things. Hopefully her indignation was one of them.

The buzzing doorbell echoed through the apartment. 'Molly, it's me. Nathan,' he added in his don't-fool-with-me attitude. 'I want to talk to you.'

Well, guess what? She didn't want to talk to him. Filling the kettle, she pushed the 'on' button.

'I know you're in there.'

Who let him into the building this time? Seemed he charmed everyone he came across. Except her. No, even her, when she stopped trying to resist him.

Buzz. Knock, knock. 'Molly.'

Persistent. No surprise there. Back to the door, growling into the speaker, 'Go away, Nathan. I have nothing to say to you right at this moment.'

Except that you've upset me, and stirred me in ways a man hasn't in a long time.

'You want me to shout until the neighbours come out to see what's going on?'

'Go for it.' She huffed at the peephole.

'Let me in.'

Definitely louder, and he wouldn't stop there. Another huff and she wrenched the door wide. 'You're not coming in.'

'Fine.' He leaned a shoulder against the doorjamb and concentrated his entire focus on her.

The cheek of him, so damned sure of himself. She stabbed his chest before she put her brain in gear and jerked her hand away. 'You think you can say what you like to me and get away with it.'

'Wrong, Molly. I know I'll never get away with anything around you.'

Her mouth dropped open. Hurriedly closing it, she swallowed hard. What did he say?

'You don't take any bull from anyone and, for some reason, especially from me.' His mouth twitched. 'I like that.'

Again her jaw dropped. Again she slammed it shut, jarring her teeth in the process. This wasn't going according to plan. Not that she'd had one other than to keep Nathan out of her apartment. 'Right. Fine. You've had your say so kindly remove yourself from my doorway so I can close the door.'

He didn't move a centimetre. 'I haven't told you why I'm here.' His eyes were locked on her as though seeing right inside to every thought crossing her confused mind. 'Can you spare me a couple of minutes?'

That couldn't be a plea. Could it? His eyes were dark, his mouth soft.

Nathan was making it hard to stay uptight and focused when he looked at her like that. This was probably the biggest mistake she'd made in a while, but she stepped back, holding the door wide, and nodded, once, abruptly.

'Thanks.'

The tenderness in his gaze made her shiver. Had he done an about-face? If so, why? No, he wouldn't have. Molly headed into her lounge, where she remained standing. To sit would give him a height advantage. The kettle whistled, clicked off. She ignored it.

Nathan stood before her, not so close as to dominate her but near enough that she was fully aware of him. Heck, she was aware of him all over the ED, so there was no way she could ignore him in her apartment even if she shut herself in the bathroom.

He reached for her hands and said, 'I'm very sorry for doubting you. I had no right to do that. Or to criticise you. If I could take those words back, Molly, they'd be gone already. Not thrashing around inside your head.'

He understood her too well. Now he'd stunned her. Nathan Lupton had said sorry—to her. The tension fell away, leaving her wobbly, with a spinning head and racing blood. Somehow her fingers had laced with Nathan's. 'Accepted,' she whispered. What else could she do? Being offside with Nathan wasn't what she wanted. Not now, not ever if possible.

His gaze remained fixed on her. The coffee shade of his eyes had lightened to tan with hints of green and black. A smile was growing on his lush mouth.

Heat expanded in her stomach, spreading tentacles of longing throughout her body, knocking at her heart, shimmering into her womanhood, weakening her knees.

'Molly?' Nathan's hands took her face to ever so gently bring her closer to his mouth. Those full lips brushed her quivering ones, apologising and teasing. Then he pulled back to again lock eyes with her. Heat sparked at her, set her blood humming, lifting her up on tiptoe.

As her mouth touched his she fell into him, winding her arms around to spread her hands over his back, pushing her awakened nipples against his solid chest. She breathed deeply. *Nathan*. His name reverberated around her skull, teasing, laughing, giving.

Oh, yes, giving. His mouth was devouring hers, his tongue plunging deeper with every lick. Hands skimmed over her arms, her waist, then held her butt tenderly while stroking, firing her up to the point of no return. Molly hesitated, her mouth stilled. Did she want this? Stupid question. Her mouth went back to kissing him hard, demanding more, sharing everything.

Then Nathan raised his head. 'Molly?' Disappointment knocked behind her ribs when he took her hands and held them tightly between his. 'I think I'd better go while I still can.'

Thump, thump went her heart. He was right. The next step would be in the direction of her bedroom, and despite feeling comfortable and safe with Nathan, she wasn't as ready as that entailed. Sure, they could make out and have fun, but the sun would rise and then she'd have plenty of misgivings to deal with. This man had got closer to her than anyone in a long time, but it had happened so fast she needed to pause, take a breath, and think about what she wanted. 'You're right. It's too soon for me.'

He squeezed her hands gently, brushed his lips across hers, and stepped back. 'Me, too.'

Chapter 8

Molly was whacked. Every muscle ached, and she'd thought she was fit. Lifting the kettle to fill it took energy she didn't have. That afternoon's basketball game had been tough. She'd worked hard to justify Coach's belief in her. They'd barely won—surprising considering the opposition team was ranked seventh compared to their second slot in the competition.

Pride lifted Molly's spirits further. Not once had she failed to take a catch or run the length of the court bouncing the ball. She'd made most of her shots count, taken some intercepts without too much difficulty. Yes, it had been a good game, and now she was worn out.

Work had been busy beyond normal all week, making everyone tired and scratchy. Though Nathan had remained friendly and easygoing with her. There'd been no more kisses or time together away from work, but lots of laughs and friendship. A very normal week for most people, and she couldn't ask for more.

Her bed looked so tempting since she'd changed the sheets and straightened up her room. The washing machine was humming in the kitchen, the pantry had some new food on the shelves, and her newly washed hair was under control. Not that that would last, the curls being the unreliable nuisances they were.

Sinking on the edge of the bed, there was no holding back the smile splitting her face. Or the soft, warm feeling settling over her. Yes, it seemed she was getting up to speed with returning to a normal life, and she had Nathan to thank for some of it. That man made her feel special. She only hoped she'd given some of the excitement and wonder back.

Without thought, she sprawled over the bed, her head snug on her pillow as she kept running images of Nathan through her mind. Laughing over something silly, stitching up a cut in an old man's arm, kissing her. They were more than friends now. But were they becoming a couple? Hardly.

The ringing phone woke her. Scrabbling around the top of her bedside table, her fingers latched onto the instrument just as the ringing stopped. Damn.

Then it started again. Nathan's name blinked out at her.

'Hi.' She scrubbed the sudden moisture from her eyes. It was *only* a phone call.

'Hey, Molly. How did the game go?'

Man, she loved that voice. Over the phone it was even more gravelly. 'It was awesome. We won.'

'So you'll be out celebrating. Though it does sound rather quiet.'

'I'm at home. Some of the girls were going to a wedding and the rest of us had other things to do.' She hadn't, but she'd fallen in with the general consensus that one weekend not celebrating wouldn't hurt.

'Bet you're exhausted. But I was wondering if you're up to meeting my mob. They've descended upon me without warning, and I need some backup.'

'You didn't know your family was coming to visit?'

Nathan's laugh was a short hoot. 'The day any of my sisters tell me they're on their way I'll buy a lotto ticket. All the nieces and nephews are here too, I might add.'

'How many?' Nathan wanted her to meet these people? Seemed they were way past being civil with each other and on to greater things.

'Eight.'

'You're pulling my leg,' she spluttered.

'Nope.' He laughed. 'Three married sisters make for eight brats to buy birthday and Christmas presents for.'

It didn't sound like he resented that. Quite the opposite. He seemed very happy he belonged to this family. 'You must have lists everywhere to keep up with what you've bought who, and what you'll get them next.'

'You have no idea. So, are you up for them? I have to be fair and warn you it won't be a quiet afternoon and you'll never have seen a meal like it. Also, dinner will be at some ridiculously early hour that's closer to lunch so that everyone can be back on the road early. Getting the ankle-biters home late causes bedlam the next morning apparently.'

'It doesn't sound as though any of this is a hardship.' Did he really want to introduce her to his family? Had he thought it through? *Grab the opportunity.* Even if they didn't go much further with whatever was happening between them, she should get out and enjoy herself while she could. 'I could come for a few minutes,' she teased. This teasing was another first. She'd forgotten how to long ago—safer that way—but apparently the ability had been hovering under the surface.

'Minutes? Oh, no, you don't. All or nothing, girl.'

She laughed. This was so different from anything she'd have expected from Nathan before Vicki's breakfast. Before V day and after V day were now her measures. 'I'm on my way. Well, I will be when I've spruced myself up a bit.'

'Don't get carried away. By the time the little horrors have finished with you you'll wish you'd saved yourself the effort.'

'This sounds like fun.'

'You have no idea.' Nathan was laughing fit to bust as he hung up.

Eight kids in one hit? Crikey. Molly stared around her cramped bedroom. What was happening to her? She'd been out more often to more places since V day than at any time throughout the last two months put together. Even better, she was happy. The only time she hadn't been was when Nathan had accused her of being drunk, and his apology more than made up for that.

Leaping off the bed, she threw the wardrobe door open. What to wear? Something to impress Nathan, even if he had warned her to downplay the outfit?

Molly settled for tight black jeans, a cream jersey, and her favourite red boots. No, cream was a magnet for grubby hands. Tossing that jersey aside, she flicked hangers from one side to the other, found the bright orange jersey and tugged it over her head, instantly feeling at ease. Orange top and red curls. Perfect. Lipstick. Red or orange? Red was the first one to land in her hand, so red it was. She had to stop singing to apply the gloss.

So much for exhaustion and muscle aches. She was going to a party of sorts. Bring it on.

Nathan's house on Saturday morning had had an air of quiet elegance about it, with the sweeping lawns and ocean view attention grabbing.

Today Molly felt as though she'd dropped into the middle of a circus. Who knew kids could make so much noise? Then there was the exuberant adult joining in all the games and flying kites and chasing balls, seemingly all at once. Gone was any vestige of Dr Lupton.

'Hey, you came.'

'You didn't think I'd turn up after saying I would?'

'I figured you'd pull into the drive, hear the racket going on and take off faster than a rocket.' Nathan wrapped an arm around her shoulders. 'I've said it before—you're one brave lady. Come and meet the tribe. I promise not to quiz you on names later.'

She felt a bit bedazzled as she was introduced to sisters, brothers-in-law and all those children, and had to pinch herself to make sure this was real. It was nothing like her family, where she was the only child, with her mother and all the expectations of grandeur and a father in New Zealand replaced by a stepdad. They loved her, but this? She looked around and swallowed. The Luptons left her speechless. It was probably just as well or she might say something so odd they'd be putting her back in her car and waving goodbye before she'd had time to relax.

'Here, get this into you.' One of the women handed

her a glass of wine. Annemarie? Or Jessie? It wasn't Allie, or was it? 'I hope you like wine, because a few hours with us will turn anyone to drink. We're enough to scare off the bravest.'

Molly accepted the glass. 'I think you might be right.'

'Try and leave, and I'll wheel-clamp your car,' Nathan called over his shoulder as two young boys tried to tackle him to the ground. 'And that's Annemarie.'

She laughed. She was doing a lot of that lately. Again Nathan had seen right through her confusion. 'Thanks, Annemarie.' Colour filled her cheeks. 'I'm in the mood for a wine, which is rare.' So much had been happening, so something, someone to relax with was perfect. Her gaze found Nathan. Having a drink made standing around talking to strangers easier, and kept her hands busy. Unless— 'You look like you need some help,' she called over to Nathan.

'Stay back, and look after those sore muscles. We have a few hours to get through yet.' When she lifted one eyebrow, he laughed. 'You're walking round like a toddler on a high.' Boys and girls fell onto Nathan, pushing him onto the lawn, tickling him as he carefully tossed one after another into the air and caught them again.

'Let's sit on the sidelines,' Annemarie said, heading for the expansive deck and some chairs, sheltered from the light, cool breeze coming off the sea. 'The men can play while the women relax with wine and nibbles. It's tiring just watching.'

Settling into a wicker chair, Molly watched Nathan and his brothers-in-law chasing kids and balls around the lawn and waited for the questions from the sisters, sipping her wine in an attempt to look the part of a friend with nothing else to do on a Saturday afternoon. That part was kind of true. When the grilling didn't come she began to enjoy herself.

'Mum, when can we eat? I'm hungry.' A little girl stood in front of them a while later, hands on hips, just like her uncle Nathan had been doing earlier.

'Ask Uncle Nathan. He's in charge of the barbecue.'

'Now,' came the call.

The women hit the kitchen, and Molly found herself taking an endless supply of salads, breads, dressings and sauces out to the huge table in the conservatory. Delicious smells wafted from the barbecue where Nathan and the guys had begun cooking steak and sausages.

'How're you doing?' Nathan came over to her. 'I've neglected you a bit.'

'It's fine. I don't need to be babysat. Anyway, I liked talking with your sisters.'

'That's a worry.' He grinned.

'You were having fun with the kids. You're just like them, getting muddy rolling around on the lawn. I half expected you to ask for a turn on the trolley.' There was a box on wheels that the men had taken turns pulling children around in.

'No one would take me on.' Another grin.

'I can see why your family descends on you.' No sign of being in control or wanting things done his way today. 'You love those kids and they love you back just as much.' She could see him with a large family of his own. Not with her—she couldn't. Her stomach squeezed a little, her mouth lost the sweet taste of the wine. 'You ever plan on having your own brood?'

Nathan turned from watching the kids arguing over a game of hopscotch to studying her a little too intently. 'Is that a loaded question?'

An important one. 'It stands to reason you might want your own family when you're so comfortable with this crowd.'

'You're right, I adore them. I fully intend on raising some kids of my own one day. What about you? You want a family some time?'

'Absolutely.' It was true. She did. People didn't always get everything they wanted, though. 'It's not something I've thought too much about lately.' Again true, because there'd never been a reason to. There hadn't been a man waiting in the wings to be a part of that life. Now there was a possibility of love happening she had to think how to go about this.

'Rosie and I had planned on starting a family as soon as I qualified.' His gaze had left her, appeared to have gone out across the lawn somewhere.

Molly touched his arm. 'Nathan? I'm sorry. I didn't mean to upset you.'

He looked at her, placing his hand over hers on his arm. 'You said sorry again.'

'Because I spoiled the moment.' He wanted a family. A bucket of cold water couldn't have chilled her any more than that information. It was the wake-up call she hated. Of course he'd want children when he fell in love again. It's what most men and women wanted. She did. Only it wasn't going to happen for her, and she wouldn't take anyone else on that ride. It would be grossly unfair to expect Nathan to drop his dream of children for her. A weight settled over her heart—

the one that wasn't supposed to be involved with this amazing man.

'Get it into your head that talking about Rosie comes as naturally to me as eating. Sure, there're moments I feel sad, but it's a whole lot worse if she's never acknowledged.' He squeezed her hand, then let it go to step aside, putting space between them. 'If it's a problem for you then there's not a lot I can do. I will never deny she was the love of my life and how hard it's been to lose her.'

Collecting a few wake-up calls today. What was next? 'I like it that you feel that way. No one should be forgotten when they've been such a special part of your life. Hearing you talk about her says a lot about you, all good.' Her smile wavered, but since he wasn't watching her she got away with it. She wasn't going to be as special to him because even if he wanted that, she couldn't allow it to happen.

Instead she had to back off in case he did start to fall for her. That's when the day would come that she'd have to tell him the very long odds of her ever getting pregnant. Already she knew a quickening of her pulse whenever she heard Nathan's voice or laugh. Felt a softening of her limbs when he touched her. This had to stop. He'd been hurt once, she wasn't giving him a second blow.

'It helps you understand.' Nathan turned back to the barbecue. 'I'd better take over before the guys burn the steaks.' He hesitated, faced her again. 'We'll have some time to ourselves later.'

'I need to head home early. Catch up on sleep. And I'm working in the charity shop tomorrow.' She needed to think all this through. Unfortunately leaving now would be awkward after she'd helped set out the food and had said she couldn't wait to sample the salads.

'If that's what you want to do.' Nathan nodded abruptly. Sensing her withdrawal?

As soon as dinner was over and the kitchen cleaned up, she'd go home and revert to the Molly he used to know. No, not that. She'd be friendly and outgoing, but no more kisses. Already, walking away wouldn't be simple. Not when she'd finally come out of a drought to find she could be aroused by a man—one in particular.

But they weren't a couple. It was presumptuous to hope there might be more to Nathan's invitations and kisses than having a good time. It was quite possible he wanted to have some uncomplicated fun, and wasn't looking for a more permanent arrangement, and that she was reading too much into his friendliness. Something she'd be better thinking about than getting her knickers in a knot because he was the one helping her step back out into the real world.

Molly shoved aside all the reasons for not spending time with Nathan and said, 'It isn't, really. I don't know what came over me.' Except she did, and it wasn't going to disappear. She should leave, now. If only it was that easy. When she finally came out of her cave she didn't want to go back into the dark, cold space that her life had become.

'Gun-shy? I'm not surprised after meeting all this lot. It's enough to scare anyone off.'

'More that I feel very comfortable with them—too comfortable, maybe.'

He ruffled her hair like she'd seen him do with his nieces. 'Nothing wrong with comfortable.'

Yes, there was, if it led to greater expectations than

were reasonable. But for tonight at least she'd relax and continue enjoying herself. And Nathan.

The family didn't leave early. It was as if they knew they were frustrating him. Nathan ground his teeth. Molly had said she'd leave after dinner, then changed her mind. Finally the brothers-in-law had made sounds about heading away and he'd had the front door open with embarrassing speed. But if they hadn't gone soon Molly might have, and he didn't want that. He wanted time with her not being interrupted by one of the children asking for more ice cream or a sister quizzing him on his next holiday plans.

'At last.' He shoved his hands in his pockets before he could haul Molly into his arms and kiss her senseless.

'You don't mean that.' She smiled as she stood in front of him, looking sensational with the riotous curls and that perfect body.

'Normally I'd agree, but tonight I just wanted to be with you for a while.' Hell, he wasn't going to be able to not kiss her.

Her breasts rose on an intake of air. 'I'm still here.'

'Tell me something I don't know.' He had to touch her. Had to. Placing his hands on her shoulders, he drew her closer. And closer. Until she was up against him, those breasts nudging his chest, her mouth so near to his. Then his mouth was on hers, kissing, tasting, drinking her in. As he kissed Molly he waited to see if she'd pull back or tense even a little, but, no, her arms were winding around his neck and her hips were pressing into his. Giving up on caution, he went deeper with the kiss, savouring Molly, her softness, her scent, all of her. Everything about her woke him up.

Then her mouth was gone. 'Nathan?' she gasped, blinking rapidly, no disappointment blazing out at him this time. But hope was, and enough desire to drown in.

'Yes, Mol. I'd like to take you to bed.'

She sank back against him, and returned to kissing the minutes away, until he couldn't take any more. Swinging her up into his arms, he asked, 'Bedroom?'

'No. Right here. Now.'

As he walked her up to the wall, he said, 'I'll be gentle.' No way did he want to frighten or hurt her.

'Don't you dare.' She lifted a leg to his thigh, freed her hands from his and wound them around his neck. 'I won't break.'

The corners of his mouth lifted. 'Tell me something I don't know.' Then he claimed her mouth, and placed his hands on her butt to lift her higher. When she wound her legs around him and settled against the growing evidence of his sex he had to take a deep breath and hold onto the need trying to break free. This wasn't just about him.

'Nathan,' she growled.

He returned to kissing, drawing out the exquisite moment for as long as possible. His mouth trailed below her ear, down her throat, to the neck of her jersey. 'Damn it. This has to go.'

How she did it he had no idea, but within moments her lace-covered breasts were before him, drying his mouth and tightening his groin to breaking point. Molly first. He pushed between them, slipped his hand under her trousers, then her underwear, and found her centre, and touched, caressed, and felt her blow apart with one hard, swift stroke.

She clung to him, hauling in gulps of air, her eyes barely open.

He waited, kissing her forehead, her breasts, her arm.

'Nathan, let me.' She wriggled in his hold, trying to unwind her legs from his torso.

'Steady,' he whispered against her feverish skin.

'Inside. I want you inside. It's your turn.'

'Shh. It's not about turns. I'm here, with you. We'll get together as soon as we remove the obstacle.' But, yes, he was more than ready.

She blinked. 'Obstacle?' Of course. 'Then let me down. I'll be quick.'

'You'd better be,' he grunted as he lowered her carefully and held her as she got rid of the rest of her clothes.

Then she was back in his arms, her legs wound around his waist. Lowering herself over his sex.

He couldn't halt the trembling throughout his body as he pushed deep inside. Molly held on tight as he withdrew and returned, winding her tighter and tighter until she exploded again. Then he let go, and rode the wave of desire, passion and need. Unbelievable.

Nathan stretched out in his bed, one hand behind his head, the other on Molly's breast as she slept. Earlier she'd been exhausted, and now after two bouts of lovemaking she'd succumbed, and had been comatose for a couple of hours.

Not that he minded. Lying here with her, listening to the soft snuffles she made, he couldn't have felt more relaxed or happy, in a way he hadn't expected to ever feel again. Though lately he'd been open to it, he just hadn't believed it might happen. Certainly not with Molly O'Keefe. Here was a woman who'd turned out to be nothing like the face she presented to the world. It could be that he hadn't known what to look for and her feisty, strong personality had been simmering in the background all along. Or it might be that with the divorce papers in her hands she'd found the hope and courage to go in search of the life she wanted.

Whatever it was, it didn't really matter, as long as he was a part of the future she unravelled. This had started as a challenge to make her like him, to be friendly towards him, but now the challenge had changed. He thought he might want her in his life—in all ways possible. Since Rosie no other woman had made him *want*. Love, a partner, family. Molly did that. *Rosie*. His heart slowed. He still missed her, but not as severely as in the past. Was he getting over the crippling loss? Did he want to have a future with another woman? Yeah, he thought he might. The only problem was that it was happening fast. Too fast?

'I'm glad your family turned up today or this might only be wishful thinking.' Molly's sleep-filled voice sounded sexy as hell.

As his body reacted in the only way it knew, he grinned, and caressed her breast, extracting a gasp of pleasure from her. 'You have an open invitation to visit any time you like.'

The sleep was rapidly disappearing from those sensational eyes, replaced with a sparkle that warmed his heart as Molly reached for him, wrapping her hand

around his obvious attraction for her. 'Knock, knock,
I'm here.'

'Can't argue with that,' he muttered as he leaned in
to kiss that exquisite mouth, before exploring her body
with his mouth. He couldn't get enough of her.

Hours later he woke suddenly as the bed rocked
sharply.

'Look at the time.' Molly sounded frantic as she
tossed the covers aside, along with the arm he'd had
around her waist. 'Ten past eight. I've got to be at the
arena by nine.'

'There's plenty of time.'

'No, there's not. I can't be late, or Coach will send
me packing permanently. I don't intend letting her
down again.' She disappeared out the door, returned
with last night's clothes, still yabbering. So unlike the
Molly of the past. 'I have to get my gear from home
and clothes to wear to the charity shop afterwards.'

Shoving the covers aside, Nathan stood up and
stretched, and she didn't stop to notice. She was definitely on a mission. 'I'll put the coffee on. You want
something to eat? Toast? Cereal?'

Finally she stopped and came to kiss him, a brief
touch of those lips on his stubble-covered chin. Nowhere near enough. 'No, thanks. I'll grab something
at home.' Then she was in the bathroom, the shower
spraying out water and the extractor fan making a
racket.

He knew when he was not needed. But if Molly
thought he'd toe the line that easily, she was going to
have to think again. In the bathroom he opened the
shower door and joined her, taking the soap from her

hands to wash her skin, starting at her neck, and working his way down to her feet. 'No complaints, madam?' He grinned through the water pouring over his head.

She waved a hand in the narrow space between them. 'How quick can you be?'

'Let me show you.'

When Molly dragged herself out of the shower not too much later and began drying her glistening skin, Nathan watched her while soaping himself. 'You're beautiful.'

Her head shot up, surprise widening her eyes.

He repeated himself. 'You are beautiful.'

Her hands hesitated in the process of towelling her stomach, and dropped to her thighs.

His gaze followed, then backed up to her lower belly. 'How'd you get that scar?' It was small, and stark against her pale skin.

The towel came up instantly, and the shutters came down over her eyes. 'I had an accident.' Then she was gone, out into his bedroom.

Snapping the shower off, Nathan picked up another towel and followed her. 'Molly, I'm sorry. I didn't mean anything by my question. I didn't even think before I asked.' The result of one of her ex's rages? Gritting his teeth, Nathan dried himself hard and fast.

Her face was blank. 'It's nothing, okay?'

No, it wasn't okay, but nothing would make him say so. His thoughtless question had already upset her. He was ready to murder someone.

Pausing in her rapid dressing, Molly looked at him with sadness pouring off her in waves. 'Sorry to rush off like this.'

He suspected she was apologising for something entirely different. It took all his strength not to wrap her in his arms and tell her everything would be all right. Because he didn't know for sure that it would be, and making false promises was not the way to go. Instead he placed a hand on her cheek. 'Go impress Coach. I'll see you later, though probably not today.' He needed some space while he thought through everything that had been happening between them.

Molly didn't look unhappy with that. 'It's fine. I've got stuff to do after basketball.' She was already making her way to the door, where she paused and looked directly at him. 'I had the best night.'

Steal his breath, why didn't she? 'So did I, Molly. So did I.' It was true. So true it was scary. And exciting. And something to think about.

Chapter 9

'Hi, Vicki. I'm not going to ask how your week-end went. It's written all over your face.' Vicki had headed north to Darwin to spend time with Cole when he wasn't on duty.

Molly banged her locker shut and pocketed her key. When Vicki didn't reply she looked closer. 'Oh, hell. Come here.' Regretting her comment, she reached to hug her friend.

Palms out towards her, Vicki shook her head. 'Don't. I'll fall apart if you're kind to me.'

'Fair enough.' How awful to have her husband head-ing away so soon for who knew how long. Molly went for a complete change of subject. 'I see you've gone all out today. Love that shade of purple in your top, and as for the boots, I'm drooling.' Relief glittered out of Vicki's sad eyes. 'Took me weeks to find boots to match my outfit. Finally found them in a second-hand shop. This is not my usual style of clothes. I'm more the black on black type. Except for the shoes.'

'Except for the shoes,' Molly said at the same time, and they burst out laughing. Leaning back against her locker, she waited while Vicki changed into her uniform. 'Hope we have a quiet night.'

'I want it so busy I don't come up for air.'

'One of us should get lucky, then.' Her ears were straining for the sound of Nathan's voice out in the department. She hadn't seen him when she'd arrived, and as he was always early he had to be tied up with a patient already.

'You been for a spin in Nathan's fancy car yet?'

'I was too busy.' Doing other things with Nathan, and avoiding certain issues that weren't going to go away no matter how much she wanted them to.

'Doing what?' Disappointment blinked out at her.

Vicki wanted her to get with Nathan? Then she'd be pleased to know what had gone on between them, but Molly wasn't spilling the beans. She didn't do juicy gossip, and when it involved herself she remained especially tight-lipped. She straightened up. 'Better get cracking and start earning my living.' Away from the questions that were likely with Vicki needing a distraction from her aching heart.

'I'll be right there.'

Joining the rest of the shift waiting for change-over, Molly still couldn't see or hear Nathan. She should be relieved, not sad. Having decided to go for friendly and easy with him, disappointed wasn't an option. Saturday night had been sensational. Not a lot of sleep, though. Instead she'd had quite a workout, and still wanted more.

'Morning, everyone. Hope you had a good weekend.' Nathan strode in with a large smile and sparkling eyes as he scanned the room, pausing for a moment when he saw her. The smile brightened briefly, then he seemed to remember where he was, who he was with, and he straightened. 'Right, let's get the show on the road.' He came to stand beside Molly, though.

Her body was doing the happy dance on the inside while externally she tried to keep her face still while listening to Mick run through the patients in the department. It wasn't easy when she was fighting the desire to curl into Nathan, struggling with the need to touch him, to feel his warm skin under her palms.

'Cubicle one, forty-two-year-old male, waiting for liver function tests to be completed. In two, fifty-six-year-old female, extreme abdo pain, query diverticulosis.' Mick continued through the list of patients, and Molly felt tired before they'd started.

'You okay?' Nathan asked quietly as everyone dispersed to get on with the shift.

Why was he asking? 'I'm good. Did you get the place cleaned up yesterday?'

'Eventually.' His smile was devastating.

'You went back to sleep.' She grinned.

'Quiet, woman, unless you want everyone knowing why I was so exhausted.' His whispered words sent a thrill of excitement down her spine.

How was she going to remain focused on not getting too close to this man who'd woken her up from her dull and cautious life?

Mick was talking to the triage nurse and now turned

to Molly. 'Can you take this one? Twenty-one-year-old male, stab wounds to his face and arms. I'll send someone else to help you in a mo.'

'On my way.' She checked which cubicle to use, glad of something to keep her busy and away from Nathan, because even standing beside him made her weak at the knees.

Got it bad, Mol?

Yeah, she was beginning to think so.

'I'll check the man out with Molly, Mick. Those stab wounds might need my sewing skills.'

So much for putting space between them. But what could she say? She liked working with him, even when they hadn't been comfortable together. He was a superb emergency specialist, and she learnt from watching him. So she went to meet her patient and settle him on the bed in cubicle eleven as the triage nurse gave them the details.

'Beau Cooper, twenty-one, stabbed with a broken bottle, significant wound to his face, minor cuts on both arms.' Sally turned to the young woman who'd accompanied him. 'Gina, here, is Beau's girlfriend. She brought him in.'

'Hi, Beau. I'm Molly, one of the nurses who's going to look after you.' She turned to Nathan. 'This is Dr Lupton.'

Nathan moved up to examine the young man's face. 'Beau, tell me what happened when you were attacked. Did you fall to the ground, bang your head? Any details are important.'

'I'm not sure. Two guys attacked me when I asked for my girlfriend's bag back. They smashed a beer bottle and got me in the head, the arms and my leg. I stayed upright, didn't hit my head on anything. That's all I can tell you.'

'How's your breathing? Are you having any difficulty with that?'

'Seems all right.'

Then the glass hadn't cut through anything vital in his throat. Holding her hand up, Molly moved it from left to right. 'Follow my hand.'

Beau's eyes slid sideways, focused on her movements.

'Good, your vision checks out.'

The curtains flicked wide and Hank joined them. 'Nathan, you're wanted in three urgently.'

'On my way.' Nathan turned to her. 'I'll be back when you've cleaned him up.'

After a quick rundown on what had happened, Hank said, 'I'll remove his jeans so we can check his legs for abrasions.'

Molly nodded. 'Might as well. Though from the small amount of blood I don't think there's anything too serious in that region, but he needs to get out of the messy clothes anyway.' The wound in Beau's neck and face was deep, his neck had damaged muscles that would require surgery that couldn't happen until the morning. She began swabbing the area, careful not to cause him any more distress.

Hank got Beau to lift his hips while he tugged the jeans off.

Their patient groaned but did as asked.

'I'll get you some penicillin next,' Hank told him. 'Who knows what was on that bottle?'

'Get something to numb the pain too.' Molly had finished cleaning the man's neck and face, and dropped the swabs into a hazardous waste bin at the head of the bed. 'I'm going to talk to Dr Lupton, Beau.'

Nathan was entering notes on a patient file on the screen. 'How's your man?'

'I'll be interested to hear what you say after you take a look at the neck and face wound. I think he needs surgery.'

Nathan's chair rolled back from the desk and those long legs pushed him upward. 'Any other serious injuries?'

'Not really. Hank's getting some drugs. The guy's in a lot of pain and trying not to show it.'

'The tough type.'

'That's because he's a boxer,' Beau's girlfriend told them minutes later. 'They're expected to take the knocks without complaining.'

'Why did those men have your handbag?' Molly asked Gina as she handed Hank the painkiller drug and checked the dates with him.

'Thought they were being clever,' Beau snarled. 'They reckoned they were better than me and could help themselves to my girlfriend.'

'Don't let them get to you. You'll only upset yourself and I'd prefer you stay calm and get on with recovering.' Nathan was at the side of the bed. 'I need to look at your wound. That all right with you?'

'Yeah.' Beau nodded, then grimaced and swore.

'Tip your head sideways. That's it.'

After a thorough examination Nathan told his patient, 'You're lucky. There's no serious damage, but a plastic surgeon will have to put it back together so you're not left with an ugly scar. In the meantime I'll put in a few temporary stitches to keep the wound closed, and the bleeding to a minimum.'

'Thanks,' Beau muttered, reaching out for his girl-friend's hand, looking scared.

'You'll be fine,' Molly said. 'I'll get the gear.'

Nathan told his patient, 'This means you'll stay in overnight.'

When Molly returned, Nathan was scrubbing his hands at the sink before pulling on gloves. She placed the suture kit on the small table next to him.

Behind her Gina was saying, 'I'll phone your mum, tell her what's happened.' Out of the corner of her eye Molly saw the girlfriend tighten her grip on Beau's hand. 'Love you,' she added as his face screwed up.

'Don't call the olds.'

'They need to know where you are. What if the police ring them?'

'I suppose.'

'Right.' Nathan stepped up to the bed. 'Let's get this out of the way.'

Molly saw Gina's face whiten. 'Why don't you go out to the waiting room to make that call? You can come back any time you like, just tell them who you're with and they'll open the security door.'

'Thanks.' Gina's relief was obvious in her speed to get away before Nathan started stitching the wound.

'Have you spoken to the police yet?' Nathan asked Beau in an attempt to distract him from the tugging and snipping as he placed stitches along the edges of the wound.

'Gina did. They're going to press charges, so I suppose they'll turn up here.'

As soon as Nathan had finished, Molly went to tell

Gina it was all right to come back, and then she went to see a ninety-three-year-old who'd been found wandering in the rain in the gardens of the rest home where she lived. 'How are you feeling, Mrs Grooby?'

The old lady opened her eyes and focused on Molly. Nothing wrong there. 'I'm good.'

'What about the last couple of days? Everything all right?' She was gaunt and looked very pale. According to the rest-home staff she'd become quite vague lately, yet right now she was alert and beginning to watch everything going on out in the department.

'I think so.'

The notes said Mrs Grooby had been disorientated when she'd arrived two hours ago. A medical event, or lonely and seeking attention? 'I'm going to ask you silly questions. Can you answer them for me?'

'Yes, dear.'

'What's our national animal?'

'A kangaroo.'

'What do people get from a library?'

'Books, of course.'

'Count backwards from ten for me.'

As the old lady muttered numbers in the correct order, Molly tidied up her bed cover and watched her patient. 'No problem. You slayed the test.'

'I heard all that. Nothing wrong with your mind, Mrs Grooby,' Nathan announced as he strolled into the cubicle.

Was he following her around? He couldn't be. Since it was a quiet night he could be trying to keep busy too. 'She's lonely,' Molly said quietly as she passed him.

He nodded. 'We see that often with the oldies.'

'You two talking about me?' Mrs Grooby's eyes lit up.

Molly chuckled. 'You're too sharp for your own good. Would you like a cup of tea?'

'Yes, please. And a biscuit?'

'Of course.' Molly headed down to the kitchen and sneaked a biscuit for herself while she waited for the tea bag to brew. Only an hour in and already she was hungry. It had to be a result of running around the basketball court Saturday and Sunday.

Mick stuck his head in the door. 'There are two ambulances on the way in with an elderly couple who were in a multiple car pile-up. Nothing serious, mostly cuts and bruises, and shock. You and Hank take them when they get here.'

'Onto it.'

The couple was shaken but alert as they were wheeled into adjacent cubicles and transferred from the stretchers to beds. The curtain between was pulled back and when Mrs Andrews tried to reach her husband's hand, Hank and Molly moved the beds closer. 'There you go.'

'Some date this turned out to be,' Colin Andrews winked at his wife. 'Should've stayed home and watched the tele.'

'I don't know. It's quite exciting in here,' his wife returned.

'Where were you off to?' There was a storm raging over the city, and it was bitterly cold out. Molly had worn her puffer jacket into work.

'It's our fifty-third wedding anniversary, and we always visit the church we were married in on the day.

We didn't have time earlier what with all the family dropping in and out like we run the best diner in town.'

Mrs Andrews's gruff voice made Molly glance at her. Something wasn't sitting right.

'Has anyone got in touch with a member of your family?' Molly asked as she sponged the lady's arms where small cuts from windscreen glass had caused bleeding.

'You don't want them descending on the ED,' Colin answered quickly. 'Too noisy.'

'You can't tell one without telling them all,' his wife hastened to add.

When Molly lifted her patient's arm she felt a tremor in the soft muscles. There was definitely something not quite right going on.

'We'll sort it,' Colin growled.

Glancing at Hank, Molly saw he'd also got the sense something was wrong. But what could they do? Their role was to patch people up and send them home again, or pass them on to specialists and wards, not to solve family problems. 'Right, I'm going to do a bit of stitching.'

'Bet you're not as good at it as Sylvia. She used to make wedding dresses for the nobs.'

'Is that so? Then she can sew you back together when I've finished with her.' Molly laughed. 'Can I get you both a cup of tea while I'm at it?'

'Best offer I've had all night.' Colin smiled, relief underlining his words. So getting in touch with their family was a no-no.

As it wasn't her place to interfere, Molly let it go with a heavy heart. Families were so important, and to lose one was beyond comprehension. When her mother had insisted she was wrong about Paul, that he'd never meant to hurt her, she'd felt she'd lost everything—her marriage *and* her family. Nowadays her mother was working hard at getting back onside, and as much as Molly wanted that, she was taking a cautious approach. 'Tea along with the needles and thread coming up.'

'Molly.' Mike appeared round the corner of the hub. 'Sixteen-year-old girl, overdosed on paracetamol. Resus, please. Hank, you okay in here?'

'Sure.'

'On my way.' Shuddering, she sped along to the well-equipped room and straight up to the bed where Nathan, a junior doctor and another nurse were working with the teen while an ambulance paramedic was filling them in on the scant details.

'The mother thinks she swallowed at least twenty tablets. When they found her she was unconscious, but has since woken and been throwing up.'

'Resultant liver damage will be the biggest concern,' Nathan explained to the other doctor as he listened to the medic reading out the obs she'd taken on the ride in. 'If she's been vomiting then I don't think it's necessary to pump the stomach. I'll give her some charcoal to soak up any remaining traces of drugs in her digestive system.'

Molly began wiping the girl to clean her up. Along with the other nurse, they stripped her and dressed her in a gown and got rid of the grubby clothes.

'Nathan, you're needed next door,' someone called.

'Now we're getting busy.' He looked to Molly, a wry smile lifting his mouth. 'That'll keep us on our toes and too busy for anything else.'

'Seems like it.' She smiled back. Why did he have

to be so sexy even when dressed in a boring green uniform? This should be the one time her mind didn't drag up images of him looking like a centrefold, or holding her against his naked body, or sitting opposite her having breakfast in the café.

When he joined her and Hank in the café for coffee and sandwiches just after eight, she was glad they weren't alone or she might've dropped her intention of keeping him at a distance—a very short one—while at work. He was near irresistible.

'You survived my lot okay.' Nathan bit into a thick bread roll filled with meat and a dash of salad. 'They can be intimidating.'

'I enjoyed myself, so thanks for inviting me along.'

Hank's eyebrows rose, before he went back to checking his phone for messages.

'You obviously like kids,' Nathan observed.

Hadn't they done this on Saturday? Because of her scar had he guessed there might be an issue with her infertility? 'Who doesn't?'

I'm not seeing where this is going.

'Not everyone thinks children are the best thing since sliced bread.'

'Certainly everyone in your family does. I'm only surprised you're capable of walking without a limp. They used you as a trampoline half the time.'

'I'm used to it. Though as they get bigger I'm going to have to tone down the level of bounce.' He was watching her like there was no one else in the room, and certainly had no qualms about Hank knowing they'd spent time together.

Hank put his phone down and picked up his mug.

'I've seen Nathan bruised and limping after a round of ball games with the Lupton bunch. He hurt for days, and got no sympathy from any of us.'

Nathan grinned. 'You were pathetic, not joining in to help me out.'

'A group of us were at Nathan's for a barbecue when some of his family showed up unexpectedly. Those kids took over like they owned the place, and we had a lot of laughs watching Uncle Nathan do his impersonation of an active seven-year-old for hours on end.'

'I know what you mean.' Obviously she wasn't the first he'd invited to his house. Why did she think she might've been when they were having a party there next weekend? It was his way of being friendly, and she'd thought there was more to it. Though he'd offered her the flat to live in. After kissing her. And now he'd made love to her. 'Kind of cute, I think.' She grinned at Nathan, who screwed his face up. 'Shows he's not always the boss.'

'I'm getting another coffee. You two need any?' Hank stood up.

'No, thanks,' Molly and Nathan answered simultaneously.

She watched Hank walk across the room, stopping to yarn with nurses from the general ward.

'I missed you yesterday.'

Knock me over with a feather.

'You did?' Warmth stole through her, softening all those knots that had begun tightening since she'd seen how much he adored his nieces and nephews and heard how he wanted to add to the bunch.

'Yes. I came that close...' he held up two fingers only millimetres apart '...to driving over to your apartment late yesterday but I know you were busy at the charity shop.' His smile hit her in the chest. 'Anyway, I sat down on the couch, and didn't know a thing until seven.'

'You old man, you.'

'You think?'

'Not for a minute.' This was fun, and relaxing, and she could do it for ever. Except—

Shut up, conscience. Let me have some fun before it's time to get real.

'Sorry I had to race away but that's how it is.' Now that she was getting a life.

'It wouldn't be if you moved into the flat.'

She hadn't seen that coming. Leaning back in the hard plastic chair, she tried to lift the blinkers and study Nathan as others might see him. There was much to like, to trust, to love even. And she couldn't help the way he turned her on, how she wanted to be with him more often. But, 'Everything's happening in a hurry. I need to keep my own space at the moment.'

'Fair enough.' His face lost its relaxed expression. 'I understand. But I'm an impatient brute at times.'

'The last thing you are is a brute, Nathan. Believe me, I know.'

He gulped, and sighed. 'It was a loose term. I need to learn to be careful of my words around you.'

She shook her head. 'No, you don't. I need to lighten up. Though I thought I was doing okay.'

'You know what? We've suddenly become serious. This isn't the place to be mentioning what's happened to you so let's relax again.' There was a plea in his eyes.

She nodded, more than happy to go along with him. 'Done.'

'So how many awkward questions did the sisters ask you?'

'Not one.' She'd been as surprised as Nathan looked. 'Not usual?'

'Not at all. My sisters believe there're no rules when it comes to their brother.' He drained his coffee.

'Families know all the buttons to push.' Would Gran have liked Nathan? She had no idea why but Molly thought she probably would have, and that gave her comfort.

'I'm glad you had a good time and enjoyed being with the kids.'

'Nathan...' She swallowed. Every time he mentioned the kids and her in the same sentence the worry intensified. It was beginning to seem like she wouldn't be able to have a few weeks of fun before telling him the truth. To be fair, that would be selfish of her. Sometime in the next few days they were going to have a full and frank conversation about her fertility—or lack of.

'Hey, guys, we're needed. All hands on deck. A van full of American tourists rolled on the highway and the first ones are expected here in ten.' Mick was already moving away in search of more ED staff.

'Mondays are supposed to be quiet,' Nathan muttered before he took a last mouthful of his roll.

Chapter 10

What was Molly's problem? She seemed all out of sync. One moment happy beyond description, the next eyeing him with trepidation. Nathan watched her calming a teenager whose friends had brought her in with numerous bee stings.

'You're not having a reaction.' Molly wiped the girl's arms. 'Yes, you copped a lot of stings, which have been removed, and you're hurting, but your windpipe is not about to close up.'

He stepped in. 'Hi, I'm Nathan, a doctor. What Molly's telling you is correct. If you'd had an allergic reaction your throat, tongue and face would be swelling by now.' He hoped that backing Molly and playing it down would quieten the shrieking, shaking girl. 'Just to make absolutely certain, let me have a look inside your mouth.'

Instant quiet returned to the area as Becky's mouth fell open for him. After his examination, he told her, 'Looking healthy. Now let me touch your neck and throat.' With gentle fingers he felt for any sign of swelling. 'Again, all good.'

Molly smiled at her, and *his* gut twisted. He had it bad. The week since his family had been in town had been sensational. Lots of laughter, shared meals and unbelievable sex. There'd been tender moments too, like when she'd made his favourite breakfast and set it out on the conservatory table with a flower in one of his beer glasses because he didn't own a vase. He did now. Molly had found him the ugliest pottery creation imaginable at the charity shop. The vase had pride of place in a hidden corner of his office. Molly had threatened to buy flowers and bring the hideous thing out for tomorrow night's party with the medical team. Who would have believed she could be such a tease? Especially with him. It was great.

'Becky, you'll soon get very itchy to go with the pain and swelling.' Molly nudged him none too gently with her elbow. 'Dr Lupton will give you something to relieve that as much as possible.'

'I'll prescribe a cream to save you having to buy one. Just apply it a couple of times until the itching stops.' Nathan nodded as he mentally ran through the available remedies, all the while trying not to laugh out loud at Molly's temerity for giving him the get-a-grip look in here. But she was right. He shouldn't get distracted by her while at work. Though how not to he had no idea. It would be better to start by staying away from patients she was involved with.

'So I'm not going to have anaphylactic shock?' Becky sounded disappointed.

'No, I'm pleased to say you're not.' Did she want attention that badly she'd risk her life? 'Have you ever seen anyone suffer one?'

'A boy at school had one once. Everyone was around him like you wouldn't believe, and he got taken away in the ambulance. He nearly died. Heaps of kids went to see him in hospital afterwards.'

Uh-huh. 'I think there are better ways of getting people to take notice of you. Like being the person who organises the others to go visiting someone who's sick. Being the sick person sucks. Apart from the pain and all the things medical staff do to you, it's boring lying around in bed all day. Especially in hospital where it's noisy and the nurses come and poke at your body any time they like.'

Molly had turned away, her sexy mouth twitching nonstop.

Becky was eyeing him warily. 'What's the food like?'

It was hard not to laugh, even though this was one mixed-up girl. 'Nothing fancy, but it passes. But you won't be finding out. You can go home shortly.' He turned away before Becky could come up with some symptom that might let her stay in overnight. 'Molly, can you get the cream for Becky when I've signed the form?'

'Sure.' She turned to their patient. 'Want your girl-friends to come in now?'

'They won't be waiting for me.'

Molly stepped closer to the bed. 'They were still there fifteen minutes ago. The triage nurse told me.'

'Really? Can they really come in?'

'I'll get them right now.' Molly headed away.

Nathan went to write up the notes on Becky. Twenty-thirty. Half an hour before he could think about heading home or to Molly's apartment. Not too long, if all went according to plan.

'Nathan.' Mick appeared in front of him. 'You're needed in Resus. Unconscious thirty-one-year-old male, fell from the third floor of an apartment, severe head injuries, punctured left lung, fractured femur both legs, and that's only the obvious.'

He moved fast, heading for Resus right on Mick's heels. So much for plans. But if he had to be waylaid then this was what he wanted to be doing more than anything.

Except it wasn't.

They worked their butts off trying to save Mason Haverstock, every staff member in Resus giving their best and more. To no avail. Mason's heart gave out due to blood loss and trauma from fractured ribs.

Nathan went into withdrawal, automatically closing everything down and signing off the case. Only when he talked to the man's wife and parents did he drag himself out of the funk the death had brought on—because he understood the pain he was inflicting by telling the crying woman what had happened. His words were intractable, and were stealing her dreams, her love, her future. These moments had always been hard, but for him they'd become almost personal since Rosie's death.

Next he went for a brisk walk around town, barely noticing the drizzle and cool breeze. What was a bit of weather when your heart was breaking?

* * *

Nearly two hours later he texted Molly from outside her apartment block. You awake? There was light behind the blinds of her bedroom so he wasn't waking her. He hoped. Anyway, if she was asleep she wouldn't hear the text land in her phone. He'd given up on the walk, had headed for home, and instead ended up here. Molly would know what he wanted. She also understood pain.

Come up. The door into the building clicked open.

'I need a hug,' Nathan said the moment he reached the third floor and found her standing in her doorway, dressed in a thick white robe.

Molly nudged the door shut with her hip and reached for him, wrapped her arms around his waist and pulled him close to nestle her face against his neck. 'That bad?'

'That bad.' He nodded against her. The guy had only been thirty-one, for Pete's sake. All his life ahead of him. A wife and two little girls left behind. Life was a bitch at times. A real ugly bitch. Nathan's arms tightened around Molly's warmth, and he absorbed her strength, the understanding, like a man starved.

Time disappeared as they stood there, Molly's soft hands beneath his shirt, caressing his back, slowly, tenderly. All he knew was that this was where he had to be, who he had to be with while the darkness roiled, then began to fade.

Finally Molly lifted her head enough to look at him. 'Tea? Or something stronger?'

He knew too well from the past that something stronger wouldn't fix his pain over losing a patient. It might blank out things if he drank enough, but those sights would return when he woke up with a mighty hangover and nothing solved. Then he'd feel a failure for being weak. 'Tea. Lots of it.'

Her smile was filled with understanding and care. Love? No, it couldn't be. Not this soon. That had to be wishful thinking. He wanted Molly to love him? Possibly. They had been having an amazing time, and he couldn't see it slowing down any time soon. But was that love? Or was he reacting to the aftermath of a gruelling night in the ED? Her smile had gone right to the tips of his toes, filling every space in his body, and his mind. His arms tightened around her again. 'In a minute.'

They drank tea, Molly's legs curled under her curvy butt on the small couch, while Nathan half lay in one of the chairs, stretching his legs across the room, his mug held in both hands as he talked out the gremlins. She asked no questions, made no comments about what he'd done for his patient, just listened, and accepted, and understood.

He hadn't had that before. Not even from Rosie. She'd hated hearing anything about his work except when they'd saved someone and even then she'd only wanted the bare, happy facts. It was the only area of his life she hadn't understood as much as he'd wanted. Yet here Molly was, totally getting his mood. As a nurse, she knew what it was like to face hell in the department.

They went to bed, holding each other like they'd never let go. Then in the early hours they made love, slowly, tenderly, and filled with so much care and—and love. Afterwards Nathan lay on his back, his hand on

Molly's butt as she lay sprawled on her stomach, sound asleep, and he stared upwards into the dark.

Love. Was that what this was? This sense of coming home, of belonging to another person in a way not even his family could give him? Love. Yes, that's what these feelings and sensations were about. Love. That softening in his belly whenever he touched Molly, listened to her sharp voice and her light laughter, smelled her scent, saw that lithe body move sometimes as though on hot coals and at others as though she was dancing through the air.

It had happened in a flash, their relationship doing a one-eighty in weeks. Who'd have believed it could happen to him again? Not again. This was different. With Rosie they'd always been in each other's lives, had grown up falling in love. With Molly, a snap of his fingers and, *voilà*, he was a goner.

Rolling onto his side, Nathan scooped Molly against the length of his body and closed his eyes.

Molly woke instantly. No slow stretching, opening her eyes one at a time. Just ping. It was Saturday morning and tonight was the work barbecue.

Nathan held her against him as though he never wanted to let her go. Soft snores told her he was out to it. Good. He needed to move on from last night's tragedy. Not that it would vanish from his mind easily. They never did. The downside to working in medicine was the toll it could take. Snuggling harder against him, she thought about last night's lovemaking. It had been very different from the other times. Slow, and caring. She'd given everything in her to Nathan, hoping to ease his pain. It must've worked, judging by his comatose state. He'd never before slept beyond sunrise with her.

Reaching for her phone, she sat up in a hurry when '08.05' blinked at her. There was a dessert to make and get into the freezer before she got ready for basketball, and then she'd promised to go round to Nathan's house straight after to help with anything he hadn't got done.

'Morning,' came a sleepy voice beside her. Then an arm began pulling her back under the covers.

'Oh, no, you don't. We've got things to do.' She pushed away.

Nathan tugged her again, causing her to sprawl across his frame. 'Starting with this.'

She gave in. How could she not?

It was the perfect way to start the day. Followed by Nathan poaching eggs and frying bacon while she made a lemon dessert. When she felt his gaze on her, she turned from whipping the cream cheese. 'What?'

'You're singing. I like it.'

'I was?' Definitely getting back to normal.

Next she hit the court with the Roos, and they stole the game fifty-eight to thirty-five.

Bypassing the after-match celebrations again, Molly headed home for a shower and to get dressed in red and white for the evening. Then she drove to Nathan's and found Vicki already there, running around with a vacuum cleaner and duster.

'I don't know why she's bothering. By the time everyone leaves tonight the place will be a lot messier than it is now.' Nathan scratched his head.

'She needs the distraction,' Molly muttered. Vicki had been valiantly trying to be cheerful all week since returning from Darwin, but everyone saw through her attempts. 'It must be hard, saying goodbye to her man so often.' She'd hate that, couldn't imagine being married to someone who was often away for long stints.

'It gets to Cole too,' Nathan admitted. 'I don't know why he went and signed up in the first place. I get wanting to do something for your country, but it's hard on family and friends, and yourself. I doubt I could do it. In a way I admire him.'

Molly's sympathy lay with Vicki, but she kept that to herself. Holding up the plastic container she'd brought, she said, 'I'll put this in the freezer and find something useful to do.'

'I hate to tell you this but everything's pretty much ready. We can kick back and relax once madam's finished making a racket with the sucky motor machine.'

'You've been spending too much time with your nephews. Sucky motor. I'll give you sucky.'

'I wish, but we're not alone.'

Molly headed for the kitchen, swallowing her laughter. Nathan was so relaxed it was hard to believe he was the same man she'd known only a couple of weeks ago.

'You two have come a long way in a short time,' Vicki said with a grin minutes later as she packed the cleaner into its cupboard.

She couldn't have overheard their banter. 'True. We're not about to kill each other any more.'

'It's great. He needs someone like you in his life. Make that he needs *you*.'

Molly looked around for Nathan. Having him overhear Vicki was the last thing she wanted.

'Relax. He's out in the conservatory, making sure there's enough gas for the barbecue. It should've been the first thing he checked. But that's Nathan.'

'What do you mean by that?'

'He can be the most disorganised male you've ever met when he's not at work. It used to drive Cole bonkers when they were flatting together.' Vicki headed for the kitchen. 'Ready for a drink? I'm not talking coffee or tea.'

'Why not? Everyone will be turning up soon.' As long as Vicki didn't start going on about Nathan she was happy to relax. Relax. A new word in her vocabulary. Suddenly relaxing had become part of her routine, along with having fun and mixing with people without looking over her shoulder. And starting to trust a man. 'I'll have a beer.'

'Coming up.'

She sank down onto the cane couch in the little nook off the kitchen where she could see out across the lawn to the sea, and if she turned her head slightly to the left Nathan out in the conservatory filled her sight, rubbing the stainless-steel lid of the state-of-the-art barbecue, bringing out the shine.

'Here.'

She took the bottle and settled down further into the thick cushions. 'This is the life.' Then she sat up straight. That might sound like she was trying to weave her way into Nathan's home for her own gain. 'I mean, how better to spend a Saturday afternoon than with friends?'

'Take it easy. You're more than a friend to Nathan.' Vicki was eyeing her over the top of her own bottle. 'I meant what I said before. You're good for him, and I think he's good for you. I don't know anything about your life before you came to work with us, but you've changed since my birthday. I'm putting some of that down to Nathan. Am I right?'

This was what good friends did. They talked, and then she'd have to give some answers back. She wasn't ready for that. Or was she? 'Yes, you're right.' Looking outside again, she sighed with happiness. Then an image of Nathan chasing his nephews across the lawn out there swiped her, and the warmth that had started filling her slowed, chilled. Children. He'd made no bones about wanting a family. He'd been honest, whereas she'd lied—if only by omission.

'Molly? What's wrong?'

Her gaze drifted back to the man tipping her world upside down. She wanted to tell Vicki nothing was wrong, but she couldn't. 'It's early days. We don't know each other very well yet.' She knew he liked having his inner thighs stroked, that it hurt deeply when he lost a patient, that he adored his nieces and nephews. Family. She stood up. 'Let's see what else needs doing.'

'Molly, sit down, and I promise to shut up.'

Because she wanted friends in her life and not just as numbers on her phone, she plonked her backside back on the couch. Anyway, she liked Vicki and didn't want to upset her. 'Here's to a great night.'

'I'm going to put some music on. I never could understand why Nathan doesn't have it playing all the time.'

'Because I like to hear myself think.' The man himself lounged against the central kitchen bench, a beer between his fingers and a lopsided smile on his face.

Molly sucked in her stomach. It was so unfair. He was gorgeous. He was everything she wanted in a man when she moved forward.

Hey, you are moving forward.

Yes, but there was some way to go before she'd allow permanence into the picture. Even though things were beginning to stack up as she wanted, it was early days.

While the other two gave each other cheek and talked about people and events she knew nothing about, Molly did some serious thinking. She had begun falling for Nathan too quickly. She trusted him as she'd once trusted Paul. He was fun, and caring, and sharing. Paul had once been fun, and caring, but sharing had been replaced by selfishness. She needed to step back, get to know Nathan better, if he hung around— and he acted as though he intended to.

Which brought her to the real problem. She had to tell him the truth. Because if she did fall in love with him, that was far too late.

'You going to daydream all afternoon?' Nathan tapped her shoulder.

If only that's what she was doing. Forcing a smile, she said, 'Got any better suggestions?'

He laughed, which went some way to lightening her mood again. But the clock was ticking. She had to tell him she couldn't have children.

'I didn't think they'd ever leave.' Nathan locked the door behind Hank and Myra before trailing into the kitchen where Molly was putting the last of the dirty glasses in the dishwasher.

'They've really gone?' Her knuckles were white as she gripped a dirty beer mug. She'd become more distant as the night had progressed.

What's up, Mol?

'The place is quiet, isn't it? Apart from the music,

and I've lowered the decibels considerably. I might have to drop leftover desserts in to the neighbours in the morning as an apology.'

'Good luck with that. I don't think there's much left.' Glasses rattled against the wire rack as she put the mug in the washer.

'Want a nightcap?' They could sit and talk in the nook, where it was warm and cosy.

'No, thanks.'

'Tea?'

'No.'

'Bed?'

Shaking her head, she shut the washer and flicked the dials. Then she leaned back against the bench, her hands gripping the edge of the counter at her sides. Apart from the low hum of water swirling inside the dishwasher the house was quiet. Too quiet. Filling with foreboding.

Nathan rushed to fill the eerie silence before Molly could ruin the warm fuzzy feeling he got when he was with her. 'Thanks for all you did tonight.' She'd been a trouper, setting out food, clearing up after everyone, making sure no one went without a drink while barely touching one herself. 'You were taught how to be the hostess with the mostest?'

Her chin jerked down once. 'Yes. Part of being my mother's daughter was the social training that went on every day, no matter what else was happening.'

Had Molly ever been herself, doing what she wanted, how she wanted? Or had the basketball, the nursing degree and whatever other things she'd achieved been done because she'd been put under pressure? Had she spent all her life trying to please others? He wouldn't expect that of her. Ever. 'Now you can do whatever you want. You could even have tipped Carry's drink over his face when he started making rude suggestions to you and Myra.'

'I came close, believe me.' She shrugged. 'It's all right. He'd had too much to drink and will probably fall over backwards apologising on Monday.'

'True. It's not the first time, and won't be the last. I'd like to not invite him to these dos, but he's one of the team, one of the best, and everyone has their issues.'

So what's yours tonight, Molly?

'He'll pay you back for the taxi you organised. You're right, he is one of the best—when he's sober.' Worry was in her gaze, making her nibble her lip and turning those knuckles whiter than ever.

'Talk to me.'

Her eyebrows lifted, fell back into place. 'Too clever for your own good, you are.'

The foreboding increased. This was about him. He'd swear on his next breakfast Molly was about to dump on him. Or walk away for ever. His gut tightened as nausea rose. They weren't an item so how could she drop him? This called for something stronger than a beer that had gone flat over the hour since he'd opened the bottle. Standing, he reached around Molly for the wine bottle.

She flinched.

Slowly withdrawing his hand without touching the bottle, he backed off two steps. 'I'd never hurt you,' he ground out through clenched jaws. 'Never.' It hurt for her to think differently.

'I know.'

'So what was that about?' They'd come far, or so

he'd thought. Guess it wasn't easy to get over what had been done to her.

'I'm sorry.'

He hated that word coming from Molly. It came loaded with the need to please, to be safe, and she did not have to do that around him. 'You don't owe me an apology for anything. But I would like an explanation.'

Her breath intake was ragged. 'You're right. You're owed one.' She was being too compliant.

He wanted to shake her gently, make her stop being that person and return to being the Molly he was getting to know, but instead he poured a small wine and returned to sit down, giving her space, wishing he could wrap her in a big hug and hold her until she never, ever felt afraid again. He should be able to without worrying he was making her uncomfortable. 'I thought we were getting close enough to talk about most things.'

Especially since you told me about your ex.

'I think I will have a drink after all.'

He started to get up to get it for her but she put up a hand in the stop signal.

When she sloshed as much wine on the bench as into her glass Nathan knew he was in trouble.

Putting his drink aside, he sat straighter, needing to focus on Molly and whatever was worrying her. He waited. His gut churned. His heart thumped hard and heavy. And he waited.

Perching on a stool, she sipped her drink and put the glass aside to jam her shaking hands between her knees. Then finally she raised her head and eyeballed him.

He wished she hadn't. He would far prefer her not to

say a word, to carry on with the silent treatment. There
was something in her look that said his world as it had
become was about to disintegrate. Rushing in, he said,
'You can trust me not to hurt you that way.'

You're repeating yourself.

'Not in any way, if I can help it.'

'Nathan. I get that. In spades. Otherwise we
wouldn't have been spending as much time together
as we have. Even though it's only been a short time, I
trust you. It's me who hasn't been up-front about everything.' Her breasts rose and the last drop of colour
drained from her face. 'I don't see me having babies
any time soon. If at all. And they're important to you.'

His heart slowed, his lungs seized, his head spun,
yet his eyes never left hers as he tried to figure out
where this was going. 'You said you wanted kids.'

'Yes. One day, maybe. Right now I'm getting back
on my feet after the horror that was my marriage. I
don't know what I want for the future. I don't trust myself to get it right straight away. It's too soon.'

'I understand that.' As much as he could, because
it was a bit like him falling in love with her after the
wonderful relationship he'd had with Rosie. But he
hadn't known fear like Molly had. Hadn't had his belief
in Rosie undermined. Hadn't seen those she should've
been able to trust not back her until later on, by which
time her heart had already been broken. So, really, he
knew nothing about where Molly was coming from.

Suddenly she was right in front of him, hands gripping hips, her eyes flashing. 'No, you don't,' she yelled.

Nathan waited, not wanting to risk upsetting her
further.

She breathed deeply, said in a quieter voice, 'I know

you've tried, but I'm still working at understanding myself, so how can you?'

He began to rise, to scoop her into his arms and hold her safe.

Her hand shot up in the stop sign again. 'No. Please, no.'

He stilled, waited.

'Sit down. Please,' she added quietly, and he knew she hadn't finished. In fact, she started before he'd taken a step, like it was a force that had to be set free. 'Watching you with your family brought it home to me that I'm being unfair to expect you to spend time with me when I can't guarantee I'll ever be ready to want to settle down, let alone have a family. If we could guarantee we'd have some fun and walk away happy then…'

She swallowed hard. 'I'm screwed up, Nathan, and while I might have stopped looking over my shoulder at every turn, I still have nightmares about being strong enough to cope with what's ahead.'

'You're stronger than anyone I know,' he ground out through the anger filling him for the man who'd done this to sweet, beautiful Molly.

'It's skin deep,' she whispered. 'Those steps I talk about taking—a toddler could do better.'

'You're taking them. That's all that matters.' Still he wanted to haul her into his arms and never let her go, to make her feel better, and stop the ache that was expanding in his chest. But the stop sign was still in her eyes, in the tight way she held herself, as though if she relaxed even a fraction she'd shatter. He also wanted, needed, to fight her gremlins for her, but Molly would never let him do that. She fought her own battles. All he could do was be there for her. 'You need more time. We don't have to stop seeing each other.'

'And if I still don't feel I can have a permanent relationship after we've spent a lot of time together?' Her curls shook as she talked. 'No, Nathan. You deserve better than that. You can love again, and have the life you want. You've been honest about your love of family and the children you want one day. I will not risk taking that opportunity away from you.'

Yeah, the news was starting to seep in around the edges of the haze in his mind, and making him begin to understand the full impact of what Molly was telling him. He had always wanted children. Growing up in a large, happy family, it had been a given he'd add to the clan, as his sisters had. Not once, not even when Rosie had died, had he given up on that dream completely. But did he want them at the cost of love? He was half in love with Molly already. Half? Now was not the time to think about it. He'd finally let a woman close for the first time since Rosie. Yeah, and look where that was getting him.

His heart was on the way to taking another battering. He didn't want to lose Molly, he wanted them to make this journey together. If at the end of it she still wasn't ready for him then he'd have to take it on the chin. But he wanted the opportunity to give it all he had. 'Why haven't you said any of this earlier?' It might've saved him falling for her. Except he'd thought that had begun the day she'd started in the department. 'You've told me so much about what happened, it would've been simple to finish it with this. I'd at least have been warned.' Anger was beginning to simmer. At her for not trusting him enough, at himself for fall-

ing for her, for finally letting go the restraints Rosie's
death had put on his heart.

'At first I didn't see what was happening. I do want
love and family. One day. If I can get past all that's
happened. I'm afraid I might be reading too much into
my feelings for you. You're everything Paul wasn't. I
want that. What I don't want is to make you into someone you're not, and I could be unwittingly doing that.
I need time, and getting out and about with people,
before I'm ready for a commitment. It's essential to
know I'm not making another horrendous mistake—
for everyone's sake.'

Pain sifted through his tight chest muscles. This
was not how he'd seen the night finishing. But life
loved throwing curveballs. He already knew that, had
dealt with it and had thought he was coming out the
other side.

'I'll always be here for you, Molly. I care a lot about
you.' Damn it. He wanted to say he'd move on and be
grateful she'd thought of him when trying to sort her
life out, but he couldn't. It wasn't true. Neither was telling her he was falling in love with her a wise idea. It'd
be putting everything back on her, and it was obvious
she already felt terrible about this. He also had to own
some of it for rushing in.

'You sure we can't continue as we are, and see how
it turns out?' He wouldn't get down on bended knee.
Only because he already knew it wouldn't work and
he had to have some pride left when she walked out.

Knuckling her eyes, she took her time answering
him. 'I'm sorry. I didn't know if we were having a
couple of dates and then getting back to life as it used

to be, though a lot friendlier, or we'd end up disliking each other.'

'Stop saying sorry. You're being truthful.'

'And that includes being sorry.' She shook her head, those blasted curls flicking in every direction. 'I wanted another week with you before I said what was bothering me.' She swallowed. 'I once believed in love so much I thought it could overcome everything, now it's hard to accept I was wrong.'

So she'd been happy with him. That put the final wedge in the situation. Molly O'Keefe had wanted to spend more time with him and she'd just made absolutely certain it wasn't going to happen.

Molly staggered into her apartment and sank to the floor. She'd lied to Nathan—again by omission, but she'd been untruthful all the same. He deserved better. Through what Paul had done to her, she'd become someone else, a person she barely recognised at times. Honesty was of paramount importance now. On the other hand, telling Nathan about the small chance she'd ever get pregnant wasn't ever going to happen. If he'd said he'd take the risk, she'd have to live with the hurt caused if it didn't happen. She was not prepared to do that. He'd thank her one day.

Her heart was shredding, her head throwing so many accusations at her about dumping Nathan, it was a wonder she'd managed to drive home safely from Coogee. But she had. There wasn't anywhere else for her to be. This was her home—small, lonely, but hers. She did not belong in Nathan's house, or in his flat.

How had she fallen in love so quickly? The answer didn't matter. She did love Nathan. Though what she'd told him was also true. It might only be a step in getting her life back. A temporary one, though judging by the agony in her chest that was complete and utter nonsense. With Paul she'd believed love would win the day. How wrong could she have been? That was the reason she was struggling to believe in herself now.

Yet, deep inside, a kernel of hope and longing and that love said this was for real. That Nathan was the right man for her. He'd always look out for her, come what may.

'I did the right thing. Especially for Nathan.'

Didn't I?

'Yes.'

She had to believe this was the right way to go or she'd never get up in the morning. But, hell, she hurt. Everywhere. Who'd have thought she'd feel like this after such a short time with Nathan? Truthfully? She'd never expected to fall in love again when Paul had blotted her thoughts of what love was meant to be. But she had. And thereby done the right thing by Nathan in walking away before they got in too deep. Except she'd already done that. Deep, then deeper, her heart was tied up in knots for him.

Her phone lit up as a text came in. You get home all right? Nathan. Caring to the end.

A waterfall cascaded down her cheeks. Something special and wonderful had ended. She had to be that strong woman he mistakenly believed she was. Fake it till she made it.

Tap, tap on the phone. Yes. Sorry. Molly paused. Stop saying sorry. She deleted the word, typed, Thanks, and pushed Send. *Fake it.*

Her bed was cold—and lonely.

Her head ached. The pillow was soon soaked.

Her heart went through the act of giving her life, all excitement and happiness gone, just a regular pumping.

So much for finally joining in on the work social scene. She'd been afraid of trusting people and had been the one to dump on Nathan's trust. Now she had to continue working with him because running away was not an option. She'd stand tall and take the knocks. *And* be strong, even if she had to fake it in the beginning.

Until now she'd believed of all the things Paul had done, taking away her baby and leaving her with only one damaged Fallopian tube was the hardest thing to deal with. Now she knew different. Walking away from Nathan was worse. He'd lost Rosie; he didn't need to lose his chance of having children with someone in the future. His nieces and nephews adored him, and the youngsters he dealt with in the ED were always in awe of him. He'd be an amazing father.

Snatching the box of tissues, she scrubbed her face, but still the tears flowed. Never before had the knowledge of not being able to have a child been quite so devastating. No children, no Nathan.

Chapter 11

'Can you look at two-year-old Lucy Charles?' Molly asked Nathan. 'She's got a plastic top from a small tube stuck in her ear. She's a right little cutie, even if she is screaming the place down.'

'You've tried oil to get the top out?' Nathan asked, ever the professional with her, though there were times he'd ask how she was doing at basketball or in the op shop.

Over the past month she'd become so used to the thudding in her chest whenever she was near him that she could answer without hesitation now. 'No. She's not letting anyone near her head, let alone the offending ear.' Maybe Nathan could charm the wee dot into letting him make her better.

'It's never easy with a toddler.' Nathan swung open the curtain to the cubicle from which shrieks emanated. 'Hello, Mrs Charles. I'm Nathan, a doctor.' He crouched down to be face to face with the little girl. 'Hey, Lucy. What's that on your shirt?' He pointed to the rabbit.

Lucy stared at him, hiccupping through her tears.

'Is it a cat?'

A headshake.

'Is it a horse?'

Another shake.

Nathan put his finger to his lips. 'I don't know, then. You'll have to tell me.'

'Wabbit.'

'So it is. Have you named it?'

'Wobby.'

'Can I look at his ear? It's so big.'

Lucy stared at him, then looked at her mother.

'Go on, show the doctor Robby's ear.'

Without touching her T-shirt, Nathan pointed to the rabbit's ear. 'Look, there's something stuck in there. I'm going to have to pull it out.' Clenching his hand tight, still without touching the shirt, he made a pulling motion and then looked into his palm. 'Yes, I've got it. Wobby didn't feel a thing. Now can I see your ear?'

Lucy shook her head.

'Not easily tricked, are you, little one?' To Lucy's mother, he said, 'I'm going to give her something to quieten her down enough so I can remove the obstruction. She'll be sleepy for an hour or two afterwards but there won't be any side effects.' Then he said to Molly, 'Can you get the drugs? I don't want to leave Lucy while she's comfortable with me.'

'Sure.' Nathan was so good with kids. Her heart skittered. She knew that. It was why she'd walked away from him, but it wasn't getting any easier to accept. Seeing him every day in the department, she was constantly questioning her ability to carry on working here. But she had to. She'd vowed not to weaken, to be that strong woman Nathan believed she was.

Once Lucy accepted the syrup she began to calm down almost immediately and the button was soon removed, then she was on her way home with her mother, and Molly went looking for someone else to help.

'Molly, ready for a break?' Vicki appeared around a corner.

'Is it time already?' She had no appetite for the soup she'd brought from the local deli but she'd go through the motions. Changing direction, she headed for her locker.

'Sure is. You were miles away. Or maybe only three cubicles down, where a certain doctor is about to examine an abscess.'

'You got nothing better to do than make up stuff?' Molly asked around the longing that wasn't in a hurry to go away.

'Better than thinking about my own problems.'

'You heard from Cole today?'

'Four times. They're heading back to Randwick late Saturday.'

Molly smiled as she opened her locker to retrieve her supper. 'That's good news.'

'It is.'

That's it? Not sure whether to press for more, Molly stayed quiet. As her soup heated in the microwave she threw out, 'You know where I am. Come round for coffee any time.'

'What time are we going to look at that apartment?'

'Eleven tomorrow morning.'

'I might watch your basketball game too.' Vicki wasn't getting her nails done, or sprucing up the apartment for Cole? There was definitely something wrong.

Molly shivered. She and her new friend made a right sorry pair.

Nathan held his breath. What apartment? Where? Molly was moving? His flat was still available.

Yes, but she doesn't want you in her life outside here.

He should be glad Vicki was going with her to check out the new place, but all he could think was, *Why didn't you ask me to go along?*

Making an abrupt turn, he headed for the lift to go downstairs to the cafeteria. Sitting in the same small room with Molly, hearing her talking and laughing with others, was too much.

She didn't ignore him at work, did her best to remain friendly and approachable without expecting any special attention, which he'd had to back off from giving or risk upsetting her further. Yet it was as though she was a stranger. Wound up in plastic wrap, visible yet unavailable, nothing changing. His life was on hold. His head spun.

Life could be horrid, throw up the worst of bad deals, and Molly had had more than her fair share. He hurt with missing her. But he also had to sort out what it was he wanted in life. For all Molly had said, she was right about one thing. He did want a family. But he wanted it with her. Which it seemed was an impossibility, for now at least.

Then again, the day would probably come when Molly was ready, and then what? If he'd walked away as she was trying to make him do then they'd have missed out on the wonderful, loving relationship that he believed was possible. The question he'd been asking himself for the past weeks was, *Do I want to miss out on love so I can have children?*

The only answer that made its way into his skull was no. Yet he hesitated to try and persuade Molly to take a chance on them. Something in the pain that had bored into him from her desperate eyes when she'd told him she might be making a mistake held him back. *He* didn't want to cause *her* any more pain.

His phone rang. 'You're lucky I'm taking a break,' he told his sister. 'You working late?' It was after midnight.

'Only time it's quiet around here.'

'The joy of having those brats.'

'We're not coming up for the weekend,' Allie said. 'Russ has pulled a murder inquiry.'

'You and the kids can still come down.'

'Or you and Molly could come here for the weekend.'

It was like a punch in the gut. His sister thought Molly was a serious part of his life. 'She's got other things on.'

'Nathan, you've let her get away, haven't you?'

'You've read too much into our relationship.'

'We all think she's wonderful. She fitted in with everyone, and that's saying something.'

How true. 'You're right on that score.' Why did Allie automatically think he was at fault for Molly no longer being on the scene?

Ever consider Molly might have dumped me?

'I'm going now. I need to eat before I get hauled back to the department for someone who had nothing better to do on a Friday night than get into a scrap somewhere.'

'Nathan.'

'If I didn't know better, I'd say that was Mum talking to me.'

Allie chuckled. 'Believe it, brother. Now, tell me what's going on.'

'I'm at work, Allie.'

'Having a break. You wouldn't be worrying what Rosie would have to say about you finding someone else, by any chance?'

'Hardly. She told me to move on and not live on my own for ever.' So why the hesitation on his part? He couldn't put it all on Molly. Was trying to save her pain an excuse for his own insecurities? Talk about mixed up. At some point they both had to take a step into the unknown, whether it was together or with other people. He wanted to do it with Molly. So *was* he worried about letting Rosie's memory down?

'Are you sure?' His sister echoed his doubts.

No, he wasn't sure about any damned thing. 'Got to go. Talk later in the week.' He ended the call before Allie said anything else disruptive to his thinking. Not that it was hard to do, he thought as he bit into the chicken roll he'd bought at his favourite bakery. Today they'd failed him. The roll was tasteless, the bread dry, and there wasn't enough mayo. Tipping the lukewarm coffee down the sink, he went back to work in search of a distraction. One that didn't have red curls and sad eyes.

Saturday morning found Nathan charging up and down the lawn with the mower as if a swarm of bees was after him. How was Molly's apartment viewing going? The place was closer to Bondi Beach than Bondi Junction. She'd shown no reticence about filling him in on the scant details she'd obtained from the agency when he'd asked. He hadn't asked what had happened to the idea of purchasing a property. Could be she wasn't as ready for something permanent after all. It's what she'd said about a relationship with him.

Nathan ran out of lawn to do battle with. Now what? If there were some waves he'd go surfing, but the sea couldn't be calmer. If only the kids had turned up. He was in his happy zone with them. Family was what it was all about.

There's more to family than just the children. You need the right woman first. Not only as the mother but for you, your partner, lover, holder of your heart.

He shook his head. When he'd finally found the woman he wanted to be with, a woman he'd started letting into his heart, it had all gone wrong.

Did I scare her off?

Nathan sank down on one of the outdoor stools and stared unseeingly out to sea. Was that why she'd pulled out? The only thing wrong with that idea was that she'd sounded so genuine about not being sure of herself, of needing more time to become comfortable with herself. A lot more comfortable. Molly didn't lie or exaggerate. She'd meant every word, so he could relax on that score. He hadn't frightened her away. But there had been more to what she'd said. He'd seen it flicker through her eyes as she'd turned to leave that night.

Could it be his need to have children that was the problem? That she was afraid of letting him down? Because she would be nervous about not getting everything right with the man she finally gave her heart to. That was a given, after what her ex had done to her.

This was getting too complicated. Overthinking everything in an attempt to find answers that only Molly could give him.

Tugging his phone from his pocket, he called Molly on speed dial, and listened to the ringing go on and on until voice mail picked up. Hearing her message to leave a number and name made his heart slow and his stomach tighten. Damn it. After Rosie had died he'd often rung her phone just to hear her voice. He hit 'end'. This was spooky. Molly was out there somewhere. He'd see her on Monday if not before. She hadn't gone away for ever. Comparing the situation with that of Rosie was desperate.

He rang Molly's number again. 'Hey, Molly, it's Nathan. Give me a buzz when you get a moment. Nothing urgent.'

She must've got that because he didn't hear back from her.

Finally, unable to focus on any of the chores that needed doing, he went for a drive. It wasn't until he was driving over the Harbour Bridge that he realised where he was going. A calm settled over him. Yes, he needed to do this, to find out if he was ready to move forward.

The house was small, tired, and didn't touch him in any way. Rosie's immaculate gardens were a riot of weeds and kids' toys, and he felt a moment of sadness for what had been. A dog lay on the front porch, too lazy to lift its head when he stopped at the front gate. He and Rosie had intended getting a dog one day when there was time to look after it properly, but seeing the setter sprawled over the spot Rosie had used to sit in the sun didn't raise any feeling other than nostalgia.

'I miss you, darling, but you've gone. As has the house with all our hopes and dreams. It's someone else's paradise now.' Like Rosie, it had morphed into something different, freeing him to get on with his life, to make a new future with Molly. He'd always miss Rosie, love her quietly, but to spend for ever mourning her was to waste the life he'd been given. As Rosie had told him in that last hideous week, 'Life's precious, Nat. Grab it and make the most of what you get. Don't spend it all thinking about what might've been. Do it for me, if not yourself.'

'Actually, Rosie, I am going to do this for me. And Molly.' There was a spring in his step as he walked away from the past.

The band was so loud her eardrums were bursting. It was also out of tune and the guy at the microphone couldn't have sung his way out of a paper bag if he'd tried.

'That's terrible.' Molly grimaced, and took a sip of her vodka. The second in one night. *Turning into a lush, girl.*

Vicki raised her glass in salute. 'At least he's still upright, unlike the drummer.'

They were at a bar in Randwick, close to the army base. Needing to be busy, Molly had offered to drive Vicki out here to meet Cole when his unit got into town early in the morning. After checking into a motel down the road, they'd come along to the pub for a meal, though Molly had barely touched her food, her stomach permanently tied in knots. Her clothes were a little looser too. Funny how once she'd have been thrilled about that, and now thought she looked better with a little weight on her hips to fill out her gorgeous trousers and skirts.

Molly looked around at the crowd and wished she'd stayed in the city. She didn't belong here. Standing up, she set her half-full glass aside. 'Let's go. I can't take any more of this.'

'Spoilsport.' But Vicki was quick to follow her. Outside they both checked their phones. Vicki scowled. 'Nothing. Where's Cole?'

Molly stared at her screen. 'One missed call.' She knew the number off by heart. 'Nathan.' They still talked, although not in a relaxed way as before. He hadn't phoned her since they'd gone their separate ways. If he hadn't said it wasn't urgent, she'd be starting to worry.

'What did he want?'

Molly shrugged. 'No idea.' She'd love to talk to him, to touch his hand, and feel his lips on her cheek. It wasn't going to happen. She'd left him. It was over.

'Here we are.' Vicki gestured to the bright neon lights flickering on and off. 'Why are we staying in a motel when I could be at home in my big comfy bed, watching TV?'

'Because Cole is about to ride into town, looking for you,' Molly said. 'Plus I don't drive after drinking.' Neither did she want to go home to her empty apartment. It echoed of Nathan. Fingers crossed, she'd be moving very soon. The owner of the place she'd inspected that morning was getting back to her tomorrow after he'd checked exactly when the current tenants were moving out. She hadn't found the strength to go looking for somewhere to buy. Seemed she wasn't as far ahead in her new life as she'd hoped.

Right then Vicki got a text. 'Cole says he'll be knocking down the door at six.'

'I'll get out of the way by a quarter to.' Molly set the alarm on her phone.

'Don't rush off on my account. Damned time of the month. The army never gets it right.'

She grinned. 'Some things we can't control. But I still don't want to be here for the reunion.' Molly stripped down to her underwear and slid under the covers of the nearest bed. 'Get some sleep so you're not dozing off on your husband.'

Molly fell asleep immediately, only to sit bolt up-right some time later, her head thumping along with her heart. Time of the month. No. Not possible. Can't be. Picking up her phone, she brought up the calendar.

Closing her eyes, she drew air into her lungs, and tried again. It had been due last week. Her periods were never reliable. This would be another example of na-ture rubbing her loss in her face. But—what if… No. She tossed the duvet aside and clambered out of bed to sit on the hard chair, her legs tucked under her, her body trembling. Sleep would be impossible. At least until she found out if she was pregnant.

She *couldn't* be.

She showered, dressed, and crept out of the unit at five thirty, leaving a note saying, 'Have a great couple of days. See you at work.'

In the car with the engine running she blew on her cold hands. Now what? It was too early for any shops to be open to buy a test kit. But she wanted to be at home when she found out the result so headed for Bondi

Junction, concentrating on driving and not what she'd do if the test was positive. Go knock on Nathan's door and apologise for walking away from him so quickly?

What had to happen was that she did not make any rushed, emotionally driven decisions that she'd come to regret.

Damn it. Her hand hurt where she'd hit the steering wheel. This was crazy. Here she was already thinking the test would be positive when in all reality there'd be no blue line. Her stomach sank. The gynaecologist had been clear about her slight chance of having a baby.

In Bondi Junction she sat outside the shopping centre, feeling ill, until it opened. With her purchase finally in her hand, she headed for home and privacy, afraid of the outcome, almost too scared to find out. Almost.

'Answer your damned phone, Molly O'Keefe,' Nathan shouted, dropping his on the bench with a clatter. 'I need to talk to you,' he added in a lower tone. 'Please.'

He paced the kitchen. Think of another way to get her attention. Climb the Harbour Bridge and threaten to jump off? Then she'd really believe he was mad. Mad for her might not work in the circumstances.

The phone rang. Hope soared. Allie's name blinked at him. Not in the mood for her wisecracks or helpful suggestions, he ignored her. She'd told him the family thought Molly was the bee's knees. His gut had been telling him the same for weeks now. If only he'd listened earlier he might not be feeling so sore and uptight.

He did need to talk to someone, just not his sister.

Molly. Snatching up the keys to his four-wheel drive, he
headed for the garage, where he paused. If she wasn't
taking his calls then what were the chances she'd let
him into her apartment? His gaze fell on the monster
car, the sparkling paintwork reminding him it hadn't
been out for a run in weeks. Not since the day he'd
brought Molly home for the first time. The day he'd
suggested a fast ride out of the city. The first time he'd
seen how excitement turned her eyes to emeralds and
brought tenderness to her face.

Now he knew what to do. His finger zipped across
the keys on his phone.

Hey, Molly, feel up to that ride in the red machine I
promised weeks ago? I'm heading for the Blue Mountains and would like some company.

He pushed Send before he had time to overthink
things. Now what? Stand here waiting for a reply that
most likely wasn't coming? Nope. He'd pack a picnic,
find a blanket to spread on the grass, and put a bottle
of wine in a chiller pack. Then he'd change into something less manky and head for Bondi Junction.

Midmorning, Molly gave up on her walk and let
herself into the apartment, automatically reaching for
the kettle to make tea. Her stomach told her it was not
taking tea or anything else right at the moment. But
she needed to eat. She had a baby on board to look out
for. She also needed sleep, but that was probably asking too much when she felt wired. And with her mind
throwing up so many questions and doubts—all to do
with Nathan. The father of her baby. He had to be told,

and soon. She wouldn't hold out on him. This new version of herself—still tinged with the old one but getting past that—would not hold back on the truth. All of it this time.

Her phone pinged. Nathan again.

Hey, Molly, feel up to that ride in the red machine I promised weeks ago? I'm heading for the Blue Mountains and would like some company.

So would I. Yours especially.

But would Nathan still be talking to her after she gave him her news? Or would he say she'd only told him to get back with him for all the wrong reasons? Only one way to find out. Shirking this was what the old Molly would've done. She was going to be a mother; she had to be tougher than she'd ever been. Starting with talking straight to Nathan.

Sinking onto a chair, she stared at the phone in her shaky hand. *Do it.*

Yes, please. Then she dug deeper. Do I get to drive?

I promised, didn't I? Ten minutes away.

Ten minutes? What was she going to wear? The most important date of her life and she had to look good. Sensational even. She was going to blow Nathan out of the water with her news and—and he wouldn't care about what she was wearing. Her shoulders dropped.

This is being tough?

The green floral dress was too loose, the black trousers and orange shirt didn't go with the new boots, the red blouse and cream trousers looked good and felt all wrong. The pile on the floor grew as her ward-robe emptied.

'What will you think of me when I tell you the rest of why I had to leave you, eh, Nathan?'

Ding-dong.

She was about to find out. Unless— No, she was not going to chicken out.

Ding-dong.

Molly ran through the apartment in her underwear and stabbed the button by the door. 'You can't come up. I'll be with you shortly.' Not waiting for his reply, she raced back to her bedroom and tugged on jeans and pulled a cream jersey over her head. But when her curls refused to be contained she stopped to stare at herself in the mirror.

What do I care about my appearance? We're going for a drive and I'm going to tell him about the baby and then he'll bring me home and life will go on as it has for the past few weeks.

Picking up a twist tie, she bundled up her hair and aimed for the door, not bothering with make-up. There'd be no drive anywhere. She couldn't sit beside Nathan pretending all was well in her world on the trip to the Blue Mountains.

Nathan was leaning against his fancy car, his arms crossed over his chest, his eyes fixed on her from the moment she stepped outside. 'Molly, I've missed you.'

She didn't bother with the rejoinder about seeing each other every day at work. They both knew that's not what he meant. Her mouth flattened. Where to start?

He continued, 'You look pale, and those shadows under your eyes are a worry.'

She stared at the man she loved, the man she was about to rock off his pedestal. 'You're not looking so perky yourself.' Then she looked harder. Wrong, Mol. There was something assured about him, a confidence— No, Nathan was always confident. Today he looked comfortable in his own skin. 'Forget I said that. You look great.' Might as well start out as she meant to go on.

'You think? I've not been sleeping very well.'

'Me neither.' Nights spent tossing and turning, trying to solve the riddle that was her life.

Come on, get this over. Before we get into the car, and then I won't have an agonising hour on the road sitting beside him as he takes in what I have to say.

The words stuck in her throat, refused to budge.

'Come on. Let's get on the road.' He held the driver's door open for her.

Finally she managed to speak. 'Nathan, I've got things to tell you first.'

'Same. But let's not do it out on the street. I'd like to take you to the mountains where we can talk all day if necessary. Please.'

The trip home afterwards might be long and cold. Or—or it might be the greatest trip she'd ever made. It might also be her last time with him. 'Okay. But you drive.' She wouldn't be focused enough.

'Now you're worrying me.'

There was a small smile coming her way and she ran with it, gave a tight one back. 'Let's go.'

They rode in silence, tension building as the kilometres flew by. At one point Molly wanted it over, then she wanted to continue driving the highway right into the night.

Nathan finally pulled into a parking area and turned off the engine. 'Want to walk a bit?'

'Yes.' It would be easier saying what was bottled up inside her if she was moving, not sitting looking directly at Nathan. But when he took her hand as they strolled along a path heading out to a bush-clad hill-side, she nearly cried. She'd missed his touch. Face it, she'd missed everything that was Nathan. Even his grumpiness, though there had been some of that at intense moments in the department.

'Molly, I've screwed up big-time.'

Hello? She tried to pull her hand free, but he tightened his grip.

'Hear me out, please?'

'Nathan, there are things you need know first.' Panic started squeezing her chest. 'I haven't been entirely honest with you.'

'Stop, Molly. I could say the same.'

What? Nathan was so honest it could be brutal. Or was that wishful thinking? By hoping for the man of her dreams to push away the past, had she overlooked his faults? No. She wouldn't believe that for a moment. This was the man she trusted completely, did not expect to turn into a monster once she'd given him her heart. 'Go on.'

He stopped walking and turned to face her, reached for her other hand. 'I love you. I think I have from the first time I set eyes on you.'

Her knees sagged. This was not what she had been expecting. Not that she knew what he'd been going to say, but it sure hadn't been this. 'I—'

He shook his head. 'Let me finish. Yes, I love you with all my heart. But I don't want to rush you into anything you're not ready for. I hear your uncertainty about being ready for a relationship. I'll wait for you, Mol, for as long as it takes.' He swallowed, tightened his hold on her hands. 'And if you decide I'm not the man for you then I'll deal with that too.'

Tears spurted down her face. Nathan loved her. The man she'd fallen for loved her. They could make this work. Be a family. She could forget the past, be happy again. Tell him first she loved him? Or about the baby? He mustn't think her love was because of the baby, and that she needed him onside for that only. 'I'm pregnant.'

'What?' He rocked forward like he'd taken a blow to the solar plexus. 'You're—*we're*—pregnant?'

'Yes.' She stepped back, tugging free of his grip. And he let her go. 'I don't know how it happened as we were always careful, and my chances of getting pregnant were slim.'

'We didn't use protection that first time. Besides, those condoms had been lying in my drawer for a while. Hang on. Why were your chances slim?' Then understanding dawned in his eyes, tightened his mouth. 'That scar on your tummy. He did that, didn't he?'

She nodded. 'I was four months along. Paul was jealous of our unborn baby. Said he wasn't sharing me with anyone, not even his own child.'

'Oh, Mol.' As Nathan wound her into his arms, he asked, 'Has that got anything to do with why you said you couldn't go on seeing me?'

Leaning back to read his expression, she nodded. 'I've only got one Fallopian tube, and even that's not in the best shape for conception. Or so the specialist thought. It seems he was wrong.' Nothing showing in Nathan's face said she shouldn't continue. 'You want a family, I couldn't guarantee you one, so in a way I lied. I didn't want to hurt you in the future when a baby didn't come along. If I'd told you, you might've felt sorry for me and pretended everything was all right.'

'I'd never do that.'

She nodded. 'Deep down I knew it, but I'm still insecure about knowing I'm right when it comes to understanding you. But I know for certain my love for you is real, and everlasting.'

'You love me?' A smile that was pure Nathan split his face, and melted the last band around her heart. For the first time in years she relaxed totally. 'You love me.' His hands were on her waist, lifting her, and then they were spinning in a circle. 'And I love you. That's all that matters.'

He believed her—he didn't think she'd said it because she needed a father for her baby. There was so much happiness in his face she knew he meant what he'd said. 'It is. You make me whole again,' she whispered, just before his mouth claimed hers.

Then he stopped. Pulled back, still holding her. 'Molly, please say you'll marry me. I promise to love you for ever and ever.'

'Yes, Nathan, I will. Because you love me. Not because of the baby.' That she'd have on her own if he didn't love her. But he did. He'd said so, and Nathan always told the truth.

'Yes, Mol, I do, with all my being and then some. And I love the baby already.'

The next kiss rolled into another and then another, and turned them towards the car and the picnic and the blanket. Especially the blanket and the thick bush not too far away.

Six weeks later

'I pronounce you man and wife,' announced the marriage celebrant. 'Nathan, you may kiss the bride.'

The house rocked with laughter and cheers as family and friends, dressed to the nines, crowded round.

'That's enough. Some of us have only got the weekend off.' Cole nudged Nathan when the kiss went on for ever.

Nathan came up for air and gave his mate a glare. 'Thank goodness for that. I couldn't put up with your crassness for any longer.'

Molly grinned as she shook her head at them. 'Boys, stop it.'

Cole hauled her in for a big hug. 'I'm so glad he found you.'

'So am I,' Molly admitted, sudden tears threatening.

'He didn't find her, I pushed them together.' Vicki grinned.

'Here, you're soaking your dress.' Nathan handed her a handkerchief.

Molly laughed. 'Who has these any more?' She carefully wiped her eyes, aware of not messing her make-up, done by a woman Vicki had hired from the cosmetic department of one of Sydney's large stores for them and Lizzie.

'You want me to produce a handful of tissues instead?' her husband asked.

Her husband. She pinched herself. No, she wasn't dreaming. This was real. She'd found love again, this time with the right man. Hadn't had to fake a thing. Looking at him as he waved to the waiter with a tray of champagne glasses, her heart swelled till it hurt. Damn, but she was so lucky.

'Molly Lupton, you lucky girl.' Lizzie swept her into a hug. 'I am so happy for you.'

'I glad you made it in time.'

Lizzie gave an awkward laugh. 'Well, you know me. Stubborn to the end.'

'You won't lose your job because you've taken these few days off?' She'd been working on intense negotiations in Hong Kong until two days ago.

'Let them try. I might be the only person to come from Perth, but I'm the best.'

Molly hugged her friend. 'You are so right.'

'Your mum's thrilled, by the way.'

Molly looked across the lawn to where her parents and Dad's new lady stood together, watching the proceedings, as though unsure how welcome they were. 'I know, and this time when she says she likes my husband I'm going to accept that. We both made mistakes, and I don't want those to ruin the future. My babies need their grandparents to be there for them like Gran was for me.'

'Babies? As in plural?' Nathan had appeared beside her, two glasses of champagne in one hand.

She stretched up on the tips of her beautiful, pointy cream shoes and whispered, 'Twins.'

He shoved the glasses at Lizzie, reached for Molly and spun her around and up into his arms. 'Twins,' he yelled. 'We're having two little blighters, not one.'

So much for keeping the pregnancy quiet until they got through the first trimester and well into the second. Clapping and cheeky comments exploded around them, glasses were raised, and finally Molly got one of her own to take, not one or two, but three small sips from before putting it aside. No more for her until the babies were born. 'My husband, baby one and baby two. I love you all.'

And months later:

Nathan rushed through the Saturday afternoon crowd, elbowing people out of his way. Typical bloody weekend. Everyone was getting out amongst it, and in his way.

The ED had been flat out, dealing with idiots who'd had too much food and alcohol when he'd got the call to go to the maternity unit. Molly had gone into labour at thirty-five weeks. It had been fast, almost too much so, but the babies were in good shape, tiny and absolutely beautiful. Like their mother.

Two teddy bears and one enormous bunch of irises was a lot to protect from these idiots who weren't looking where they were going, but at last the main entrance to the hospital loomed up in his line of vision. Why the hospital gift shop had to be closed today of all days he didn't know.

The lift was slow to arrive, and when it came, people surged past him to fill it to capacity. 'Typical,' he muttered as he charged up the stairs, reaching the maternity floor out of breath and having to bend over double while his lungs recovered.

Then he was racing down the corridor, out of breath for a different reason. Excitement gripped him, and his face ached as his smile knew no boundaries. 'I'm a dad, I'm a dad.' Spinning into Molly's room, he rushed up to the bed to hug her, forgetting he had his arms full.

Slamming on the brakes, he swallowed. Both babies were snuggled against her breasts, eyes closed, cute little pink noses. He couldn't hug her anyway. 'I'm married to the most wonderful woman on the planet. Mrs-Beautiful-Molly-Mother-of-Two-Lupton.'

'Glad you remembered.' Molly laughed tiredly. 'Want to hold someone?'

'Yes, you.' He placed the teddies on the only chair and held out the flowers. 'I bought every last Dutch iris in the shop.'

'Did you get some vases? There's only one jar in here.' She was grinning at him now, sending his stomach into a riot of longing and happiness.

Damn, he loved this woman so much. His son and daughter were a bonus. It was Molly he woke up for every day. 'I love you, Molly Lupton.'

She nodded. 'I know. Love you back. Now, about names.'

That was an ongoing debate. Hopefully they'd have it sorted by the time everyone went home. Tomorrow.

Tomorrow.

'Joshua and Karina?'

Molly nodded, a look of glee at having won the battle on her face. 'Joshua and Karina.'

How could he refuse her anything?

* * * * *

**IF YOU ENJOYED THIS BOOK
WE THINK YOU WILL ALSO LOVE**

SPECIAL
EDITION

Believe in love. Overcome obstacles. Find happiness.

Relate to finding comfort and strength in the
support of loved ones and enjoy the journey
no matter what life throws your way.

6 NEW BOOKS AVAILABLE EVERY MONTH!

"You're welcome to join me if you'd like. Unless you have plans. It's Saturday, after all."

Plans as in a date? Yeah, not so much these days. In fact, she hadn't been in a serious relationship since she and James had broken up over two years ago.

"I don't date," she blurted before she could stop herself. "I mean, I can, but I don't. Or I haven't been. Um, lately."

She consciously pressed her lips together to stop herself from babbling like an idiot, despite the fact that the damage was done.

"So, dinner?" Desmond asked, rescuing her without commenting on her babbling.

"I'd like that. After I shower. Meet back down here in half an hour?"

"Perfect."

There was an awkward moment when they both tried to go through the kitchen door at the same time. Desmond stepped back and waved her in front of him. She hurried out, then raced up the stairs and practically ran for her bedroom. Once there, she closed the door and leaned against it.

"Talking isn't hard," she whispered to herself. "You've been doing it since you were two. You know how to do this."

But when it came to being around Desmond, knowing and doing were two different things.

Don't miss
Before Summer Ends *by Susan Mallery,*
available May 2021 wherever
Harlequin Special Edition books and ebooks are sold.

Harlequin.com

Love Harlequin romance?

DISCOVER.

Be the first to find out about promotions,
news and exclusive content!

Facebook.com/HarlequinBooks

Twitter.com/HarlequinBooks

Instagram.com/HarlequinBooks

Pinterest.com/HarlequinBooks

You Tube YouTube.com/HarlequinBooks

ReaderService.com

EXPLORE.

Sign up for the Harlequin e-newsletter and
download a free book from any series at
TryHarlequin.com

CONNECT.

Join our Harlequin community to
share your thoughts and connect
with other romance readers!
Facebook.com/groups/HarlequinConnection

HARLEQUIN

HSOCIAL2021